"Unpredictable Risk"

R.I.S.C. Series

Book 5

Anna Blakely

"Unpredictable Risk"
R.I.S.C. Series
Book 5

First Edition

Other Books by Anna Blakely

R.I.S.C. SERIES

Taking A Risk, Part One
Taking A Risk, Part Two
Beautiful Risk
Intentional Risk

R.I.S.C. Bravo Team Series

(Special Forces: Operation Alpha World)

Rescuing Gracelynn

Dedication

To my ARC team.

Thank you SO much for all you do to help
make these stories the best they can be.

Y'all are truly the best!

Prologue

Afghanistan, Six Years Ago...

"It's gonna disintegrate, you keep lookin' at it all the time."

Staff Sergeant Jordan Wright glanced away from the tiny picture in his hand, his smile reaching his eyes. "You're probably right, Briggs." He shrugged. "Can't help it."

Strands of her short, blonde hair peeked out from beneath her helmet as the young petty officer shook her head. "I swear, every time I see you lately, you're staring down at that thing."

"That *thing* is my son." Wright looked down at the black and white image again. Beaming with pride, he ran his gloved thumb over the once-smooth photo. "Jordan Charles, Junior will be here in a little over two months. Still can't believe our tour will be completed in time for his birth."

"Careful, Sir. Don't want to jinx yourself. You never know what could happen between now and then. After all, this is the Army."

"No, shit," their driver, Master Sergeant Owens, chuckled from behind the wheel. "Good thing you've learned that lesson early on, Briggs. Just make sure you don't forget it."

The higher-ranking officer was their escort, as was typical

1

for a ground convoy of this nature. Though theirs was smaller than most, the rough terrain the squad was traveling through had seen a lot of action recently. And none of it was good.

Today, Jordan and the others were making the nearly hundred-mile trek from their base at Bagram to Phoenix, a U.S. Army base located in the Kunar province. The area had finally been liberated from ISIS. With the United States' help, its people were making great strides to rebuild what was once thought to be doomed.

Jordan's squad was split up between three cargo trucks. Five were riding in the Deuce-and-a-half in front of them, another five in the truck behind them, and the M36 carrying Jordan, Owens, and Briggs was sandwiched in the middle.

"I don't know how your wife does it, Staff Sergeant."

"What do you mean?" Jordan asked Briggs.

"Having to take care of everything back home while you're over here for months on end."

Jordan grinned. "Stacey's a saint, that's for sure."

The woman snorted. "She must be."

"What's the matter, Briggs?" Owens asked. "Don't you and your new husband want kids?"

"Sure, I guess. Someday." She looked out at the sharp, rugged mountains surrounding them. "We've talked about it, but we've been married for less than a year. I'm thinkin' maybe once I've done a few more tours."

"Why wait so long?" Jordan asked.

Briggs rolled her pretty eyes. "I'm only twenty-four, Wright. We have plenty of time. Plus, I'm pretty sure Corban would have himself committed if he had to be a stay-at-home dad. I love my husband dearly, but he's too much of a busy-body."

"Oh, he'd be busy, all right." Their Master Chief smirked. "But, there's nothing better in the world than raising a child. Hard as hell sometimes, but still the most rewarding thing I've ever done in my life."

"That's saying a lot for a man like you, Master Chief," Jordan commented, knowing all Owens had done in his military career.

"It's the truth. Of course, like you, I couldn't have accomplished half the stuff I've done if it weren't for the unwavering support of my wife." The middle-aged man grinned. "My Bree is the sweetest, most patient woman in the world."

"If you don't mind me asking, Master Chief"—Briggs slid a glance his way—"how many children do you and Mrs. Owens have?"

"Four." Their leader's smile grew wider. "Plus, seven grandchildren and another one due next spring."

In his mid-fifties, Owens had salt-and-pepper hair and a few well-earned wrinkles. He was one of the best military leaders Jordan had ever had the pleasure of working with.

Briggs' brows rose at that. "Wow."

"Yep. Wasn't always easy. But you just wait and see. There's no love like the one you feel the moment you meet your child for the first time. Doesn't matter if it's your first or your fourth. The love just grows and grows. Ain't that so, Wright?"

"Yes, sir." Jordan looked down at the ultrasound image of his unborn son again. "Heck, I already love this little guy, and he's still cookin'."

"Cooking?" Briggs laughed.

"Well, what would you call it?"

"Uh..." the young woman thought for a moment. "You

know what? Cooking works pretty well, I guess."

All three laughed as they followed the truck in front of them onto a three-arched, concrete bridge.

"God, I hate these things."

Jordan glanced over Briggs. "You're kidding. You've been over here in the thick of war, and you're worried about a bridge? Aren't you from California? That place is loaded with them."

"Do you know what an earthquake could do to a bridge like this one?"

"You been in one before? An earthquake, I mean?"

"Sure. You live in California long enough, you're bound to. I've never been in a bad one, but I grew up seeing them on the news and in pictures. Whole freeway overpasses collapsing, crushing the cars beneath them or dumping the ones driving on them over the edge. The school I went to had monthly earthquake drills. Used to give me nightmares just thinking about that sort of thing happening to me and my parents."

"Well, you can relax, Petty Officer," Owens assured her. "This part of the country isn't really known for its earthquakes."

"I'm just ready to get this stuff to Phoenix and get back," Briggs brushed her fears away.

"Yeah?" Jordan glanced over at her before putting his eyes back on the road in front of them. "Why's that?"

"Corban and I have a dinner date scheduled."

Jordan smiled. "Thank God for Skype, right?"

"Hooah, Staff Sergeant."

"Hooah," Owens and Briggs repeated in unison.

All three occupants laughed together as they continued driving slowly across the extended structure. Almost to the middle of the bridge now, Jordan glanced out his window to the river below.

It was more like a large creek, but the distance from them to the water was enough to make even him a little nervous.

He'd just put the ultrasound picture back into his chest pocket when the truck jerked as though it had hit something. *What the hell?* He looked at Owens. "What was that?"

"I don't know." The other man looked up into the rearview mirror. "I didn't see anything on the road."

"Oh, shit," Briggs exclaimed breathlessly. "Look."

Jordan's eyes moved to where her finger was pointing. He couldn't believe what he saw.

"The b-bridge," Briggs barely stuttered out. "I-it's going to collapse!"

Horrified, Jordan watched as the portion of the road beneath the Deuce-and-a-half in front of them began to crack and tip sideways. Seconds later, the concrete slab broke completely away from the rest of the bridge and fell, taking the truck and its five occupants with it.

"No!" Briggs screamed. She began to cry.

At this height, there was no doubt the men in that truck had just fallen to their deaths.

"Reverse! Reverse! Reverse!" Jordan yelled at Owens to back up.

Owens slammed the truck into reverse and pushed the gas pedal down to the floorboard. The truck behind them did the same, both vehicles making a few feet back toward safety. But it was already too late.

Jordan and the others felt the portion of the bridge both trucks were on beginning to sway. Briggs screamed again as they were jerked back and forth.

Left…Right…Forward.

"Oh, my god," Master Chief stated, his tone knowing. The formidable man began reciting the Lord's Prayer just as the bridge beneath their spinning tires gave way.

Much like the time his friends talked him into riding his first roller coaster, Jordan's stomach flew into his throat. Briggs screamed again, shouting for her husband and saying she didn't want to die. Owens prayed louder, and Jordan braced himself as best he could.

The vehicle tipped mid-air, water and rocks rushing toward them at a deadly speed. In the seconds that followed, Jordan was both astonished and heartbroken as everything seemed to move in slow motion.

Scenes from his thirty-two years began flashing through his mind.

His mother's loving kisses and hugs. His father teaching him how to fish. The moment he saw his beloved wife for the very first time. Watching her walk toward him in a flowing, white gown.

He could still hear the words, "I'm pregnant" coming through the speakers of his computer screen back at base.

As they continued to fall, Jordan thought of his unborn son. A son he'd never get the chance to meet. Stacey would be a fantastic mother, just as his own had been before cancer stole her away from him.

Knowing he'd be with his mom again offered him a tiny sliver of peace. The knowledge that he'd never see the love of his life again shattered that peace all to hell.

I love you, Stacey. I'm so sorry, baby.

In his final moments, Jordan yanked the picture back out of his pocket. He prayed with everything he had that his son would grow up knowing just how much he loved him.

He prayed for Stacey, hoping she would somehow find a

way to move on from this and be happy again.

Jordan was still staring at the picture, praying for his family, when the truck crashed into the unforgiving riverbed, destroying every dream he'd had ever had.

Chapter 1

Six Years Later…

Grant Hill pushed open the glass door and stepped into his place of employment. R.I.S.C.—which stood for Rescue, Intel, Security, and Capture. The former SEAL had worked for the elite, private security company a few years now, after he'd decided to leave the Navy.

Working closely with Homeland, both Alpha and Bravo— R.I.S.C.'s two security teams—were made up of former-military operators recruited for their specific skills and expertise.

Executing both government sanctioned ops and jobs for private citizens, the teams' duties include everything from playing bodyguard to finding and eliminating enemies of the United States.

It was like being a SEAL without all the red-tape, bureaucracy bullshit. And Grant loved it.

"Good morning, Grant."

He looked up to find Gracie McDaniels, R.I.S.C.'s public relations liaison, smiling at him from behind the reception desk. The petite blonde was way too fucking cheery for this early in the morning.

"Hey." He gave her a nod.

"Everyone's in the conference room." She tilted her head toward the office hallway. "Oh, and I made a fresh pot of coffee a few minutes ago, so there should be plenty left."

Now, *that* was almost enough to make even him want to smile.

"Thanks," he mumbled as he walked by the desk.

She grinned even wider. "Of course."

Grant forced himself not to shake his head in wonder. He'd never understand how someone who had gone through what Gracie had could still be so happy.

Just a few short months ago, the woman had been kidnapped and almost died. Had it not been for Nate Carter—one of R.I.S.C.'s Bravo Team members—she would have.

Now Gracie and Nate were in love and engaged to be married. Something that seemed to be a theme with the men at R.I.S.C. Too many of the fuckers had risked their lives to protect and save a woman, only to fall in love in the process.

Screw that.

First, there was Jake McQueen, their fearless leader and owner of R.I.S.C. When the former Delta badass thought Olivia—his best friend's little sister and now Jake's wife—had been brutally murdered, Grant and the rest of Alpha Team traveled with Jake into the belly of Hell to take out the fuckers responsible. Instead, they found Olivia alive and literally running for her life.

Later, when she was taken again and nearly tortured to death, Jake had been able to end the bastard once and for all. Fast-forward to a year later and the two were now married and had a baby on the way.

But Jake wasn't the only R.I.S.C. man to fall into that sort of torturous trap.

Trevor Matthews—Alpha Team's medic and Jake's SIC, or Second In Charge—went through a similar situation when the woman he'd just started dating was used as a sick fuck's tool for revenge. After that it was Nate and Gracie and most recently, Derek West and his childhood friend-turned-fiancée, Charlotte "Charlie" Stone.

Come to think of it, the men of R.I.S.C. were dropping like fucking flies. As far as Alpha Team went, Grant, Coop, and Mac were the only single members left.

He had no idea what Coop's and Mac's feelings on the topic were, but as far as Grant was concerned, he wanted no part of that shit. Shaking those pointless thoughts away, he entered the conference room on the right.

Sitting in his regular seat at the head of the large, oval table was Jake. To his right was Trevor who, like Jake, was a former Delta Force operator.

At the side of the table opposite Grant sat the team's two snipers. Sean "Coop" Cooper and McKenna "Mac" Kelley were among the best marksmen Grant had ever worked with.

"Hey, big guy." Derek—a former SEAL and the team's genius computer geek—looked up at him from his seat next to Trevor. "Nice of you to finally join us."

Checking his watch, Grant looked at his teammate. "I'm three minutes early."

Derek looked at the clock on the wall. "So you are. I stand corrected."

"Listen up," Jake addressed the room. "As I'm sure you've already figured out, we have another job. Not as intense as the last few we've had but no less important."

They all waited while he picked up a small, black remote and pushed a button. The retractable screen behind him lit up with the picture of a man Grant instantly recognized.

"This guy again?" Coop groaned.

"This *guy* is a United States Senator," Mac chastised her partner.

"Okay. But seriously, Jake." Coop looked at their boss. "What's he trying to do, turn us into his permanent entourage or something?"

Jake smirked. "One, we will never become anyone's permanent anything. And two, this job is going to entail a little more than just being an extra watchdog at political rallies and fundraisers."

"How so?" Derek asked from beside Grant.

With a somber expression, Jake explained. "Trevor and I met with Senator Cantrell earlier this morning. Apparently, someone has been sending him threats."

"Okay." Mac looked around and back to Jake. "I mean, that sucks, but isn't that sort of an occupational hazard for someone in his position?"

"Can be," Trevor piped in. "But these threats seem more personal in nature."

"He has his own team of guys, though. Right?" Coop asked. "Why does he need us?"

"The senator wants someone from the outside on this."

"Does he not trust his people?" Mac asked, curious.

"Cantrell just wants some extra eyes on him," Jake answered for Trevor. "One of you will be assigned to his detail. Those who stay behind will work to try to find the source of the threats and determine whether or not they're legit."

"Hell, I'll do it," Coop volunteered. "Watching over the guy may be boring as hell, but it'll still beat sifting through emails and all that shit."

Jake nodded. "All right. I'll let the senator know and set up a time for you to meet with him and his head of security." He looked Grant's way. "Anything you think will help Coop better protect Cantrell be sure to let him know."

Grant tipped his chin. He and the others started to stand, stopping when Jake spoke again.

"Hold up. There's one other thing." He pushed another button on the remote, and the image on the screen changed.

"Whoa. Who's that?" Coop asked with blatant interest.

"This is Brynnon Cantrell, William Cantrell's daughter."

"Nice."

Grant was hit with the sudden urge to jump across the table and beat the shit out of his teammate.

What the hell?

Schooling his expression, he clamped his jaw shut and kept quiet. Mac, however, didn't bother to hide her eye-roll.

"What's her play in all this?" the pretty blonde asked. "Cantrell think she's the one behind the threats?"

"On the contrary"—Jake shook his head— "He also wants someone from the team to serve as Miss Cantrell's personal bodyguard. Just until we determine whether or not the threats are valid."

"Damn," Coop exhaled and sat back in his chair. "I spoke too soon."

The room filled with laughter, but Grant was still focused on the redhead smiling back at them from the screen.

"Has she been threatened, too?" he asked roughly, the thought pissing him off. The primal need to protect her made no sense. He'd only met the woman once.

Yeah, but she'd left one hell of an impression.

"Not according to Cantrell. Said he just wants someone on her as an extra precaution."

Mac smacked Coop's arm when he snickered. "Seriously?" She glared.

Coop gave her an innocent shrug. "Someone's got to pick up the slack around here. Ever since D over there got engaged, he's been acting like a damn choir boy."

Derek shot back with an unapologetic grin. "Just wait. When you find the woman you want to spend the rest of your life with, you'll cool your jets, too."

When Mac scoffed, Coop gave the petite blonde a funny look.

"I'll do it," she told Jake.

"Just so we're clear"—D leaned his elbows onto the table—"are you volunteering for the bodyguard gig or to be Coop's one and only?"

"Funny." Mac flipped the computer geek off.

Coop's expression tightened, but he recovered before anyone other than Grant noticed.

"I thought so." Derek leaned back in his chair with a grin. "And you still haven't answered the question."

Mac sighed loudly, her patience waning. "The bodyguard job, smartass." She looked over at Trevor and Jake again. "Like I was saying, I'll watch over the senator's da—"

"I'll do it," Grant cut his teammate off.

All eyes shot to him.

"You sure?" Jake asked, looking as confused as everyone else in the room. "I figured you'd want a break from Cantrell duty, seeing as how you've done it twice already."

From across the table, Mac's blue eyes met his. "I don't mind doing it, Grant. Really."

"I said I'll do it."

His curtness left her blinking.

Damn, man. Take it easy.

Grant cleared his throat. "It makes sense for me to take on one of the assignments. I already know the players."

Trevor gave him a curious glance. "Except this time, you'll be watching the daughter not the senator. Totally different players in that game."

"Maybe." He shrugged. "Maybe not. Either way, Cantrell trusts me, and I've already met his daughter, which may help put her more at ease." An odd desperation pushed him to continue. "This will keep me in the loop. Plus, it'll give me a chance to see if the threats are coming from anyone within her circle."

Jake and Trevor shared a look before Jake nodded. "Okay. Coop, you're with the Senator, and Hill will take his daughter."

"Lucky bastard." Coop gave him a sideways smirk.

Their boss grinned. "You two stick around, and I'll give you some basic intel you'll need. Trevor has some information Ryker sent over for the rest of you to start going through. Anything suspicious stands out, let Trev know ASAP. I'm going to give Coop and Hill what they need and head back home."

"Speakin' of home"—Derek stood as he spoke— "I'm surprised to see you here. Liv feelin' better?"

"She's better now that the second trimester has passed," Jake answered. "We're both just hoping these last three months go by quickly."

Mac smiled. "I keep trying to get her to change her mind on the gender reveal thing, but she's dead set on not finding out the baby's gender until it's born."

"We both are." Jake beamed. "Plus, Mike is supposed to be back for the birth, and Liv thought it would be more exciting for him if we wait."

"About damn time her brother came back," Trevor commented. "I'm hoping to talk him into joining the team."

"Me, too," Jake nodded. "He wasn't too receptive when he left. I figure I'll wait until after Liv delivers to open that conversation again."

Back in the day, Olivia's brother, Mike had been on the same Delta Force team as Jake until he was pulled into a deep cover assignment that lasted over a decade. It also required everyone in his life to believe he was dead.

Mac squealed. "I can't wait for the baby to get here. My vote's for a girl, by the way. And I'm totally going to teach her all the kick-ass sniper tricks I know."

Grant tried not to grumble. He was happy for Jake and his wife, especially after everything those two had been through. But he had a sense of urgency to get this job started as soon as possible.

Wonder why.

Finally, after the baby talk ceased and the others left to go meet in Trevor's office, Jake, Coop, and Grant went over some basic info.

For the next several minutes, Grant shared with Coop any pertinent information he'd learned from his time spent guarding the senator. Once that was covered, Jake handed Grant a folder with intel regarding Brynnon Cantrell. Basic information they needed when taking any personal bodyguard assignment.

Age. Date of birth. Place of residence. Occupation…

"She flips houses?" Grant asked aloud. He couldn't help but be a bit surprised by that fact.

"She does," Jake confirmed. "And she makes a pretty good living doing it."

That explains the calluses.

Grant had been serving as extra security detail for the senator while he'd gone on a two-week event tour.

The final event had been held at the senator's mansion. Grant had noticed the man's daughter the second she walked into the large ballroom.

When Cantrell had introduced him to the stunning redhead, Grant had felt something he hadn't in a very long time.

Even though they'd only spoken briefly that night, he hadn't been able to shake the memory. So why the hell he volunteered to be her personal fucking bodyguard was beyond him.

"Impressive." Coop's comment on Brynnon's occupation snapped him out of his thoughts. "Although, she probably just pays someone else to do the work while she sips her triple caramel whatever-the-fuck women drink now."

"What makes you think that?" Grant challenged the other man.

Coop's hazel eyes looked back at him like he'd lost his damn mind. "Uh, because her dad's a senator? Plus, according to this"—he looked at one of the papers in the folder Jake gave him— "the guy used to own some big-time construction company. Made millions working military contract jobs overseas. Cantrell sold it for a hefty profit when he decided to go into politics. The man's loa-ded."

"No, shit. I've worked for him already, remember?" Grant bit back. "Just because the man has money doesn't mean the guy's daughter is a spoiled brat."

Coop threw his hands up defensively. "Okay. Geez. Who pissed in your cornflakes this morning?"

He's right, dumbass. Chill the fuck out already.

"Hill's got a point, Coop," Jake stated. "We don't want to

go into this thing making assumptions about anything or anyone. If these threats are the real deal, we need to be on our A-game."

The young sniper nodded. "Understood, Boss."

Jake gave him a nod. "You two have any questions?"

"Nope." Coop stood. "I'll head over to Cantrell's place now to get the lay of the land and go from there."

"I'll call to let his people know to expect you." Jake turned to Grant. "What about you? You good?"

"Yep."

"Okay. Cantrell told me his daughter is currently working on a house over on Hopkins Street. If she's not there, try her condo. Both addresses are in the folder."

"Got it."

"Either of you find anything you think's worth looking into, let Trevor know immediately. He's going to continue manning the office, but I'll be reachable by phone, too. Don't hesitate to call if you need anything. And watch your backs, just in case."

"Roger that."

All three men left the room. Both Grant and Coop were parked in the parking garage adjacent to the building, so they took the elevator down to the garage together.

"So. You and Cantrell's daughter, huh?"

Grant's eyes shot to Coop. "What?"

"It's cool. Not like I'm gonna rat you out or anything."

"What the fuck are you talking about?"

"You're not, you know"—Coop waggled his brows—"bumpin' uglies?"

He's your teammate. Don't kill him.

Grant shook his head, afraid if he spoke he'd rip into the assuming bastard.

17

Coop muttered under his breath. "If you say so."

Smacking his palm against the stop button on the elevator's control board, Grant pinned the former Ranger down with a glare.

"You got something you want to say to me, Sean?"

"Whoa." Coop held his hands palms-up. "You were just pretty damn quick on the draw taking the job from Mac like that. I figured you and Red had a thing going from when you worked for Cantrell a few months ago."

A muscle in Grant's jaw bulged. "You figured wrong."

"All right." He shook his head. "Jesus, man."

Fuck. Coop was right. What the hell was wrong with him? He'd never ripped into his teammate like that.

Grant started the elevator's descent again. "I met her once. For about five minutes."

"Okay."

"Cantrell trusts me, which will make it easier to get his *daughter* to trust me."

"You don't have to keep explaining yourself, Hill. I get it, all right?"

Damn it. He didn't want Coop or anyone else on Alpha Team thinking he had a thing for Brynnon Cantrell. She was no different than any other client.

Keep telling yourself that shit, asshole. Maybe one day, you'll actually believe it.

With a couple of shared nods, the two men parted ways. Grant climbed into his black GMC Sierra and entered the flip house address into his phone's GPS.

Twenty minutes later, he was parking in front of a single-story home. As he got out, he gave the property an assessing glance.

Picture-perfect bushes and mulched landscaping trimmed

the front of the house. Two pots filled with bright yellow mums framed each side of the bottom step, and what appeared to be a brand-new sidewalk led from the paved driveway to the small, covered porch.

Grant's apartment was small and bare. A place to shower, sleep, and eat. But even someone like him could appreciate the curb appeal this small house held.

Raising a fist, he knocked on the pristine, white door. From behind the decorative glass, he heard a muffled female.

"Come in."

She couldn't be that stupid. Grant tried the doorknob. Sure enough, it was unlocked.

"Seriously?" He let himself in and closed the door behind him. Grant took a few seconds to study the space in front of him.

The living room was small, yet the wood floors combined with the way the furniture had been arranged made it appear spacious. It was also unoccupied.

Opening his mouth, he was about to ask where she was when the voice of his dreams called out. "I'm in here!"

Grant closed his eyes and took a deep breath, willing himself not to go storming in and let the fool woman know the billion and one reasons she was putting herself at risk.

Remembering he had no claim over her, he quietly made his way toward the open archway at the far left of the room.

Once there, he had the choice to either go left or right. To his right was a narrow hallway with four closed doors. Bedrooms and bathrooms, he assumed. To his left was the kitchen.

There, sticking out from beneath the sink, were two lean, jean-clad legs. A pair of dirty, women's work boots were attached to the feet.

"You can just leave the food on the table," she instructed without bothering to come out. "The check's already made out and signed, tip included. Thanks."

Grant shook his head in disbelief. She was in a vulnerable position with absolutely no clue about who'd just walked into her house, and she didn't seem bothered in the least.

Jesus. He could be a fucking serial rapist or some shit, and she'd just let him waltz right in.

He took a few steps closer but still remained silent. A few strained grunts and muddled curses came from beneath the sink as she struggled with whatever it was she was trying to do.

"I called the bakery this morning to double-check the amount. Just leave the food, and I'll deal with it all when I'm done here."

More pissed than he had the right to be, Grant decided the first thing they were going to discuss—if she ever came out from under that damn sink—was her lack of self-preservation.

A clanging sound preceded a loud, "Damn it!"

Standing with his booted feet shoulder-width apart, he crossed his arms and waited for her to wiggle herself free.

"If there's a problem with the check"—she grunted—"you'll have to call your boss, because I…"

Wide, emerald eyes that had haunted his dreams for months stared up at him.

"Oh. It's you." Brynnon Cantrell whispered.

She remembers you. A sliver of warmth nearly penetrated the space where his heart used to be.

Blinking, the startled woman climbed awkwardly to her feet. She was taller than the average woman, but with his six-five frame, her eyes still only met him at chin-level.

Brushing some wild, auburn strands from her face, she straightened her shoulders in an attempt to compose herself. The flush filling her porcelain cheeks betrayed her.

"Sorry." She looked up at him. "I thought you were someone else."

"Obviously." Grant glanced over her shoulder then back to her. "You always leave the front door unlocked when you're here by yourself?"

She blinked at his abruptness. "Um...yeah. Usually. It's a nice neighborhood."

"And nothing bad ever happens in those, does it?"

Perfectly groomed brows turned inward as confusion replaced her earlier embarrassment. "You work security for my dad, right?"

"Grant Hill." He held out a hand to reintroduce himself. "And I work for R.I.S.C. Your father is a client of ours."

"Brynnon." She nodded, returning the gesture.

"I remember," he admitted before he could stop himself.

They stood there, shaking hands in awkward silence before her round eyes went wide again. For a second, Grant thought it was a reaction to the same, sizzling zip of electricity he'd felt the first time they'd met.

Suddenly in a near panic, she blurted, "Oh, crap! Did something happen? Is my dad okay?"

"Your father's fine, Miss Cantrell."

She blew out a breath. "Thank God." Wheels spinning, the naturally beautiful woman looked back up at him questioningly. "So why are you here, Mr. Hill? I mean, other than to lecture me about unlocked doors."

Ignoring the smart-ass comment, he let go of her hand. "Call me Grant. And it's more about what I can do for you."

Her bow-shaped lips parted slightly before she cleared her

throat, asking, "And what is that, exactly?"

"I'm here at your father's request."

Disappointment flittered behind those seas of green before a look of understanding crossed her face. "You've been assigned to guard me." It was a statement, not a question.

"Yes, ma'am. I have."

Taking a deep breath, Brynnon put on the same forced smile he'd seen the night they met.

"Well, let me save you some time, Mr....err...Grant. I don't want, nor do I need a bodyguard. I'm sorry you wasted a trip coming here."

She has a stubborn streak. *Good to know.*

"Your father seems to think otherwise."

Lifting her slightly dimpled chin, Brynnon crossed her arms. "Yes, well, I guess it's a good thing I'm over eighteen and can make my own decisions."

Oddly, Grant found her bit of attitude appealing. He liked that she wanted to be independent. However, given how easily he'd strolled on in here, she definitely needed a keeper.

"Your father received a threat."

"Not to sound uncaring, but my father receives about a hundred threats a year. An unfortunate side effect of being a politician, I guess."

"The senator seems to be taking this one a little more seriously. He hired R.I.S.C. to protect you, for the time being."

She rolled her lips inward, visibly unhappy with that bit of news. "I appreciate the concern, but like I said, I can take care of myself. Now, if you'll excuse me, I have a house I need to get ready to sell."

Brynnon took a step toward the room's entrance, but

Grant didn't budge. He just stood there, waiting for her to realize she wasn't getting her way. Not surprising, the woman didn't give up that easily.

"I apologize again for having wasted your time, but I will talk with my father and make sure you are paid for the entire day. Now, if there's nothing else, I really do need to get back to work."

Brynnon held her hand out, indicating he should leave the way he came.

One corner of his lip twitched. "I'm not leaving."

Her pretty brows rose. "Uh, yes. You are."

Grant's only response was to cross his arms and raise a brow. With her hands on her jean-clad hips, the senator's daughter stood her ground.

"I said I don't need you here."

Grant took a slight step forward. "And I said, I'm not leaving. Your dad hired me to do a job, Princess. That's exactly what I'm going to do."

Anger flashed in her eyes. The red in her cheeks darkened. "Did you seriously just call me *Princess?*"

When he didn't bother answering the rhetorical question, she became even more upset.

"My father may have hired you, Mr. Hill. But I just fired you."

He shook his head. "Can't."

"I'm sorry. I *can't?*" She chuckled humorlessly. "Last I checked this was a free country, and I'm a grown-ass woman. If I don't want a bodyguard, I don't have to have one."

The childish statement made her wince. She tried like hell to hide it, but was half a second too late.

Knowing they'd just keep going in circles if he continued the pointless argument, Grant reached into his jeans pocket and pulled out his phone.

Looking appalled, Brynnon asked, "What are you doing?"

"Calling your father."

Remaining silent, Grant held the phone to his ear and waited as it rang.

"Good. While you two are chatting, you can tell him thanks but no thanks."

Ignoring the comment, he kept his eyes on hers as he waited for the senator to answer. After what felt like an eternity, the other man answered the call.

"Cantrell."

"It's me."

Her father sighed. "Let me guess. She's balking at my order for protection and says she can take care of herself."

"Yes, sir."

"Hand her the phone."

Grant held it out for Brynnon, who yanked it from his hand.

"Will you please tell your watchdog his services are not needed?" There was a pause before her voice rose an octave. "Protection from what? *You're* the one who got the threat not me. If anything, he should be guarding you." Another pause. "Fine. Then he can come give the other guy back up or something."

The angrier she got, the more prominent the red in her cheeks became. Grant refused to admit how adorable it was.

"But, Dad," she paused. "If you'd just listen..." Another pause. Brynnon rolled her dazzling eyes. "That's not fair, and you know it. We've talked about this, Dad. You can't use Mom as an excuse every time you want to..."

There was one final pause before Brynnon's shoulders fell in defeat. "Fine," she huffed. "But he'd better not get in my way. I have an open house here tomorrow, and I want to get my place finished so I can list the condo."

Grant watched as Brynnon turned away from him. This time when she spoke, her voice turned lower. Softer.

"I know, and I appreciate that you're worried about me." There were a few seconds of silence before he heard her say, "I love you, too, Daddy. Bye."

After ending the call, Brynnon drew in a deep breath, exhaling slowly before turning back around to face him. "Here," she offered him back his phone.

Their fingers brushed lightly as he reached for it. Ignoring that same damn zing from before, he shoved it into his pocket and waited for her to speak.

"Okay." She relented, as if the choice had ever really been hers. "You can stay. But I meant what I said to Dad. I have to get this place ready for the potential buyers who will be here tomorrow. If I can't get this damn sink fixed, I'm screwed."

"What's wrong with it?"

"There's a leak, and I can't get the threads to seal enough to stop it."

He looked behind her. "Give me the wrench."

She scowled at his gruff order, but then her eyes fell over his chest and biceps. Deciding he may actually be able to do what needed to be done, Brynnon grabbed the tool from the countertop behind her and held it out to him.

"Knock yourself out."

Chapter 2

"Thanks for your help."

Brynnon leaned back against the kitchen counter and took a drink from her water bottle.

Grant gave her a single nod. "No problem."

Lordy. The man's voice was every bit as sexy as she remembered. Maybe more so. Too bad he was so damn bossy.

Admit it. Even that turns you on.

Brynnon shook the ridiculous thoughts away. After all, they'd only met once…months ago. Which made her reaction to the infuriating man that much more confusing.

He'd been working extra security at one of her father's benefit balls, and for reasons beyond her understanding, her dad had insisted they be introduced.

She and Grant had shaken hands and shared polite introductions. That was it. The entire interaction lasting a couple minutes, at best.

For some reason, however, Brynnon hadn't been able to get the tall, dark, and broody security expert out of her mind.

Never before had a single handshake consumed her thoughts like the one with this man. Yet here she was, three months later, and she still found herself thinking about the way he'd looked at her that night.

"Here."

Grant handed her back the wrench. Their fingers touched again, making her pulse skyrocket. Brynnon's gaze rose to meet his and suddenly, it was as if everything around them had vanished, leaving them inside a bubble.

A very large, very sexually-charged bubble.

"We need to go over how this is going to work." He stared down at her. "I'll need the names of contractors you use, as well as anyone who works with you on a regular basis. You also need to put together a detailed schedule for the next couple of weeks."

Aaaaand...there it went. Like a giant needle, his words punctured the bubble she'd been enjoying more than she should, deflating it in an instant.

Much to her dismay, Brynnon had spent many a night since fantasizing about the expressionless man. Apparently, she'd over-romanticized him. By a whole hell of a lot.

This man was here because he was being paid to do a job. Not because he wanted to be.

God, I need to get a life.

"Why do you need all that if my dad was the one who received the threats?"

"Precaution. Someone wants to get to him, they could use you to do it."

Brynnon set the wrench back into her tool bag by her feet. "I don't mean to sound insensitive or like I don't care, but you realize this is probably nothing, right?"

"I do." He tipped his head.

"Oh." His answer surprised her. "Well, good. Because most threats politicians receive are nothing to worry about.

Just a bunch of keyboard warriors who don't like this law or that. They send my dad and other members of Congress threats thinking they'll get it changed. Honestly, it's scary how ridiculous some people are these days."

"Agreed. However, on the off chance there is some validity to these threats, I still need to do the job I've been hired to do to the best of my ability. That means you do what I say when I say. No arguments."

Brynnon watched as he walked to the kitchen door leading to the back yard and flipped the deadbolt before turning back to her.

"Starting with keeping all your doors locked while you're in the house."

Excuse me? Brynnon's jaw nearly dropped from his arrogance. He might appear to be a sexy, scruff-covered god of a man, but she was beginning to think he was nothing more than an a condescending ass.

Brynnon crossed her arms and put on the sweetest smile she could muster. "Well, that's going to be kind of hard to do during tomorrow's open house. The name kind of implies the doors will be, you know…open."

His rolled lips and deep breath gave away his irritation, bringing her a sense of childish satisfaction.

"I think you should postpone it until after this situation has been resolved."

Brynnon laughed at that. "Have you ever bought a house, Mr. Hill?" His silence answered for him. "No? Well, let me enlighten you. The longer this house is in my name, the more interest it accrues. That means I lose money. I'm already a week and a half behind schedule due to unexpected issues that kept popping up. I can't afford to wait."

Grant ran a large hand across his chiseled jaw. "There's no

way I can control who comes in and out of here in a situation like that."

"No," she agreed. "There isn't. However, given the trust my father has put in you in the past, I have full faith you'll be able to handle it just fine."

A mouth she'd described in her mind as kissable tightened, making Brynnon felt a little bad. She knew he was just trying to do his job, but damn it. She had a job to do, too.

"Okay, look." She dropped the attitude a smidge. "How about a compromise? I'll do what you say *if* my safety truly becomes a concern. Otherwise, I have a business to run. I hope you can respect that."

"My job is to protect you, Princess. Can't do that if I'm busy worrying about stepping on your toes. I hope you can respect *that.*"

Don't slug him. Don't slug him.

Brynnon narrowed her eyes, no longer feeling bad. "That's another thing. Quit calling me Princess. It's demeaning, and I don't like it."

Not wanting to give the big jerk a chance to get the last word in, she went about putting the rest of her tools away and wiping down the kitchen counters. After that, she swept the floor and went back through each room to make sure everything was set up exactly as she wanted.

When the real delivery boy showed up during her walk-through, Brynnon started for the door. Blocking her, Grant held up a hand to stop her.

"From now on, I answer the door."

Biting her tongue, she let him. The young man's eyes nearly bugged out of their sockets when he laid eyes on the big man opening the door.

Putting the poor kid out of his misery, Brynnon quickly

grabbed the check from the kitchen and paid him.

After putting the food in the refrigerator, she did one final walk-through. Satisfied with the way the house looked, she was about to tell Grant tomorrow's schedule when her stomach growled.

"Hungry?"

Now that you mention it...

"I'm starved."

His dark brows turned inward. "When was the last time you ate?"

Brynnon thought for a moment. "I don't know. I've been so busy today I guess I forgot to eat." For reasons she didn't understand, this angered him.

"You shouldn't do that."

"I didn't do it on purpose, I assure you. I told you I got busy."

He let out a frustrated sigh. "Do you have food at home, or do you need to stop and pick something up?"

What's with this guy? None of her previous bodyguards had ever given a shit whether she ate or not. But with him, it was like having a second father around.

Growing up, she and her brother, Billy, had both endured bodyguards. First, when her father became a multimillionaire almost overnight, thanks to his construction company's military contracts. Later, when he ran for Congress, he insisted they have them during the weeks leading up to the election, as well as after.

Each time, Brynnon felt the same. She hated it.

"I can just hit a drive-thru on the way home."

The beast of a man sounded almost horrified at the thought. "Fast food?"

"I take it you prefer something else?"

"Yes."

"Okay." She let the word hang there. "What do you suggest?"

"There's a restaurant not far from here. They have steak."

Brynnon looked down at herself. Her jeans were dirty and ripped, her flannel faded, and the t-shirt beneath it was stained. She didn't need a mirror to know her hair was also a total wreck.

"Um, I'm not really dressed for that sort of thing."

"It isn't fancy. You're fine."

Her schedule was so hectic, she usually just grabbed something quick while driving to the hardware store and back. She couldn't remember the last time she'd eaten a decent meal and had to admit the idea was more than a little appealing.

"Okay," she told him. "If you say so."

"I do. Let's go." Grant started toward the front door. "While we eat, you can give me that information I asked you about."

"Fine. But I'm driving."

"We both are." He looked over his shoulder. "You're following me."

Already sick of his bossy ass, Brynnon fought the urge to stick out her tongue. How she ever thought he was potential dating material was beyond her.

This is what you get for putting a guy you've talked to for all of thirty seconds on a sexual pedestal.

Knowing the tiny voice was right, she did as she was told and followed him to the restaurant. Less than forty-five minutes later, she was enjoying the best meal she'd had in a very long time.

Brynnon took another bite of her grilled club sandwich,

the crispy bacon and freshly sliced tomato putting the heavenly concoction over the top.

"Okay, you were right." She covered her full mouth with her hand. "This is so much better than fast-food."

Grant swallowed a bite of his enormous T-bone. "Told you."

While he was focused on his food, Brynnon took a moment to study the formidable man.

His brown hair was almost military-short in the back and on the sides with slightly longer layers on top. A dusting of dark scruff covered his square jaw and strong chin and his perfect lips had two settings: flat or pursed.

Brynnon glanced down at the edge of what she assumed was a full-sleeve tattoo peeking out from beneath his rolled cuff. Her heart thumped a little harder, and muscles she hadn't used in far too long clenched, wishing she could see more of his ink.

I want to see all of it.

Pretending she hadn't just thought that, she returned her focus to his face. More specifically, to the set of gray-blue eyes that seemed to penetrate her soul.

There was something in them she hadn't noticed the first time they met. She couldn't exactly name it, but whatever it was made her heart sad.

As they continued eating, Brynnon shared with him what she could about the people she hired to help with her business, promising to write down their names and contact information when she got home.

"What about your social life?"

Brynnon halted her sandwich mid-bite. "What about it?"

"Who's in your circle?"

She smirked. "My circle?"

His eyes gave a slight roll. "Friends. Boyfriends. Who do you hang out with?"

"Oh." She sat her sandwich back down. "Well, seeing as how I'm always working, I don't really have a *circle*. No boyfriend, and really the only close friend I have is Angie. She's kind of my unofficial assistant. Helps me manage the business email and stage the houses. And, when she's able, she helps me host the open houses. She won't be there tomorrow, though. Her husband has the weekend off, so they're taking their two boys on a weekend getaway."

"I'll need Angie's information, too, then."

Brynnon snorted. "Okay."

Brow arched, he asked, "Is that going to be a problem?"

"No," she chuckled. "It's just that...it's Angie. She's a total soccer mom. A cool-as-hell soccer mom, but still. We've been friends for years, and she's like a second daughter to my dad. I can promise you, Angie didn't send him any threats."

"Still need to rule her out."

"Fine." Brynnon gave him a tight smile. "I'll include her information."

Once that was settled, they finished the rest of their food in relative silence. After taking care of the check—she'd insisted on paying for her own meal—they walked to their cars parked by the sidewalk out front.

A cool breeze hit, and Brynnon wrapped her opened flannel shirt around herself a little tighter. Brushing some wind-blown hair from her eyes, she spoke as they approached his truck.

"I'm assuming you'll follow me home, make sure it's safe, and then meet me at the flip house tomorrow morning?"

Grant looked back at her as if she'd missed something big, his answer shocking to say the least. "I'm staying with you."

She nearly choked on her own breath. "Excuse me?"

"Standard protocol."

When the wind blew another chunk of hair into her face, Brynnon slapped it away. "Uh, not for me, it isn't."

"Too bad." He shrugged one of his big shoulders. "This is how I work."

Through clenched teeth she informed him, "Well, it isn't the way *I* work. Except for when I was still in high school, no other bodyguard assigned to me has slept inside my house."

"Just means they were shitty at their jobs."

Grant's stare was unwavering, and he spoke with a confidence she found both attractive and frustrating.

"Well, seeing as how the condo is mine"—she dug her keys from her purse— "I'm pretty sure I get the final say about who stays in it and who doesn't."

Seemingly aloof, Grant pulled his own keys from his pocket and pressed the fob to unlock his truck. "Sorry, sweetheart, but my job is to be your bodyguard." His eyes locked with hers. "The name kind of implies that your body is, you know…guarded."

Irritated he'd twisted her words from earlier to fit with his agenda, Brynnon squeezed her fist around her keys. "Do you even have a change of clothes?"

"I packed enough for a week. If this goes longer than that, I can either do my laundry at your place, or run by my apartment for more."

Damn. The guy had an answer for freaking everything.

An image of his boxers mixed with her panties left her flustered. If she had that sort of reaction to his laundry, there was absolutely no way he could stay under the same roof as her.

"Fine." She smiled up at him. "I'll compromise. You can

stay parked out front."

He shook his head. "Not good enough."

With a shrug of her own, she said, "It's gonna have to be."

Spinning on her toes, Brynnon went to her car, got in, and slammed the door harder than necessary. Wrestling with the urge to scream, she started the ignition and shoved the gear shift into drive.

Not bothering to wait on him, she peeled out of the parking lot and headed toward home.

Once there, she parked in her drive and walked quickly to her front door. Rather than pulling in directly behind her, as she'd expected, Grant parked his truck in the street against the curb.

His long legs made it easy to catch up to her, so by the time she'd unlocked the door and was reaching for the knob, he was there. Putting his hand over hers to stop her.

"I need to clear the house and perimeter."

With a quick intake of air, she glanced down at where their hands met.

"Right. Sorry."

Brynnon jerked her hand away and stepped back giving the large man plenty of room to get by.

"You can come inside, but stay by the door until I'm finished."

Not waiting for her to respond, Grant removed a gun from his back waistband—one she hadn't even realized he'd been carrying—and began to swiftly and efficiently check each room in her condo.

She'd never understood how some women could get turned on by a man with a gun…until now.

Brynnon watched as he held his weapon out with ease, as though it were a natural extension of his body. Flexing right along with his taut, sinewy forearm, that damn tattoo peeking out from beneath his sleeve continued to tease her.

When he finally went upstairs to check the bedroom and her office, she took a few seconds to get her head on straight. She needed to get a grip on her neglected hormones now, before she did something stupid like ask him to take off his shirt.

He could barely stand being around her as it was. Something like that would surely send him running for the hills.

Maybe if I did ask to see the rest of his tattoo, he'd leave and never come back.

Disappointment from the thought of never seeing him again was immediate. And ridiculous.

Brynnon didn't want him here, and he didn't want to be here. So why the hell would she care if he left?

"I don't," she whispered to herself.

"What?"

Brynnon's head swung up to see Grant walking toward her from the base of the stairs.

"What?" Her mind worked like crazy to figure out which part she'd actually verbalized.

"Thought you said something."

"Oh," she chuckled nervously, willing her pulse back to normal. "No. I mean, I did, but I was just talking to myself." *Yeah, because that sounds perfectly normal.*

"The place is clear. I'm going to check outside. Don't open the door for anyone other than me."

"Yes, sir," Brynnon gave him a flimsy salute, then cringed inwardly.

Again, the man was only doing his job. A job he probably wished he'd never agreed to. So why was she acting like such a bitch?

Because you like him.

No. That couldn't be right.

Sure, when she'd first laid eyes on him at her father's party, she'd thought he was incredibly sexy. And okay, so maybe she'd thought about that night way more than she should have these past few months.

But she could see now they were totally incompatible. Brynnon didn't know how they could manage to be friends, let alone lovers.

A rush of cold air tore her away from her thoughts as he let himself back inside.

"Perimeter's clear as well." He returned the gun to his waistband.

"Okay."

"Give me your phone."

The blunt order took her off guard. "Why?"

Taking a deep breath, he very patiently explained. "I'd like to put my number in it in case you need me during the night."

"You're not...staying here? With me, I mean?"

His expression was unreadable. "You made it pretty clear you didn't want me inside your home."

"I didn't think it mattered what I wanted."

Grant's lips pressed into a hard line. "During the drive here, I thought about what you said. While it's not how I would prefer to do things, I understand your hesitation."

"You do?"

"You're a single woman living alone. I could easily overpower you if I wanted."

The image of him lying on top of her formed in her mind's eye. Brynnon wasn't sure which she felt more...fear or arousal.

Licking her dry lips, she shook her head. "Exactly. Okay, then." She handed him her phone. "So you'll go home, and I'll call you if I need anything?"

He finished adding his name and number to her contact list before answering. "No. I'll be out front in my truck."

"Your truck?" She looked at him as if he'd lost his marbles. "It's like twenty-nine degrees outside. You'll freeze!"

Typically, Decembers in Dallas weren't horrifically cold. This year, however, the area had already been experiencing record lows.

"I'll be fine."

"This is stupid, Grant. You've already checked the place out and as we discussed earlier, the threats my father received were directed toward him not me. So go home and sleep in your nice, warm bed. I promise if something happens, you'll be the first person I call."

Ignoring her pleas, Grant turned for the door. "Lock this behind me, set the alarm, and work on that list of contacts before you go to bed. I need it by morning."

Brynnon shook her head at the stubborn man. If he was expecting her to beg, he could think again.

"Fine. Whatever. Just don't oversleep. Open house starts at nine, but I need to be there no later than eight."

She thought he may have responded with a low grunt, but wasn't sure. What she did know was she wasn't going to waste any more time worrying about his stubborn ass.

As soon as the door was locked and the alarm set, Brynnon went upstairs into her office and quickly made the list of names and phone numbers he'd requested. After that, she took a hot shower to help ease the tension in her tight muscles.

Tomorrow was an important day, and she needed to be

well-rested and welcoming when the potential buyers arrived.

Feeling relaxed for the first time all day, Brynnon slid under the covers and laid back on her soft pillow. Closing her eyes, she tried to clear her mind of anything stressful or worrisome, but thoughts of Grant sitting outside in a freezing-cold car kept barging in.

After nearly an hour of tossing and turning and staring at a blank ceiling, Brynnon gave up. Throwing her covers off, she grabbed her thick robe from the bathroom and stomped back downstairs.

Not bothering to tie her work boots, she slid them on and stormed outside. Sucking in a breath of cold air, Brynnon held her robe tightly closed and clomped her way down the front steps and through the crunchy grass.

Grant spotted her immediately and turned his key enough to bring power to the windows.

Sliding his down, he asked, "What's wrong?"

"My conscience is being a nagging bitch."

His brows arched. "I'm sorry?"

Brynnon huffed out a breath, sending a silvery cloud into the air in front of her. "You can come inside, but you're staying on the couch."

Understanding crossed over his handsome face. He shook his head. "Don't want to put you out, Princess."

"I told you not to call me that," she glared. "Look, do you want to come inside or not?" When Grant still didn't budge, she fought the urge to stomp her foot. "You know what? Forget it. I take it back. You want to freeze your ass off out here, be my guest."

Spinning around, Brynnon walked away swiftly. Halfway to the front stoop, she heard his truck door open and shut.

She smiled in spite of herself, wiping it away before

turning to hold the door open for him.

"Thanks." He stepped past.

Heat from his body assaulted her, as did the woodsy scent of soap and something else she couldn't quite name. Whatever it was, the man smelled positively delicious.

After re-engaging the locks on her door, Brynnon started for the alarm system on the wall, but Grant had already beaten her to it. She watched, shell-shocked as he entered the correct sequence of numbers.

"H-how'd you do that?"

"With my fingers." He looked at her deadpan.

A heated flush crawled up her neck as she gave him a sarcastic smile. "Cute. I meant, how do you know my security code?"

Grant shrugged but remained silent.

"You're seriously not going to tell me?"

"Nope."

Too tired to start a whole new argument, Brynnon walked over to a large ottoman she kept in the corner of the living room. She pulled out a blanket and extra pillow before tossing them onto the couch.

"Bathroom's in the little hallway behind the stairs as you go to the kitchen. There are plenty of towels and extra toiletries in the closet next to it."

"I know."

"Right." Because he'd already cleared the place. "I guess you know where everything is."

He gave her a silent nod.

"If you get hungry, you're welcome to whatever you can find in the fridge or cabinets. Although, I should probably warn you...I don't cook much, so there's not a whole lot in there right now."

Another nod.

Brynnon glanced over at the couch and back to him. There was no way a man of his size was going to be comfortable sleeping on it.

Feeling a little guilty—but not enough to offer up her own bed—she said, "I'd give you the second bedroom except it's set up as my office, so there isn't a bed in there."

"I've slept on much worse. I'm sure I'll manage."

"Okay. Oh, and also, I use the master bathroom connected to my bedroom." When he didn't respond, she added, "I just don't want you worrying about me walking in on you or anything."

"Wasn't worried."

"Good. I mean, I wasn't either. I just wanted you to know."

"Glad we got that settled."

"Me, too." Okay, she seriously needed to stop talking. "Well, I guess that's it. Goodnight."

Brynnon turned away and headed up the stairs. At the top, she thought she heard a quiet, deep voice say, "Goodnight, Princess."

Chapter 3

"Let me show you the master closet. You won't believe what I was able to do with the space."

Grant watched as Brynnon took yet another couple down the hallway toward the bedrooms. Trying his best to look like another interested buyer—as she'd requested—he skimmed through the before-and-after photo album.

She'd set it out on the kitchen table to show what the house looked like when she bought it compared to now. He had to admit, she was damn good at her job.

When they'd first learned what Brynnon did for a living. Coop had assumed she was a silver-spooned brat beauty who paid someone else to be the brawn. Grant had known better.

The calluses he'd felt on her hands months ago told him she did more than hang a few pictures and smile for the buyers. Watching the way she went about last night and this morning to get things ready for the public showing, he could tell she took great pride in her work.

Not wanting to step on any toes, he'd done his best to stay out of the way throughout the day. Still, he got a few looks here and there...mainly from the female visitors.

He caught Brynnon scowling at a few when they'd blatantly flirted with him. But, then she had simply put on that fake-as-fuck smile he'd seen her wear the night they first met and went back to being the gracious hostess.

For some reason, it pissed him off when she did that. She should be able to be herself all the time and not just when it suited the public eye.

Still waiting for her to get done, Grant grabbed a water bottle from the fridge. Leaning back against the counter, he took a few sips and thought of the way she'd looked when she came outside last night.

He damn near laughed when he saw her storming toward him in her bathrobe and work boots. Goddamn, she looked adorable. Not that he could tell her that.

She'd gotten all huffy and basically told him to fuck off, making him unable to sit in that damn truck any longer.

He told himself he was only taking her up on her offer to sleep on the couch for professional reasons.

Yeah, right. That's why your dick was as hard as a goddamn two-by-four the entire night and most of today.

Grant glanced down at his strained zipper. After checking to make sure Brynnon and the others were still in the bedroom, he adjusted himself as best he could.

Usually, he had complete control over his body. It was imperative when he was a SEAL and even now as a R.I.S.C. operative. Of course, he could just blame it on the way she was dressed.

The form-fitting pencil skirt and thin, white blouse was professional and not revealing in the least. Still, he'd nearly swallowed his tongue when he caught his first glimpse of her this morning.

He'd seen nuns wearing less than she had on, yet his dick had still taken notice. The fucker had been half-hard ever since.

The pull this woman had on him was confusing as shit, and he fucking hated it. *The sooner this assignment is over, the better.*

Even as Grant thought it, a tiny string tugged at the place where his heart used to be. The thought of walking away from her again was unsettling, which was confusing as hell.

Frustrated with the unfamiliar emotions, he tipped the plastic bottle up, chugging the rest of its contents in one long gulp.

Using the trash compactor Brynnon had installed to save floor space—one of many brilliant moves on her part—he pressed his booted toe down onto black pedal and waited for its rectangular drawer to slide open before crushing the bottle in his fist and tossing it inside.

When he shoved the contraption closed a little harder than necessary, it made a loud banging sound right as Brynnon and the couple returned from the bedroom. The three stopped in their tracks, Brynnon's eyes growing wide as they met his.

Scrambling for an excuse other than being pissed at his overactive libido, Grant offered an awkward apology.

"Sorry. This one closes a lot easier than the one at my place."

There was no trash compactor at his apartment, but they'd never know that.

"So." Brynnon tore the young couple's attention away from him. "What do you think of the house?"

The woman looked up at her husband with a hopeful grin. "I love it."

He smiled back down at her. "I do, too." The man turned to Brynnon. "It's a bit smaller than I'd originally planned on, but I think it would be perfect for our first home."

"Great!" Brynnon pulled a card from her skirt pocket.

"Here's my contact information. If you two decide you want to make an offer, just email it to me and I'll get back with you as quickly as I can. But don't wait too long. There was another couple here earlier who were planning to talk to the bank after they left. I'm expecting an offer from them, as well."

The man looked back at his wife, who appeared nervous at the thought of losing the house to someone else. "We'll be in touch shortly," he assured them both. "Don't worry."

The wife's shoulders relaxed, and though he couldn't see her face, Grant heard the smile in Brynnon's voice.

"Excellent. I look forward to hearing from you."

After handshakes were exchanged and goodbyes were given, Brynnon shut the door behind the excited couple and leaned her back against it. Closing her eyes, she let out a loud exhale and gave herself a moment to recharge.

"That seemed to go well."

She looked back at him and smiled. "It went really well." Excitement lit up her eyes as she pushed herself off the door. "I've been doing this long enough to tell the looky-loos from the serious buyers. My gut says I'll have at least two offers before bedtime."

He gave her a nod of approval. "Nice."

"Yeah." She nodded. "It is."

Placing her hands on her lower back, Brynnon arched her chest forward and moved her neck to one side and to other to stretch her tired muscles. Though the action was innocent in nature, it pushed her firm breasts forward tightening the thin silk covering them.

Grant had to fist his hands at his sides to keep from reaching out and taking what he had no business wanting. Luckily, she started to lower her arms before opening her eyes, giving him half a second to raise his gaze back up to her face, where it belonged.

When Brynnon looked back at him, however, he could've sworn she somehow knew what he'd been thinking. Or maybe she was thinking the same about him. *Maybe it doesn't matter because even if you wanted to do something about it—which you don't—you couldn't, because she's a fucking client.*

"Are you hungry?"

The question was innocent, but Jesus. H. Christ. She had no idea what she was doing to him.

"Very."

"Good. So am I." She looked down at her watch. "I'd really like to make a quick trip to my cabin before we go home." Her eyes shot to his. "I mean, to my home. To the condo."

Her rambling was too fucking cute. "I know what you meant."

"Right. Sorry." She inhaled deeply before letting the air out slowly. "I always get wound up on open house days. So much is riding on them, you know? Or maybe you don't know."

"I get what you're saying." Something hit him, then. "Wait. What cabin?"

"Oh." Her brows went up. "I guess I haven't told you about that yet. I'm flipping a cabin in the woods. When it's done, I'm going to sell the condo and live there."

The fact that she preferred a cabin in the woods over a plush condo in the city was even more proof that she wasn't the high-maintenance diva Coop tried making her out to be. But Grant wished he'd been told about it sooner.

"Where is it located?" he asked roughly.

His concern over the fact that they were about to go to an

unknown, unsecured location sounded more like irritation. Her smile dimmed slightly making him want to kick his own ass.

"Sixty-seven miles north of here, off thirty-five."

That surprised him even more. "That's damn near Oklahoma."

"I know." She grinned. "But just wait until you see it. The property is just north of Gainesville, and it's so beautiful and peaceful. No traffic or sirens. No reporters waiting around the corner to ambush me with questions about my dad." Her voice turned wistful when she added, "Just me and the quiet sounds of nature."

Professionally speaking, he hated the idea of her being in the middle of the fucking woods by herself. Personally, the place she described sounded like a dream.

"I know it's a drive," she spoke up again. "I don't need to stay long. I've just been so busy getting this place ready for today I haven't had a chance to get up there in over a week. I don't like to stay away for too long, in case someone's eyeing the place. I want people to know someone lives there. Or, will be, anyway."

"Makes sense."

She blew out a breath of relief. "Good. Let me just pack up the food and tidy the kitchen, and I'll be ready to go." Brynnon started to leave the room but turned around. "I know you aren't big on fast food, but—"

"It's fine."

"Yeah?"

He nodded. "We can leave your car here. I'll drive."

Her face scrunched. "No offense, but that thing looks like a major gas guzzler. Wouldn't it be smarter to take my car?"

"It's not a problem."

"You sure, because I can—"

"I'll drive."

One of her brows arched, and she put her hands palms-up. "I was just trying to save you some money." Thinking about her comment, Brynnon's round eyes widened as she babbled. "Not that you need to. I didn't mean to imply that you were short on money."

Jesus, she really needed to learn to relax. *Says the pot to the kettle.*

Grant quickly put her at ease. "I appreciate the offer, Brynnon. I just prefer to drive my truck."

"Okay." She smiled shyly.

Grant watched her leave the room, surprised at her uncertainty. She'd had no problem standing up to him or trying to put him in his place yesterday. But just then, she'd acted as though the idea of offending him bothered her.

Women.

He shook his head. They were a confusing-as-fuck species, which was one of the billion reasons he didn't do relationships.

As promised, Grant stopped for food on the way to Brynnon's cabin. He ordered four chicken, bacon, and avocado wraps and a large ice water. He was already on his third while she'd barely made a dent in her enormous cheeseburger and fries.

"How can you eat that crap?"

She looked at him like he was nuts. "Are you kidding? This is heaven."

His stomach turned. "It's loaded with carbs and saturated fat."

"I know." Brynnon surprised him with a broad smile before taking another big bite.

"You should take better care of yourself."

"Like what? Drink protein shakes and work out six hours a day?" She shook her head, her thick, red hair swaying across her shoulders. "I don't have time for that. Besides, I burn more than enough calories doing what I do."

"Eating healthy isn't just about weight, Princess. Heart disease is the number one killer of women in this country."

Letting the nickname slide, Brynnon pouted. "You're killing my burger buzz." She swallowed another bite. "Let's talk about something else."

Deciding to save his fourth wrap for later, Grant crumpled the paper from his current one into a ball and tossed it into the sack on the floor between them.

"What do you want to talk about?"

"You."

Shit. He should've kept his mouth shut. "Not happening."

"Oh, come on," she pleaded. "You probably know everything there is to know about me."

Not as much as I want to.

Grant cleared his throat. "Didn't know you had a cabin in the woods."

"Okay, fine. You didn't know that *one* thing. But I only bought it a few months ago. Besides, I bet there's a file somewhere at your office that has all sorts of personal information about me."

Grant remained silent, unwilling to admit he did have a file on her. It just wasn't at the office.

Brynnon turned toward him a little more. "You have to give me *something*. We'll start small like…where'd you grow up?"

She was like a dog with a fucking bone. Grant knew if he didn't give her something, she'd just keep prodding.

"Nebraska."

"Nice." She put a fist in the air. "Go, Cornhuskers!"

Grant glanced over at her then back to the road. "You follow football?"

A tiny snort escaped the back of her throat. "Please. I'm from Texas. It's practically a religion here."

A gorgeous woman who liked football. Damn, he was in trouble.

"Favorite team?"

Brynnon's eyes narrowed. "Nice try, but we're supposed to be talking about you, remember?"

One corner of his mouth twitched as he fought a smile. A gorgeous, *smart* woman who liked football. He was so fucked.

"Where in Nebraska?" Brynnon kept on with the questioning.

"Bellevue. It's just north of Offutt Air Force Base."

"Cool." Wrapping up what remained of her burger, she threw it in the sack with the rest of their trash. "Is that why you went into the military?"

"Yep." *Liar.*

"Did you always know you wanted to be a SEAL?"

He glanced over at her again. "How'd you know I was with the Teams?"

"My dad told me. He was very impressed with you, by the way. Said he loved your no-nonsense attitude."

"Your dad seems solid."

Affection filled her voice. "He is. But you still haven't answered my question about being a SEAL. Did you know from the start you wanted to go that route?"

No. "Yep."

"Okay. Let's see. What else?" She thought for a moment. "Oh, I know. Have you ever been married?"

His chest tightened. "Nope."

Her line of questioning was creeping into dangerous territory and needed to be derailed before he said shit he had no business sharing.

"Girlfriend?"

Let's see how well she does when the table is turned.

With a cocky brow, he looked over at her. "You asking out of curiosity or personal interest?"

Grant damn near did smile when he saw the dark blush creep into her neck and cheeks.

Score one for the bodyguard.

Laughing it off nervously, she shook her head. "You wish."

"What about you?" he continued his attempts to thwart her interrogation. "Ever been married?"

"Came close once, but no."

Grant didn't care for the change in her tone. "What happened?"

She paused, her eyes skittering to his. "You really want to know?"

Actually, he did. "Wouldn't have asked, otherwise."

Biting her bottom lip—something she really shouldn't do around him—Brynnon took a deep breath and blew it out.

"Growing up with money has its perks, but it also has a lot of downsides. Stuff people don't think about."

"Such as?"

"My dad's construction company took off my freshman year of high school. Not long after, boys started noticing me. I thought it was because they liked me, you know? But it wasn't. They liked my money…or, rather, my *parents'* money. They'd stick around long enough to be invited to dinner or outings on the boat. Things like that." She smiled sadly. "I always seemed to get especially popular around Christmas time."

"They were using you." The thought pissed him the hell off.

She nodded. "I finally wizened up and quit dating altogether. I didn't even go to prom."

Grant schooled his expression as he realized they had more in common than he'd initially thought.

"And after high school?"

Brynnon shrugged. "I focused on my college classes. Made it to my junior year before I fell for a guy again."

"Must have been pretty serious if you were going to marry him."

Grant was hit with a sudden wave of jealousy. It spiraled through his system at the thought of her wearing another man's ring, making him want to find the bastard and beat the shit out of him.

What. The. Fuck?

"It was." Her sweet voice broke through his shocking thoughts. "At least, I thought so." Looking down at her lap, she shook her head. "I still can't believe what an idiot I was."

He didn't like the sound of that. "What makes you think you're the idiot?"

"Because I fell for it. Hook, line, and sinker." She laughed humorlessly. "In the beginning, I thought Lucas was the perfect guy. He was incredibly smart, especially when it came to computers. He was witty and handsome. Plus, he was a Campbell."

When he gave her a look, Brynnon took time to explain. "Around here, being a Campbell means he came from money."

Understanding sunk in. "So unlike your boyfriend in high

school, that was a non-issue."

"Exactly," she nodded, her gaze dropping to her lap. Using a softened tone he hadn't heard before, she said, "I guess you could say Lucas swept me off my feet."

Unable to hide his bearish tone, Grant asked, "What did he do to you?"

Her eyes rose to his. "His love was computers and gaming, but Lucas knew making a lot of money at that sort of thing was a long shot. His uncle owned a lucrative building supply company and promised him the CEO position if he could land a deal with my dad's construction company."

Grant's hands tightened around the wheel. "He used you to make a business deal?"

Embarrassed, Brynnon looked out the passenger window and nodded. "It was second semester of my senior year at SMU. I'd come home for the weekend and had been staying at his apartment. I left that Sunday afternoon to go back to school, but before I got into the elevator, I realized I'd forgotten my backpack. So I went back inside."

She looked over at him, apparently feeling the need to explain. "We weren't engaged, but we'd been dating for nearly a year. He'd been talking about marriage and had given me a key to his place."

Ignoring the way she licked her lips again, Grant put his eyes back on the road and listened while she continued.

"Lucas didn't realize I'd come back in, and I overheard him on the phone with his uncle." One corner of her mouth rose as she shook her head. "The dumbass had the call on speakerphone."

Grant probably would have smiled had he not been dreading whatever was coming.

"Anyway, his uncle was talking about my dad, and I heard

him tell Lucas to"—she made air quotes— "hurry the hell up and marry the redheaded bitch so we can seal the deal before the next quarter starts."

Grant ground his teeth together but stayed quiet, not wanting her to see how much the screwed up story pissed him off.

"The worst part was hearing the response Lucas gave." With a sharp bite in her voice, Brynnon finished the rest of the story. "He told his uncle he'd planned on proposing the following week, but his *other* girlfriend had already paid for a weekend cruise for the two of them."

"Are you fucking kidding me?" Grant growled before he could stop himself. So much for hiding his anger.

Not bothered by his profane outburst, Brynnon gave him a half smile. "I wish I were." She immediately changed her mind. "Actually, no, I don't. I mean, it sucked at the time. I'd given a lot of myself to Lucas." Her eyes dropped to her lap again. "Some things you can only give away once."

Grant was surprised the steering wheel didn't break. The motherfucker had taken her virginity, knowing he was scamming her the entire time? It was enough to make Grant want to hunt the bastard down.

"Looking back, I realize the signs were always there. I think I just didn't want to see them."

He pinned her down with his eyes. "What he did wasn't your fault."

"Maybe." She shrugged, sitting back in her seat. "Doesn't matter, now. I truly believe everything happens for a reason. Sometimes it just sucks when you have to wait to figure out what that reason is."

Grant didn't believe that. He'd lost too much to think there was a reason behind all that pain. No divine intervention ever came through when he needed it.

It was another one of those billion reasons he didn't get involved in a serious relationship.

Guys like Jake, Trevor, and Derek…they were cut out for shit like that. Not him.

Chapter 4

"What do you think?"

Standing just inside the entryway, Brynnon held her breath while waiting for the muscle-bound man to finish clearing the cabin's interior.

The nerves fluttering inside were confusing. She wasn't sure why, but for some reason, she really wanted Grant to like her little piece of heaven as much as she did.

From the tiny entryway you could see the open living room, kitchen, and staircase leading up to what would soon be her bedroom and private bath. At the far end of the kitchen was a hallway leading back to the two bedrooms, full bath, and laundry closet.

It wasn't huge but to her, it was perfect.

Except for the occasional contractor and Angie—her one and only girlfriend—she'd never had anyone else out here until now. Even her dad had yet to find time in his busy schedule to come by and see the place.

Deeming it safe, Grant's gorgeous eyes began scanning the cabin's interior, taking it all in. After what felt like forever, he turned and gave her an approving nod.

"It's nice."

Her heart thumped. "You really think so?"

"Don't say things I don't mean, Princess."

She crossed her arms. "Again, with the nickname?"

Blowing her off, he simply shrugged and began walking around slowly, staring up at the exposed beams. "The woodwork is impressive. You do all that, yourself?"

"I'd like to say yes, but no. Before this one, I had no experience with an all-wood home. I searched around and found a local guy with a small crew to clean, repair, and re-seal it all. Cost more to do that than it did putting in the floors and cabinets."

"I bet." He walked over to one wall. Running a hand across one of the logs, he nodded again. "They did good work."

"Heck yeah, they did. You should've seen this place when I first bought it. Talk about a buyer's remorse."

For just a second, Brynnon thought she may have seen an actual smile trying to peek through.

Man, he's a tough nut to crack.

"Well, this is it. Oh and just ignore the scaffolding behind me."

She used her thumb to point to the monstrosity of a structure ruining the otherwise perfect room.

Unfortunately, the smaller, two-story windows on each side of the stone fireplace were too high for her regular ladder to reach, so she'd borrowed the elevated frame from a guy she'd used for some of her other projects.

"I finished staining the trim and window sill the last time I was here," she continued. "It was the last thing I did before leaving, and I didn't have the energy to break the scaffolding back down."

Grant tipped his chin toward the top of the small staircase that ran along the north wall.

"What are you doing with the space up there?"

Brynnon smiled. "That's the master suite."

"Master *suite*?"

"It's just a fancy way of saying my bedroom and bathroom," she chuckled. "It was originally used as attic space. After I bought it, I decided to utilize the space for a better purpose."

He put his hands in his pockets and turned his brows inward. "Why three bedrooms?"

"What do you mean?"

"Just that there are already two bedrooms down here. It's just you, right?"

"Well, yeah. But I'm hoping someday the right guy will come along and love the cabin as much as I do. For now, one of the other bedrooms will be a spare and the other my office. At least until..." Brynnon trailed off.

"Until what?"

She blushed. "Until a baby comes along."

A shadow she didn't understand fell over his face. "You want kids?"

"Sure." She smiled. "Don't you?"

Rather than answer the question, Grant pulled his hands from his pockets and started looking around again. "So what is it you need to get done here today? I'd rather not be too late getting back on the road. Nighttime means less visibility, which in turn means we're more vulnerable."

Wow. Whiplash much?

Blinking, Brynnon recovered from the sudden change in topic. "Um, not much. I need to take a few measurements in the room upstairs. The furniture I ordered will be in soon and I want to make sure I know where I want everything to make the set-up easier. Once my bedroom's done and I clean a few things up, this place will be ready to go."

"Let's get that done so we can get back to the city."

Resisting a roll of her eyes, Brynnon went to the kitchen. Just when she thought she was making headway with the guy, he turns back into Oscar the Grouch.

"I still think you're taking this whole bodyguard business a little too seriously," she spoke over her shoulder as she removed her jacket.

Laying it over the back of one of her bar stools, she walked to the sink and opened the cabinet below. Brynnon reached for the small tool bag she kept there, continuing her thoughts as she began digging for her measuring tape.

"I mean, you've been with me nearly two full days and there hasn't been the slightest sign of danger."

She stood back up just in time to see Grant's eyes shift away quickly. Fully aware he'd been checking her out, Brynnon fought a smug smile, pretending as if she hadn't noticed.

Walking past him, she put a slight wiggle into her walk as she moved up the stairs a little more slowly than usual. When he cleared his throat from behind her, Brynnon had to literally bite her lip to keep from laughing.

Once inside the empty room, she quickly went to work, trying to measure the areas she wanted to put her dresser, bed, and twin nightstands. When the metal tape decided not to stay put, she stood to find something to help keep it in place…and ran into a solid wall of muscle.

"Oh!" she exclaimed, startled.

Grant looked down at her, his gaze impossible to read. "Need some help?"

"Um, yeah," she swallowed. "That would be great. Thanks."

A few seconds later, Brynnon realized not only had she not moved, but her hand was still resting against his rock-hard chest.

"Sorry." She jumped back, nearly stumbling in the process. "Where do you want me?"

The deep, rumbled words left her aching in all the right places. And flustered. "I...um...what?"

He glanced at the tape still in her hand. "What do you need to measure?"

Wanting to slap herself upside the head, Brynnon laughed it off. "Oh." She smiled. "Right. Sorry."

Good grief. Could she be any more lame?

Turning back around, she closed her eyes for a couple of seconds to compose herself before returning to the task at hand.

"If you could hold the end here, I'll pull it to where I need to stop."

Freeing enough tape to ensure they wouldn't touch, Brynnon held out the metal end for him. There were a few times during the process she thought she'd caught him staring at her exposed cleavage—an unfortunate and not-at-all intentional happenstance when she had to bend over to get the correct measurement.

She had to admit it was nice to know there was an actual human inside all that cold, rough exterior.

When she had all that was needed, Brynnon dropped the tape back into the bag and zipped it up. After heading back downstairs and putting it away, she excused herself to go to the restroom before the hour-plus trip back home.

Once she was finished, Grant took a cue from her and did the same. While waiting for him in the living room, a cool breeze brushed over Brynnon, taking her by surprise.

Remembering her furnace had kicked back off just before they came downstairs and her ceiling fans were all turned off to save electricity, she looked up to try to determine where the breeze would have come from. It only took a couple of seconds for her to spot the source.

"Damn it."

Walking over to the scaffolding, Brynnon kicked off her heels and began climbing the metal rungs attached to its frame. The window to the right of the fireplace—the same one she'd worked on the last time she was here—was cracked open at the top.

In her bare feet, Brynnon pulled herself up to the wooden platform and went to the window. She was usually meticulous about this sort of thing. Then again, she *had* been working day and night, lately. It was very possible she'd forgotten to shut it before she left.

Pushing it closed, she'd just secured the latch when a deep voice boomed from behind her.

"What the hell are you doing up there?"

Startled, Brynnon spun around quickly and squealed. Grant was glaring at her from the doorway just under the stairs. He looked extremely pissed off, though she had no idea why.

"Jesus, Grant!" she put a hand to her beating chest. "You scared the hell out of m—"

Before she could finish the sentence, the structure below her began to sway and give. Brynnon tried reaching for the metal frame, but it was already buckling beneath her feet. She was thrown off balance, the edge moving just out of her reach.

Terrified, she swung her gaze back to his. Grant's eyes grew wide as they both realized what was about to happen.

"Jump!" He yelled as he started to run across the room.

What? "Are you crazy?"

The wooden platform began to tip forward.

"I'll catch you," he promised. "Just do it!"

I'll do what you say if my safety is truly a concern. Damn. She should've known those words would come back to bite her in the ass.

Not wanting to fall amid the hard, metal pipes, Brynnon threw up a quick prayer and did as Grant ordered just as the entire scaffolding collapsed.

Screaming as she went, she leapt toward his outstretched arms. As promised, Grant caught her, but her force of motion caused him to fly backward. Luckily, the couch was directly behind him.

With a loud *oof,* Grant landed awkwardly over the arm of the couch, the momentum bouncing them both from the cushions down onto the floor. When it was all said and done, Brynnon was on the area rug in front of the couch...and Grant was lying on top of her.

It took her a second to realize he'd somehow managed to place his hand between her head and the floor, protecting her as they fell. *Man, he's good.*

"Are you okay?" He stared down at her with genuine concern.

"Yeah," she squeezed the word out. "I just can't breathe."

Cursing under his breath, Grant hopped off her much more quickly than she'd expect a man of his size. "Sorry. Here." He held out his hand for her to take.

Accepting the help, Brynnon was pulled gently to her feet. Grant went over and studied the fallen scaffolding closely. When he was finished, he turned back to her.

With his hands resting on his hips, he asked, "You sure

you're okay?"

"I-I think so." She nodded, but looked down at herself just to be sure. Her right arm was a little sore, but other than that, she was fine. "Yeah. I-I'm good."

She glanced over his shoulder toward the massive pile of metal and broken wood. A shiver ran down her spine, knowing how much worse it could've been.

"Are you?" When Brynnon brought her eyes back to his, the hard expression on his face damn near caused her to recoil.

"What the hell were you thinking?" he hissed through his teeth. "You could've been killed."

Great. Her valiant protector was back in pissed-off bodyguard mode. *Just when I thought he was softening up to me a little.*

"Uh, I was thinking that the window up there needed to be closed."

A muscle beneath his dark scruff bulged as he clenched his handsome jaw together. "What if you'd been alone?"

She thought about all the times she had worked on the scaffolding with no one else around but decided that was definitely not something she intended to share with Grumpy McGrumperson. Instead, she gave him another truth.

"I always keep my phone in my pocket while I'm working." From the fire shooting from his eyes, that was not the right answer.

"And if it breaks or you're knocked unconscious?"

The same frustration she felt last night started to seep back in. "Look, Grant. I appreciate your concern, but I'm a big girl. I've been doing this sort of thing for years, and that's the first time anything like this has ever happened."

Nostrils still flaring, he looked as though he wanted to

continue reprimanding her. Instead, he rolled his lips inward before telling her, "From now on, you need something done up there, I'll do it."

"Excuse me?"

"You heard me. You have no business being up on that death trap."

"Why? Because I'm a woman?"

"It has nothing to do with your gender. You're not going back up there because it's not safe."

"Says the Navy SEAL who's probably gone into some of the world's most dangerous places."

"That was my job."

"And this is mine!" A few seconds passed before Brynnon broke the uncomfortable silence. "Look, I told you last night. I don't take orders from you."

"Wrong." His gray eyes pinned her down. "You agreed to when it came to your safety.

"From a perceived threat against my *father*, which has nothing to do with what just happened. The things I have to do for my job or to get this place ready do not concern you."

"My job is to protect you. Which means *any* threat against your safety concerns me."

They were still staring each other down when Brynnon's phone rang. Pulling it from her pocket, she couldn't resist showing him the screen. "Oh, look. It's not broken."

With a smart-ass smile, she answered Angie's call. "Hey, Ang. What's up?"

"Have you checked your email lately?"

"No, I've been…" Brynnon glanced back up at Grant. "Busy."

"Busy, huh? That hunk of a bodyguard you told me about still hanging around?"

She didn't miss the woman's mischievous tone. She should've known better than to mention Grant when Angie called before the open house this morning.

"Ang," she warned her friend not to go there.

"What?" The other woman's tone changed from devilish to angelic in a snap. "I'm just anxious to hear how *busy* you've been. That's all."

Brynnon rolled her eyes. "Uh, huh. You mentioned an email?"

Angie sighed. "Fine. Be a killjoy. And there are email*s*. Plural."

"Okay, I'll bite. What were they?"

"Offers from today. Three, to be exact."

Forgetting for a moment they'd just been arguing, Brynnon shot a smile in Grant's direction. "Seriously? That's great! Were they reasonable?"

"Well, considering one was for the asking price and the two others were over it, yeah. I'd say they were pretty reasonable."

"Sweet! Okay, listen. I'm at the cabin right now. We're about to leave, but I won't be home for over an hour, so can you please write each of them back with the usual counter? We'll see if any write back and go from there."

"Sure thing. And listen…anything happens between you and the guarder of your body, I'd better be the first to hear about it."

Knowing she was probably blushing, Brynnon told her friend, "I'm hanging up now."

"I'm serious!"

Laughing, Brynnon said goodbye and ended the call.

"Good news?"

He wasn't smiling—*shocker*—but he wasn't scowling quite

as fiercely, either.

"We got three offers on the house. All at or above the asking price."

Grant tipped his head. "Congratulations."

"Thanks." Feeling badly about the way she'd treated him after he'd practically saved her life, Brynnon sighed. "Listen. In all the excitement with…*that*"—she motioned toward the death trap that used to be her friend's scaffolding—"I never did say thank you. You could have been seriously hurt, jumping under me like that, but you didn't hesitate."

He shrugged. "It's my job."

His job. Right. She really needed to remember that's all she was to him.

Ignoring the sting she shouldn't feel, Brynnon said, "Regardless. Thank you."

Grant gave her another nod. "We should get going."

"Okay."

"What do you want to do about that?" He nodded toward the heap.

"Leave it. I'll deal with it later. I should probably call the owner and let him know what happened, though. I'll offer to pay for a replacement."

"You're kidding."

"No, actually, I'm not. He let me borrow it and I broke it."

"You didn't break it. It broke. There's a difference. The guy's lucky you didn't get hurt."

"But I'm the one who put it together. Not him." Brynnon looked over at the mess again. "I must not have tightened something down enough."

Even as she said it, she knew that wasn't what happened. She'd used scaffoldings just like that one several times over the years. Not once had she ever had one wobble, let alone collapse like that one had.

"It could've been a manufacturing issue, for all we know." She looked back at Grant. "I'll deal with it later."

Grabbing her jacket from the barstool where she'd left it, Brynnon put it on and followed him out the door. The chill in the air had more of a bite to it than when they first got there, making Brynnon excited for the impending winter weather.

Texas wasn't known for getting much snow, but the farmer's almanac, along with every weather forecaster around the country, were predicting a much higher-than-average amount this year. As a kid, she'd always wished for a few feet of the stuff so she could build a snowman or throw snowballs at her brother. Unfortunately, the only time she ever got to play in the snow was when her family went to Colorado on the occasional skiing trip.

Grant started the truck but didn't put it in drive right away. Instead, he sat there, looking at her cabin and the immediate area around it.

"You're awfully secluded out here."

She glanced over at him. "That's kind of the whole point."

"What are your plans for security?"

Brynnon wondered when he was going to bring that up. "I keep meaning to get a security system installed." She looked at her cabin's front door and back to him. An idea struck. "Hey, doesn't your firm install those?"

"We do."

"Great. I'll just hire you guys to do it, then. Can you get me in touch with whoever I need to talk with to get it all set up?"

"I'll take care of it."

She wanted to argue about him taking over, but something

in his eyes told Brynnon he was actually pleased she wanted his company to handle that end of things.

"Okay. Just get me some quotes on the systems you think are the best and let me know what it costs. We can go from there."

With his signature nod, Grant began driving them back to the city. "I still need a schedule from you that covers the next two weeks, at least."

Crap. She'd given him the list of contacts but completely forgot about the schedule. "I'll get that done as soon as we get to the condo."

"That's fine. What's on the agenda for tomorrow?"

She hesitated, unsure of how he would react to her plans. "Sunday brunch at my father's at ten-thirty. After that, we need to make a trip to Children's Medical."

"Children's Medical?" He actually sounded concerned. "Someone sick?"

She smiled sadly. "Almost every kiddo there." When he gave her a *no shit* look, Brynnon figured she should explain.

"A nonprofit group I'm associated with delivers Christmas gifts to the cancer wing each year. Tomorrow's the day we scheduled for this year."

Grant's lips became pinched, and his right eye twitched slightly.

"Seriously? You're going to get upset about this, too?"

"I'm not upset," he grumbled.

"Could've fooled me."

The confusing man's chest rose and fell with a deep breath. "It's not ideal, from a security standpoint. But what you're doing"—he glanced over at her, his expression softening a tad— "It's a good thing."

"Oh." With a chagrined smile, she offered a soft, "Thanks."

Okay, so maybe she needed to quit jumping to conclusions where he was concerned. Of course, it would help if the man changed his expression once in a while, rather than wearing that perpetual scowl all the freaking time.

After a few minutes of awkward silence, she spoke again. "One of the few things I like about my father being a senator is the charity work I've been given access to through his platforms. Among collecting and delivering presents to the children at the hospital, this particular charity works throughout the year to help Children's Medical raise money for juvenile cancer research."

At the mention of cancer, a shadow crossed over Grant's face. Before Brynnon could ask him about it, he changed the subject.

"After I drop you off at your car, I'll follow you to your condo. Once we get there, I need to—"

"Clear the inside and check the perimeter." She smiled over at him. "I know."

Though he didn't actually smile, there was a small twitch at the corner of his mouth. She swallowed hard, thinking of what it would feel like to kiss him there. To kiss him *everywhere.*

Thoughts of earlier ran through her head, and she couldn't help but be impressed with what she'd felt while he was lying on top of her. There'd been a definite bulge pressing against her thigh. Unless he was hiding a second gun in the crotch of his jeans, the man was seriously blessed.

You're just a job, remember? Brynnon's spirit was instantly dulled. Damn that tiny voice, anyway.

For the rest of the ride, she tried to forget all about the

way his warm, hard chest felt beneath her palm while standing in the upstairs room. Focusing instead on a mental to-do list, she worked diligently to erase the memory of the other hard body part she'd felt.

It worked, too. Until later.

Lying in bed, she kept fighting against memories of him racing to her rescue. Wrapping himself protectively around her. His body pressing against hers on the cabin floor.

Her body ached for his touch, but she knew that was impossible. For a minute, she thought about quietly getting herself off but then felt weird doing that knowing he was lying downstairs, asleep on her couch. Plus, knowing her luck—and him—the hard-ass would probably decide to do an impromptu intruder drill and burst into her room mid-orgasm.

More than a little frustrated, Brynnon turned onto her side, punched her pillow harder than necessary, and forced her eyes closed. Instead of thinking about how incredible sex with Grant would almost certainly be, she began plotting ways she could talk her dad into forgetting about this whole bodyguard nonsense when she saw him at brunch tomorrow.

Chapter 5

"Hey, man. Good to see ya."

"Hey." Grant shook Coop's outstretched hand as he and Brynnon stepped inside her father's home. Having worked closely with Senator Cantrell a couple of times now, he was familiar with the mansion's setup.

"And you must be Brynnon." The former ranger gave her a sideways grin. "Hi. Sean Cooper. You can call me Coop."

"Hi, Coop." Brynnon smiled as she returned the handshake. "It's nice to meet you."

"Likewise. Your father told me a lot about you."

Rolling her captivating eyes, Brynnon chuckled. "Great."

"Nah. All good things, I promise."

The handsome sniper winked, and Brynnon's lips curved even higher. Grant pushed back the urge to punch the fucker for being able to make her smile like that.

"Let me take your coats," Coop offered.

"Thank you." Brynnon began unbuttoning her coat.

When she came downstairs this morning with it already on, Grant had taken notice of the way it's dark green color matched perfectly with her eyes. Since when did he notice shit like that?

Since her.

Coop helped her slide the thick wool from her shoulders, and Grant wanted to kick himself for not thinking to do that. Again, the question of why he gave a damn about something like that struck.

He didn't ponder the thought for long, however. Mainly because—though he didn't want to admit it—he already knew the answer.

"You're pretty good at that." Brynnon smiled up at Coop. "Has my dad been using you as a bodyguard or a butler?"

The younger man smirked. "A little of both, actually."

What the actual fuck? She was flirting. With *Coop*. Right in fucking front of him.

"Well, don't let him try to push you around." Brynnon's voice went all smooth and creamy. "He may act serious and tough, but the guy's a complete softy."

"I was about to say the same thing about this guy." Coop used his thumb to point toward Grant.

Brynnon laughed a little too loudly at the joke, adding to Grant's frustration. He'd barely gotten two words out of her this morning—way out of character for her—but now she was practically falling all over his teammate? What the hell?

Grant tried to tell himself the distance she was putting between them was a good thing. He hadn't missed the interest behind her smoldering gaze last night when she'd bumped into him upstairs. Hell, for a second there, he'd actually thought about kissing her.

If she hadn't pulled away first, he honestly sure he wouldn't have leaned down for a taste. Afterward, when he'd seen her up on that goddamn scaffolding and completely lost his cool. Not because he was a controlling bastard—like she probably thought—but because the idea of something happening to her scared the fuck out of him.

When he realized she was going to fall, his heart had come back to life for the first time in over a decade. Somehow, Brynnon Cantrell was starting to slither between his carefully placed defenses. That terrified him even more.

Coop laughed at something she said, snapping Grant out of his jumbled thoughts. He blinked, his eyes connecting with hers. The light in her eyes dimmed slightly before skittering away.

What the fuck?

He wasn't sure what happened between last night and today, but her demeanor with him was definitely different. The silence on the ride here had given him time to wrack his brain for what he'd done to piss her off, but he couldn't pinpoint anything out of the norm.

Now, she was flirting it up with Sniper Boy, which made no goddamn sense to him whatsoever. Something was definitely bothering her, and he had full intentions of calling her out on it the first chance he got.

"There's my girl!"

All heads turned to see William Cantrell walking across the tiled floor toward them. "Hi, sweetheart." With his hands on Brynnon's shoulders, the prestigious man kissed his daughter on the cheek. "Good to see you."

Grant watched, envious of the embrace Brynnon gave to her father.

"You too, Daddy. Is Billy here?"

The senator's smile faltered at the mention of his son's name. *Interesting.*

"Not yet, but he promised he'd come."

"I'm sure he will."

Brynnon smiled again, but Grant had been around her long enough now to recognize the uncertainty behind her eyes. She hadn't talked about her brother much, and he had a feeling there was some tension there.

Her father held his hand out for Grant. "Grant, my boy. Good to see you again. I take it you and my daughter are no longer butting heads?"

"No, sir," Grant lied to the man.

"Well, just wait." Cantrell chuckled. "You stick around this one long enough, it's bound to happen again."

"Hello…" a blushing Brynnon waved a hand back and forth in her dad's peripheral. "*This one* is standing right here."

The senator simply laughed again, speaking a little lower when he added, "See? I swear, she's the spitting image of her mother. Got both her beautiful looks and attitude."

Looking appalled, Brynnon's voice rose an octave. "Dad!"

Laughing, her father simply wrapped an arm around Brynnon and gave her a squeeze. "Oh, calm down, sweetheart. You know I'm only telling our new friend the truth."

"He's not our *friend*. He's my bodyguard. One you insist I have, even though I don't need him."

Grant hid his reaction to the statement, her words stinging a hell of a lot more than they should.

Blatantly bypassing Brynnon's continued objection to Grant's presence, the senator smiled at them both. "The food is just about ready. Why don't we all go have a seat in the dining room while we wait?"

Brynnon started in that direction but stopped when she realized Grant wasn't following.

Her pretty brows turned inward. "You're not coming?"

He was surprised that didn't make her happy and wanted to tell her so. Instead, Grant did his best to control his irritation. "In a minute. I need to go over a couple of things with Coop first."

Without another word, the confusing woman turned and followed her father across the large entry toward the hallway leading to the dining room.

Waiting until they were out of earshot, Coop grinned. "Brynnon seems great. I totally expected her to be all hoity-toity and stuck up, but she acted genuinely nice. I guess I shouldn't be all that surprised. Her dad's pretty cool. You two really getting along okay?"

Grant tore his eyes from the entryway where Brynnon had just disappeared to and looked back at his teammate. "Any new threats?"

Coop blinked at Grant's obvious change of subject. "Not in the last two days." The other man's brows scrunched together. "You seem grumpy, even for you. What's the matter...do you not like her, or something?"

I like *her* too *much*. "She's fine."

"Fine?" The other man looked confused. "If you say so."

Done with the topic, Grant let out a frustrated breath. "I say so. Now, can we please focus on the reason we're here instead of how fucking sweet you think Cantrell's daughter is? It's bad enough I had to stand here and watch your mutual fucking flirting session."

Coop put a hand up between them. "Whoa, take it easy, man. I was just asking if you two were getting along. Jesus."

Shit. Coop was right. He needed to get his head in the fucking game. Otherwise, he'd risk letting his true feelings for the woman show. The slow upturn of Coop's mouth told him he was already too late.

"Holy shit."

"What?" Grant kept his expression flat.

Coop's eyes grew as big as saucers. Blurting much too

loudly, "Dude, you like her!"

"Shut the fuck up," Grant growled, his eyes flying over to the direction where Brynnon and her father had vanished. Glaring back at Coop, he whispered angrily, "Are you seriously that stupid, or are you trying to get us both fired?"

The idea that Grant may have an actual romantic interest in someone apparently trumped any threat of reprimand from the senator because Coop began to chuckle. "Oh, my god." He covered his mouth but then held his hands up as though he were praying or some shit. "This is the best news I've ever heard. Like, seriously epic."

"There is no news," Grant hissed. "You're assuming shit you have no business assuming."

"Oh, no," Coop shook his head, amusement flickering in the young sniper's hazel eyes. "You like her. It makes perfects sense now."

"The fuck are you talking about?"

"You." Coop pointed at him. "Ever since your last gig with the Senator, you've been walking around like you're pissed off at the world." He shrugged. "Well, more than usual anyway."

"No. I haven't."

Ignoring his false denial, Coop continued with his hushed rant. "Plus, you practically jumped all over Mac's ass to get this assignment."

"I didn't jump." Grant took a step forward, his hands curling into tight fists at his sides. "I explained to you why I volunteered for this job."

Not backing down, Coop grinned. "Oh, you explained alright. I'm just not buying it."

Grant wanted to shove his knuckles into the other man's teeth. "You seem to be under the impression I give a shit what you buy or don't buy."

Snapping his fingers, Coop pointed at him for the second time. "That's another thing. You've been on the defensive with this case from day one." Straightening his shoulders, he spoke with a piss-poor British accent. "I think thou doth protest a little too much."

Grant took a step back and forced himself not to reach out and break the man's finger right the fuck off. "I'm protesting because your accusations are completely unfounded. And, we've only been working this for three days, dumbass."

"Deflect all you want, man. I saw the way you were looking at her."

What the hell? "When?" Grant challenged.

"When she was hugging her dad. You got this look in your eye. One I've never seen you wear. Almost like you wished she was hugging you instead."

Shit. Goddamn it. Shit. "So I glanced Brynnon's way. Doesn't mean I like her."

"Bullshit." Coop smirked. "It was only there for a second, but I saw it. You got that same look Jake has when he looks at Olivia. And Trev with Lexi, or D with Charlie."

Anxiety began to seep through his pores. Coop couldn't be right. He wasn't falling for her. Was he?

Fuck. Fuck, fuck, fuck.

Grant gave himself a mental shake. What the hell was he worried about? It wasn't the same look. Even if it were, it wouldn't matter. He didn't do the whole committed, romantic shit those other guys did.

He tried that once. Still bore the scars inside his soul because of it.

More than ready to end the pointless conversation, Grant

decided to turn the tables on the know-it-all.

"Speaking of looks, Sean…how's Mac doing?"

Coop blinked. "What?"

"You wanna talk about the way a guy looks at a woman, take a look in the fucking mirror."

The other man shook his head. "Mac and I are teammates. Partners. That's all."

"But you want to be more, right?"

"Fuck, no!"

Grant nearly smiled. "Now who's protesting, asshole?"

"Because you're way off base with this shit."

"Right. And I suppose I've imagined all those stolen glances I've seen you throw her way. Or the ones she's given you."

Coop's brows raised, and the guy's cheeks actually became slightly flushed. His physical reaction to Grant's statement made him wonder if Coop genuinely didn't realize the way Mac looked at him when she thought no one was watching.

After recovering from the apparent bomb drop, the other man tried stumbling his way out of it. "She doesn't…you don't…I haven't been throwing Mac anything."

"Only because, from what I've seen, she hasn't been willing to play catch. Yet." He tossed that last word in there, just to keep Coop's melting pot of thoughts boiling.

Flustered, the only thing the former Ranger could come back with was, "You don't know what you're talking about."

Grant locked eyes with his teammate. "But you do?" Running a hand over his jaw, he took a step back. "Tell you what. Instead of worrying about what you *think* is going on in my personal life, maybe you should man up and get your own shit in order."

Grant spun on his heels and walked away, more pissed at

himself than anyone. Just as he started to enter the hallway, Brynnon appeared from around the corner. The two nearly collided.

"Oh!" She exclaimed. "Sorry."

"Sorry." Grant grabbed her upper arms to keep her from falling over.

For the next thirty seconds, they both just stood there, staring into each other's eyes. Grant had no idea what he was revealing, but Brynnon's oozed with a mixture of turmoil and heat.

The source of her conflict was a mystery, but one thing was clear…she was definitely attracted to him.

Heat radiated from beneath her thin, hunter-green sweater, penetrating his palms. Its V-neck was just low enough to give him a glimpse of her cleavage. Despite his cock twitching behind his zipper, it was Grant who pulled away first.

Dropping his hands, he put some space between them. "Sorry, Princess. Didn't see you coming."

Her rosy lips pursed together. "Why do you insist on calling me that?"

"Why are you acting so standoffish with me today?"

The question was out before he even realized it. Christ, it was like he had no control when she was around.

"I-I haven't been standoffish."

Nice try, sweetheart. This was neither the time nor the place for this conversation, but the cat was already out of the fucking bag, so…

"Bullshit. You barely said two words to me this morning, yet you were all laughs and giggles with Coop a few minutes ago."

Her pretty eyes narrowed. "I was not all *laughs and giggles.*

It's called being polite. You should try it sometime."

"It's called flirting your ass off."

Brynnon's jaw dropped, and her cheeks became flushed like they always did when she got pissed. Grant found himself wondering if they got that way during sex, too.

Lowering her voice, her eyes slid to where Coop was probably still standing and clamped her teeth together. "I most certainly was *not* flirting, and I resent the implication suggesting otherwise."

Grant's own jaw tensed. "There's the politician's daughter. I was wondering when she would make an appearance." She opened her mouth to let him have it, but Grant didn't give her the chance. "You can resent anything you want, sweetheart. I've got two eyes, and they both work just fine."

Raising a brow, she gave him a humorless smirk. "Yeah? Well, tell me if they can see this."

In an unexpected—not to mention unladylike—move, Brynnon flipped him the bird before turning around and storming back into the dining room. Grant had never been into BDSM or anything of that nature, but his palm suddenly itched to reach out and smack that fine, jean-clad ass as it swayed back and forth across the floor.

The thought, along with the image of her giving him the finger, pulled a low chuckle from the back of his throat. It felt rough and unfamiliar, those particular muscles having laid dormant for far too long. But damn, if it didn't feel good.

Grant knew he should probably be concerned about losing the protection detail, but at the moment, that was the farthest thing from his mind. Instead, he stood there, thinking about the fiery redhead and how she frustrated him more than anyone he'd ever known.

She also takes you from limp to loaded in mere seconds.

The annoying-as-shit voice was right. Brynnon surprised him at every fucking turn, but for reasons he may never understand, Grant liked it. A lot.

He pulled on the crotch of his jeans, attempting to shift his swollen cock, which was pressed painfully against the inside of his zipper. It screamed to get out and bury itself inside her hot, wet heat. Grant had no doubt if he were to ever get the chance, Brynnon would burn him alive the second their bodies united.

It may very well make him a sick bastard, but the fire he'd just lit under the auburn vixen turned him on like never before. Too bad he couldn't do anything about it.

Yet.

The same taunting word he'd thrown at Coop a few minutes ago echoed through Grant's ears. From over his shoulder, he glanced back, not surprised to see the smug bastard standing by the door, watching. A wide, shit-eating grin spread across the man's face.

"Enjoy your brunch."

Without a word, Grant raised his right hand and offered the guy the same gesture Brynnon had just bestowed upon him and made his way down the hall toward his unknown fate.

Chapter 6

"Do you want some potatoes, sweetheart?"

Brynnon looked across the table to where her father was sitting. Her mother had been gone several years now, but it still made Brynnon sad to see the empty chair where she used to sit.

"I have plenty. Thank you."

Sitting in the chair beside her, Grant took the offered bowl and began spooning some onto his plate. Brynnon had half-expected him to leave and never look back after that particularly heated conversation.

While he and her father discussed random topics, she ate her food quietly, using that time to try and get her head on straight where the sexy-as-sin man was concerned.

She didn't know what it was about Grant Hill, but he sure as hell knew how to rile her up. It was like he'd tapped into her psyche and knew exactly which buttons to push at the exact right moment. No other man had ever done that to her before.

That's not all he does to you.

That part made her even more frustrated. How, after chewing her ass out and accusing her of flirting with his teammate, could she possibly still find him attractive? Better yet, why hadn't she ratted him out to her father? If he knew the way Grant had spoken to her, he would have fired him on the spot and saved them both the trouble.

Because everything Grant said was true.

Brynnon grabbed her iced tea and took a big gulp, wishing she could punch the tiny voice in her head in the throat.

Fine, so maybe she'd flirted a *little*. So what? It shouldn't even matter to him, anyway. Grant wasn't interested in her like that. She was a job to him, and nothing more. Except...

If that's true, why did seeing you flirt with another man bother him so damn much?

Brynnon also hadn't missed the way those mysterious, blue-gray eyes of his had slid down to her cleavage, right in the middle of an argument. Not to mention the unmistakable heat she'd seen in them when they'd risen back up to meet hers.

She could just chalk it up to the fact that he was a guy, but her gut said he was more interested in her than he was trying to let on. Which only added to the frustrating mix of emotions she experienced every time Grant was in the room. Or, in her thoughts.

Brynnon had tried being distant this morning, thinking maybe that would help. Instead, all her self-induced silence had given her was more time to think about other things. Like, the way it felt to be wrapped in his protective arms, or how she'd laid in bed last night, pathetically wishing he'd burst into her room and ravish her until they were both physically spent.

"What do you think, Brynnon?"

Her father's mentioning of her name snapped her out of it. Glancing up from her plate, she realized both he and

Grant were looking at her as if they were waiting for an answer.

"I'm sorry, what?"

Her father set his fork down, his silver eyebrows curved inward. "Are you okay? You don't quite seem yourself today."

"I'm fine," she lied, praying the smile she was giving him seemed legit.

Her dad shook his head. "I hope you aren't coming down with a cold. Have you been wearing your coat?" He looked at Grant. "I swear, that girl has never worn a winter coat like she should. Ever since she was a little girl, her mother and I have had to get on to her about the dangers of being stuck in the cold without proper clothing. Well, I'm sure you know, with your training and such. Hypothermia is nothing to mess around with."

"No, sir," Grant agreed. "It's not."

His deep voice rumbled from beside her, and Brynnon could swear she could feel it vibrating through her. A familiar tingling began to spread in her lower belly, making it difficult not to react.

Seriously?

Her father was treating her as if she were a child, and Grant was going right along with it and *still* her body was reacting to him. It was like every time the man opened his mouth to speak Brynnon instantly thought of sex.

It didn't matter what he was saying, either. God, that was frustrating. It was also weird, given that her dad was less than five feet away from them both.

"I wore my coat today, Dad." She tried not to snap. "Ask Grant. He could probably even tell you its color."

Brynnon looked over at him for the first time since he'd

entered the room. She half-expected him to lie about her earlier behavior. Instead, he backed her up…and then some.

With his eyes still on her, he nodded. "She did. It's dark green."

"See?" Brynnon gave her father an I-told-you-so look. "I—"

"It has six buttons down the front," Grant cut her off, his eyes remaining locked with hers while he continued giving the detailed description. "At the top"—he brushed one of his hands across his collarbone—" there's an oversized collar that folds down with two long straps connected to its hood. It comes in at the waist and the bottom flares out, stopping about mid-calf."

Brynnon stared back at him in silence. She wasn't sure what her dad was thinking, but she found it fascinating. And a total turn-on.

"Excellent attention to detail, son." Her father finally broke the silence. "They teach you that in BUD/s?"

Grant blinked, breaking their connection. "Among other things." He looked back at her father.

"You know, I wanted to go into the military. Even signed the dotted line."

"What happened?"

"Flat feet," Brynnon answered for her dad. She'd heard the story enough times she knew it by heart.

Her dad chuckled. "Can you believe that?"

"Yes, sir. Actually, I can." In typical, Grant fashion, he kept his tone flat. Even.

It sure wasn't flat when he was yelling at you for flirting. Determined to let it go and smooth things over with him, Brynnon decided to use the odd conversation as a starting point.

"Do they still do that?" She directed the question to him. "Not let people join the military if they have flat feet?"

Grant's large shoulder rose and fell as he brought his eyes back to hers. "Depends. Used to be an automatic red stamp."

"But not anymore?"

"Some branches accept it more easily than others. Just depends on whether or not the candidate has any debilitating symptoms related to the issue. If they can't stand for long periods or have back pain when they walk or run long distances, they're usually out. But, they also look at which branch and job the individual is interested in. If it's one that involves more sitting than standing, for example, they may let it slide."

"Interesting."

Grant's forehead creased as though he was surprised by her comment. "Is it?"

Unable to keep up with the charade, Brynnon shook her head. "No," she snickered. "Not really. I mean, come on. We're talking about feet."

Warmth seeped into his eyes, along with a tiny spark of light. She could have sworn he was about to smile back, but a loud voice interrupted the moment.

"Look who I found!"

All heads turned to the two men who'd just entered the room.

Martin Downing, the man who spoke, had worked for her father for years. First, as his personal assistant at the construction company her dad used to own. Then after he sold that business and became Senator, her father made Martin his Chief of Staff.

At thirty-two—only three years older than Brynnon—most women found his square jaw, dark brown hair, and eyes, and winning smile attractive. She had, too, until Martin opened his mouth and ruined it.

For her father's sake, Brynnon had learned to play nice with the condescending jerk. In truth, she couldn't stand the guy.

Next to Martin stood her brother, Billy. On the outside, he was a handsome, successful entrepreneur. Unfortunately, Brynnon was more than a little aware of the internal struggles the man faced but wouldn't admit.

Billy was tall and lean, his features long and sharp. His reddish-brown hair, full lips, and green eyes, which were identical to Brynnon's, had made many a girl swoon. That, and his natural charisma.

The guy could charm the pants off almost any woman he met...and probably had. He was always smiling and joking, entertaining whoever was around to listen with his witty humor. But, Brynnon knew it was all a big show. She'd seen his other side, and it wasn't pretty.

"Billy." Brynnon's dad gave her brother a tight smile. "You decided to join us, after all."

"Yeah, sorry I'm late. There was a wreck on the highway. Traffic was backed up for over an hour."

"You couldn't call?" Brynnon asked, not bothering to hide her annoyance. Her brother had no respect for anyone's schedule but his own.

Billy's green eyes met hers. "Hey, sis. You know, I would have, but my phone died."

"Right." Brynnon rolled her eyes and took a drink of her tea.

"It did!" her brother insisted. Noticing the man sitting next to her, he tipped his chin in Grant's direction. "Who the hell are you?"

"Jesus, Billy," Brynnon chastised him. "Rude much?"

He scoffed. "What? I can't ask who the strange man sitting next to my sister is?"

"Your sister's right. You could at least try to be a little more tactful." Her dad shook his head before looking at Grant. "I apologize for my son."

Billy rolled his eyes. "I don't need you to apologize for me, Dad. I'm not twelve."

Her father pressed his lips together. "Then stop acting as if you were."

Deciding it was time to step in, Brynnon said, "Billy, this is Grant. Grant, meet my brother, Billy."

"Wow." Billy walked around the table to where she and Grant were sitting. "It's been a long time since Bryn brought a boyfriend home to meet the family." When Grant stood to shake Billy's hand, her brother leaned toward him and fake-whispered, "Between you and me, my sister has a tendency to run men off. Not sure why. Could be the stick she has shoved up her ass, but who knows. Either way, I wouldn't get too comfortable if I were you."

Mortified that her brother would say something so demeaning, Brynnon swung her eyes to his. "What the hell?"

Hating that Grant had to bear witness to her shitshow of a brother, she felt a familiar warmth spreading through her cheeks. Brynnon glared at Billy, letting him know without words he'd better knock it off.

"That's quite enough, William," her father intervened.

Typical Billy, he simply laughed and slapped Grant on the shoulder. He then turned to Brynnon. "Oh, I'm just teasin'. You know I love you, sis." Leaning down, he kissed the top of her head before walking back around to take his seat.

Brynnon gave Grant a quick glance before staring back

down at her plate and muttering, "Sorry."

He put his arm across the top of her chair, his natural heat warming her upper back as he leaned toward her. With his lips precariously close to her ear, he whispered, "Nothing you need to apologize for, Princess."

Surprisingly, his use of the nickname didn't bother her like before. Maybe it was the softer tone he'd used or the way his hot breath and lips had brushed against her ear when he spoke. Either way, her heart began beating a little faster.

Forgetting how close they still were, Brynnon turned her head to thank him. When she did, their noses nearly touched. She should have pulled away but was too entranced by the way his pupils had begun to dilate. A classic sign of arousal.

Brynnon inhaled quickly, the catch in her breath breaking whatever spell they'd both been under.

Looking as taken aback as she felt, Grant practically jerked away, returning his attention to the three men sitting across from them.

Thankfully, Martin, Billy, and her father had all been focused on their own conversation and hadn't noticed the exhilarating exchange.

"So Brynnon." Martin's smooth voice matched his TV-ready smile. "Your father tells me you sold another house. Congratulations."

"Thank you." Brynnon returned a forced smile.

"It's good to know your little business is holding its own."

Beneath the table, Brynnon's fist tightened in her lap. Sensing her struggle to maintain her cool, Grant discretely reached over and covered her hand with his.

Under his breath, he whispered, "Easy."

It all went completely unnoticed by the others, but Brynnon couldn't help but be appreciative.

Feeling more in control now, she forced her lips into a smile. "Actually, Martin, my little business is doing much more than just holding its own."

"Of course, it is." He smiled arrogantly. "I'd expect nothing less from you."

Rather than respond to the jerk's fake compliment, Brynnon started to introduce him to Grant. "Martin, this is—"

"Mr. Hill," he cut her off. "Good to see you again."

"Downing."

Confused for a moment, Brynnon looked back and forth between the two men before realizing her mistake. "Oh, of course. You two have already met."

"We have." Martin nodded. "Your man, here, does good work."

"Oh, he's not my—"

"Bodyguard?" His pristinely manicured brows turned inward as he glanced at her father. "I thought you hired him to look out for Brynnon after receiving that last threat."

"I did. That's why he's with her now."

"Dad's making you have a bodyguard again?" Billy grinned over at her. "Better you than me."

Brynnon's eyes flew to her brother's. "Wait. You don't have one, too?"

"Nope."

She shot her dad a look. "Seriously?"

"We've discussed this before, sweetheart. You know how Billy is. He's given every guard I've hired the slip within the first twenty-four hours. Frankly, it's a waste of money."

"That's not the point."

"Ah, come on, sis," Billy popped a green bean in his mouth. "Don't be mad. Dad just knows I can take care of myself."

"Are you implying I can't?"

Billy looked at Grant. "I'm sure my sister doesn't mean to sound ungrateful for your services. She's just pissed because she's the baby, which means she gets special treatment."

"That's not true!" Brynnon nearly yelled.

"Whatever. You've always been a daddy's girl."

"Yeah? And you were a mama's boy!"

The room went silent. Realizing what she'd just said made Brynnon want to crawl in a hole somewhere and never come out.

"Billy, I'm sorry. I-I didn't mean to say that."

In typical Billy fashion, he blew it off with a grin. "Ain't no thing, Sis." Standing, he looked to their father. "I just remembered I have somewhere to be."

Guilt shot through Brynnon's heart. "You're leaving?"

The performance began again. "As much fun as this little family reunion has been, I do have a personal life I can't ignore. Who knows? This girl may be the one." He gave Grant a wink. "Guard my sister's body well." Turning to the other two men in the room, he tipped his head. "Dad. Martin. Enjoyable, as always."

Without another word, he walked out of the room.

Brynnon shot up from her chair and began speed-walking after him. Luckily, she was able to catch up before he reached the other end of the long hall.

"Billy, wait!"

Her brother stopped and turned, his smile not nearly as brilliant as before. "What is it, Brynnon?"

"I'm sorry about what I said in there. I didn't mean to bring Mom into it."

"It's okay." He gave her a sheepish grin. "I started it."

He turned away, but Brynnon stopped him with a hand to

his arm. "I'm serious. I've been under a lot of stress getting my last house ready to sell, plus trying to sell my condo and get my cabin ready, but…that's no excuse."

"Yeah, well, I deserved it after what I said to your boyfriend in there."

"He's not my—"

"I'm *teasing*. Geez. Maybe that's what you need to help with all this stress."

"What?"

"To get laid."

"Billy!" Brynnon smacked his upper arm, ignoring the image of Grant's face flashing through her mind.

Despite the spat they'd just had, both siblings began to chuckle. Brynnon looked up at her brother. "I miss this. Us. We should get together for lunch. Just me and you."

"What about your watchdog?"

"He can sit at another table or outside in his truck. I don't know. I'll figure something out." Brynnon gave her brother a hug. "I love you, you big jerk."

"Love ya, too, Sis," he hugged her back. "Uh, oh. I think that's my cue."

"What?" Brynnon pulled away. Noticing her brother's gaze was focusing on something behind her, she turned around to find Grant strolling toward them.

She looked at her brother again, but he was already walking toward the front door. "I'm serious about getting together soon!" she hollered after him.

With a casual wave in the air, Billy hollered back, "Call me."

She watched her brother walk around the corner and out of her sight.

"You okay?"

Drawing in a slow, deep breath, Brynnon took a second to compose herself. Between their earlier argument, her brother's ridiculous behavior, and her overactive hormones, she wasn't sure what she was.

"You worried about me, big guy?" She turned to face him.

"It's in my job description."

There it was again. The job. Tired of feeling like she was walking on eggshells around the man, Brynnon decided to go for broke and just ask.

"Is that all I am to you, Grant? A job?"

Not expecting the question, Grant blinked. He opened his mouth to answer, but closed it. When he started to open it again, Brynnon realized hearing the truth would be worse than not knowing. At least if she didn't actually hear him say it, she could still hang on to the fantasy a little longer.

"Never mind." She shook her head. "Forget I said anything." Stepping past him, Brynnon started back for the dining room. "We still have to go to the hospital after this and I can't be late, so we should probably—"

A large hand grabbed her wrist, interrupting both her words and her forward progress. Glancing down to where his fingers gently held her, Brynnon tried to ignore the electrical current burning its way through her thin sweater.

"Brynnon, wait."

Grant must have felt the same, thrilling jolt because he let go of her arm as though she'd shocked him. *He does feel it.*

"I'm not..." he started to speak. Brynnon watched his large Adam's apple bob up and down as he swallowed before beginning again. "I'm not the man for you."

She forced herself not to react to those disappointing words. "Really?" Brynnon stepped closer. "Tell me, Grant. What kind of man do you think I need?"

He shook his head, and for a minute, Brynnon expected him to shut down and walk away. Instead, he stared down at her, showing a side of himself she thought she'd never see. "I want you, Princess." Heat flared behind his gray eyes. "I shouldn't, but I do."

Holy crap. "W-why shouldn't you want me?"

Running a hand over his scruff-covered jaw, he glanced away before bringing his eyes back to hers. "Too many reasons. And like it or not, this *is* a job. Your father hired me to protect you. Not sleep with you."

Brynnon's most intimate muscles clenched. Just hearing him talk about it left her wanting him even more. Feeling bold, she lifted her chin and asked, "Why can't you do both?"

Grant's chest swelled, and his nostrils flared, their topic of conversation affecting him just as strongly. Even so, he came back with, "Having sex with a client isn't just unprofessional, it's against policy."

"Policy?"

"It's put in place for a reason." Grant swallowed again. "Look, Bryn. We come from two different worlds. In yours, you screw something up on the job, it may take longer for you to sell a house. I fuck up, someone dies."

"Except I'm not in any danger. We're on day three, and there's been nothing. How long are you going to continue to watch me before you admit to my father—and yourself—that this assignment is completely unnecessary?"

"I will watch over you until my boss tells me otherwise."

Hoping he'd take the bait, Brynnon decided to throw him a line. Licking her lips, she asked, "And after that?"

Looking conflicted, he shook his head. "I already told you. I'm not the—"

"Man for me. Yeah, I got that. It's too bad, really." She

shrugged. "I think we could've been great together."

Refusing to come off as needy—any more than she probably already had—Brynnon turned and started back down the hall. "I'm going to tell Dad we're leaving."

She made it a few steps before facing him again. "Oh, and Grant?"

Still standing where she'd left him, the frustratingly sexy man gave her a low, "Yeah?"

"Those neat little lines you've drawn for yourself are great and all. But if you don't cross one every once in a while, what's the point?"

His brow creased. "The point of what?"

She smiled sadly. "Life."

With that, Brynnon went back into the dining room to tell her father goodbye. She hoped, with time, Grant would see she was right.

He'd admitted he wanted her, which was a massive step in the right direction. Now, she just had to figure out a way to get him to put actions to words.

Chapter 7

Grant took his eyes from the road just long enough to give Brynnon a quick, sideways glance. To say things had been awkward between them since their hallway confessions would be a major fucking understatement.

He was just thankful Senator Cantrell and that kiss-ass Downing hadn't decided to come looking for them. Or worse, Coop. Explaining away the shit that had poured from his mouth would've been damn near impossible.

Grant still couldn't believe he'd admitted to wanting to sleep with her. Never in his life had he had less control than he did around that woman. Every time she got near, he found himself wanting to share shit with her. What the fuck was that all about anyway?

There'd only ever been one person he truly felt he could bare his soul to. And she'd been his guardian angel for more than sixteen years now.

Hell, Grant hadn't even given all of himself to Baylee, and he'd come damn close to asking her to marry him. *Thank fuck for small favors.*

A sharp pain radiated through his chest, the memory of what she'd done still as fresh as the day it had happened. He must not have done a good job of hiding it, because

Brynnon's voice sounded worried when she spoke to him. "You okay?"

Having already revealed too much, Grant kept his mouth shut and tipped his head.

Assuming his foul expression had something to do with her, Brynnon apologized again for her brother. "I'm sorry Billy acted like such a jerk."

Grant kept his eyes on the road. "Can't control what your family does."

"I guess not." She sighed. "You talking from experience?"

She was fishing, but this time he damn sure wasn't gonna bite. "Everyone has had family issues at one point or another."

"A vague, non-answer," Brynnon teased. "I think you've been hanging around politicians too long."

Wanting to talk about anything other than his family, Grant spun the conversation back to hers. "So what's your brother's story?"

Thanks to the file he had on Brynnon, he already knew the basics but was interested to see what she'd share.

A laugh escaped from her lips, the sweet sound one he could listen to endlessly. "Going with the spin. You *have* been around politicians too much." She sighed again. "Fine. We won't talk about you. Let's see…the cliff-notes version of Billy is, he's a brilliant man with the potential to do great things."

"But?"

"But, over time, he's gotten…lost."

"Lost?" Grant slid his eyes to her and back again. "He seemed pretty confident to me."

"I think the word you're looking for is *cocky*. And that's what you saw because it's what Billy wanted you to see."

Brynnon frowned. "It breaks my heart, really. Back when my dad still owned his construction company..." She paused and turned to him. "Wait, did you know about that?"

"Cantrell Construction?" Grant nodded. "Your dad told me about it the last time I worked security for him. He sold it about six years ago, right?"

"A little over five, yeah. Anyway"—she got back on track— "Billy used to work for Dad. Was in charge of the supply orders for the bigger jobs. It was an important position, and he was great at it."

Grant thought for a moment. "Billy's a couple of years younger than me, right? So he would've only been, what, twenty-nine when the company was bought out?"

"Yep. He was twenty-four when Dad promoted him to head sales manager."

Grant blew out a low whistle. "Bet that pissed some people off."

Brynnon chuckled. "Oh, yeah. There were a handful of employees who resented him for it at first. But, over time, Billy proved himself to be a solid asset to the company."

"So, what happened?"

"When Dad decided to run for office, he didn't want his personal business to be viewed as a conflict or a distraction. The way he explained it, too many politicians in the past had been accused of mixing company finances and contacts with their political agendas. Could make things murky. Anyway, a couple of larger companies had been sniffing around for several months, wanting to buy us out, so Dad contacted them when he was ready to sell. The company with the top bid won and my father never looked back."

"And Billy?"

"He signed on as Dad's co-chief of staff with Martin. I

could never work with the man, but those two seemed to do really well together. At first."

"What happened?"

Her face fell. "Our mother died. It happened shortly after Dad first took office."

Grant's fists tightened over the steering wheel. "I'm sorry."

"Thanks. It's been almost five years now, but it still hurts, you know?"

More than you realize. "How'd she die?"

"Car wreck. Dad had only been a senator for a few weeks. He had a meeting with a bunch of big-wig politicians that day. About forty-five minutes before it was scheduled to start, he realized he'd left some documents at home that he needed. Dad called mom and asked if she could bring them to him. Told her to hurry."

Brynnon turned to face the passenger window, but Grant still saw the tears in her reflection. The sight hit him with such force he damn near pulled the truck over just so he could pull her into his arms just so he could make them go away.

Discretely swiping one away, she cleared her throat and told him the rest. "Mom knew how crucial Dad's meeting was, so she rushed to get the papers to him. She took a curve too fast and lost control of the car. The doctors told us she died instantly."

"Damn, Bryn. I'm sorry."

She offered him a watery grin. "Thanks."

"So, Billy took it hard, huh?"

Brynnon sniffed, blinking away her unshed tears. "Oh, yeah. I wasn't kidding when I said Billy was a total mama's boy. Don't get me wrong, my mother loved me very much.

But my family had stereotypical dynamics. Dad and I always had a special bond, as did Billy and Mom. After she died, my brother started going downhill almost immediately."

"How so?"

"Well, for starters, he quit working for my dad. He'd never admit it, but I'm pretty sure Billy blamed Dad for what happened. He started hanging with the wrong crowd, partying all the time...that sort of thing. Dad tells everyone Billy's a 'free spirit' but the truth is, he's a mess."

Brynnon got quiet for a moment before sharing some more. "My dad loves Billy. There's just a lot of animosity between the two. On both sides. Dad blames himself for Mom's accident and Billy's subsequent fall down the rabbit hole, but at the same time, he knows Billy is old enough to make his own choices. Although, my brother's last stint at rehab seems to have paid off." Brynnon gave him a small smile. "He just got his year chip three weeks ago."

"That's good."

"Yeah. It is." She paused a moment and then, "You know, everyone thinks having a lot of money makes life easy, but it doesn't."

"You don't have to explain anything to me."

"I want to. I need you to understand why I was so opposed to having you assigned to watch me. Well, not you, personally. I would've balked at anyone."

She took a deep breath and explained. "I'd just started high school when the construction company took off. When Dad's net worth grew into the millions, Billy and I had to be escorted to and from school, sporting events, birthday parties...I couldn't even go to a school dance without having one of Dad's security team there with us. Do you know how hard it was to dance like that, knowing someone's watching your every move?"

Before he could answer, Brynnon chuckled. "Of course, you don't. You were probably the quarterback prom king dancing with the cheerleader queen."

Memories of a prom night much different than the one she'd just described assaulted him, but Grant somehow dialed back the pain. Averting the comment, he simply uttered, "I don't dance."

Shock filled her beautiful eyes. "Like, ever?"

"Nope."

"Oh." Brynnon's face fell a little. "That's too bad."

"Why's that?"

"The charity ball is in two days. I put it on the agenda I gave you."

Shit. He'd seen it written down but hadn't had a chance to talk with her about it. The last thing he wanted to do was spend another night in a huge room full of pretentious people throwing around their money like it was water. He'd had his fill of that shit the last time he worked for Cantrell.

Yeah, but that's how you met her.

Ignoring the memory of that particular night, Grant asked, "How important is it that you be there?"

She chuckled. "Very."

"Define very."

"I'm giving a speech and kicking off the dance contest."

"There's a contest?"

Brynnon smiled wide. "It's part of the fundraiser. Every year, couples can sign up, either ahead of time or at the ball. All proceeds from the required entry fee go to the charity we're supporting. Couples dance simultaneously while the rest of the attendees watch. When the song is over, the couples line up, and the winner is determined by whichever one gets the biggest applause. It's fun!"

Sounds like the sixth version of Hell.

Brynnon laughed. "Obviously, you don't feel the same."

"I don't dance," he repeated.

"Yeah. I got that." She paused before her eyes filled with alarm. "Crap. We'll still need to get you a tux. It's a black-tie event, and everyone's required to wear one, but it's in three days. We've got to get you fitted, and—"

"Relax, Bryn. I may know someone who can help us with that."

"You do?"

Grant nodded. "Her name's Charlie. She owns a party planning business."

Sounding skeptical, she asked, "You're friends with a party planner?"

"She's married to one of my teammates."

"Oh." Brynnon's shoulders relaxed. "Okay. We'll need to call her ASAP."

"I'll take care of it."

The last thing he wanted was to have to put on a monkey suit, but evidently the event was pretty important to her. Which made him curious…

"Do you compete?"

Her smile returned. "For the past three years. My partner and I have never won, but it's still a lot of fun. I'm bummed I won't be competing this year."

He didn't miss the disappointment in her voice. "Why not?"

"My partner broke his foot last week and had to back out. That reminds me…" she turned to him. "Don't let me forget to call the dance committee chairperson later and let her know to take Danny and me off the list."

Doing his best not to sound like a jealous asshole, Grant cleared his throat. "Who, uh...who's Danny?"

"One of the guys I contract out for all of my landscaping. Apparently he was working on another project and missed a patio step. Broke his foot in two places."

What he responded with was, "That's too bad." What he was thinking was, *thank fuck for clumsy landscapers.*

It was an asshole thought to have, especially since the guy's misfortune meant Brynnon couldn't compete. It also meant he didn't have to spend Tuesday night watching another man cozying up to her on the dance floor.

Grant knew his caveman attitude was asinine, given his earlier spiel about not being the right guy for her. What did he expect her to do, anyway? Wait around for him to change his mind?

Yes.

No. He'd never ask her to do that. Brynnon was too full of life. She needed to be able to have one that made her happy. Grant suddenly wished he could be the man to give that to her.

Turning his truck into the hospital's visitor parking lot, he pulled into an empty spot and turned off the ignition. Grant started to open his door, but Brynnon stopped him with a hand to his arm.

"Wait." Her fingers squeezed his forearm.

He looked back at her. "Yeah?"

"Before we go inside, I wanted to clear the air."

Ah, fuck. Grant didn't think he could take more deep discussions. "About?"

"Us."

There is no us.

The words were on the tip of his tongue, but Grant kept

his trap shut for fear he'd come off as an uncaring asshole. Right or wrong, her opinion of him was starting to matter. A lot.

Instead, he asked, "What about us?"

"I feel like we got off on the wrong foot. Between my resistance to having you assigned to me and today, my shitshow of a brother, and the discussion about us..." She sighed. "Anyway, I was just wondering if we could maybe, I don't know...start over?"

He stared back at the adorable woman, the nervous blush in her cheeks nearly dark enough to match her hair. He'd spent the last few months imagining how it would feel to run his fingers through her long, auburn locks. How soft it would feel inside his fist as he held onto the back of her head while she—

"So?"

From the passenger seat, Brynnon stared back at him expectantly. Those deep forest eyes filled with nervous hope while waiting for his response. And he'd been over here imagining her on her knees, his engorged cock sliding between those luscious lips.

On cue, his dick jumped inside his jeans. *Jesus Christ.* He really needed to stop doing that shit.

Realizing he still hadn't said a fucking word, Grant choked out, "Sure."

"Really?" Her shoulders relaxed. "Good. Because I really do appreciate what you're trying to do. I still don't think it's necessary, but I promise I'm not trying to make your job any harder than it needs to be. And as for the other..." She licked her lips nervously. "If something happens between us after this bodyguard gig, great. If not, that's okay, too."

Swallowing back the urge to reach out and pull her to him,

Grant offered a low, "Okay."

He should probably tell her nothing could ever happen between them. Brynnon wasn't like the picket fence women he'd met in the past. She also wasn't the kind to have a one-night-stand and just walk away the next morning, either.

She was different than any other woman he'd ever known. Brynnon was a cabin-in-the-woods kind of gal full of intelligence, confidence, and passion. And though he'd chosen years ago to never allow a woman into his heart, she was getting closer and closer with each moment Grant spent with her.

Oblivious to his thoughts, Brynnon smiled back at him with a sweet, "Okay."

Chapter 8

"Look how happy they are."

Brynnon turned to Angie—her best friend and self-proclaimed partner in crime—and smiled widely. Family drama momentarily forgotten, her heart felt full from the little bit of happiness they'd brought with them today.

"It's my favorite day of the year."

The attractive, brunette woman smiled back. "I'm so glad you asked me to help."

"I'm so glad you agreed to," Brynnon teased, nudging her shoulder.

Both women laughed as they continued watching the room full of children open their presents with glee. They'd all been admitted to the cancer wing—some new patients, others all-too-familiar.

"Thanks again for storing and hauling all of the presents. Between my tiny garage and the cabin being so far away, it was so much easier keeping them all at your place."

"My pleasure." Angie looked back over the smiling children. On a low whisper, she said, "It's so sad knowing some of these kiddos will have to spend Christmas here."

"I know," Brynnon agreed. "That's why we do this. For those who won't get to go home by Christmas. Or ever."

Angie swiped at the corner of her eye and shook the negative thoughts away. "All right, enough of the sad crap. Tell me about Mr. Muscles over there."

Brynnon glanced over to the far wall where Grant was standing. With his arms crossed in front of him, he had his back against the wall, and the scowl she'd thought was starting to vanish more prevalent than ever. And he was staring at her.

Looking away, Brynnon had thought the olive branch she'd offered in the truck had done the trick. Apparently not. *Maybe he just hates kids.*

Her gut tightened at the thought. Which was a ridiculous reaction because, hello, it wasn't like they were ever going to date, let alone get to the point where they'd discuss having kids.

You need to get laid.

Billy's earlier words ran through her mind, and Brynnon was starting to think he was right. Too bad the one man she wanted to fix that particular issue was about as hands-off as a guy could get.

"You weren't kidding about him being grumpy," Angie continued. "The guy looks absolutely miserable."

"Told ya." Brynnon pushed away her worthless thoughts of sex with Grant.

"Maybe it's been a while."

"A while?"

"You know. Sex."

"Angie!" Brynnon looked to make sure the kids weren't listening. "There are children here."

"Who are all too busy playing with their new toys to give a damn about what we're saying."

"Still. They might hear you."

"Quit trying to divert the conversation." Her knowledgeable friend smirked. "I'm telling you, the second you two get back to your place, you need to jump his bones."

"He's my bodyguard, Ang. Not a date."

"So tell him you need him to guard your body a little closer."

Brynnon couldn't help but laugh. "You're insufferable."

"And you're suffer*ing*. From lackofdickitis."

Barking out a laugh, Brynnon covered her mouth to keep from drawing attention their way. "Stop," she laughed behind her palm. "Seriously."

"I *am* serious. When was the last time you had sex with something that didn't require batteries."

Brynnon glanced around again, praying no one was listening. "I'm not having this conversation. Besides, he's not even my type."

"Yeah, you're right," her friend agreed. "I can't imagine you being attracted to such a tall, dark, and seriously built sex machine like him."

Refusing to comment, Brynnon stood silently while Angie continued fueling the fire. "Come on, Bryn. Look at him. He's like a buff, walking, talking, life-size sex doll."

"That may be, but he's also the most impatient, grumpy, bossy-ass man I've ever known."

Angie's lips curled into a slow smile. "Oh, man. It's worse than I thought."

Brynnon's brows knitted together. "What's worse?"

"You." The other woman grinned. "You've got it bad for the man. Way worse than I thought."

"I do not."

"Oh, yes, you do. And I'd be willing to bet, from the way he keeps looking at you, the man would be more than happy to offer up a cure for what ails you."

"Sorry to be the one to tell you, my well-intentioned friend, but you'd lose your ass on that bet."

Angie crossed her flannel-covered arms. "And you know that how?"

"He told me."

Her brown brows grew into high arches. "He *told* you? Wait, so have you two actually talked about this? When? What was said? Good God, woman, why haven't you told me any of this?"

"Shh…" Brynnon hushed her friend. "I haven't told you because the conversation only happened a couple hours ago."

Dark brows rose. "Seriously?"

Rolling her eyes, Brynnon nodded. "I know. It was stupid. I never should've opened my big mouth."

Angie grinned. "*You* initiated it?"

"Like an idiot, yes. Unfortunately, I did."

Throwing her hands on her narrow hips, Brynnon's friend demanded, "Details, woman. Now."

On a sigh, Brynnon proceeded to share all about the conversation she'd had with Grant. Saying it out loud made the possibility of them becoming more seem less promising than she'd initially thought. On the other hand, she was pretty proud for putting herself out there, regardless.

"He wants you." Angie grinned from ear to ear.

"So?"

"So? He's a man, and he verbally admitted that he wants to sleep with you."

"Weren't you listening? Yes, he admitted he wanted me. But right after that, he basically told me nothing could happen between us. At least not while he's still my bodyguard, and who knows how long that ordeal is going to last. So none of it matters."

"Like hell, it doesn't. You just have to tear down his defenses."

"Right," Brynnon scoffed. "Look at the guy, Ang. Does he look like a man who's easy to break?"

When her friend turned her gaze toward where Grant was still standing, Brynnon shot out her hand and grabbed the other woman's arm. "I didn't mean that literally! Now he's probably going to know we're talking about him."

"Oh, he knows, sweetie."

Unable to help it herself, Brynnon slid a glance his way. Sure, enough, he was staring right back at her. Even from this distance, she could feel the electrical current running between them.

Maybe it was best if they didn't sleep together. If the guy made her feel this way with twenty feet spanning between them, she'd probably spontaneously combust if they so much as kissed.

Brynnon groaned. "I'm going to the restroom." When Angie started to say something else, Brynnon raised her palm. "Alone."

"Fine." Angie smirked. "But there's only one cure for lackofdickitis, and it sure as hell ain't your dildo."

"Jesus." Brynnon shook her head. "Remind me again why I invited you here?"

"Because you love me."

With a hand on her arm, Brynnon smiled. "Yeah. I really do." She stepped past her friend. "I'll be right back."

Though it took a lot of strength, she forced herself to look straight ahead, not relaxing until she made her way around the corner out of his line of sight. Ducking into the ladies' room, she did her thing and took her time washing her hands.

When she'd given Grant the whole 'neat lines' spiel, she'd felt confident in her ability to wear him down. Now, she wasn't so sure. Angie's words rang past her ears…

He verbally admitted he wants to sleep with you.

Shaking her head at her reflection, Brynnon quickly rinsed the soap from her hands and ran them under the automatic hand dryer. Reminding herself why she was here, she decided to focus on the kids and not the object of her desire for the rest of their time here.

Pushing the swinging door open, she stepped out into the hallway. It was empty, save for an older gentleman standing against the wall in front of her. He looked right at her, so Brynnon gave him a polite smile and turned back in the direction from which she came.

"Miss Cantrell?"

Surprised the man knew her name, Brynnon stopped mid-step and turned back around. The older man—she guess to be in his sixties—approached her.

"You are Senator Cantrell's daughter, aren't you?"

"I'm sorry, have we met?"

The man shook his head, his blue eyes zeroed in on hers.

Okay… Calling upon years of experience dealing with the public, Brynnon held out her hand and smiled. "I'm afraid you have me at a disadvantage. I'm Brynnon."

"I know who you are," he spoke sharply, refusing to take her hand.

Alarm bells started going off in her head. Returning her arm to her side, she asked, "And you are?"

"Charles Miller. I'm"—he paused half a second before blurting, "I'm a reporter.

Brynnon glanced down at the generic press badge hanging around the man's collared neck. "It's nice to meet you, Mr.

Miller. Who do you write for?"

The man's eyes skittered away for only a second before finding hers again. "The, uh, Dallas Observer."

"I'm familiar with it." Brynnon offered the man a smile. "Are you wanting to know more about the children's Christmas party we're putting on today?"

"Actually, I want to know how your father sleeps at night."

The man's statement took her completely off guard. "Excuse me?"

"Cantrell Construction built the bridge that collapsed near Kunar six years ago, correct?"

Brynnon's heart thumped hard inside her chest at the memory of such a tragic event in the U.S. military's history. "Y-yes, but—"

"Twelve soldiers died that day because your father decided to use low-quality supplies."

She recoiled as if she'd been struck. It had been years since anyone had asked her about that day. "I'm sorry, Mr. Miller, was it? I don't know who your source is, but I can assure you, my father's company used only the highest quality supplies for *every* project they took on. Furthermore, there was a full investigation into the cause of the collapse, and Cantrell Construction was not found liable in any way. I'm sure your boss can get you a copy of the report. Honestly"—she shook her head— "I'm not sure why your editor would even send you here to question me about something that's old news."

Rather than appease him, the man's eyes flared with anger. "Old news?"

"Yes. As you, yourself stated, the incident happened over six years ago. Now, if you'll excuse me, I really do need to get back to the children."

With a snarl, the reporter got in her face. "Your father is a murderer, and I'm going to make sure the world knows it."

****

Grant watched Brynnon say something more to her friend and head for the wing's entrance. He took a step in that direction, but Angie—the woman Brynnon had introduced to him as her best friend when they'd first arrived—mouthed the word, *Bathroom.*

Glancing to where Brynnon had disappeared, he hesitated before deciding to stay put. He hated having her out of his sight for even a minute, but he'd already noticed the dead-end hallway as they'd walked in earlier. The only things down there were the two restrooms with a water fountain in between. And it wasn't like he could follow her into the bathroom.

I'll give her five minutes, then I'm going after her.

With a nod, Grant let her friend know he understood and stayed where he'd been posted for the past hour. Two minutes later, a young, African American boy he'd seen opening presents earlier approached him. Wearing a pair of Transformers pajamas, the kid appeared to be about eight years old.

Only two years younger than—No. He was *not* going to go there.

"You Miss Brynnon's boyfriend?" the boy asked boldly.

Grant dialed back his emotions, his deep voice answering, "Depends. Who's asking?"

"I'm Kenny." The young man held out his hand.

Dwarfed inside Grant's fist, the two shook hands. "Grant."

"Nice to meet you. But you still didn't answer my question."

Letting go of the boy's hand, Grant shook his head. "No. I'm not her boyfriend."

Confused, Kenny tilted his head. "So why do you keep staring at her like that?"

Damn, this kid's observant. "I'm her bodyguard."

"Bodyguard." Kenny's round eyes grew wide. "She in danger?"

"No. It's just a precaution."

A tiny pair of shoulders sagged as relief flooded the young boy. "Good." Milk chocolate eyes slid down to Grant's waist. "You carrying?"

Jesus, this kid damn near made him want to smile. "Maybe."

His eyes rose to Grant's again. "Good," he used a serious tone. "Someone tries to hurt Miss Brynnon, you gonna shoot them?"

"If I have to," Grant answered honestly. *I'll take out anyone who dares to bring her harm.*

"Good," the kid said again. "That's really good."

When Brynnon had first mentioned coming here, Grant had wanted nothing to do with it. The kid part was hard enough. Throw cancer in the mix, and it was like dropping him in the middle of his own personal hell. Even so, he was actually starting to enjoy talking with Kenny.

"Yeah? Why's that?"

Looking up at him as if he'd lost his damn mind, Kenny asked, "Don't you two ever talk? She's the nicest lady I know, besides my mom."

"You think so?"

"Heck, yeah. Miss Brynnon's a really busy lady, but she

still takes the time to come by and see me." Looking around to make sure no one was listening, Kenny whispered, "Well, technically, she comes to see all the kids. But I know I'm her favorite."

Grant felt the corner of his mouth turn upward. "That so?"

The kid gave him a no shit look. "Duh. It's probably because we have so much in common since she works on houses and all that." Standing a little taller—which wasn't saying much since he was all of four feet—Kenny told him proudly, "I want to be an architect when I grow up."

Before Grant could respond, the boy looked over at the group of kids and gasped. "Oh, they're lining up for cookies and stuff! I gotta go!"

Grant watched as Kenny started to run off, but the boy stopped and turned back around.

"You promise you won't let anyone hurt Miss Brynnon?"

A warm feeling spread throughout his chest. "Not while I'm around."

Kenny smiled. "Then I hope you stay around her forever. She's special."

With that, the boy turned back around and joined the other kids in line.

"Yeah," Grant whispered to himself. "She is."

Speaking of which…

He checked his watch. Nearly ten minutes had passed since Brynnon left to go to the bathroom. He scanned the room to make sure he hadn't missed her return. Angie was over at the nurse's station, helping serve the kids cookies and drinks, but the object of his search was nowhere to be seen.

Damn it.

Walking swiftly across the room, Grant headed for the

restrooms. The sound of a man's angry voice hit his ears just as he rounded the corner. The sight before him sending an immediate surge of anger through his system.

"Your father is a murder, and I'm going to make sure the world knows it."

A man appearing to be about sixty or so was in Brynnon's face, and it was clear the guy was pissed.

What the fuck?

"You're wrong," Brynnon's sharp voice seethed. "And you need to leave before I call for security."

"That won't be necessary," Grant's voice grated. He was by her side in seconds. The relief in her eyes when she swung her gaze to his was like a punch to his gut.

"The truth *will* come out." With that, the man walked away, disappearing down the hall. Grant started to go after him, but a small hand on his chest stopped him.

"Let him go."

"Who was he?" Grant demanded.

"Just a reporter."

"What the fuck did he want?"

Though she tried to hide it, Grant saw the tremor in her hand as she removed it from his chest. "Nothing."

"Sure as hell didn't look like nothing." He did a visual sweep of her body. *If he hurt her, I'll fucking kill him.*

"Whatever you're thinking, stop."

His eyes shot to hers.

"I'm fine, Grant. Really." Brynnon lowered her arm. "He was just after a story that doesn't exist. That's all."

"Apparently, he didn't get the memo."

"Right?" She shook her head. "That came out of nowhere, for sure."

"What's the non-existent story?"

116

Brynnon took a breath to compose herself. "Nothing important. I promise." Seeing he wasn't convinced, she added, "This sort of thing happens all the time. An overzealous reporter catches wind of something they *think* might be their chance to land a big story. They try to dig up dirt on a U.S. Senator or his family only to find out it's completely bogus. Seriously, let's just forget about it and go see Angie and the kids. After, we need to call your friend and set up an appointment to get you fitted for your tux."

Begrudgingly, Grant agreed and walked her back to the party. But as he waited for Brynnon to say her goodbyes and give out hugs, he thought more about the man he'd seen talking to her. He'd appeared bitter. Angry. Not exactly characteristics he'd expect to find in an overzealous reporter. Maybe a trip to the paper where the guy worked would help put the uneasy feeling in his gut to rest.

Grant stood back as Brynnon doled out hugs to each and every child there. As they started to leave, he heard a voice holler out for him.

"Bye, Grant! Remember what we talked about!"

He turned and gave Kenny a wave.

A look of shock spread over Brynnon's face. "Shut the front door. Is that an actual smile I see?"

Clearing his throat, Grant returned to his usual state of indifference, muttering, "Cute kid."

Brynnon gave him a knowing grin. "I see you met Kenny. That explains it."

"What's his story?"

Her lips flattened slightly. "When Kenny was four, he was diagnosed with Neuroblastoma. It's a rare type of cancer that most commonly affects children. From everything I've read, most don't even survive past the age of five, but Kenny's a fighter. His doctors chose an aggressive course of treatment that took him to the brink of death. But, he went into remission three years ago."

"How old is he, now?"

"He just turned eight last month."

Grant pushed the elevator button and waited. "So, if he's in remission, why is he a patient here?"

What was left of Brynnon's smile vanished. "He went in for one of his bi-yearly checkups. Completely routine. The scan showed another tumor. You wouldn't know it to talk with him, but the cancer is spreading rapidly this time."

"What's the prognosis?"

"I spoke to his mother the last time I was here. The Dr.'s only give him another month or two."

The unexpected news hit Grant in the chest. Reflexively, he swung his gaze back to the end of the hall where he could still hear the children laughing. "Damn."

"Yeah."

Inhaling deeply, he could still hear Kenny's earlier comment as they stepped into the empty elevator. *I want to be an architect when I grow up.*

Smacking the lower level button, Grant turned to Brynnon. "Does he know?"

"He does, but he refuses to believe the doctors are right." She gave him a watery smile. "Like I said, he's a fighter."

They were both silent, lost in their thoughts as the elevator descended. On the way out to Grant's truck, he shook his head. "How do you do it?"

Her forehead bunched. "Do what?"

He pushed the unlock button on his fob. "Come here and hang out with those kids and their parents, but still want children of your own. I'd think it would make you want to avoid the possibility of that type of pain and loss altogether."

"The exact opposite, actually."

Grant and Brynnon both climbed into the truck and shut their doors. As he drove away, Brynnon explained, "I thought the same thing, at first. Every kid in there is different. From their diseases and prognosis to their families and backgrounds…no two are alike. But after spending time with some of their parents, I realized there was one thing they all had in common."

"What's that?"

"Love."

Grant scoffed. "Love?"

"I'm serious. It's the one thing that gets them through it all. I mean, sure, they get upset. Sometimes, they get very angry. At the doctors, themselves. God. But in the end, every single parent I've spoken with has told me the same thing. They'd rather go through all that a million times over than to have never experienced the love they shared with their children at all."

His hands curled around the steering wheel, his fists tightening as forceful emotions threatened to take him over. Fearful he'd spout off something that had nothing to do with Brynnon but would probably hurt her, anyway, Grant remained silent for the rest of the ride.

Back at her condo, he quickly went through the routine of clearing the place, using the time to get his shit under control. When he returned to the entryway where Brynnon had remained, as asked, he found her thanking someone on the phone before ending the call.

"Who was that?"

"I ordered some pizza. It'll be here in twenty. I probably should've asked first, but I'm starving."

"Pizza's fine."

He was hungry, too. And, truth be told, pizza was his weakness. *Well, one of them.* Grant stared at the woman standing before him.

He thought of the way she'd looked at him when they'd been discussing the possibility—or impossibility—of them being together. The way her eyes reflexively found his when she and Angie had been talking about him while at the kids' party.

It wasn't the first time a woman had propositioned him or indiscreetly talked about him with her friends. But it was the relief Grant saw in her eyes the moment she saw him, and that dumbass reporter walked away that really hit home.

She trusts me.

Just a few short days ago, he wouldn't have cared one way or another. Now, Grant realized it mattered. A lot.

Even the way she'd talked about still wanting kids, despite knowing everything the ones in the hospital were going through. At first, he'd thought her crazy, but now...

If he was being completely honest with himself, Grant was in fucking awe of her. Though their situations were different, she too, had experienced loss and heartache. Unlike him, however, Brynnon hadn't let hers define who she was as a human being.

She still believed in the possibility of love and happiness. A future filled with joy and peace. Happily ever after. All the things he'd closed his eyes to for so many years.

The more time he spent with her, the more Grant found himself reconsidering everything he'd come to believe as truth. He just wasn't sure what to do with it all.

"I got two meat-lovers." Her voice broke through his thoughts. "I hope that's okay."

Meat lovers? A woman after my own heart.

His heart.

The saying had been around for years, but had never rang more true for Grant than in that moment. And if he wasn't careful, this woman could very well take his.

Chapter 9

Sitting with her legs crisscrossed on one end of her couch, Brynnon moaned as she took a bite. After swallowing it, she licked her lips in appreciation. "I swear, pizza is the most perfect food in the entire world."

Next to her, Grant gave her an odd look before returning his focus to his own slice. He'd been acting a little strange ever since they left the hospital. She just wasn't sure why.

Deciding to go for a semi-normal conversation, Brynnon reached for the open box on the coffee table and grabbed another piece. "My dad's not a big fan, so Mom would wait until a night she knew he wouldn't be home for dinner to order it. When we were tiny, Billy and I used to be fascinated by the fact that she could just make a phone call, and within a few minutes, someone would be at the door with our food. Mom would always tell us not to tell dad, and she'd hide the empty box at the bottom of the trash so he wouldn't see it." She smiled. "It's silly, but those are some of my favorite memories with my mom."

"Why do you think that's silly?"

Brynnon swallowed a bite. "I don't know. I guess with all the fancy trips and things we took, I'd expect something like that to be at the top of the list, but they're not. Don't get me wrong, I loved that time with her, too. I guess maybe those nights at home stick out because, somehow, they just seem more...real." She blinked and looked back up at him. "Sorry. I'm probably not making much sense."

"No, I get what you're saying."

That surprised her. "You do?"

Grant hesitated, almost as if he weren't sure whether or not he wanted to say whatever it was he was going to tell her. But then he began to open up more than he had the entire time they'd been together.

"My mom died of cancer my senior year in high school."

"Oh, Grant." She reached out and placed her hand on his knee. "I'm so sorry."

He shook his head. "It was a long time ago."

"What about your dad?"

He let out a silent laugh. "Dad's a whole other story."

"I've got time." She removed the hand from his leg. "Plus, I've been told I'm a pretty good listener."

One corner of his mouth rose. Damn, the man was even more gorgeous when that happened. She couldn't imagine what he'd look like with a full-blown smile spread across his face.

With a deep breath, he opened up some. "Not much to tell. He's a truck driver. Or, at least he was. I don't really know."

"You don't know what your father does for a living?"

"He never was much of a father. As in, at all."

"Oh."

"Yeah. When mom found out she was pregnant with me, he denied I was his and took off. I saw him a handful of times growing up, but he married someone else who already had two kids, and that became his only family."

"Do you two ever talk?"

Grant tossed his empty paper plate onto the coffee table and shook his head. "Haven't spoken to the man in over twenty years."

That broke Brynnon's heart and pissed her off, all at the same time. "What a gigantic asshole." She quickly added, "Him. Not you."

A low chuckle escaped the back of his throat. "Pretty much."

She thought for a moment. "He didn't even reach out to you after your mom passed away?"

"Nope."

Brynnon pictured Grant as a young man. A boy who'd lost everything just as he was preparing for his future.

"Did your mother ever marry?"

"Once. When I was about nine. Jack was an abusive asshole, though. At the time, I was too young and too small to do anything to stop it. Mom put up with it for a while."

"Oh, God. What happened? How did she get away?"

"One night, the bastard came home drunk and decided to lay into me." Pain from the heart-wrenching memory was crystal clear in his eyes. "The next morning, after Jack went to work, Mom packed up what little stuff was ours, and we left. We stayed with her parents for a while until she could afford an apartment of her own. Grandma and Grandpa helped us out as much as they could, but it was still hard for mom. Being a single mother, especially back then, was tough. There was more of a stigma those days, which made it even harder."

"Where are your grandparents now?"

"Buried in the cemetery next to my mom."

"I'm sorry."

For the next several minutes, the two sat in silence. Grant

lost in his memories, Brynnon absorbing everything she'd just learned. When her thoughts returned to his dick of a father, renewed anger against a man she'd never met began to boil over.

"How could your dad abandon you like that? I don't understand how *any* parent could do that. And he's even worse because he denied his own son his love but then turned around and gave it all to someone else's kids."

Typical Grant, he just blew it off. "It's no big deal, Bryn. It doesn't matter."

Brynnon loved hearing him use the shortened version of her name, but ignored it. She needed him to see she could feel his pain. That the anger and resentment he kept buried inside wasn't his to bear alone.

"Like hell, it doesn't. It's obvious it still bothers you, and it should."

Brynnon slid closer to him. So close, in fact, her crossed feet were now touching his outer thigh.

"You said it was mainly just you and your mom growing up, right? And you were, what, eighteen when she died? I can't imagine how hard that must have been. How did you get through it?" She asked.

Sadness mixed with the bluish gray in his eyes as he stared back at her. "The day after I graduated high school, I enlisted in the Navy."

Without thinking, she placed her hand back onto his leg. "A lot of kids—especially boys—that age would have acted out. They would've turned to violence or drugs. Dropped out of school, but you didn't. Despite the loss you've suffered, you went on to make something of yourself."

Grant huffed out a breath. "I wouldn't exactly say I didn't act out." He gave her the tiniest of smirks. "After all, I went on to specialize in explosives so I could blow shit up."

Brynnon grinned. "You went on to serve your country and risk your life protecting those who couldn't protect themselves." She slid her hand over his fist and squeezed. "I know I didn't know your mom, but I do know she would've been very proud of the man you turned out to be."

Choking back tears, she suddenly wished his mom was still here so she could see what an amazing son she'd raised. Despite her best efforts, a tear escaped the corner of her eye.

Grant turned, shifting against the cushion to face her more directly. With his free hand, he cupped her cheek, his thumb gently wiping away the tear. "Don't cry for me, Princess," he whispered softly.

"I can't help it," she admitted shakily.

With more tears threatening to fall, Grant moved his thumb down to her quivering lip. Swiping it back and forth slowly, his gaze dropped to her mouth before rising back up to her watery eyes. It was the only warning she had before he kissed her.

Leaning in, Grant pressed his lips to hers. The powerful surge arching between them was so strong it was almost as if she'd been struck by lightning. Brynnon nearly jerked away for fear it was too much. Before she could, his tongue began running along the seam of her lips.

Without hesitation, she opened up for him. Her tongue reached out, joining his in the most sensual, sexually charged kiss she'd ever experienced. Desire flared inside her, and before she knew what she was doing, Brynnon had risen to her knees and was framing his face with her hands.

A deep grunt escaped his throat, and Brynnon swallowed it whole as she let out a tiny mewling sound of her own. The kiss had started out slow, tentative. But it didn't take long for it to become all lips and teeth and tongues as they both finally allowed their mutual attraction for one another to come to life.

Before she realized what she was doing, Brynnon swung her left leg up over his and climbed onto his lap. Straddling him, now, she could feel his swollen cock pressing against her needy core. Grant grunted again, his hips thrusting upward, his body searching for the release she was more than willing to give him.

"Brynnon," he moaned her name as his lips traveled across her jawline and lower. His rough whiskers only added to the already incredible sensation.

As if they had a mind of their own, Brynnon's hands moved from his face and began their journey downward. She could feel his sculpted chest and abs through his button-up shirt and couldn't wait to see what he looked like without it.

With that in mind, she began to untuck the shirt from his belted waistband. The second she'd pulled enough of the material free, Brynnon slid her hands underneath and felt skin-to-skin what she'd only been able to imagine.

On a hiss, Grant's muscles contracted beneath her touch as he brought his mouth back to hers. Brynnon moaned loudly as she began tasting him again, knowing right then, she'd never get enough.

Without conscious thought, she ground her denim-covered sex against the hard bulge beneath her, desperate to relieve the explosive pressure causing her most intimate muscles to ache to the point of pain.

"God, Grant," she panted against his lips. "I want you."

Brynnon dropped her hands to his belt and began pulling the tight leather free from its metal buckle. She'd never felt this way before. It was as if she'd die if she didn't find release soon. From what she could feel pressing against her throbbing pussy, Grant was in the same boat as she was.

The end of the belt popped free. Brynnon began frantically working to undo the button on the waist of his dress pants when a large hand clamped down over hers, stopping her. Tearing his lips from hers, Grant let out a guttural groan.

"What's the matter?" she choked out.

"Stop."

The rough order left her blinking. "What?"

"Jesus. Fuck." Grant looked up at her, both astonished and confused, almost as though he had no clue where he even was. "I'm sorry." He shook his head. Cursing under his breath, he made a move to get up. To get away from her.

What the hell? Without much choice, Brynnon slid awkwardly back onto the couch and let him stand. She watched as Grant began pacing back and forth.

"God, Brynnon. I'm sorry." He stopped and ran a hand through his hair, regret pouring out of him as he looked back at her. "I'm so sorry. That was—"

"Incredible." She answered for him.

His chest heaved with each of his ragged breaths. "I was going to say a mistake."

Ignoring the sharp dagger piercing her heart, Brynnon shook her head. "I disagree." Legs still trembling from the most incredible kiss she'd ever experienced, she stood and walked toward him.

"You don't understand. I've never done that before." Lips pressed into a thin line, Grant shook his head. Pissed at himself for actually acting human for a change.

In an attempt to lighten the mood, Brynnon gave him a sly smirk. "You've never kissed someone before?"

The scowl she'd grown accustomed to returned as he ran his hand over the same scruff she'd felt against her skin only seconds before. "You know what I mean. I've never crossed the line on a job like that." He exhaled loudly. "It was unprofessional, and I would understand if you want to have me replaced by a different R.I.S.C. operative."

"Are you serious?"

"You have every right to be upset."

"The only thing I'm upset about is the fact that you stopped."

Grant swallowed, regret swimming in his eyes as they locked with hers. "I never should have started."

"I think you need to ease up on yourself just a tad. It was just a kiss, Grant. Not a proposal. Besides, it's not like you were the only one participating.

The muscles in his jaw bulged as he clenched his teeth together. "Doesn't matter. But regardless, I assure you it won't happen again."

Wanna bet?

Those two little words damn near fell off her tongue, but Brynnon held them in. She knew he'd felt the same, heart-stirring connection she had. He just needed a little more time to accept the inevitable.

Deciding to let it go—for now—Brynnon went back to the coffee table and began cleaning up the mess from their dinner. From behind her, his deep voice reverberated through the small room.

"I'm going to go check the perimeter one last time. I'll…see you tomorrow."

Without turning back around, she answered, "Okay."

He cleared his throat before asking, "Did that reporter happen to tell you which newspaper he works for?"

Closing her eyes for a moment, Brynnon forced the sting in her eyes away. Taking more time than she really needed to pick up the napkins, plates, and leftover pizza, she told him, "The Dallas Observer."

"While we were at the hospital, I texted my friend about getting a tux. She found a rental place downtown that keeps several in stock. She checked, and they have a few in my size. I have an appointment there at eight-thirty."

Great. So not only had the man kissed her senseless and then pull away before they could get to the really good part, she now had to spend tomorrow morning watching him parade around in a tux.

Freaking fantastic.

"Also"—his deep voice rumbled again—"I noticed you didn't have anything in particular scheduled for the afternoon, so I'd like to go to the Observer."

Brynnon turned around. "Why?"

"I want to speak to the reporter. At the very least, he needs to understand approaching you the way he did is unacceptable."

"I don't need you fighting my battles for me, Grant. Besides, I told you it was nothing. I already handled it."

"Still, you said the guy was sniffing around for a story about your father. I'd like to find out if whatever story he's working on has anything to do with the threats the senator has received."

"Okay, but it's a waste of time."

She walked past him toward her kitchen. There was a pause, and she thought maybe he was going to say something more about the two of them. Instead, the next thing Brynnon heard was Grant disarming the alarm before opening the door and walking outside.

The next day, after a very, *very* restless night's sleep, Brynnon rode with Grant to the tuxedo shop. Thankfully, he had her wait in the front while he went with the owner to try a few on.

With the massively awkward tension that had been between them, the last thing Brynnon needed was to have the God of Kissing filling her head with suit porn. It was bad enough he'd gone for well-worn jeans, a black T-shirt, and a black leather jacket. The man looked like a damn model for Bad Boys R Us.

Her dreams hadn't helped her already-grouchy mood, either. During the few short stretches of sleep she'd been able to cling on to, her head had been filled with scenes like those she'd read in her favorite romance novels.

In the first one, Brynnon dreamed she and Grant were back on her couch. Only that time, in her subconscious fantasy, he hadn't stopped.

Another was of the two of them in her bed. His hard body hovering over hers as he pumped himself in and out of her welcoming heat.

Then there was *the* dream. The one with the shower. In it, Brynnon had been standing beneath the water, rinsing out her hair when Grant startled her by opening the door. Already stripped bare, he'd joined her, using his mouth to give her the most intense climax ever.

That dream, in particular, had left her hot, wet, and more aroused than she'd ever remembered feeling. Her clit had been so swollen, Brynnon had been forced into an almost frantic self-gratification session.

The result? A mediocre orgasm. One that did very little to combat her body's need for the pleasure, she instinctively knew only one man could bring her. The same man currently undressing somewhere in the back of this very store.

Sitting in the store's small waiting area, Brynnon crossed her legs, pinched them together in an attempt to try and ease the almost painful throbbing that had returned. If she couldn't get the man on board with her no-strings sex idea soon, she didn't know what she was going to do.

"You feel ok?"

Grant's voice broke through her X-rated thoughts, causing Brynnon to jump. Her gaze swung up to his. "I'm sorry, what?"

"I asked if you were feeling okay."

"Yeah." She stood a little too quickly. Wiping her hands down the front of her long, maxi skirt, Brynnon cleared her throat and plastered on a smile. "I'm good. Why do you ask?"

His brows turned slightly inward. "You sure? Your cheeks are all flushed, and you were sitting there, looking as though you were in pain."

Her mind raced. "It's just a little too warm in here, that's all."

"Really?" He seemed surprised by her explanation. "I thought it was a little cold, myself."

"Well, yeah, but that's probably because you were taking your clothes off."

Holy hell in a hot air balloon. Could she sound like more of a blubbering idiot?

With an urgent need to change the subject to *anything* else, Brynnon nodded to the plastic suit bag draped over one of his forearms.

Don't think about his sexy forearms. Ignore. The. Forearms.

"You"—her voice cracked, so she cleared her throat and tried again— "you find one?"

"Yeah." Grant nodded, his all-seeing eyes still staring back at her as though he were trying to decipher some big mystery.

"Good. We'd better get going, then. You wanted to run by the paper, plus I need to sit down and search through some listings for some more flip house options when we get to the condo."

He nodded. "Let's go."

Less than forty minutes later, the two were pulling into Brynnon's driveway. Parked behind her car, she turned to him, still stunned by what they'd discovered.

"I still don't get it. Why would Charles Miller lie about where he worked?"

She couldn't believe it when the woman at the paper had told them she'd never heard of him. The nice lady had even searched the Observer's employee database and assured them no one by the name of Charles Miller had ever worked for them, as a reporter or otherwise.

Grant pulled the key out of the ignition. "Who knows. Hell, his real name probably isn't Miller."

"It's so bizarre."

Pissed at himself, Grant shook his head. "Should've gone after him when I had the chance."

"Uh, no. You shouldn't have. We were in a children's hospital with a Christmas party taking place twenty feet away. Letting the creep walk away was the smart thing to do."

She could tell he still wasn't convinced, but Grant made no further comment. Instead, he pulled his phone from his pocket, went into his contacts, and tapped a name she couldn't see.

"Who are you calling?"

"Derek West. He's Alpha Team's computer guy. I'm going to have him access the hospital's security cams in that hallway. He should be able to pull facial rec on the guy and find out who he really is."

Brynnon's brows rose. "He can do that?"

Grant scoffed, "And then some."

Okay, so that was a little more than impressive. "Wow. I thought that sort of thing was made up for TV and the movies."

He looked over at her again, his expression serious. "You spot that guy again, I don't care where we are, you let me know. And stay as far away from him as you can, you hear me?"

"Yes, sir."

"I'm serious, Bryn."

"I said okay," she repeated. Brynnon would admit she could be stubborn, but she wasn't stupid. Nor did she have a death wish.

She heard a muffled voice answer the call and Grant mumble, "It's me."

Feeling as though she should give them some privacy, Brynnon started to open her door, but Grant stopped her. "Hold on," he told his friend. To her, he asked, "Where are you going?"

"I forgot to check the mail when we got back last night. Figured I'd go do that while you talked with your friend."

Grant's eyes slid to his rearview mirror, no doubt looking at the multiple mailbox post across the street. Brynnon resisted the urge to roll her eyes.

"It's just the mailbox, Grant. I'll grab it and come right back over." She raised two fingers. "Scout's honor."

He looked back at her, deadpan. "The Girl Scouts use three fingers."

She smirked, glad to see his pseudo-sense of humor had returned. "I never joined." With that, she slid out of the truck and headed down the gentle slope of her drive. Looking both ways like a good girl, she deemed it safe and casually walked across the street.

Opening her box's metal flap, Brynnon pulled out a larger-than-normal stack of mail and realized she'd not only forgotten to grab it last night, but also the night before. *The first night Grant stayed with me.*

No wonder. Her brain had experienced all sorts of misfires since the frustrating man had barged into her life.

As she always did, Brynnon stood at the edge of the street near her mailbox—which was on one end—and began sifting through the numerous envelopes.

Some were bills she'd been expecting, others some political flyers she'd never read. At the bottom, however, there was a large, manila envelope that caught her eye.

Her name was hand-written on the front, but there was no address or return address. She looked the rest of it over and realized it didn't have any postage or a post-mark from the USPS.

Thoughts of the non-reporter ran through her head. She knew she should probably hand it straight over to Grant, but Brynnon's curiosity got the better of her. Instead, she stayed put and began ripping the envelope open.

Seeing multiple items inside, she balanced the rest of the mail in her arms, she slid her hand inside and pulled out what felt like a picture. The glossy image left her momentarily stunned.

It was an image of her at the flip house she'd just sold. Only, from the looks of it, it had been taken several weeks prior.

Heart pounding, she dropped the rest of the mail onto the pavement at her feet and began pulling out the other pictures.

There was a thick stack of them. Some as recent as two days ago while others had been taken well over a month ago. And they were all of her.

Sick to her stomach, Brynnon's mind began to whirl with what this meant. Someone had been following her. For a while, from the looks of it.

She started to put the pictures back into the envelope, but her fingertips hit another piece of paper inside. Pulling it out, Brynnon read the ominous words typed out there.

Your father did not heed his warning. He was told what would happen if he didn't confess his sins. Now, you will atone for the sins of your father.

"What the hell?"

There was a loud noise coming from somewhere down the road, but she was still too lost in her thoughts to pay it any attention. One by one, she went back through each of the pictures. Her stomach pitched at the knowledge that the threats her father had received were actually against her.

Brynnon felt nauseated and was suddenly lightheaded. *How could I not have known?*

The sound in the background grew louder. Brynnon's fear-induced fog had just started to clear when she heard Grant yelling her name. Looking up, she was surprised to see him running wide-eyed down her driveway.

"Move!"

Everything happened in slow motion.

Grant looked to his left—her right—as he continued sprinting toward her. Brynnon followed his gaze, a wave of terror crashing over her as she realized the noise she'd heard was a car. And it was coming straight for her.

Frozen with fear, she looked back at Grant, who'd made it just past the middle of the street. He was waving his arm and screaming for her to get out of the way. With determination etched all over his face, he threw his arms open and jumped.

Grant's rock-solid body slammed into hers just as a red blur sped past, taking the post holding the mailboxes out in the process. The force of the tackle sent Brynnon flying backward, her head slamming hard against her neighbor's front lawn. White stars flashed behind her eyes before everything began to fade away.

Chapter 10

"Ouch!"

Grant repositioned the towel full of ice against the back of Brynnon's head as gently as he could, thankful as fuck she couldn't see the way his hand still shook. "Sorry."

"S'okay." Her fingers brushed his as she took over the job of keeping the makeshift ice pack in place.

Confident she had a good hold, Grant positioned the kitchen chair next to Brynnon so it faced her and sat down. Nearly knee-to-knee, he stared into her eyes. For what felt like the millionth time since they'd come inside, he checked for the slightest change in her pupils or any other sign of a concussion.

"You don't have to keep checking. I told you I'm fine."

I'm not. "I've seen concussions go sideways fast. They're not something to dick around with."

She worried her bottom lip before asking him, "That car…that was no accident, was it?"

"No." He shook his head. "It wasn't."

The terrifying scene ran through his head again. He'd been sitting in the truck, talking to D about Charles Miller—or whatever the fuck the man's name was—when he heard the rev of an engine. With an uneasy feeling in his gut, Grant had told D he'd call him back and got out of the truck just in time to see the small, burgundy car pull away from the curb where it had been parked and head in their direction.

His heart damn near stopped as it sped up and swerved over the center of the road. Putting Brynnon directly in its path.

He'd immediately started running for her, screaming to get the hell out of the way, afraid he was already too late.

Those goddamn pictures had her so scared, she hadn't been able to comprehend what was going on around her. Thankfully, Grant was able to push her out of the way just in time, but she'd hit her head pretty hard when they landed, damn near losing consciousness.

Fearful the car would come back for a second try, he'd scooped Brynnon into his arms and carried her straight into her condo. After making sure she was okay, he'd then called Derek back to explain what had happened.

"We should call the police." There was a slight tremor present in her quiet voice.

Hearing her fear made Grant want to hunt down the bastard responsible and rip his fucking heart out.

"Derek's on his way."

"He's not the police."

"No." Grant shook his head. "He's better."

The trepidation reflecting back at him settled like a brick of C4 in his gut. He understood her concerns with not calling DPD. Grant also got why she'd probably lost faith in his ability to protect her.

The image of that fucking car heading straight for her played through his mind again. *Goddamn it!*

He should have been with her. Hell, he should have gotten the mail for her or...

"This wasn't your fault."

Grant's eyes rose to hers. "Never said it was."

"You didn't have to." She sat the towel down onto the table. "I can tell that's what you're thinking."

She sees too damn much. "I didn't..." His low-pitched voice nearly cracked. Raising his hand to her face, he cupped her soft cheek and started again, "I didn't think I was going to get to you in time."

Wrapping her delicate fingers around his thick wrist, Brynnon stared back at him with laser focus. "But you did. You saved my life, Grant. Don't lose sight of that."

Jesus, he wanted to taste her again. Had thought of little else since sharing that first, mind-blowing kiss last night. From the radiating heat staring back at him, Grant knew she wanted it, too.

God, she was something else. Most women would be melted in a puddle of hysterical tears by now. Not Brynnon. No, his woman was strong. Fierce. And she...

What. The. Fuck?

Grant shot to his feet and went to the door, putting some much-needed space between them. She wasn't his. No woman had been his. Not since—

"Grant? Are you okay?"

Concern laced her sweet voice, but Grant refused to look at her for fear he'd give in to his desire to take what he wanted. What he knew she was willing to give. Hell, the woman had nearly died less than an hour ago, but here she was, worried about him.

"You need to put that ice back on your head."

The words came out much harsher than intended, making

him feel like a complete asshat. He knew he was giving her a fuckton of mixed signals and felt like a total asshat because of it, but *fuck*.

As much as he wanted her—God, he couldn't remember ever wanting a woman so much—Grant would not allow himself to act on his desires. Not now, while she was vulnerable and scared.

He may be a Grade-A prick, but he was not the kind of man to take advantage of a woman's fragile, emotional state. No matter how badly he wanted her.

Grant heard Derek's car before he saw it. A few seconds later, the computer geek parked his silver Hellcat in front of Brynnon's condo.

"Hey, man," the blond greeted Grant as he opened the door for his teammate. Carrying a pile of folders underneath one arm, he asked, "How is she?"

"Bump on the head and a little sore, but she says she's fine."

"Because *she* is."

The sound of her voice had both men turning to see Brynnon walking toward them.

"You shouldn't be up walking around," Grant told her brusquely.

Purposely ignoring him, Brynnon held out her hand. "Hi. I'm Brynnon. You must be Derek."

"Dude, she just totally blew you off." With a wider-than-necessary smile, Derek chuckled as he reached for Brynnon's offered hand. "Nice to meet you. I'm Derek. And, for the record, I love you, already."

Her eyes fell to the front of the guy's t-shirt. Today's pick was white with black lettering. With a sketch-style laptop in the center, it read, 'Mine's so big, you have to use two hands'.

141

Brynnon laughed but then immediately winced. She may not have a concussion, but she was definitely hurting.

Seeing her face etched in pain brought Grant's murderous desires back to life. Turning his voice lower, he glowered at Derek. "We need to find this fucker."

"That's why I'm here."

"You find our reporter?"

"I did." Turning to Brynnon, he asked, "Does the name Charles Wright mean anything to you?"

Both men waited while she tried to place the name. The skin between her brows bunched together in that cute-as-fuck way it did as she thought hard.

"It sounds familiar, but I can't place it."

"What about Jordan Wright?"

It took all of two seconds for the lines on her forehead to smooth out as recognition sank in. "He was one of the soldiers who died in that accident." She blinked a few times and looked back up at Derek. "That man, the one who claimed to be a reporter...he's really Charles Wright?"

Derek nodded. "Facial rec confirms it."

Brynnon's shoulders sagged. "That's why he was asking about the accident."

Feeling as though he were missing something, Grant's focus bounced back and forth between the two of them. "What are you two talking about? What accident?"

It was Brynnon who answered. "Jordan was one of the twelve soldiers killed when a bridge collapsed in the mountains near Kunar six years ago."

"I remember that," Grant remarked.

It was just after he'd left the SEALs to join R.I.S.C. Though he hadn't known any of the ill-fated soldiers personally, he and the rest of the military family still felt the loss to their core.

To Derek, he asked, "What does any of that have to do with Bryn?"

The shortened version of her name slipped out before he could stop it. Derek gave him a funny look, but surprisingly, the guy didn't comment.

Not giving Derek the chance to answer him, Brynnon spoke first. "I'm assuming Charles Wright was Jordan's father?"

"He was." Derek nodded. He handed her a piece of paper that was on top of the stack of folders.

A look of sadness washed over Brynnon, and Grant had to shove his fists into his pockets to keep from reaching out for her.

"That's him." She handed the paper to Grant to look over. "That's the man from the hospital."

Grant looked down at Charles Wright's picture. It was definitely the same guy. "He was asking you about a story?"

She hesitated. Grant could tell she was uncomfortable, but he had to force himself to ignore it. To treat this just like any other job.

"Brynnon, we need to know what he said to you. Exactly."

"Not much, really. H-he accused my father of being a murderer."

The hell? "Do you know why he would say that?"

Her eyes skittered to Derek then back to his as if trying to decide whether or not to answer the question. Derek responded, instead.

"Cantrell Construction built the bridge that collapsed."

"But it wasn't Dad's fault," Brynnon blurted. "At the hospital yesterday, Charles Wright claimed the company used low-quality materials, and that's why the bridge gave way. But that's not true." She drew in a deep breath. "An investigation showed the foundation had been compromised during a recent bomb attack the week before, but it wasn't discovered until after the collapse. My father contacted the military the second he found out about what happened and voluntarily provided them with all of the purchase orders and other records from that job."

"Easy." Grant attempted to calm her. "We're not accusing your father of anything."

"No, but Charles Wright is." Her eyes pleaded with his. "You have to understand. When that bridge fell, the first person everyone looked at was my dad. Reporters hounded all of us for days until, finally, the news reported the actual cause. Dad's business was built on the pride he took in what they did. Cantrell Construction was known for its *high*-quality work. Not the other way around."

"Where do you think Wright got the notion they'd cut corners on that job?" Derek asked her.

"I have no idea." She shook her head. "My guess is, he's still mourning the loss of his son and wants someone to blame."

Like every other emotion the man had, Derek's skepticism was evident. "Maybe. Still seems wonky to me."

"Why's that?" Grant asked his teammate.

"It's been over half a decade. Why go after Cantrell now? And why use Brynnon to do it?"

"The sins of your father," she whispered more to herself than to them.

When Derek looked to Grant for an explanation, he went over to the table and retrieved the bagged note. Brynnon's prints would most likely be the only ones on it, but he still wanted to try and preserve it as best he could. Just in case.

"Your father did not heed his warning," Derek read the note aloud. "He was told what would happen to you if he didn't confess. Now, you will atone for the sins of your father." The man's crystal blue eyes shot to Grant's. "That last part is a version from a quote by the famous Roman poet, Horace. Our guy worded it a bit differently, but it's basically the same thing. What the fuck?"

With a grim nod, Grant agreed. Charles Wright, or whoever sent that letter, wasn't playing around.

"It all makes sense now." Brynnon broke the silence. "Jordan's dad blames mine for the death of his son." She looked up at him, that damn fear now stronger than ever. "He wants to kill me, so my dad suffers the loss of a child, just like he did."

Grant closed the distance between them in one long stride. With his hands on her shoulders, he locked eyes with hers. "That's not going to happen."

There was a short pause before Derek cleared his throat. Grant should probably be embarrassed by his blatant show of emotion in front of his teammate, but surprisingly, he wasn't.

Acting as if nothing out of the ordinary had occurred—thank Christ—the computer whiz looked at him and asked, "This note was in an envelope full of pictures?"

"Yes," Brynnon answered for him as she grabbed the stack of pictures from the table and brought them to Derek.

Cursing under his breath, he flipped through a few before handing them back to her. "According to the message, your dad was warned."

"Well, yeah. I mean, that's why Grant's here in the first place, right? He was hired to watch over me as a precaution because Dad received some sort of threat?"

"Some sort," Derek parroted her words. When the former

SEAL shared a look with Grant, he knew exactly what D was thinking.

Understanding hit him like a kick to the nuts. "Sonofabitch."

"What?" Brynnon looked between both men. "What is it?"

Still talking to his teammate, Grant had to work hard to control his temper. "Cantrell fucking lied." He swung his gaze to the man's daughter. "This wasn't just some vague threat like your father claimed. It was a threat against *you*."

"What? No." She adamantly denied the accusation. "My father wouldn't do that. That doesn't even make any sense. Why would he keep something like that from you? Or, me, for that matter?"

Grant's eyes bore down on hers. "That's what I intend to find out." To Derek, he asked, "Can you stay with her until I get back?"

"Didn't even have to ask, brother."

"Thanks." Grant went to get his coat from the hook near Brynnon's door.

"You're leaving?"

It was shit timing, but he had to find out what the hell was going on. Starting with a conversation between him and Senator Cantrell.

After a quick text to Coop to verify the senator was at his office, Grant told Brynnon, "I'll be back soon. Derek will keep you safe." When she started to argue, he added, "He's a former SEAL, like me, and he's well-trained."

"I don't care about that." She shook her head. "I just want you to calm down and think about this for a second before you go storming off to my father's office."

"Nothing to think about, Princess. Your father

146

intentionally left out vital information that could very well have affected your safety. I need to know why."

"Not to step on any toes, here, but I have to agree with your man, Brynnon. What your dad did wasn't cool."

Her wheels turned. "*If* he did what you're saying, I'm sure there was a reasonable explanation as to why. Dad would never knowingly put me in danger."

Like Brynnon, Grant ignored Derek's claim that he was her man. "That's exactly why I'm going to see him. To give your father a chance to explain."

But if Grant found out the senator had purposely allowed his daughter to be in more danger than he'd let on, then God help him.

"You got this, D?" he asked his teammate.

"I'll protect her like she's my own."

Knowing just how much those words meant, Grant gave his friend a nod of thanks.

"While you're gone"—Derek added— "I'll run the note and pics through the scanner to see if anything pops up, and I'll leave these for you to look through." He held the folders up a little higher.

"What's in them?"

"Information on the twelve soldiers who died on the bridge. I have copies of it all at my place." He shrugged. "If Wright's claims are true, there are eleven other families out there with motive. Figured between the two of us, we may be able to find something that sticks out."

"Sounds good." With one final glance in Brynnon's direction, Grant left.

Less than twenty minutes later, he found himself arguing with Cantrell's personal assistant. The girl was young and probably good at her job, but she sure as hell wasn't going to keep him from seeing the senator.

"I told you he's in a meeting." The well-intended woman brazenly stepped into his path. "If you'd like to have a seat, I'm sure he will be more than happy to speak to you after—"

"I don't have time to wait."

Grant sidestepped her and reached for the expensive doorknob.

"Sir, please stop." She turned to Coop, who was standing nonchalantly to the side. "Don't just stand there, stop him!"

"Sorry, Jaynee." Coop folded his arms. "Grant's right. What he needs to discuss with your boss can't wait."

Having zero patience or time for this bullshit, Grant turned the knob and barged into Cantrell's private office.

Brynnon's father was sitting behind his desk and Martin Downing was in one of the two leather chairs facing him. Both men immediately stopped speaking and turned their attention onto him.

"We need to talk," he growled not giving two fucks who the guy was or what political power the man had.

Scowling, Martin stood abruptly. "You can't just walk in here like this and interrupt us. Just who do you think you are?"

Wanting to flick the stuck-up bastard like the annoying bug he was, Grant shot back, "The man trying to keep the senator's daughter alive."

"I am so sorry, Senator," a worried Jaynee piped in. "I tried to tell him to wait, but he—"

"It's okay, Jaynee." William Cantrell held his hand palm-up to calm the woman down. He looked back at Grant. "What happened?" His eyes widened with concern. "Is she all right?"

Never one to pull any punches, Grant spouted off, "No

thanks to you."

Guilt permeated from the man, but his little sidekick kept coming at him. "How dare you talk to the senator like that!"

Ignoring him, Grant kept his focus on Cantrell. "When were you planning on telling me the truth?"

The senator blinked before telling his assistant, "We're good here, Jaynee. Thank you."

Both scared of him and confused by her boss's directive, the girl's hesitant eyes moved from his to Cantrell's. "A-are you sure?"

"I'm sure."

"O-okay, Sir. If you say so." With a final, wary glance in Grant's direction, Jaynee turned and left the office.

To Martin, Grant said, "You can leave, too, Downing."

Red-faced, Cantrell's Chief of Staff appeared to be on the verge of a serious tantrum. "Now wait just a damn minute. I don't take orders from you." Martin spun on his expensive shoes and faced Cantrell. "Sir, I really think I—"

"Martin should stay." The senator looked at Grant. "If you're here for the reason I think you are, he needs to know what you've discovered."

Grant didn't like it, but refused to waste any more time arguing. "Fine." He turned to Martin, "Shut the door."

Downing looked to his boss, and only after Cantrell gave him a single nod of his head, did he do as he'd been asked. *Jesus, what a prick.*

The second the door closed, Grant laid into Brynnon's father. "When you called Jake looking for protection, you told him the threat was against you, but Brynnon's the real target, isn't she?"

"Yes," Cantrell sighed.

"Why did you lie?"

"First, tell me what happened," her father pleaded. "Is she really okay?"

"Do you even care?"

Grant knew he should probably watch his mouth, given the powerful position the man was in, but at the moment, it didn't matter. The only thing that mattered to him was finding out the truth, so he could keep Brynnon safe.

"Of course, I care. She's my daughter. Now, tell me what happened!"

"Someone just tried running her over with a fucking car!" Grant's voice echoed off the thick walls. "*That's* what happened."

Suddenly looking much older than before, Cantrell plopped down into his high-back chair and shook his head. "Oh, God." With unshed tears filling his eyes, he looked up at Grant. "But she's okay? She wasn't hurt, was she?"

"A bump on the head. I was able to push her out of the way at the last second."

The man put his head in his hands and held it there. After a few seconds, he wiped his reddened eyes dry and straightened his shoulders.

"Thank you."

"You can thank me by telling me what's really going on."

"It's my fault," Martin spoke up. "I advised the senator to keep the nature of the threat from Brynnon."

"No, Martin. You were only trying to help. It was my decision not to tell her."

Bypassing Cantrell's comment, Grant narrowed his eyes to Downing. "Why the hell would you do something like that?"

"Because I know Bryn."

That raised Grant's shackles. "What's that supposed to mean?"

"It means I've known her a hell of a lot longer than you. If she knew the threat was against her, she would've been even more stressed than she already was."

"You kept this from her so she wouldn't be fucking *stressed?*" Grant wasn't buying it.

"Brynnon's always been a bit of a worrier," her father tried to explain. "After her mother died, she was constantly worried about me. Always checking up on me to make sure I was eating right and getting enough rest. That sort of thing. When her brother started acting out, she worried about him. Made sure he went to his meetings, had food in his refrigerator."

"That doesn't sound like a worrier to me, Senator. That sounds like a loving daughter and sister."

"She has a life now. A successful business. I didn't want her to constantly be looking over her shoulder. That's no way to spend your days. Trust me, I've had to do it more often than I'd have liked. I didn't want that for her."

"So why hire me at all?"

"That was also my idea," Martin butted in again. "I knew the senator would feel better with someone watching over her."

Grant ran a hand over his jaw. "So you didn't want her to worry, yet you still tell her there's a threat against you and coerce her into accepting my help? Didn't you think she'd be just as worried about you and your safety?"

The older man smiled. "Do you have children, Grant?"

A familiar pain cut through his chest. "No, sir."

"When you do, you'll understand. As a parent, you have to make a million different decisions. Sometimes, it's clear which direction you need to go. Others, you do what you think is best and pray you were right." The man stood and came around to the front of his desk. "I've had numerous threats via phone calls, letters, emails throughout the years. Do you know how many of those came to fruition?"

"No, sir."

"None. Not a single one."

Grant began to understand. "You assumed this was just like all those other times."

He nodded, and Martin finished the explanation.

"If Brynnon thought the threat was against her father, she'd blow it off as nothing more than an annoyance. I knew he could convince her to go along with having a security detail, at least for a week or two. Our hope was, by that time, we would've been able to ferret out whoever sent the message to start with, and you and she could go on with your lives as if nothing ever happened."

Cantrell looked back at Grant. "She could focus on her career rather than spending every single day in fear."

Shit. Grant still thought it was a dumbass move, but as misguided as it had been, he was beginning to understand why the senator did what he did.

"That's why you didn't put a guard on Billy," he stated. "It wasn't because you knew he'd fight you tooth and nail; it was because he's not the one in danger. She is."

"I've still been keeping an eye on Billy, just in case," Martin told Grant. "I text or call regularly. Go by his place now and again."

"Martin and my son have been friends for years, so it wouldn't be suspicious for him to call Billy or drop by to see him."

Grant took a deep breath and let it out slowly but remained quiet.

"I love my children, Grant. They mean more to me than

any of this," Cantrell waved his arms around his office. "I realize I may not have gone about this the right way, but I can assure you...every decision I've ever made in regards to Billy and Brynnon has been out of love."

No, he sure as hell hadn't gone about this the right way, but Grant wasn't going to keep beating a dead horse. The guy knew he screwed up, and from the look on his face, there was nothing more Grant could say or do to make him feel any worse than he already did.

"Does Brynnon know whoever sent the senator that first threat is after her?" Martin asked.

"She does now."

Grant proceeded to tell them about Charles Wright and why he had a grudge against Cantrell. He also told them about the pictures and letter Brynnon received, and that he had a guy scanning them for prints as they spoke.

"Do the police know?" Martin asked, sounding alarmed. "Have they arrested this Charles Wright guy?"

"There isn't any hard evidence against him."

Again, it was Martin who asked, "Well, what about the car that almost hit Brynnon? Were you able to get a license plate or see the driver?"

"The driver was wearing a hood, and I only got a partial. My associate is working on that, as well." Grant turned to the senator. "I'm going to pay Charles Wright a visit after I leave here. I'll let you know what I find out."

"Do you think that's wise?" Martin inserted himself again. "Shouldn't the police handle this? I have several contacts in the department. I could contact one of them."

"I have contacts of my own, but I'd like to talk with Wright first before bringing in the DPD."

"I really think this is a matter for the police, now," Martin looked to his boss. "You know I can push things through on that front."

"With all due respect, Senator," Grant jumped right back in. "You came to R.I.S.C. because you know what we're capable of. So trust me to do my job."

Cantrell looked from him to Martin, and back again. "You're right. I do trust you, and I'm well aware of what you and your team can do. I'll support whatever you think is best for the safety of my daughter."

Grant could tell Martin wasn't happy his boss sided with him, but he couldn't give two fucks less.

"Thank you, sir." He looked at Martin. "It's my understanding the charity event tomorrow night is one endorsed by this office. Brynnon still insists on going, so if you really want to help, you'll get me a list of everyone attending, as well as any of your staff and the catering crew."

The man looked as though he wanted to say more, but instead, made his smartest decision yet by answering with, "I'll take care of that."

"I'll need it within the next hour so my guy can run backgrounds on each of the names."

Martin shook his head. "The guests and staff have already been vetted by our office."

"We'll have the list to you within the hour," Cantrell assured him. "Martin, why don't you go ahead and get started on that, so Mr. Hill and his team have plenty of time to go through it."

Begrudgingly, the other man gave his boss a nod. "Yes, sir." Knowing he'd just been dismissed, Martin left Grant and the senator alone.

Turning to leave, Grant was surprised when Cantrell closed the door and turned to him. "I wanted to have a word with you, alone, if that's okay."

"Of course."

He'd do his best to control his temper, mainly because he genuinely liked his job and wanted to keep it. But if the guy thought Grant was going to take an ass-chewing sitting down when Cantrell was the one who'd fucked up, he had another think coming.

"I'm not usually a man to mix words, so I'm just going to get right to it. Are you sleeping with my daughter?"

Grant's eyes flew to Brynnon's father's. *What the actual fuck?* "No, sir," he answered honestly. "I'm not."

Cantrell gave him an assessing glance. "Huh. Well, I'll be damned."

"Sir?"

"I'm rarely wrong about these things, but for some reason, I believe you."

The guy actually sounded disappointed—which sure as hell couldn't be right. Grant cleared his throat. "If there's nothing else, I should be going."

"Not so fast."

Cantrell stepped closer. Grant towered over the older man, yet he still felt like he was about to be scolded like a child. *Well, this should be fun.*

"You may not have slept with her yet, but you do have feelings for my daughter, don't you?"

Feeling as though he'd fallen down a rabbit hole of epic proportions, Grant did his best to sound indifferent. "Sir, you hired me to protect Brynnon. Sleeping with a client is against R.I.S.C. policy, and would be grounds for—"

A bark of laughter burst from William Cantrell's chest. "Spare me the corporate CYA bullshit, Grant. Your job isn't in danger here. We're just two men having a conversation. That's all."

Yeah…a conversation about having sex with your daughter.

How the fuck was he supposed to respond to that? Was this a set-up? As he spoke, Grant had to force himself not to scan the room for hidden cameras.

"Sir, I'm a little confused by your line of questioning."

"Christ, son," Cantrell chuckled. "I guess it's true what they say…you can take the man out of the military, but you can't take the military out of the man." Shaking his head, the man slapped Grant on the shoulder. "How about I talk, and you listen?"

Grant blinked. "Okay."

"Here's the short of it. I've seen the way you look at my daughter and vice versa. I understand you have a job to do, and there's nothing more important to me than my daughter's safety. But after, if you want and she's willing, I thought you should know I'm okay with it."

Holy. Fucking. Shitballs. Confused as hell, now, Grant's brows turned inward as he asked, "You're giving me permission to date your daughter?"

Cantrell nodded. "Brynnon's had a hard time finding the right man. Someone who can appreciate and support her independence. Someone who isn't just interested in the family's bank account, if you catch my drift."

"I do."

"Good." Brynnon's father walked to the door. "Now that that's settled, please be sure to let me know what you find out when you speak to Charles Wright. Hopefully, once you two have had that conversation, the threats to Brynnon will stop and we can all go on with our lives."

"Yes, sir."

After a brief conversation with Coop, Grant left the building. He called Derek on the way to his truck.

"It's me."

"You talk to Cantrell?"

"I did."

"And? How'd it go?"

"It was…" Grant searched for the right word. "Enlightening."

"Enlightening?" Derek's voice perked up. "Do tell."

He got into his truck and made his way through the parking lot. Bypassing the incredibly awkward conversation at the end, Grant told him what he knew.

"Cantrell claims he didn't tell us Bryn was the target because he didn't want her to worry. Speaking of, how is she?"

"Worried." Derek sighed. "I swear, the woman hasn't stopped pacing since you left."

Grant cursed under his breath. "Send me Wright's address. I want to drop in and see what I can learn."

"Hang on." There was a pause and then, "There. I just sent it."

"Thanks. I'll be back at the condo as soon as I'm finished grilling Wright."

"You want backup?"

"No. Stay with her. I'll let you know when I'm done." With that, Grant ended the call and began following the GPS directions to Charles Wright's home.

As he drove, Grant replayed the conversation with Senator Cantrell. *You do have feelings for my daughter, don't you?*

The man's words ran on a continuous loop through his mind. The closer he got to Wright's place, the more he began to admit the answer…

Yes.

Despite his best efforts against it, the fiery redhead had wormed her way into a heart he'd thought no longer existed. And damn if he knew what to do about it.

Chapter 11

"What the hell are you two doing here?"

Brynnon watched an angry Grant march down the broken sidewalk toward her. Derek was right. The guy was not happy to see them there.

"Cool your jets, big guy," she told him. "And don't be mad at Derek. I made him bring me."

Grant's gray eyes shot to his teammate. "She *made* you?"

"What can I say?" The other man shrugged. "Your gal made a good argument."

When Grant opened his mouth, no doubt to lay into Derek, Brynnon slid between the two men. "Derek told me my father admitted the threat was against me not him. With everything that's happened, I think it's pretty clear whoever sent it means business."

Lips she'd had the pleasure of tasting pressed together as Grant's nostrils began to flare. "Which is exactly why you shouldn't be here."

Yep. He's mad. Well, he wasn't the only one.

"I have a right to question him."

The handsome man looked back at her as if she were crazy. "Are you even listening to yourself? The man is trying to kill you, and you want to just what? Stroll right on up and knock on his goddamn door?" He shook his head. "No. Not happening." To Derek, he ordered, "Take her back to the condo."

Brynnon knew Grant's overbearing bossiness stemmed from concern for her. But as sweet as it was, she wasn't giving up. Her gut was telling her she needed to talk with Charles Wright.

Straightening her shoulders, Brynnon lifted her chin. "First, we don't know for sure he's the one who sent the threats or tried to run me over. Second, I'm going in there, whether you like it or not."

Resting his hands on his narrow hips, he leaned down until they were nearly nose-to-nose. "Like hell."

Refusing to back down, Brynnon looked him right in the eye. "Charles Wright approached me for a reason."

"Yeah, because the guy's fucked in the head and wants to kill you to get back at your dad."

"I don't think so." When he started to argue again, she quickly explained why it would be a good idea to let her stay. "Look, just listen to me for a second, okay? I did a lot of thinking while you were gone. You're right. Someone is trying to use me as revenge for what they believe my dad did, but if Wright truly wanted to kill me, why didn't he do it at the hospital?"

"She has a point," Derek gave his two cents, something Grant didn't appreciate.

He zeroed in on his friend. "You're kidding me. You seriously think this is a good idea?"

"Fuck, no." Derek made a face. "I think it's a terrible idea."

"See?" Grant raised an arrogant brow her way.

"But—" Derek interjected— "I also think she's right. At

least, about Wright. I watched the tape from the hospital. He had more than enough time to kill Brynnon. Hell, Wright was close enough to her the guy could've easily stabbed her and walked away before you ever came around that corner. But he never even laid a hand on her. Why?"

"See?" Brynnon shot back, mimicking Grant with her own arched brow.

Grant huffed out a breath and ran a frustrated hand through his hair. "Christ. It's like trying to reason with a fucking ten-year-old."

"You're just pissed because you know I'm right," Brynnon hissed. "The man is grieving the loss of his son, Grant." After drawing in a deep breath, she reached out, squeezing his taut forearm. "You and I both know what it feels like to have lost someone we loved. Charles Wright needs someone to blame, and for some reason, my father's the person he chose. If I go in there, I *know* I can get him to listen. Or…"

"Or what?"

"Maybe…" She paused. "Maybe he *did* find something that implicates Cantrell Construction. I know in my heart, my father didn't do anything wrong, but there were a lot of employees working on that project. What if…" She licked her lips nervously. "What if one of them did?" She took a step closer to him. "I need to know the truth. So does Charles Wright."

Conflicted, Grant stared back down at her. "And if he's not just a grieving father and he really is the one trying to kill you? Then what?"

She gave him a crooked smile and shrugged. "Then you protect me."

A second later, Brynnon knew she'd won.

Grant shook his head. "Fine," he huffed. "We'll do things

your way. But the second I sense something's off, we're gone."

"Okay." Brynnon nodded. With a hand to his bicep, she whispered, "Thank you."

He turned to Derek. "Things go sideways, you get her the hell out of there."

"Roger that."

With a low curse, Grant began walking toward Wright's house. "Let's go."

They'd parked a few houses down, Brynnon assumed to keep from being spotted. If Charles Wright really was the one who'd tried to run her over, he'd most likely take off running the second he saw them.

"I don't see the car from earlier. Do you?"

"No, but that doesn't mean anything. The guy could've ditched it."

Derek spoke up first. "There's no record of Wright ever owning a vehicle matching the description you gave me. But, like you said, that doesn't necessarily mean anything."

As they approached the small, one-level home, Grant instinctively moved his body closer to hers. He rested a hand on the small of her back, the protective gesture comforting.

All of a sudden, Brynnon was hit with the image of his hard body slamming into hers, the two of them flying toward the ground. A shudder of fear raced down her spine.

"You good?"

"Yeah," she lied. "Just cold." If she let him know her nerves had kicked in, he'd make her wait in the car for sure.

With his free hand, Grant knocked on the front door. While they waited for its owner to answer, Brynnon looked back up at him. "Remember. Let me do the talking."

His gaze was intense as he handed her the keys to his

truck. "He tries anything, you get your ass out."

Brynnon shook her head. "I'm not going to leave you behind."

"That's the deal. Otherwise, you and D can leave right now."

Sensing he wasn't budging on this one, Brynnon took the keys. She started to lie and agree to his terms, because there was no way in hell she'd leave him or Derek in any sort of mortal danger. Before she could, Charles Wright answered the door.

Looking worn down, he appeared confused at first. When he realized who she was, he scowled. "What the hell are you doing here?"

"I was hoping we could talk."

The older man shook his head. "I said all I wanted to say to you yesterday."

"Well, I didn't." She sighed. "I wish you'd told me who you really were."

"Why?" he snarled. "So you could keep making excuses for your murdering father?"

"Mr. Wright, someone sent a letter to Miss Cantrell's father threatening to harm her," Grant spoke up. "And today, after speaking with you at the hospital, they tried to run her over. You wouldn't know anything about that, would you?"

"Go to hell." To Brynnon, he added, "And take your father with you."

The bitter man tried to shut the door, but a quick move of Brynnon's hand kept it from closing. "Mr. Wright, please. Someone's been following me. They left pictures of me in my mailbox, along with this." She pulled the baggie with the note out of her coat pocket to show him.

Wright shook his head. "Well, it certainly wasn't me."

"You got an alibi that can back that up?" Derek asked.

The man lifted his chin. "As a matter of fact, I do. The nursing staff at Dallas Regional's cancer treatment center. So if you came here hoping to pin that on me so you could shut me up, you're going to be very disappointed."

Brynnon sucked in a breath. "You have cancer? I'm so sorry."

"I don't need your pity. What I need is for my son to get justice."

"We want that, too," Brynnon assured him. "Please, Mr. Wright." She glanced up at Grant and then back to Charles. "Can we come inside and talk about this? I promise we won't stay long." She smiled. "Plus, it's freezing out here. I can't imagine it would be good if you were to get sick."

The man shook his head. "Now, you're starting to sound like those damn doctors." Eyeing the three of them suspiciously, he said, "I don't know what your game is, but I have a gun, and I still know how to use it."

Grant and Derek both stiffened beside her. *Ah, hell.* Sensing the former SEALs' impending outbursts, Brynnon put a hand to Grant's arm and intervened.

"I can assure you, Mr. Wright. We're just here to talk."

The man hesitated a few more seconds before stepping aside and letting them into his home. The place was small and not very well kept. There was laundry strewn about, and it hadn't appeared to have been dusted for quite some time.

"You'll have to excuse the mess. It's the cleaning lady's day off."

"We don't care about the state of your house, Mr. Wright," Grant spoke sternly. "We want to know why you blame Cantrell Construction for the death of your son."

"Like I told her"—he looked Brynnon's way—"the

materials they used weren't up to snuff."

Picking up a framed photo, Brynnon asked, "Is this him?" It was amongst several scattered about a tall bookshelf. "Is this Jordan?"

In the one she'd chosen, a handsome groom and his bride were smiling for the camera. The same woman was in several other pictures, only without her husband. In some, she was holding a small baby. Others, the child was older.

"Yes." The female voice took them all by surprise. "That's my brother and Stacey. His widow."

Brynnon and her two guards turned to see a woman about her age standing in the doorway between the kitchen and living room. She was petite with short, blonde hair. The woman was attractive...and the spitting image of Charles Wright.

"This is Jessica Price. My daughter."

"Daughter?" Derek looked confused. "None of the reports I ran mentioned anything about you having a daughter."

"That's probably because Dad didn't know I existed until a few years ago."

"She's right," Charles spoke up. "Back in the day, Jessica's mother and I...well, we had a moment of indiscretion. It was a one-time thing, and we lost touch afterward."

"I take it your wife knew nothing about the affair?" Grant asked.

Wright lifted his chin. "It's not something I'm proud of, but Jordan's mom and I were going through a rough patch. I needed someone to talk to, and Camille, Jessica's mom, was there. She and I worked together. We went out one night after work and..."

"They made me." Jessica smiled, but her expression was

odd. Almost nervous.

Charles looked ashamed. "After, I told Camille it was a mistake. That I loved my wife, and it could never happen again."

Brynnon frowned. "And Camille never told you she was pregnant?"

"No. She got a promotion a couple of weeks later and was transferred out of state. I didn't know I had a daughter until Jessica showed up at my door a couple of years back."

"After my mom finally told me the truth about who my father was, I paid to have a DNA test done so there wouldn't be any doubts." She glanced at her father. "For either of us."

"Do you live here with your father, Jessica?" Grant grumbled.

"No. I have an apartment. I come by to check on him a few times a week."

Brynnon's expression softened. "So you never knew Jordan?"

"No." Jessica shook her head. "I wish I had, though. To hear Dad talk, my brother was amazing."

Genuine sadness filled Brynnon's heart. "I'm sorry."

Wright huffed out a breath. "If you were truly sorry, you'd be doing everything you could to find the truth, just like I've been doing for the past six years." He pressed his lips together tightly before shaking his head in disgust. "The military claimed that what happened was nothing more than a tragic accident. The case was closed, and everybody went on about their business, but not me. I knew something wasn't right, so I started looking into it more."

"What did you find?" Derek asked the disgruntled man.

Continuing on with his round-about answer, Wright scoffed. "At first? Not much. I knew someone like me wasn't going to get very far on my own, so after about a year, I hired a private investigator. He's former military. I call him once a week to see if he's found anything new. For the last five years, he's been researching what happened with no luck. But a few days ago, the guy called *me*. Said he'd found something interesting. That he was almost certain he'd found the proof I'd been looking for all along."

"What kind of proof?"

"Something about paperwork not matching up. He wouldn't give me any details over the phone."

"What's his name?" Derek asked.

"Oh, no." Wright smirked. "I'm not telling you that."

"Why not?" Grant challenged.

"Why should I? You'll probably just go try and strong-arm him the way you are me."

"No one's trying to strong-arm you, Mr. Wright," Brynnon tried to assure him. "We all want the same thing here."

"Yeah? What's that?"

Brynnon looked him square in the eye. "To get to the truth."

"Dad, you need to calm down," Jessica put an arm on her father's shoulder. "Remember the doctors' warnings about your heart."

Chest heaving, Wright kept his eyes locked on Brynnon's but kept quiet. A few seconds passed before Grant broke the silence.

"Did your investigator send you what he found?"

Wright shook his head, his gaze sliding to Grant. "He was supposed to come by yesterday morning, but he never did."

"Yet, you still showed up at the hospital to confront Miss Cantrell."

The man's hard eyes became narrowed slits. "It's not like I could just waltz into her father's office." He looked back at her. "I read about the party for the kids in the paper. I thought…" He paused. "I thought maybe you would actually listen."

"You pretended to be a reporter to get close to her," Derek responded. "Doesn't instill a lot of trust when you start the whole thing off by lying about who you were."

His eyes shot to Grant's. "I'm on borrowed time, son. And when my time comes, I want to go to the good Lord knowing my son got the justice he deserved."

With a gentle voice, Brynnon told him, "I'm listening, now." She glanced at the other two men then back to Wright. "We all are."

The ball was in his court now. She'd tried to get him to understand they were only trying to help. If he didn't want to believe her, there was nothing more she could do about it.

A single nod was the only response he gave, but it was enough.

Brynnon's mouth turned up in a slight smile. "Thank you." After he gave her another nod, she said, "Your PI didn't show up, but you must have other information you've gathered over the years."

"I do," Wright confirmed her thoughts.

"May we see it?" When he hesitated, she added, "We're not going to take it and run, Mr. Wright. I promise. I just want to see what has you so convinced my father's actions caused Jordan and those other brave men and women to lose their lives."

After a moment's hesitation, Wright turned away from her and gave his daughter a look. "Come help me get the files." To Brynnon, he said, "I'll be right back."

Brynnon drew in a deep breath before letting it out slowly. "Well, at least he didn't outright refuse."

"You know, you're pretty good at this," Derek commented with a crooked smile. "You and Hill are like the perfect good cop, bad cop duo."

She grinned, but Grant simply grunted and walked over to the small end table near the couch. Picking up one of several prescription bottles, he studied the label before holding it up.

"He's telling the truth. About having cancer, at least. My mom used to take this same medicine when she was going through treatments. Supposed to help boost the immune system."

Brynnon's heart ached as she watched him set the bottle back down. It was hard to imagine the strong, formidable man before her as a broken, grieving teenager.

"Here." Wright came back into the room. He and Jessica each handed her a bulging folder. "This is everything I've found over the last six years."

Grant and Derek both stood over her shoulder as she began to look over the folders' contents. Some of what she saw made sense, like the copies of the purchase orders Cantrell Construction had used. Others, such as the topographical map with scribbled notes, would take more time to go over.

When Brynnon got to a picture of the bridge post-collapse, her chest tightened. "I can't imagine how scared they must have been," she spoke absentmindedly.

"It's all I think about," Jordan's father stared at the photo. "What must've gone through my boy's mind as he fell to his death. He had to have known he wouldn't survive a fall like that. That he'd never see his wife again or meet his baby boy. Jordan had no idea he had a sister…"

169

The older man's voice cracked. He blinked a few times before clearing his throat and looking back up at her. "It's not right. It's not right that your father continued on with his life as if nothing ever happened. Not when so many others lost theirs."

"Mr. Wright," Brynnon addressed him as she closed the folder. "Obviously I can't begin to imagine the pain Jordan's death caused you—"

"No," he shot back. "You can't."

Giving him a sad smile, she did her best to empathize. "But I do know what it's like to lose someone you loved so dearly." She took a step closer. "With your permission, I'd like to take this folder home and look through it. See if there's anything there you may have missed."

"Why? So you can cover it up like your old man has?"

Brynnon shook her head, hating that life had taught this man to be so untrusting. "No. I want to help you get to the truth, so you can find the peace you're searching for. And these two men are going to help me. They're both former military, so they understand better than most the sacrifice your son gave that day. What every soldier on that bridge gave. They have resources beyond yours and mine that can help us find out if there is any truth to your suspicions."

With a leery glance, Wright asked, "What branch?"

"Navy," Derek answered for both men.

He eyed Grant more closely. "SEALs?"

Grant nodded. "We were both with the Teams."

A smidge of respect replaced some of Wright's animosity. "Then I hope what she's saying is true."

"We will find out what happened to your son and the others," Grant promised. Turning his voice deadly, he warned the older man, "But the threats and the violence toward Miss

Cantrell ends now."

Silver brows bunched together as he looked back at Brynnon. "I've harbored a lot of hate toward your father for quite some time, but I would never threaten or harm a woman." He shook his head. "That's not how I was raised."

"Do you know anyone who drives a maroon sedan?" Derek asked.

Wright blinked quickly before stammering, "I...um, no. I don't..."

"It was you, wasn't it?" Grant growled. "You were pissed off because Brynnon didn't give you the answers you were looking for, so you waited until we left the hospital and followed us to her house."

"No." Wright shook his head. "You're wrong."

Ignoring the man's claim, Grant rested his hands on his narrow hips and continued sharing his theory. "Then when she was standing by herself next to the mailbox, you saw your chance and tried to run her over. Hell, you damn near killed us both."

The older man continued to adamantly deny the accusation. "It wasn't me! I told you, I was in chemo." He looked to Brynnon, pleading for her to believe him. "That's why I talked to you when I did. I was already going to be near the hospital for my treatment. I saw that you'd be there, too, so I went to see you. But I never tried to hurt you. I give you my word."

"Your word?"

"Grant," Brynnon tried to intervene, but the angry warrior didn't back down.

"No." Shaking his head, her angry bodyguard took a step forward and glared down at the agitated man. "You cornered an innocent woman in the hallway of a children's hospital and then lied about who you were. Sorry, but your word doesn't mean jack shit to me."

"I swear, I didn't—"

"It was me," Jessica blurted loudly. All eyes turned to her, the young woman's shoulders sagging with defeat. To Brynnon, she admitted, "I did it." She looked at Brynnon. "I'm the one who sent the threats to your dad. I took the pictures and…I-I was the one driving the car."

Brynnon grabbed Grant's hand when she felt him stiffen in anger in an attempt to keep him calm.

"Jessica." Her father looked up at her, stunned. "Why?"

. "Why?" the other woman gave her father an incredulous look. "Because I'm so sick of this! The stress and anger. Watching you get your hopes up every single week when you call that worthless P.I. only to be let down again and again. Your heart can't take it much longer, Dad. Not with the added strain from the cancer and chemo."

Jessica knelt down in front of her father's frail form. Tears fell from her eyes when she took his hands in hers and continued on.

"I just found you, and now…" Her voice broke. "I'm going to lose you, soon. I did what I did because I couldn't stand to see you spend one more precious second, the seconds we have left together, being consumed by this hateful, anger-driven need for what you think may be the truth."

Jessica had been stalking her. Had sent threats to her father, and just today had come damn close to killing both her and Grant. But despite all that, Brynnon felt her heart breaking for the poor woman.

She watched as Jessica stood. Wiping her tears away, she faced Brynnon again. "I'm sorry. I didn't mean to get that close to you. I swear. I only meant to scare you. And the pictures..." she looked chagrined. "My dad has spent nearly every penny of his savings trying to find the truth about my brother's death. Not knowing is tearing him apart, and I—"

"Jessica." Charles shook his head. It was obvious he'd had no idea what his daughter had been up to.

Tears formed in the woman's pleading blue eyes again. "I-I didn't know what else to do. I thought maybe if your dad believed one of his own kids was in danger, he'd confess. My father could finally be at peace and live his last days focusing on other things."

"Like you," Brynnon surmised.

"Yes." The torn woman nodded. "As selfish as it sounds, I want us to be able to appreciate the time we have left instead of chasing ghosts." When Jessica took a step toward her, Brynnon squeezed Grant's hand to keep him from charging the other woman. "I really am sorry for what I did. I swear, I won't do anything like that again. I just..." She looked at Charles again, the love she felt for her father unmistakable. "I can't bear to see him like this. You know?"

A tear escaped the corner of Brynnon's eye before she could stop it. Using her free hand, she wiped it away. "I do know. And, I'm not going to say what you did was okay—"

"No," Grant interrupted. "It sure as hell wasn't okay."

"*But...*" She looked back at Jessica. "I understand your need to protect your father."

"Mr. Wright"—she drew her focus back to him— "I know you have no reason to trust me, but I'm asking you to, anyway. Or, at least to trust them." She tipped her head toward Grant and Derek. "Please. Let us talk with your private investigator so we can see for ourselves what evidence he thinks he has."

"What if you don't like what you find?" he challenged her. "Are you really going to stand there and tell me you'd sell out your own father for the sake of my son? Someone you never even met?"

Straightening her spine, Brynnon looked Charles Wright in the eye and told him the God's honest truth. "I promise you, if I find out someone at father's company was in any way responsible for what happened to Jordan and the others, I will tell you. And if that's the case, I'll hand over every scrap of evidence to you. After that, you'll be free to use it however you deem fit."

The broken man studied her a few seconds longer before giving up the name. "Hank Mitchell. He's the one who's been working this case for me. Lives in Phoenix, but I'll call him and let him know it's okay to talk with you about what he found."

"Thank you for trusting me." Brynnon looked up at Grant before adding, "Trusting us."

Wright's jaw muscles bulged. "Just don't make me regret it."

"You won't," Grant assured him. "But cancer or no cancer, you or your daughter ever come near Brynnon without a personal invitation again, I guarantee that's a decision you *will* regret."

With his final warning given, the three of them left Charles Wright and his daughter and headed back to the condo. Without a word to either man, Brynnon went upstairs to her office, shut the door, and called her father.

Hours later while lying in bed, she found herself struggling to shut her mind off enough to sleep. Along with the day's emotional roller coaster of events, the conversation with her dad played over again in her head.

At first, he'd begun by falling all over himself, apologizing and trying to make her understand he'd only kept the threat against her a secret out of his innate need to protect her. Brynnon told him she understood but quickly reminded him she was a grown-ass woman who needed his honesty more than his protection.

With that issue out of the way, she'd then shared what they knew about Wright and his daughter. She'd only just begun to talk when Martin entered her dad's office. Deciding this was information his Chief of Staff needed to hear, her dad put the phone on speaker.

Brynnon went through the entire thing, starting from the moment Wright opened the door and ending at the point when they'd left. Understandably, her father had wanted to file charges against Jessica for the threats and stalking, but Brynnon eventually talked him out of it.

What Jessica Price did was wrong, but Brynnon couldn't help but understand the roots from which the woman's desperation had grown.

With Martin's unsolicited support, her dad had blown off what Wright said about his private investigator's so-called proof, claiming if there was something off with the paperwork, it was likely a simple clerical error.

Of course, Martin had thrown his two-cents in when he could. After practically grilling her on what exactly Mitchell supposedly found—which she didn't know because Wright didn't have that information—Martin told her under no circumstances could Mitchell have anything showing that Cantrell Construction was liable for the bridge collapse. He also insisted any mistake found was most assuredly on the supply company's end. Not theirs.

Since Jessica had sworn she'd leave Brynnon alone from

here on out, she'd fully expected her dad to relieve Grant of his duties. Surprisingly, he'd insisted Grant remain as her bodyguard a while longer, just in case.

The relief she felt from knowing Grant would still be with her had hit with an almost shocking force. When the overbearing man had shown up unannounced that first day, she'd been ready to fight tooth and nail to get rid of him. Now, Brynnon found it hard to imagine not having the quiet, broody security expert around.

She glanced at the clock on her bedside table. *One thirty-three.* Knowing sleep was an impossible goal to achieve, she threw her covers off with a groan and stood.

Wearing a pair of striped cotton pajama bottoms and a fitted tank top, she contemplated whether or not to get her robe from behind the bathroom door. Given the hour and how quiet the condo was, Grant was most likely asleep. Besides, she'd only be down there long enough to make a cup of hot tea.

Deciding to forgo the robe, Brynnon quietly made her way downstairs. The living room was dark, but the light in the kitchen was still on.

Assuming Grant had forgotten to turn it off before falling asleep, she stepped softly on her bare toes so she wouldn't wake him. When Brynnon walked into the kitchen, she nearly jumped out of her skin when she found him awake and sitting at her table.

He glanced up at her, his brows furrowing inward. "What are you doing up?"

The tattoo. Before now, she'd only seen small glimpses of its edge where it stopped at his wrist. But now, wearing only his black V-neck T and jeans, Brynnon could see much more of the ink decorating every inch of his right arm.

The intricate design disappeared beneath his short sleeve, and she had to fight the urge to reach down and rip the damn thing off.

"Bryn? Are you okay?" Grant asked, his voice now laced with concern. "Is it your head? Are you hurting?"

Finally snapping out of it, she answered with a casual, "Couldn't sleep." Walking over to the table, Brynnon's eyes fell on the photos and papers there. "Are those the files Derek brought over earlier?"

Grant looked back down at the organized mess. "Yeah."

She noticed Jordan Wright's folder was open and resting front and center above all the others. "He was so young," she stated quietly.

"Two years younger than I am now."

Moving her gaze from the picture to Grant's face, Brynnon realized how tired and worn he looked. Almost as though the weight of the world was on his shoulders.

With a hand to his muscular shoulder, she asked, "What about you? Are you okay?"

Blinking, he looked up at her and nodded. "Yeah."

"You sure? Because I was about to make myself some tea and everyone knows tea and conversation go together." She gave him a tiny smile, hoping it would get him to open up a little. Surprisingly, it worked.

"I've been reading over Jordan Wright's file. It's crazy how much we have in common. Hell." He huffed out a breath. "I could've been him."

Pulling out a chair, Brynnon sat beside him. "What do you mean?"

"We were close in age, and he was an only child. His mom died from lung cancer shortly after he graduated from high school." His eyes met hers. "I can't tell you the number of times I traveled over bridges just like that one while in Afghanistan or some other middle-eastern country. Something like that could've just as easily happened to me and my team."

Sensing he wasn't finished purging, Brynnon remained quiet and let him finish out his darkened thoughts. When Grant looked back down at Jordan Wright's service photo, his face filled with heartbreaking affliction.

"I've seen a lot of friends and teammates die. I accepted that part of the job a long time ago. We all did." He swallowed hard, his eyes still focusing on Jordan's picture. "But sitting here and reading through his file, I just keep thinking, why didn't he get to come home? He was the all-American guy. Good son, great soldier…married with a baby on the way. So why did I make it out, but he didn't? It just doesn't make any sense. The guy barely had a chance to live."

Oh, Grant. Reaching over, Brynnon covered his tight fist with her hand. "I can't answer that. I wish I could, but the truth is it was just his time. And you…" She paused. "You do have a chance to live."

Grant looked up at her but didn't say anything, so she kept going.

"Sure, you and Jordan have a lot in common, but the difference is you *did* make it out alive. And, I know you may not agree, but I truly believe there's a reason you didn't die over there."

He stood abruptly, his chair squeaked against her wooden floors. As he walked over to the sink, Grant gripped his hands around its edge and locked his elbows. "I appreciate what you're trying to do, but I don't believe in all that shit." He turned his head toward her. "Not anymore."

"Well, I do." She stood and went to him. "I know there's a

reason you're still here."

He turned and leaned back against the counter, crossing his arms in front of his chest. "First introductions aside, you've known me less than a week. Don't really think you're qualified to make that sort of judgment about me."

"Doesn't matter." She shook her head. "I see more than you think, Grant. I've seen the friendship you have with Derek. The way you risked yourself for me. First when the scaffolding fell and again today."

He opened his mouth, but she put a hand up to stop him. Moving in even closer, Brynnon left only a few inches between them when she wrapped her fingers around one of his sinewy forearms.

"I would've died today had you not been there to push me out of the way. Now, I'm not arrogant enough to think the reason you survived your overseas tours and all your black ops missions was simply so you could save me. But, like it or not, there are people in this world who need you." One corner of her mouth rose. "I just happen to be one of them."

Emotion flared behind his guarded eyes and Grant raised his hand to brush some hair from her face. Appearing bewildered, he tucked the wayward curls behind her ear before closing his eyes and leaning toward her.

At first, Brynnon was sure he was going to kiss her again. Instead, he rested his forehead against hers and whispered, "What am I going to do with you?"

With her heart threatening to leap from her chest, she teased, "Pretty sure I could think of a few things."

Grant's hot breath hit her chin as he released a silent laugh. Lifting his head, he let one corner of his delectable mouth raise. "Don't tempt me, Princess."

God, it would be so easy. All she'd have to do would be to

raise up on her tiptoes and take what she wanted. Brynnon had a feeling this time he wouldn't be so quick to hit the brakes.

He's hurting.

Damn. That nagging little voice was right. As surprising as it seemed, the gentle giant was in a vulnerable state. If and when the time came to take things further, she sure as hell didn't want to be something he regretted.

Ignoring the reasons that brought her down here in the first place, Brynnon took a step back. Licking her suddenly dry lips, she forced a smile.

"I guess we should probably try to get some sleep. Can't very well show up at tomorrow's ball with bags under our eyes."

A flicker of disappointment flashed across his chiseled face but was gone as quickly as it had appeared. "Right," he cleared his throat. "The ball."

Brynnon chuckled. "Don't worry, tough guy. You just have to stand there and look pretty. Shouldn't be too hard for a guy like you." With a pat on his solid chest, she turned to leave the room but stopped when Grant reached out and grabbed her hand.

Taken off guard, she spun her head back toward him. "What—"

"You never did answer my question."

Brynnon wracked her brain, trying to remember what he'd asked her. "What question?"

With her hand still in his, Grant took a step toward her. "Are. You. Okay?"

"Oh." She laughed nervously. "Of course. I'm fine."

Brynnon tried moving again, but he kept her in place.

"Really?" He looked back at her expectantly. "I just spilled my guts like a pansy, and you're gonna pull the whole 'I'm fine' routine?"

She scoffed. "Sharing your thoughts and emotions does *not* make you a pansy."

Grant locked eyes with hers. "So why won't you tell me what really brought you down here?"

Damn. She walked right into that one.

Drawing in a shaky breath, Brynnon let it out slowly before admitting, "I keep seeing that car. Every time I close my eyes, it's there. And you're there, and..."

She looked away, taking another deep breath to gain control over her sudden rush of emotions. "I see how close it came to hitting you because I was so freaked out by those damn pictures I didn't realize what was happening." Brynnon brought her gaze back up to his. "I don't think Wright's daughter will try anything else, but what if she does?"

"I'll stop her. Just like I did today."

Brynnon shook her head. "I don't want you getting hurt because of me, Grant. When I think about what could've happened to you had that car been going just a little faster, or if you'd jumped out of the way a second later..." Her voice cracked, and a tear fell from the corner of her eye.

"Hey," he rumbled softly, pulling her into his warm embrace. Grant tucked her head beneath his chin and held her closely. "I'm okay, sweetheart. We're both okay."

When she nodded, her cheek brushed back and forth against his shirt, stirring up even more of his woodsy, masculine scent.

"I'm not going to let anything happen to you."

The declaration was so solid. Definite. And Brynnon knew he meant every word.

She pulled back so she could look up at him. "Just

promise you won't put yourself in harm's way for me."

He gave her another crooked grin, having no idea how those sent her heart racing. "That's kinda my job."

"I don't care," she argued, stepping out of his embrace. Crossing her arms in front of herself, she lifted her chin and stared him down. "I don't want you risking yourself for me."

"Not your choice, Bryn."

She exhaled loudly. "God, you are so stubborn."

Grant barked out a laugh. "You're one to talk."

Brynnon wanted to respond, to come back with some sort of witty comment, but she was too busy trying to catch her breath. Both sides of his lips were curved, the broad smile lighting up his entire face.

God, he's beautiful.

Mistaking her silence to mean she was still upset, Grant's smile slowly vanished, and he walked slowly toward her. "Come on," he ordered, taking her hand in his.

Before she could explain, he began walking them both out of the kitchen. With a flick of his wrist, he reached up and flipped the light switch off, carefully leading her upstairs.

"Um, Grant? W-why are you taking me to my bedroom?"

"Just relax," he uttered quietly, reading her mind. "It's not about that."

Not sure if she should be disappointed or relieved, Brynnon continued to follow the confusing man. Once they were in her room, he walked over to her side of the bed and turned to face her.

"Lay down."

"Excuse me?"

"You need sleep, right?"

"Yes…" she let the word hang there.

"Then lay. Down."

Still unsure of what his plan was, Brynnon did as she was told and crawled into bed. She had to bite her cheek to keep from smiling when the gruff man reached down and pulled the covers over her body, tucking her in as if she were a small child.

He's taking care of me.

Even more surprising was when, instead of leaving, he walked around the foot of the bed and crawled in beside her.

Propping herself up on an elbow, she looked over her shoulder at him. "What are you doing?"

"Don't worry. My clothes are staying on."

Without warning, he reached across her waist and pulled her back to his front. As promised, his shirt and jeans were still on, but Brynnon still felt guilty. She didn't want him feeling forced into an uncomfortable situation simply because he was trying to help her get to sleep.

Facing away from him again, she rested her head on her pillow and tried one last time to give him an out.

"Seriously, Grant. this is above and beyond your required duties, and you're under no obligation to—"

"Does this bother you?"

"No." She shook her head. "Not at all. Actually, it's nice. I feel…safe."

He gave her a little squeeze. "Then I'm right where I want to be."

His protective embrace helped ease her anxiety about today's close call. However, there was something else still rolling through her mind.

"Grant?"

"Yeah?"

"I think Jessica was telling the truth."

"About?"

"I don't think she meant to kill me today, but..." She shifted onto her back and looked over at him. "What if she was lying? What if she tries something like that again?"

The moonlight reflected off his eyes as his thumb brushed lazily against her side. "If she does, my team will stop her."

She nodded, her hair making a swishing sound as it brushed against her pillow. "I know you will."

Brynnon turned back onto her side and settled herself against him. With her arm resting on his, she waited a beat before whispering his name.

"Grant?"

"Yeah?"

"Thank you."

He gave her a little squeeze and whispered back, "You're welcome."

Chapter 12

Using the small mirror on the wall by Brynnon's front door, Grant checked to make sure his bow tie was straight. It was the fifth time he'd done so in as many minutes.

He didn't know why the hell he felt so nervous. This charity ball wasn't any different than the other ones he'd worked when assigned to her father. Of course, his having spent last night cuddled up to the man's daughter may be why he felt so different this time.

It's different because you're going with her. Everything's different with her.

His subconscious was right. Pacing the condo's small living room, Grant thought about last night. It was all he'd thought about the entire fucking day.

Once they'd gotten settled, Brynnon had fallen asleep quickly. He, however, had not.

Instead, he'd laid there, watching her sleep as he relished in how right it felt to hold her in his arms. To press his body against hers for the sole purpose of helping her feel safe. Protected.

It was the first time in years he'd gone to bed with a woman for reasons other than a quick one-off. Yet, even just lying next to Brynnon—fully dressed and all—Grant had

185

found himself content. Something he hadn't been in a long fucking time.

And it was all thanks to her.

Grant was never much of a talker or one to share his feelings and all that shit. Except with his mom. He always felt safe with her, because he knew she would never judge him. Once she was gone, he just...shut down.

After joining the Navy, he stayed focused on what he needed to do to get the job done. Since then, he'd kept everything close to the vest. Never talked with anyone about his thoughts or feelings in regards to surviving his time overseas when so many others hadn't. Not his fellow SEALS. Not even Jake or the other members of R.I.S.C.'s Alpha Team.

So why he'd opened up the way he had last night, Grant had no fucking idea. When she first came downstairs, he could tell she was worried about something. But rather than asking him for support and guidance, she'd given it to him instead.

Talking to Brynnon had been so damn effortless, too. She just sat there quietly, listening as he told her what he was feeling. And the words she'd said to him once he was finished had been running through his mind the whole damn day.

Like it or not, there are people in this world who need you. I just happen to be one of them.

Hearing her say she needed him triggered something somewhere deep inside. Grant began to break open as Brynnon's comforting words brought him more peace and solace than he'd felt since his mom's untimely death.

Even though she'd been talking about his ability to protect her, Grant still couldn't shake the feeling that Brynnon meant so much more. And damn, if he wasn't starting to think he needed her, too.

Lying beside her last night, holding her against him while she slept had been both heaven and pure fucking torture wrapped into one. He'd spent the entire night hard as a goddamn rock…in jeans. The second dawn snuck in through the curtains, he carefully slipped out of bed and came back down here, heading straight for the shower.

Before Brynnon, that had always worked to take the edge off for a while. But even after jerking off this morning to thoughts of her, he'd still walked around all damn day, half-hard and needing more.

You need her.

Shaking those thoughts away, Grant checked his watch and walked back over to the mirror. He'd just started messing with his tie again when the reflection of something red caught his eye.

His lungs suddenly ceased to work, and Grant froze where he stood, having spotted the most beautiful vision he'd ever seen. Still staring at her through the mirror, he watched as Brynnon slowly began making her way down the staircase. She was halfway to the bottom when he turned, taking in the full view.

Her hair was pulled up into a mound of soft curls, a few wisps of hair framing her face. Rather than caking on her makeup like so many of the women he'd seen at similar events, she'd applied just enough to highlight her natural beauty. Simple diamond studs and a matching bracelet added a little sparkle.

She had some sort of matching wrap hanging over one of her forearms, that same hand carrying a small purse in the same color. But the dress… *Holy fuck.*

It literally left him breathless.

The bright red was a magnificent compliment to her creamy skin tone and auburn hair. Its low-cut halter top was sexy as sin, showcasing her perky breasts but still what he would consider acceptable.

The body of the dress hugged her ribcage and small waist with perfection, and the long, ball gown-style skirt flared out from her narrow hips, falling gracefully to the floor. Even Brynnon's delicate, bare shoulders caught his attention. And since when had a woman's shoulders ever caused his dick to stand up and take notice?

The answer was they hadn't. Only this woman had ever affected him this way. In torn jeans and a t-shirt, Brynnon Cantrell was more than just attractive as hell. Wearing this dress? The woman was a sinful temptation.

One Grant knew he wouldn't be able to resist much longer.

By the time she sauntered over to where he stood, Grant was finally able to put his tongue back into his mouth. Still, even after swallowing twice and clearing his throat, all he managed to say was, "Wow."

Her smile reached all the way to her eyes, making the masterpiece complete. "Thank you." Her eyes traveled up and down his body slowly. "You don't look so bad yourself."

The two stood there a few seconds longer, taking in each other's beauty. Grant damn near reached out for her, but thankfully—or unfortunately—Coop chose that minute to send him a text asking what was taking so long.

Senator Cantrell had called a little bit ago saying he wouldn't be attending tonight's event. Apparently, there was some sort of political emergency meeting, but the man was sending Coop to pick them up, instead.

When Grant questioned him about not having Coop with

him at the meeting, Brynnon's dad explained this sort of meeting would last well into the night. He wanted Coop at the ball, too, as added protection for Brynnon. Just in case.

The sound of an impatient car horn blared and Brynnon smirked. "I take it Coop's getting antsy?"

Grant grunted. "Yeah. I guess we should probably get going."

With an outstretched arm, Brynnon said, "Lead the way."

The second their feet hit the sidewalk, Coop exited the stretch limo. He walked around the back of the car to the rear passenger door. With a loud whistle, shook his head and smiled.

"Damn. You clean up real nice."

"Bite me," Grant growled.

Suffering from the worst case of blue balls he'd ever had, Grant also had to worry about concealing his raging hard-on and his out-of-control emotions. He sure as shit was not in the mood to be teased.

Coop opened the door for Brynnon with a crooked grin. "I was talking about her, asshole."

Giggling, Brynnon patted Coop on the chest. "Hey, Coop. Good to see you again."

"Good to see you, too, Brynnon."

Still scowling, Grant waited until she'd slid inside, and his teammate shut the door before making his way to the other side. Coop smacked his arm as he passed on his way to the front of the car.

"If you still haven't hit that yet, there's something seriously wrong with you."

Grabbing the door handle, Grant gave his friend a low warning. "Don't."

"What? You'd be a fool to pass up a woman that fine."

"Just drive the fucking car."

With that, Grant opened his door and got inside. He glanced over at her, his eyes falling on her left leg that had become visible through a slit he hadn't realized existed. And the damn thing ran the entire length of her leg.

God, what he wouldn't give to run his hand along her smooth, toned skin. He could practically feel his fingers slipping beneath the slit's edge...and beyond.

His aching cock jumped, and Grant had to fist his hands in his lap to fight against the sudden urge to know what she had on underneath all that red satin.

It was like a goddamn test. One he was destined to fail miserably. *Fuck. Me.*

Coop started the car and began making small talk, but instead of responding, Grant simply reached over to the control panel on his side and closed the tinted and soundproof glass partition.

"Not in the mood for conversation, I take it?"

His damn lungs threatened to shut down again just from looking at her. "Not with him," he growled more harshly than intended.

Get your ass under control.

Assuming his lousy mood had to do with Coop, Brynnon's shoulders shook with silent laughter. "You two remind me of my brother and me when we were younger. Always bickered back and forth, but deep down, we both knew we loved each other."

"Speaking of your brother, is he coming tonight?"

"He's supposed to. Why?"

"I wanted to ask him about the bridge." According to Brynnon, her brother had been in charge of all supply orders at that time, and Grant wanted to see what he could remember.

"A charity ball isn't really the place to conduct an interrogation, Grant."

"I'm not going to interrogate him," Grant assured her. "I just have a couple of questions."

He could tell she wanted to say more, but thankfully Brynnon didn't press the issue. Instead she turned toward her window and watched the scenery passing them by.

What he'd told her had been the truth. Grant had no intentions of grilling her brother, but he did want to gauge Billy's reaction when he brought up what happened in Afghanistan. See if he showed any signs of guilt. For Brynnon's sake, he hoped not.

"When we get there—" Her voice broke through his thoughts— "I'll have to go straight to the stage to give the welcome speech. After that, it'll mainly be mingling with the crowd until the dance competition. Once that's over, we can say our goodbyes and leave."

"Sounds good."

"Also, I thought maybe, as long as you're okay with it, I should introduce you to people as my date, rather than my bodyguard." She quickly added, "Strictly for appearances. I just don't want to spook any of the contributors. It's hard enough raising the money these kids need. The last thing the charity needs is for people to shy away from attending future events because they think it's not safe. I spoke with my father, and he agreed."

Of course, he did. "Okay."

A few more minutes of silence passed before she began talking again. "Derek already ran the background checks on those attending and serving, so I'm assuming that's a non-issue?

Grant looked back over at her. "He did, but it's still very much an issue. If Wright's daughter was lying and she decides to come after you again, she could use someone else to do it. Just because a person's record is clean up to this point, doesn't mean it's going to stay that way."

Brynnon worried her bottom lip with her teeth. Jesus, she really had no idea how much he wished it were *his* teeth doing the biting.

"But most of these people are friends or acquaintances with my father. His staff, other politicians, and important public figures. There are even a few priests who help out each year."

"Most. You said yourself there will be people there you've never met before or ones who sign up last-minute."

Hating the sliver of fear that had returned behind those emerald eyes, Grant reached over and rested his hand over hers. His dick pulsed again when his knuckles brushed against her bare leg.

Stay focused.

"I'm not trying to scare you, Bryn, but if someone wants to get to you badly enough, they're going to use any means necessary to do so. The truth is, almost everyone has a price or a skeleton in their closet. This is why you have to be aware of your surroundings and make smart choices. For example, you don't go anywhere by yourself or set your drink down."

"What about the bathroom?"

"Mac, our female operative, will be there. She can escort you to and from."

Brynnon drew in a deep, calming breath, her tantalizing breasts rising and falling with the movement.

Not for the first time, Grant wondered how they would feel beneath his palms. They were so close, and the partition was up. All he'd have to do would be to reach out and—

"Okay."

He blinked, unsure of what she'd just agreed to. For a second, he thought maybe he'd voiced his thoughts aloud— and that she'd just given him permission to touch her.

"I'll stick to your side and keep my eyes out for anyone who doesn't seem to belong."

Running a hand down his jaw, Grant looked straight ahead, his only response a hoarse, "Good."

For the remainder of the drive, Grant kept quiet for fear he'd open his mouth and say something stupid like telling her again just how badly he wanted her. Or worse, he'd admit to having feelings for her. That shit would open up a whole new can of fucking worms.

So instead, he remained quiet.

Seemingly lost in her own thoughts, Brynnon didn't seem to mind the silence. Of course, that only made Grant start to wonder what *she* was thinking, filling him with a tailspin of hopes and fears.

Jesus H. Christ, Hill. Get your shit under control. The thought had barely entered his mind when the car slowed to a stop.

She looked over at him with a smirk, "Showtime."

Coop opened the door on Brynnon's side, and almost immediately they were bombarded with a barrage of flashing lights. Grant didn't understand the fascination with politicians and their families, but clearly some held them at almost the same level as famous celebrities.

With his hand resting protectively on Brynnon's lower back—something he found himself doing a lot—he did his best to act as a regular date would, rather than a bodyguard.

But when one overzealous onlooker slid under the security rope and approached Brynnon for an autograph, Grant's instincts took over.

In less than a second, he was in front of her with his hand held out, preventing the woman from coming any closer. Thankfully, the guards at the door quickly escorted the woman back to her place in the crowd.

"Jesus," Grant commented under his breath. "That shit happen to you a lot?"

"Only at events like this or at my father's rallies. The poor woman probably doesn't even know who I am."

"Well, that *poor woman* better keep her ass behind the line."

Brynnon slid him a sideways glance. With a half-smile, she leaned in and whispered, "Easy, big guy."

To both his enjoyment and his dismay, the tempting woman reached back and grabbed his hand, sliding her fingers between his. Grant's eyes shot to hers.

She smiled. "Appearances, remember?"

Goddamn, she was adorable.

Upon entering the large, historical building, Brynnon guided them over to where a young man was checking in the guests' coats. Billy and his date came up behind them as they waited for their ticket.

"Hey, sis. Lookin' good."

Brynnon spun around, a large grin spreading across her face. "Billy! I was hoping you'd make it."

After giving him a hug, she pulled back and tilted her head toward Grant. "You remember Grant."

"Of course." The other man held out his hand. "Glad to see you're still keeping my sister safe."

"About that," Brynnon pulled Billy down to her and lowered her voice. "I don't want anyone to know he's my bodyguard, so we're pretending he's my date."

"Ah, working undercover. I like it." Billy gave him a playful wink. "Don't worry, Grant. Your secret's safe with me." Straightening back up, he glanced toward the woman on his arm. "Speaking of dates, this is Victoria. Tori, this is my sister and Grant. Her...date."

The bleach blonde Barbie wanna-be completely ignored Brynnon as she locked her sights on Grant. In a blatant display of interest, she let her eyes slide up and down the length of his body.

With a seductive smile, she held out her perfectly manicured hand. "It's very nice to meet you."

Though he had no desire to, Grant lifted his hand. Before he could make contact, Brynnon quickly grabbed his hand and gave the other woman an obviously fake smile.

"Will you please excuse us for a moment? Grant and I need to discuss something with Billy...in private."

Surprised by Brynnon's abruptness, Victoria batted her fake lashes a couple of times before curling her red lips into a contemptuous grin. "Of course."

To Billy, Brynnon then tipped her head to the side and walked far enough away to ensure the other woman wouldn't overhear their conversation. Following the silent instruction, her brother joined them.

Turning his brows inward, Billy commented, "Wow, sis. Rude much?"

"Like I care," Brynnon scrunched her face in displeasure. "Where do you even find these women?"

He shot back with, "At least, unlike you, I'm here with a real date. Do you even remember what that's like, or has it been so long since you've had one of those you've forgotten?" To Grant, he smirked. "No offense."

Brynnon immediately blushed. Her eyes slid to Grant's before glaring back at her brother.

Sensing an explosive retort, Grant quickly intervened. "What do you know about Kunar?"

Billy stared back at him. Confused, he asked, "The country?"

"The bridge."

Rather than answer him, the man looked at Brynnon. "What the hell? Why are you bringing that shit back up?"

"A man approached me at the hospital yesterday. He pretended to be a reporter and started asking questions about it. Grant's teammate used the hospital's security feed and a face recognition program to figure out his real identity. His name is Charles Wright."

Billy looked genuinely lost. "Should that name mean something to me?"

With a sad expression, Brynnon said, "His son was one of the soldiers who died on the bridge that day. He hired a private investigator," she continued to explain. "Apparently, that man's been working on it ever since."

"Well, he's not gonna find anything," Billy assured her. "All the guy's doing is wasting his money. That investigation was closed a long time ago."

"Wright claims the P.I. found proof that your father's company used par-standard materials when building the bridge, causing it to collapse under the convoy's weight."

Grant thought he saw a flutter of fear shining behind the man's eyes, but it was gone before he could be certain.

"That's ridiculous," Billy protested. "We used the same materials on that bridge as all the other ones. The guy's probably trying to get money or something. Trust me, sis. This Wright character's just playing you."

"It's not a fucking game."

His sharp tone had Brynnon's eyes rising to his. Grant could tell she didn't care for it, but right now, that didn't matter. Her brother needed to know how serious the situation was.

"Excuse me?"

"This isn't about money, Billy." Brynnon turned her attention back to her brother. "Wright's daughter has been following me."

"What?" Billy frowned.

Grant explained. "The threat your father received was directed toward Brynnon. Not him. That's why he didn't hire security for you."

Billy's eyes widened. "H-how do you know?"

"She left a bunch of pictures in my mailbox, along with a threatening note," Brynnon swallowed. "The pictures were of me."

"She also came damn close to running her over."

Her brother's eyes shot to his. "You're serious." It wasn't a question.

"This is as serious as it gets."

"Thankfully, Grant was there. He pushed me out of the way just in time."

Sweat began beading on Billy's forehead. "Did you call the police? Have they arrested the crazy bitch?"

"We went to his house," Brynnon told him. "I'm not going to go into it all now, but my gut's telling me neither Charles nor his daughter really wanted to hurt me. I think Charles just wants to find out what happened to his son and the others, and Jessica wants him to finally be able to come to peace with it all."

"I agree," Grant backed her up. "Wright definitely has an

agenda, but I didn't get the vibe he or his daughter actually wanted to harm your sister."

With his hands on his hips, Billy asked, "What about the P.I. Have you talked with him or seen any of this so-called evidence?"

"One of my guys put a call in to him. He's waiting to hear back."

"What's his name?" Billy's chest heaved. "I'll go talk with him right now."

"Hank Mitchell," Brynnon tried defusing her brother's rising anger. "But he lives in Arizona. Don't worry, Billy. I know you and Dad would never do something like what Charles is saying. He's just a grieving father. That's all."

Her brother stared down at her. "You'll let me know as soon as you find something out?"

"Of course, we will," Brynnon laid a hand on his arm.

Eyes almost identical to Brynnon's met Grant's again. Swallowing nervously, the other man asked, "In the meantime, you'll keep protecting my sister?"

"With my life," Grant promised. "Trust me, Billy. My team and I will put an end to all of this."

"How do you plan to do that?"

"By finding out the truth about what happened in Kunar."

Visibly upset at the thought of his sister being harmed, Billy pulled Brynnon into a rough hug. "You stay safe, sis. Do whatever this guy tells you. No matter what, you have to stay safe."

From over her brother's shoulder, Brynnon's eyes met Grant's. "I will, Billy. I promise. And, hey." She pulled back. "As soon as we talk with Hank Mitchell and see whatever evidence he thinks he has, this will all be cleared up."

Billy nodded, even though he didn't seem convinced. "Bryn, listen. I—"

"I thought you said this was going to be fun."

All three turned their heads toward the source of the whiney, interrupting voice. Victoria approached them, her bottom lip protruding in an exaggerated pout.

"It is," Brynnon assured her brother's date. "Billy, why don't you take Victoria over to the bar?"

The man studied his sister a few seconds longer before pasting on his crowd-ready smile and focusing on his date. "Of course. Come on, Tori. Time to let the good times roll."

As the two walked away, Billy gave his sister a final, odd glance. One Grant couldn't quite decipher.

Chapter 13

Two hours later, Brynnon had given the welcome speech, they'd eaten a meal that wasn't that great, but probably cost a month's pay per plate, and the two had spent far too long walking around the large crowd.

After introducing him to a bunch of people whose names he'd already forgotten, the pair made their way over to the bar. Grant was sitting on a stool next to Coop while Brynnon, Mac, and Brynnon's friend, Angie, chatted it up a few feet away at end of the bar.

Just like at the hospital, Angie or Mac would glance his way and soon, they'd start giggling like schoolgirls.

He should probably be annoyed by their juvenile behavior, but Grant found it oddly endearing. Although, he was sure to suffer some hardcore ribbing from Mac later.

As Alpha Team's one and only female member, the woman looked about as girl-next-door as they came. In reality, she was one of the best damn snipers he'd ever seen.

"You talk to the brother yet?"

Grant turned to Coop. "Yeah. Saw him earlier."

"And?"

"Claims Wright is full of shit and the materials Cantrell Construction used on the bridge near Kunar were the same as every other bridge the company built overseas."

"You believe him?"

Grant sighed. "I don't know. He seemed taken off guard by the question."

"Could just be because it came out of nowhere."

"Maybe. Part of me feels like he knows more than he's saying."

"Why's that?"

Grant took a sip of his whiskey. Normally, they didn't drink while on duty, but since Brynnon and her father wanted them to blend in with the crowd, the two men had each ordered one to help solidify their covers.

"He seemed sort of nervous at first," he told Coop. "Then again, the guy's a bit odd, so who the fuck knows?"

"How'd Brynnon take you questioning her brother?"

He shrugged. "Fine. Not like I grilled the guy. Plus, she wants to find out if Wright was telling the truth, so there's that."

Coop thought for a moment. "Well, if there's any truth to Wright's allegations, D will find it."

Grant nodded. "Yeah. I talked with him earlier today. He left a message for the P.I. and is just waiting to hear back. Derek said Trevor also put a call into Ryker."

Jason Ryker was the Homeland Security agent in charge of a special task force. He was also R.I.S.C.'s handler and often hired them for ops the government couldn't officially become involved in.

"Hopefully Jason can get his hands on the investigation file. That should shed some light on the whole deal."

With a nod, Grant and Coop continued to keep an eye on the girls. A few minutes later, they watched as a man about Grant's age approached them. He was six-one, maybe six-two, head full of dark, brown hair, and a winning smile.

The stranger introduced himself to the other two women, but the guy's focus was clearly on Brynnon. Every muscle in Grant's body tensed.

"Who's that?" Coop asked casually, sipping his own drink.

"No idea."

Coop gave the man an assessing glance. "He seems really familiar, but I can't place him." He took another sip. "Looks like you may have competition, though."

Tearing his attention away from the women, Grant glared at his other teammate. "There is no competition."

Scoffing, Coop swallowed another sip. "Not so sure about that."

"Well, I am." Grant turned to him. "I've told you, there's nothing going on between me and Bryn."

Coop's hazel eyes looked back at him as if he were confused. "So?"

"*So...*" Grant tried to get through to the hard-head. "There's no competition."

His teammate hid a smirk behind his glass. "That's probably good, 'cause they're both walking this way."

Grant turned his head, and sure enough, Brynnon and the unknown man were headed straight for him. With a smile he'd come to relish, she stopped a few inches in front of him.

"Grant, I'd like you to meet Lucas Campbell. Lucas, this is Grant, the former SEAL I was telling you about."

Lucas. Fucking. Campbell.

For Brynnon's sake only, Grant didn't react to being introduced to her douchebag ex-boyfriend. He also didn't punch his fist down the guy's throat like he wanted.

"It's an honor to meet you." Lucas held out his hand. "And let me just say, thank you for your service."

Standing, Grant shook the man's outstretched hand, squeezing harder than necessary. "Thanks." When he didn't let go, Brynnon quickly jumped in.

"And this is Coop. He's also former military. Army Ranger, I believe." Brynnon looked to Coop for confirmation.

"Yes, ma'am." Coop stood and shook the guy's hand, as well. "Nice to meet you."

Lucas returned the gesture. "You, too. And, thank you, as well."

"You're welcome," Coop smiled back. "It's nice to meet someone who appreciates what the troops do for our country."

The other man smiled. "That's why I try to make the scenes in my games as realistic as possible."

Coop's eyes grew wide as saucers as he snapped his finger. "That's where I've seen you. You're *The* Lucas Campbell." He turned to Grant. "This is the guy who created War & Retribution."

Not having a clue what his friend was talking about, Grant gave him a blank stare.

His teammate's jaw nearly dropped. "Please tell me you know what WR is."

"Sorry." Grant shook his head.

"Dude. You've got to check it out. It's literally the top-rated military action game on the market. It's made this guy millions, it's that good."

"I take it you play?" Lucas asked Coop.

"Are you kidding? Every chance I get. Your graphics are incredible. It's great you care enough about the military to get the details right."

"Well, I try my best."

"You serve?" Grant asked, already sure he knew the answer.

Lucas brought his blue eyes back to Grant's. "No, sir. I wanted to, but unfortunately, my asthma kept me out."

Asthma. *Right.*

If he had a dollar for every badass wannabe who'd claimed their 'dream' of joining the military was crushed by a sudden asthma diagnosis, he could've retired years ago.

"I didn't know you had asthma," Brynnon frowned.

"It wasn't diagnosed until after you and I…well. I didn't find out until later."

"Oh." Brynnon nodded, buying the pretentious prick's story. "My dad was turned away for medical reasons, as well. I don't know if I ever told you that." She smiled at Lucas again. "But I believe everything happens for a reason, so that means there was something else you were meant to do. And seeing the generous gift you've given to the hospital's juvenile cancer research foundation, I think I know what that reason was. Or, at least part of it, anyway."

Feigning humility, Lucas shook his head. "Oh, well. I don't know about all that. I do have something else in the works, though."

"A new game?" Coop asked anxiously.

The guy chuckled. "Well, I can't really talk about it yet, but yeah."

"Sounds mysterious," Brynnon commented, still smiling at the fucker. "Come on. I'd like to introduce to you a few more people within the organization. I know they're going to be thrilled to meet you."

Before walking away with her ex, she gave Grant a wink and a nod, telling him without words not to worry.

Not likely, Princess.

204

He kept his eyes glued to the pair as they stopped to talk with an older couple. When Brynnon placed one of her hands on the other man's bicep as she laughed, Grant's curled into tight fists at his sides.

"Jesus," Coop exclaimed from beside him. "You'd better wipe that look off your ugly mug before she sees it."

Grant looked away from her long enough to glower down at his teammate. "What look?"

Coop pointed at him. "*That* one. You look like you're about to go rip the guy's arm clean off." His teammate tilted his head. "Funny. I never really took you for the jealous type."

Shit. Grant had been so focused on Brynnon's laugh and the way the asshole was smiling down at her, he'd forgotten all about trying to school his expression.

"I'm not fucking jealous. I'm…concerned." He glanced at Campbell then back to Coop. "Brynnon dated that guy in college. He screwed her over, and now all of a sudden, he shows up here? I don't know." Grant shook his head. "Something about him bothers me."

"Yeah," his friend snickered. "Like the fact that he's hitting on your girl."

With a seething glare, Grant worked to control his temper. "Told you before, she's not my girl. She's—"

"Looks like Brynnon may have found herself an admirer."

Both men turned to see Mac walking toward them. Grant still couldn't get used to seeing her with her long, blonde hair down. It was a much different look than the ponytail she usually wore. Of course, everything about her was different, tonight.

Typically, the former Ranger wore jeans or cargo pants, and either a T-shirt or tank top, depending on the weather.

Tonight, Mac had definitely dressed for the occasion. The low-cut, sequin black dress was tight and stopped just above her knees. The high-as-fuck heels she was wearing added a few inches of height, but the kick-ass operative still only stood all of five-four.

Yeah, she may look like the All-American cheerleader type, but Grant—and the rest of R.I.S.C.—knew better. When needed, Mac could play the sweet and innocent role perfectly. But put her in a shooting competition, or hell, even hand-to-hand, and Grant's money was on her. Every. Single. Time.

"Hey." Coop stared back at her. "I, uh, meant to tell you earlier. You look...great."

"Thanks." Mac tucked some hair behind her ear. "You clean up pretty well yourself."

Grant watched the somewhat awkward exchange, thankful their focus was no longer on him, but each other.

"So." Mac looked up at him and smiled. "You gonna go kick that guy's ass, or do you want me to do it?"

Damn. Spoke too soon.

"Why would I kick his ass?"

"Seriously?" Mac's brows arched. "The guy's hot, loaded, and charming as hell. And he clearly has Brynnon in his sights."

Grant's spine stiffened. "What do you mean?"

Mac studied him a minute, a knowing smile slowly forming. "There it is."

"There's what?"

Using a perfectly manicured finger, Mac made circles in the air up toward his face. "You've got this whole, silent jealous thing going on. Surprised the hell out of me when I first looked over here and saw it, but I get it." She shrugged.

"Brynnon seems really great. Plus, I think she may have just enough spunk to keep you in line."

"Jesus Christ," Grant spat out the words. "You're just as bad as he is." He used his thumb to point toward Coop. "For the last fucking time, there's nothing going on between Brynnon and me. Got it?"

"If you say so." Mac shrugged one of her petite shoulders. It was obvious she thought he was full of shit.

Rather than continue on with the pointless argument, Grant looked back to where Brynnon had been standing. Only, she wasn't there.

His heart began to thump against his ribcage as he immediately began scanning the room. "Where'd she go?"

Mac and Coop both turned their heads on a swivel. Coop shook his head. "She was right there a second ago."

"I know where she *was*," he spouted back. "I need to know where she *is*."

Grant knew he was being even more of an ass than usual, but fuck. He'd only taken his eyes off her for a second, and now…

"Ladies and gentlemen, may I have your attention, please?"

Grant, Coop, and Mac all turned their focus to the temporary stage that had been set up at the end of the large ballroom. There, standing at the podium, was Brynnon.

"See?" Coop squeezed his shoulder. "Nothing to worry about."

Slowly, Grant let out the breath he'd been holding, mentally chastising himself for not keeping a better eye on her. He'd let Coop's and Mac's taunts about Campbell fuck with his head, but he needed to get control of that shit. Now.

He'd never lost a client, and he sure as hell wasn't going to start with this one.

Not her. I can't ever lose her.

Clearing his throat, he listened as Brynnon continued to speak.

"First of all, I'd like to thank each and every one of you again for coming tonight. I just spoke with our treasurer, and we not only made our goal for this evening, we surpassed it. So please, give yourselves a round of applause."

Once the clapping died down, she began again. "I know it's hard to believe, but our time together is quickly coming to an end. Just as we've done in year's past, our event tonight will end with the annual charity dancing competition. If you have not signed up yet, there's still time. And, as with our earlier silent auction, all proceeds will go directly to the foundation."

Brynnon waited for another short round of applause before continuing. "This year's dance will be the waltz."

Grant's chest tightened and he had to force himself to take in a long, slow breaths as Brynnon went on with her spiel.

"For those who have never participated before, you and your partner will go out onto the dance floor. Once the music begins, each couple will dance until the end of the song. Afterward, the couples will line up, and the winners will be chosen by applause. The lucky winners will not only receive the beautiful trophies donated to us for this evening"—she held up a golden silhouette of a couple dancing— "but more importantly, they'll have bragging rights for the entire year."

The crowd laughed and Brynnon explained there were only a few more minutes to sign up if there was anyone who still wanted to join in. After pointing out the sign-up table at the opposite end of the room, she thanked everyone again for coming and wished them a safe trip home.

Carefully stepping off the stage, she looked over the crowd to him. Their eyes met, and she smiled as she began making her way back to him.

Good girl.

She was almost to the end of the bar when Lucas stepped into her path. Grant couldn't tell what he was asking her, but he didn't miss the disappointing look Brynnon gave the other man as she shook her head.

Maybe the fucknut asked her out, and she turned him down.

Convinced that was it, Grant relaxed his shoulders and waited for her return. A second later, Angie came up to them, eyes wide with shock as she began whispering loudly to Mac.

"Did you hear that? Lucas Campbell just asked Brynnon if she wanted to be dancing partners for the competition."

Grant forced a steady breath into his lungs, refusing to react.

"Seriously?" Mac's voice turned high-pitched. "Is she going to do it?"

"God, I hope not," Angie fumed. "That man put her through hell once, already."

"Really?" Mac seemed surprised. "Well, with those looks and his money and charm...she may decide to give him another chance. I know I would."

Grant's eyes flew back to where Brynnon and Richie Rich were talking. The guy was still trying to talk her into dancing with him, and from the look in Brynnon's eyes, she was actually considering it.

As Mac continued listing off reasons Brynnon should rethink giving Lucas the brush-off, Coop leaned over and whispered into his ear.

"You gonna let this happen?"

He turned to face him. "What can I do about it?"

"Gee, Hill. I don't know. Maybe you should"—Coop made a shooing motion with his hands— "go ask her to dance with you, instead?"

The pressure in his chest worsened. Grant shook his head. "I don't dance."

"Too bad 'cause it looks like ol' Campbell, there, is about to go in for the kill. I mean, sure it's just a dance, but who knows what it'll lead to? All that soft music playing in the background. His arms wrapped tightly around her waist. Their bodies pressed up against each other as they reminisce about old times."

"Shut the fuck up."

The order came out much louder than intended. Thankfully, Brynnon was far enough away, she hadn't heard it. However, the bartender, Mac, and Angie all abruptly stopped what they were doing and stared up at him.

With a sideways grin, Coop suggested, "Better hurry."

Goddamnit.

Grant pressed his lips together as he looked at Brynnon and Campbell again. She was definitely wavering in her resolve, and…sonofabitch. She was going to do it.

"Fuck it."

Before he could change his mind, Grant slammed his glass down onto the bar and stormed toward her. Brynnon had just opened her mouth—probably to tell the prick yes—when she spotted him.

Her pretty eyes widened in alarm, no doubt a result of his pissed-at-the-world expression. Yeah, he knew he should probably control that shit, but right now Grant couldn't bring himself to care.

For years, as both a former SEAL and now a R.I.S.C. operative, he'd come face-to-face with deadly explosives. Had been in countless situations where his life literally depended on his ability to maintain his cool.

This was not one of those times.

"Grant?" Brynnon looked up at him, concern filling those gorgeous seas of green "Are you okay? Is something wrong?"

Ignoring her questions, Grant stepped right in front of Campbell, nearly knocking the guy over in the process. Locking eyes with the other man, he grabbed Brynnon's hand and rumbled, "She already has a partner."

Careful not to be too rough, he pulled her with him as he began walking away.

Brynnon's heels clicked loudly, working to keep up as he marched them both across the room to the competition sign-ups.

Chapter 14

"What are you doing?" Brynnon hissed. She couldn't decide which she felt more...pissed off or embarrassed.

Grant grabbed a pen from the table and leaned down, adding both their names to the bottom of the registration list. The list filled with couples who were about to compete.

"I'm signing us up," he grumbled. "What does it look like I'm doing?"

"I know what you're doing," she whispered back. "It was a rhetorical question."

Grant sat the pen down and reached for his wallet. "If you already knew the answer, why'd you ask?"

He pulled out enough cash to cover the registration fee before returning his wallet to his back pocket.

The woman at the table smiled up at him. "Thank you so much for your donation, sir. You know, I was just about to close the registration, so you got here just in time." She turned to Brynnon. "You're the last couple to sign up."

Brynnon forced a smile in return and looked back at Grant. With a tug to his jacket sleeve, she moved them out of earshot from the kind woman.

"I meant, *why* are you doing this?"

Grant shrugged one of his large shoulders. "You wanted

to compete, right?"

Brynnon blinked. "Well, yes, but—"

Before she could finish, he'd grabbed her hand and was pulling her along with him once more. With no other choice but to follow—unless she wanted to cause a scene, which she didn't—Brynnon walked twice as fast to keep up with his long stride.

They weaved their way through the other couples waiting for the music to start, finally stopping in an open area at the other end of the dance floor, near the stage. Letting go of her hand, Grant turned to face her.

"Put your left hand on my right shoulder."

Feeling as though her eyes were going to bug out of her head, Brynnon looked up at him as if he were nuts.

"You're kidding, right?"

He didn't respond. Instead, the frustratingly handsome man simply raised that damn brow of his.

Doing her best to keep her voice down, she said, "Look, I don't know what's going on, but this is not the time or place to try and make some sort of point."

Grant suddenly looked grumpier than usual. "I'm not trying to prove a point."

Could've fooled me. "Is this because Lucas asked me to dance with him?" She looked at him for another second, and then gasped. "Holy crap." Brynnon looked around to make sure no one was listening before whispering, "Are you jealous?"

Grant swallowed but remained quiet.

"Well, if this is some sort of pissing match, you can stop. I told you what that man put me through. I was only talking to him and introducing him because tonight is about the kids and causing a scene with my ex wouldn't exactly go over well with the donors. And yes, Lucas is apparently one of those donors, but there is no way in hell I'd even think about getting back together with him. So you've won." When he still didn't respond, she gave him a pointed look. "Seriously, Grant. The music's about to start and people are looking at us."

Sighing loudly, he wrapped an arm around her waist and pulled her to him. Brynnon let out a tiny squeal as their bodies nearly became flush with one another's.

Without a word, Grant reached over with his left hand and lifted hers, resting it just below his right shoulder. Conflict mixed with determination in his eyes, making her wonder if maybe this was about something more than simply jealousy.

A thought hit, making her feel like an ungrateful bitch.

The orchestra began playing the song's intro, those first few notes creating a sudden sense of urgency. Brynnon shook her head as she started to ramble.

"If you're doing this because my partner backed out at the last minute and you feel sorry for me, don't. Seriously, Grant. It's a sweet thought and a kind gesture, but I don't want you to—"

"What?" He raised a brow. "Embarrass myself?"

She winced. "I-I didn't mean it like that. I promise, I didn't. It's just that, this is supposed to be a waltz, and when we talked before about dancing, you—"

"Brynnon!" he spoke her name sternly, cutting her off.

She blinked and stared back up at him.

"Do you want to dance?" Grant emphasized each word as he spoke.

After a moment's hesitation, she nodded. "Y-yes."

His metallic eyes bore deep into her own. "Do you trust me?"

"Yes." Her whispered answer was immediate. It was also

the truth. "I do."

One corner of his desirable mouth curled slowly. With his right hand already on her back, Grant clasped their free hands together. He raised them high, creating the perfect waltz position.

Leaning closer, he turned his voice low and sultry before ordering, "Then stop talking and follow my lead."

A second later, with a spine-tingling wink, Grant Hill began to dance.

His feet glided seamlessly over the dance floor, matching the rhythmic beat of the music.

One, two, three...one, two, three...one, two three.

His callused palm pressed gently against the bare skin of her back, a stimulating jolt of electricity running straight to her core. Inner muscles clenched on reflex. Her body responding to his touch as though it was a lifeline she desperately needed.

A warm, tingling sensation began to spread in her lower belly as Brynnon fell in line and followed his lead. She and Grant swayed elegantly, keeping in time to the soft, wistful music.

Spellbound, she moved as he slid them side-to-side. Forward and back. Together, they whirled amongst the other dancers. Not as a couple, but as one.

Holy hell. The man couldn't just dance. He was really *good* at it.

Brynnon was still trying to wrap her mind around that fact when she felt their bodies start to turn. Pulling her in even closer, the surprisingly gentle man held on a little tighter as he led them into their first spin.

Not missing a beat, Grant's feet moved expertly as they traveled across the hardwood floor, the bottom of her full dress swishing around their legs as they twirled. Before long, the spin was over, and in another surprise move, the former SEAL leaned in toward her.

With Grant's protective arm wrapped securely around her waist, Brynnon arched her back with the movement. The two worked together to lower into a slight dip before returning to an upright position.

The pattern continued on…Dance. Twirl. Dip. At some point—she wasn't sure exactly when—they'd both subconsciously moved their hands from the classic waltz position to a more intimate yet acceptable variation.

With their bodies even closer now, his rugged jaw brushed against her temple. Brynnon could feel his hot breath on her shoulder. The way it moved in and out with as much speed and force as her own was a telling sign.

He feels it, too.

Grant's fingertips dug into her back and hip as the song reached its intense crescendo. Losing herself in the impassioned embrace, Brynnon closed her eyes, welcoming the power and strength the man exuded.

The former SEAL often came off brusque and unemotional. But in that moment, the fierce warrior danced with the grace and ease rivaling the great Fred Astaire.

When the music softened and the song's ending drew near, Grant leaned forward moving them into their final dip. Trusting the arms wrapped snuggly around her, Brynnon slowly let her head tip backward, arching even farther than before.

Without question, she knew this man would always keep her from falling.

Feeling a sudden need to see his handsome face, Brynnon lifted her lids. The raw hunger staring back at her seized the breath inside her frozen lungs.

An intense wave of arousal washed over her with such force, it most assuredly would've brought Brynnon to her knees had Grant not been holding on so tightly.

Consumed by their desire for one another, it took several seconds for either of them to realize the music had stopped, and the crowd had broken into a loud applause.

Clearing his throat, Grant glanced away as he pulled Brynnon back to her feet, breaking the almost staggering connection they'd just shared.

Remembering where they were, and who was watching, Brynnon put on a smile and turned to face those cheering, realizing they were the only couple left on the dance floor.

"Well," a woman's voice boomed over the sound system.

Brynnon looked to the stage, immediately recognizing Leslie, the woman in charge of the charity.

With a toothy grin, she said, "I think we all know who the winning couple is this year. Let's hear it for our very own Brynnon Cantrell and her date"—Leslie double-checked the list of names— "Grant."

One of their regular volunteers walked over and handed Brynnon the small trophy. The crowd erupted in cheers, Angie's voice ringing out above them all.

Brynnon's cheeks became heated as Coop put his thumb and middle finger between his lips and let out a high-pitched whistle. The knowing look he was giving Grant made her wonder exactly what kind of show they'd had just given.

Clearing his throat again, Grant whispered in her ear, "Time to go, Princess."

Smiling up at him, Brynnon refused to let her disappointment show when she realized his usual mask of indifference was back in place. "Okay."

"Holy Dancing With the Stars!" Angie ran over and gave her a hug. "That was amazing!"

"Thanks, Ang," Brynnon hugged her friend back.

"Seriously." Angie released her. "You two are incredible together. Everyone was saying so."

Grinning, Brynnon asked, "Really?"

"Yes, really."

"She's right," Coop came up behind Angie. "The whole crowd was rooting for you two."

"Well, maybe not the *whole* crowd," Mac pointed out as she approached them. "Campbell didn't seem too happy you stole Brynnon away from him."

"Lucas?" Brynnon asked, surprised by the statement. "He only asked to be polite."

"I don't know," Angie chimed in. "He did look pretty upset when you two started dancing."

Coop gave the two women a look. "Just say it, ladies. The guy was pissed."

Angie chuckled. "Okay, fine. He was pissed."

"So much so, the guy skirted out of here mid-dance," Mac gave her a look.

"That makes no sense," Brynnon shook her head. "We haven't seen each other in years. I'm sure there's another reason he left that had absolutely nothing to do with me."

Angie grinned. "I think he was just butt hurt because Grant ruined his chances at a reconciliation. *That's* why he left." To Grant, she mouthed a silent, "Thank you."

After, she turned and gave Mac a high five.

Realizing he'd been set up, Grant ignored the two women's smug expressions and asked Coop, "Can you go get the car? I want to get out of here before traffic gets bad."

"Sure," Coop nodded. With a smirk, he told Grant, "But

don't think you're getting off that easily."

"Meaning?"

"Meaning"—Coop motioned toward the dance floor—"you've got some 'splaining to do, brother."

With that, Grant's teammate bid Mac and Angie farewell and went to get the car.

"That's my cue, too." Mac gave Grant a serious look. "Be careful. You two need anything, just call."

"Appreciate it," Grant offered the other woman.

"Thanks, Mac. It was really nice meeting you."

"You, too. And, uh…don't let this guy boss you around too much." With a wink, the other woman left.

After giving Brynnon another hug and a whispered order to share any interesting details that may arise later, Angie left Grant and Brynnon alone on the dance floor. They both spoke at the same time.

"We should—"

"You ready?"

Brynnon laughed nervously. "You first."

Grant's mouth twitched. "I was just going to say, we should get our coats."

"Right." She smirked. "Don't want Coop to start honking his horn again."

One corner of Grant's mouth rose slightly, and man, Brynnon wished she could see him smile like he had the night before.

With his hand resting against her lower back—God, she loved it when he did that—they made their way to the coat check. While she waited for Grant to get their coats, Brynnon caught sight of her brother and another man through the glass doors.

They were across the street, standing on the sidewalk, and

from what she could see, it appeared as though they were arguing. She tried to see who he was talking to, but the other man wore a dark coat and hat, and was facing away from her.

Old fears for her brother threatened to ruin her good mood. She thought about going out there to make sure he was okay, but Grant's deep voice rang through her ears.

"Everything okay?" He held her coat open for her.

Refusing to let her brother's never-ending drama ruin her night, she put her arms through the sleeves and gave Grant a smile. "Yeah. Thank you."

Peering down at her, a sliver of hunger returned as he slipped on his own coat. "You ready?"

For more than you know.

Praying he could see the real meaning behind her answer, she whispered back, "Yes."

Grant held the door open and stood close to her while they waited. A minute later, Coop turned the corner and pulled up next to the curb.

The handsome operative got out and made his way around the front of the car. He spoke to Grant as he opened the back door.

"My traffic app just sent a notification. There's a bad wreck on Seventy-Five. The entire northbound lane is shut down. I'm going to have to head down to Thirty and loop around to Thirty-Five East, so the ride home is going to take longer than usual."

Brynnon frowned as she climbed in. "That's awful. I hope everyone's okay."

"Yeah. Awful."

Coop give Grant a funny look before whispering something in his ear. Grant blew off whatever his teammate said and walked around the back of the car to his side.

As he opened the door and slid in next to her, Coop leaned down through her still-open door and smiled.

"I'll leave the partition up for the duration of the ride. You know, so you two can talk in private." With an ornery smirk, the other man closed the door and made his way back behind the wheel.

"Well, that wasn't obvious," Brynnon joked sarcastically.

A low grunt resounded from Grant's chest, but he didn't say anything. For the next few minutes, the small, dark space became saturated with an awkward silence as neither one spoke.

Fidgeting nervously with the trophy, Brynnon decided to tackle the one question that had been burning through her mind since the moment the music started.

Biting her bottom lip, she glanced over at him and asked, "Why did you lie?"

Deep lines appeared on his forehead, confusion filling in his deep voice. "When did I lie?"

"The other day." Shifting in her seat, Brynnon faced him more directly. "I was talking about the ball, and you told me you couldn't dance."

The deep lines became smooth and his tempting mouth quirked. "Wrong. I told you I *don't* dance. Never said I couldn't."

She had a feeling there was a story there, one she intended to discover. Letting it go, for now, Brynnon allowed her lips to curl into a slow smile. "My mistake."

They held the shared look a little longer before she glanced back down at the trophy. Then in a somewhat bold move, she slid across the black leather seat and pressed her lips against his coarse cheek.

"Thank you," she whispered, moving back just enough to

look him in the eye.

Grant turned his head toward her, their noses nearly touching as his heated gaze beheld hers. Deep seas of gray darkened in a way that made her heart race.

"It was my pleasure," he breathed softly.

The tantalizing sound stirred something inside her, heightening the aching need she felt for this man. Fixated on his tempting lips, Brynnon subconsciously licked hers. God, she wanted to taste him again.

"Brynnon."

Perceiving her whispered name as a warning, she broke eye contact. After offering a quick apology, she began to slide back to her own seat when Grant's hand snaked out and covered hers.

"Don't be sorry."

The surprising words left her puzzled, but hope bloomed when she saw his gaze sweeping slowly across her mouth before landing on the low dip of her exposed cleavage. Brynnon's heart pounded inside her chest, the sound of its forceful rhythm filling her ears.

A slight pull on her hand brought her back to his side. The soft swooshing of her dress as it brushed across the leather seat was the only sound in the electrified space. With a creased forehead, Grant worked his jaw, but the tormented expression crossing his face vanished as quickly as it had appeared.

On a slow exhale, he brought his eyes back up to hers. The pain and indecision she'd just seen had been replaced with a primal need matching her own. Brynnon had heard him say the words before, but now she could actually feel it.

He wants me. The realization of what she hoped was about to happen was intoxicating. Still, she had to know…

"What about all those lines of yours?"

Reaching up with his free hand, Grant cupped the back of her head and asked, "What lines?" Then he slammed his mouth against hers.

Chapter 15

She tasted of strawberries and champagne, and Grant couldn't get enough. No longer caring about possible regrets or professional reprimand, he closed his eyes and gave in to his unprecedented desire.

He'd come damn close to kissing her earlier, in front of God and everyone. The way she'd moved, her body perfectly in sync with his, he'd nearly forgotten all about where they were and the other people around them.

At first, Grant had been worried he'd fuck something up. It had been a long ass time since he'd waltzed. But it was like his mom had once told him...*Dancing is like riding a bike, son. Once you have it down, the muscles will remember. Even if the mind doesn't.*

As always, she'd been right. Of course, it didn't hurt to have such a willing partner.

Once she finally got over the shock that he actually knew what the hell he was doing, the entrancing woman had handed him the reigns. After that, dancing with Brynnon had become effortless.

It was almost as if she'd finally given herself to him, and he to her. Though he'd slept with his fair share of women throughout the years, he'd never had a more intimate connection than in those few, stolen moments with her.

It was all he could do not to throw her over his shoulder and haul her off to the nearest, private room where he could finally do the things that, up until this moment, he'd only dreamed of. Grant had spent the entire dance with his dick hard and throbbing ready to burst through his rented suit at any second.

It hadn't cared that he'd already gotten himself off that morning or that they were in the middle of a fucking crowd. The greedy thing only wanted one thing: to find the pleasure it knew this woman would give.

You're alone, now.

His cock twitched. Though Grant was dying for release, he'd be damned if their first time would be in the back seat of a limo with Coop on the other side of that thin, glass divider. He could, however, give her a little preview.

Before getting into the car, Coop had assured him the ride to Brynnon's condo would take at least forty-five minutes, thanks to their forced detour. They'd only been on the road for five.

Plenty of time to give her the first of many orgasms.

With his tongue still dominating hers, Grant released her hand to cup one of her satin-covered breasts. He swallowed Brynnon's throaty moan, the erotic sound provoking.

Sliding the same hand to the back of her neck, he tugged on the bow. A dull thud reached his ears as the slick material loosened with ease, and he knew she'd just dropped the forgotten trophy onto the carpeted floor.

Grant continued to feast on the sweetness of her mouth, nibbling her bottom lip while he pulled the top of her dress down, exposing her bare breasts. The need to finally see them tore him away, his eyes lowering to take in the glorious sight. Allowing him to take his fill, Brynnon sat still. A guy on his SEAL team had a saying… *"Tits are tits, doesn't matter who they belong to."* Looking at the perfection before him, Grant knew the jackass had never been more wrong.

"Beautiful," he whispered more to himself than her.

They were the perfect size, just big enough to fill his large hands, and the dusty rose nipples were exactly how he'd imagined. Standing at attention, the erect nubs told Grant she was every bit as aroused as he was.

The continued rise and fall of her chest was too great a temptation, so he bent down and took one of her hard-as-fuck nipples between his lips. Brynnon moaned again, her back instinctively arching as she searched for more. Something he was more than happy to give.

Sucking more of her breast into the wet heat of his mouth, Grant used his tongue to pleasure and tease, while gently kneading the other side. Delicate fingers combed through his hair as Brynnon grabbed ahold of his head, spurring him on.

After giving the other breast the same attention, Grant began leaving a trail of wet kisses up along her neck. When Brynnon tilted her head to the side, he took full advantage, gently nibbling the sensitive pulse point where her neck and shoulder met.

On a gasp, she released his hair and began slowly lowering her hand toward his belt. More than anything, he wanted her to touch him there. To feel himself between her fist as she pumped him again and again, until he exploded.

But Grant knew all it would take was that first brush of her hand on his swollen shaft and he'd have his pants down and be buried balls-deep inside her within seconds. That was *not* how their first time was going to go.

Determined to make tonight as good for her as he possibly could, Grant covered her hand with his.

"Grant," she whispered his name as a frustrated plea.

He kissed her jawline. "Touch me now, this is over before we even get started. And I plan on taking my time with you." Her body shivered. *Trust me, sweetheart. I know the feeling.*

"Please," Brynnon begged. "I need you."

"Don't worry, baby." He kissed the edge of her delicate chin. "I know exactly what you need."

Taking even more control, Grant began devouring her mouth as he reached for her leg. Slipping his hand between the open slit in her dress, he slid his fingers up along her bare thigh.

He thanked God when Brynnon sat back in her seat more fully and opened her legs to give him better access. Wanting to get her off at least once before they reached her place, Grant wasted no time.

With the slit's height and her relaxed position, he easily made his way up to the apex of her thighs. He could feel her heat before he even made contact, and just knowing she was burning alive for him was enough to nearly set him off.

As their tongues continued their erotic dance, Grant slipped his fingers beneath the lacey edge of her barely-there panties. That first touch was nothing short of explosive.

Brynnon's smooth, bare sex was drenched with her essence. The musky sent of her arousal filled his senses, threatening to send him into a frenzied state of lust and primal need.

He couldn't wait to slide into her silken flesh. It took everything he had to not say fuck it and drive himself inside her as hard as he could. If it were any other woman, he would have. But this was Brynnon, and she was…

227

Mine.

Her breath hitched. She was so incredibly responsive to his touch, he wished the ride would take forever so they never had to stop.

Goddamn, he wanted to see what was under all that red satin. Wanted to take his time exploring every inch of her body. To lick her slit and taste her arousal on the tip of his tongue. And he would, the minute they stepped foot into her bedroom.

Knowing their time here was limited, Grant moved his middle finger along her bare slit before sliding it into her molten core. Brynnon cried out, her hot, velvet muscles clenching hard around on his digit.

Fuck. Me.

Even behind his pants and boxers, Grant could tell his dick was already weeping with anticipation. Why wouldn't it? She was hot, wet, and as tight as a goddamn vise.

How he was going to make it through this without completely embarrassing himself was beyond him. But he sure as hell was going to give it the old college try.

Pumping slowly, Grant waited a few beats before adding a second finger. He picked up speed, his fingers thrusting in and out of her body with a little more force.

The sounds of her wet sex filled the air, bringing him dangerously close to the edge. Grant knew he needed to get her there and fast, before he did something stupid like fuck her right here. Right now.

He moved his hand faster. Harder. Brynnon began panting loudly, her pelvis instinctively lifting to meet his every thrust, searching wildly for the release he was about to give.

"Please, Grant," she begged again.

"Tell me what you want," His lips moved against hers as he spoke.

Round, frustrated eyes met his. "You know what I want."

"Say it."

Grant wasn't sure why he gave the rough order. He'd never been a talker during sex. But with Brynnon, he found himself wanting to hear the erotic words dripping from her lips.

Brynnon licked her lips, her words breaking free with each panted breath. "I want...more."

His dick twitched again, but again Grant forced himself to hold off. They'd get there, but right now he had a sudden urgency to feel her come apart on his hand.

He gently stretched her opening to accommodate a third finger. *In. Out. In. Out.* Tilting her head onto the back of the seat, Brynnon closed her eyes and purred.

"That enough?" he asked, knowing damn well it wasn't.

"Almost," she barely whispered. "God, that feels so good."

She was so close. He could feel her inner muscles trembling and knew exactly what she needed to fall over the edge. But first...

I need more room to work.

Taking a chance, Grant withdrew his fingers from her body and grabbed hold of the scrap of lace hindering his movements.

With an almost indiscernible nod, she gave the green light. "Do it."

Grant ripped the lace away from her bare sex, and she opened her legs even wider. A low growl reverberated from his chest as he slid two of his fingers back into her blazing pussy.

"You want me to make you come?" he asked, his hand nearly slamming into her now.

She nodded, her eyes closing again. "God, yes. Please, Grant. Make me come."

Seeing her lying back like that, legs spread with his hand between them and her bare tits in plain view for him to enjoy…it was hands-down the most gorgeous sight he'd ever seen.

Pumping his fingers at a more rapid pace, Grant slid his thumb up to her distended clit. Brynnon cried out even louder than before, that first touch nearly shooting her off the edge of the seat.

He rubbed her again, the sensitive bundle of nerves so swollen and hot, just begging for attention. Grant knew from both the way it was peeking out and her heavy breathing, it would only take a few more swipes to send her flying.

Keeping his rhythm, he thrust his fingers in and out of her trembling pussy while continuing to gently press against her clit. Soon, he began moving the pad of his thumb in small, tight circles. The combination was explosive.

A rush of blazing moisture drenched his fingers. Brynnon's entire lower body thrust against his hand as her mouth formed a silent "O". A low, keening sound traveled from somewhere deep inside her.

Grant couldn't take his eyes off her.

Determined to draw out every ounce of her explosive climax, he continued fucking her with his fingers. After a few more seconds, he regrettably pulled himself free of her body, the muscles there slowly starting to relax.

Brynnon opened her eyes, her satiated stare one he wanted to commit to memory.

Holding her heavy gaze, Grant lifted the same fingers that

had just been inside her to his mouth. With her still watching, he slid them between his lips and savored her sweet and salty essence.

A primal groan rumbled through his chest. Holy *fuck*, he couldn't wait to actually get his mouth on her. To lick and suck every drop of her next orgasm while she came against his mouth.

"That…was…" Brynnon worked to catch her breath.

"Fuck, yeah, it was," Grant agreed to her unspoken thought. Leaning over her, he pressed his mouth against hers, kissing her slowly while he carefully tied the satin halter back into place. Pulling away enough to see her face, he lifted one corner of his mouth. "And we're just getting started."

****

Like a good girl, Brynnon waited just inside her front door while Grant and Coop cleared the property. Coop took the building's perimeter while Grant rushed to make his way through each room in her condo.

With her clutch and the trophy in one hand, she raised the quivering fingers of her other to her lips. She still couldn't believe what they'd just done.

Brynnon wasn't a virgin by any means, but she'd never had an orgasm like the one her sexy bodyguard had just given her. Her legs were still shaky from the glorious eruption.

Never before had her body responded to a man's touch the way it had with his. The man's fingers had played her body as though she were a finely tuned instrument and Grant was the owner.

He does own you.

She shook her head, reminding herself to be careful. Just

because he'd thrown all his rules and policies out the window for sex didn't mean he planned to stick around once the job was done.

God, I hope he does.

Movement from the top of the stairs caught her eye, and Brynnon watched as Grant made his way back down to her. With his gun held loosely by his side, the tuxedo-wearing protector reminded her of an incredibly sexy James Bond.

He'd buttoned his jacket and ran his hand over the top of his head before getting out of the limo to keep Coop from knowing what they'd been doing behind the partition. Brynnon had done her best to tidy herself up, too, but she knew they weren't fooling anyone.

Though the other R.I.S.C. operative hadn't commented, the look Coop had given them booth when they stepped out of the car told Brynnon he suspected they'd shared more than just polite conversation. She should probably be embarrassed, but she wasn't. And from the way Grant was looking at her now, neither was he.

"We're clear." He came to a stop just in front of her.

Brynnon nodded. "Good."

"Coop called while I was upstairs. The outside is clear, so he's heading back to your dad's place."

They were finally alone. "Okay."

Shit. Why was she suddenly so nervous? The man had literally just had his fingers inside her.

Inner muscles clenched from the recent memory, and her gaze inadvertently fell to his hands. She watched as he tucked the gun into his back waistband, her heart beating faster as she began to wonder if he'd changed his mind.

"Look at me."

The low order brought her eyes back up to his. Closing

the distance between them, Grant rested a palm against one side of her face. "We don't have to do this."

Her heart dropped. Had he changed his mind?

Not wanting him to know how utterly disappointed she would be if that were true, Brynnon gave her chin a slight lift and started to say, "I-if you don't want to—"

His lips were suddenly on hers and whatever else she was going to say became lost. Grant moved forward, gently forcing her toward the wall behind her.

With her back pressed against the smooth surface, she opened her mouth to allow him in. Their tongues danced and teased, the passionate kiss continuing for what felt like forever before he finally broke away.

Resting his forehead against hers, Grant's hot breath joined hers as the pair worked to bring their breathing back to a more normal rate. In a shocking move, he took her free hand and placed it over his bulging zipper.

"Does that feel like I don't want to?"

Brynnon gasped from what she felt beneath her palm. Even through the barrier his pants provided, she could tell he was hard as stone. And very, very large.

Licking her nervous lips, she shook her head and whispered, "It feels like you want me as much as I want you." Curling her fingers around him, she tightened her grip and slowly rubbed against him.

A deep growl rolled through his chest and Brynnon couldn't help but smile when his eyes slid closed.

"God, help me, I do want you," he rumbled before lifting his lids again. With his eyes locked on hers he admitted, "I want you more than anything."

Brynnon stared back at him and whispered, "Then take me."

Moving faster than she'd imagined he could, Grant bent down and scooped her up in to his arms. She yelped, the unexpected move taking her off guard.

"I can walk," she told him as he started for the stairs.

All she got back was a grumbled, "I know."

Enjoying this particular caveman side of him, Brynnon simply smiled and rested her head against his shoulder. She shouldn't have been surprised at the ease with which he carried her up the staircase. The guy was the strongest, most formidable man she'd ever known.

Once inside her bedroom, Grant gently set her back onto her feet. With the moonlight shining from the window onto the bed, there was no need to turn on any lights.

She watched silently as he walked over and placed his gun on the nightstand. He removed his jacket, laying both it and his now-loosened bow tie over the arm of the small chair at the corner of her room. Brynnon half-expected him to continue undressing himself—a show she was more than happy to see—but instead he came back over to her and started to talk.

"We should probably discuss protection." Not giving her a chance to respond, he told her, "We get tested every six months for the job. I haven't been with anyone since before our last round. I've always been clean, and I've never gone bareback. That being said, I have a condom in my wallet for added protection…for you."

Sharing that information wasn't a mood-killer like it easily could've been. Instead, knowing this man wanted to protect her in every way made Brynnon fall for him a little more.

"I'm clean, too," she blurted, quickly adding, "And I'm on the pill. I stayed on it to keep things regulated, but I promise it's been a really long time since I've been with anyone. Like, over a year."

A corner of his mouth turned into a delectable smirk. "I could tell."

"Oh." Fire burned inside her cheeks.

Running his knuckles along her blushing skin, he assured her, "I didn't say that to embarrass you, Bryn. I fucking love how tight you felt around my fingers."

Heat crawled up Brynnon's neck, but this time it was more from arousal than embarrassment. "Well," she smiled. "I'm glad you enjoyed yourself."

Grant threw his head back, barking out with laughter. "Oh, Princess. You have no idea how much." She barely had time to enjoy the rare smile before he slid his hand to the back of her neck. With his mouth almost touching hers, he whispered, "I'm going to enjoy what happens now, even more."

"Me, too," she nodded. Deciding to take the lead, Brynnon leaned up and kissed him. With their mouths deliciously occupied, she began to unbutton his crisp, white shirt. When she got to his waistband, Grant helped out by pulling it loose and shrugging it off his shoulders.

Tossing it onto the chair with his jacket, he stood still, giving her time to look at him the way he had her. With the soft light behind him, it was too dark to make out the details, but she finally got her first look at the tattoo that had been teasing her for days.

Covering his right shoulder, the markings ran the entire length of his arm. She never really pictured herself a tat gal, but holy *hell*, that was sexy.

She could tell he had a couple other tattoos on his chest, but again, it was too dark to see exactly what they were. The larger one was centered on Grant's left peck, and there was a smaller one just over his heart.

Brynnon made a mental note to look at them all more closely later, but right now, she was too busy taking in his magnificent body. The man looked like a God, his muscles so detailed they almost didn't look real.

Unable to keep from it, she placed both hands over his chest. Her fingertips burned from his natural heat as they slowly made their way lower, over his impressive six-pack. Grant's muscles flexed beneath her touch.

"You're so beautiful," she whispered softly.

"So are you."

Her eyes rose to his again, and this time, when she reached for his belt, he didn't stop her. Pulling the tight leather loose from the buckle, Brynnon immediately went to work on the formal pants' metal clasps and inner button before slowly lowering his zipper.

The stuttered metallic sound seemed deafening in the silent room, it's only company their heavy breathing. When she got to the end, Brynnon reached for his loosened waistband, but he took over.

With his hands at his waist, Grant removed both his pants and boxers at the same time. Once they were free from his legs, he threw them back onto the chair, as well.

His erection was even larger than she'd expected, the sight leaving Brynnon speechless. Her sex clenched with anticipation as she focused on his cock. It was full and angry looking, pointing toward her as though it knew the way.

Brynnon stood there, relishing in the fact that—at least for tonight—this perfect male specimen was hers.

"I'm not gonna last, you keep looking at me like that."

His voice snapped her out of the sexual trance. "Sorry," she lied.

"Don't be. Later, after this first time, I'll let you look as long as you want."

First time? So he was planning on a repeat performance. Good to know.

"For now, though," he continued talking. "We really need to lose this dress."

With a smirk, Brynnon took care of the issue herself. With a quick pull, she released the bow behind her neck before reaching around to lower the short zipper resting against her lower back.

Letting the top fall loose, Brynnon pushed the dress and what was left of her lace panties down the length of her legs. Stepping out of the belled poof of material, she stood straight, completely naked and unashamed.

Like any woman, she had her flaws. But Brynnon also knew she'd been blessed with pretty good genes. Those, along with the physical labor her job often entailed and the occasional run, kept her body toned and at a healthy weight for her height.

"Holy fuck." Grant froze, his eyes widening slightly.

Brynnon smiled. "Like what you see?"

He stared back at her hungrily. "Like isn't exactly the word I'd use."

"Maybe you should just show me how much you like it."

Her words spurred something inside him and before Brynnon knew what was happening, she found herself being lifted back into his arms. A man on a mission, Grant carried her over to the bed where he laid her down gently.

The mattress dipped below her as he crawled onto the bed. Leaning down, he kissed her before giving a soft warning.

"This first time isn't going to last very long."

"That's okay." She cupped his rough cheek. "You've already taken care of me, so this part should be about you."

"Wrong." He shook his head. "I can't wait to be inside you, but there's something I have to do first."

For a second, she thought maybe he was talking about getting the condom, but then Grant began sliding his body lower, leaving hot, wet kisses in his wake. Brynnon's pulse began to race when she realized his true intentions.

Spreading her legs wide for him, Grant made a guttural moan of satisfaction when he settled himself between her thighs. His hot breath puffed against her bare sex and though he'd already made her come once—and recently—her body ached for his touch.

As though he could read her mind, Grant began lazily tracing her slit with his finger before adding his other hand and parting her folds. Without warning, he leaned up and ran his tongue along her opening.

Brynnon cried out, her body reacting instantly. On reflex, her pelvis rose to meet his every touch. She moaned, writhing beneath his mouth. Her hands fisted the bedding at her sides as Grant mercilessly continued lapping up juices he alone had created.

"Jesus," his deep voice vibrated against her swollen pussy. "Never tasted anything like it."

His words sent another rush of arousal to her entrance, and Grant moaned loudly as he licked her clean. The sounds he made and the soft, gentle way he was touching her was like a road map to his deepest desires.

"Grant, please," she begged. "I want you inside me."

"Not done," he growled, continuing his exquisite torture. "Need you ready."

Brynnon squeezed the blankets tighter. "Trust me," she

panted. "I'm more than ready."

"Almost."

The single word response was her only warning before he speared her with one of his large fingers. Brynnon cried out again, her head bowing back against the soft mattress as he pumped in and out of her body like before.

He growled again, the sound bringing her focus back on him. Like the operative he was, Grant's entire concentration was on the task at hand...Literally.

With hungry eyes, he watched his finger pumping in and out of her body. With his head between her legs, Grant remained intently focused on her pleasure. Knowing that brought *him* pleasure aroused her even more.

Adding a second finger, Grant leaned down and swiped her clit with the tip of his tongue.

"Grant!" she practically shouted his name. When her lower belly began to tingle, Brynnon knew she was about to come again. "I'm so close."

Hearing this, he pumped his fingers harder. Faster. His tongue pressed down, flicking her bundle of nerves a few times before Grant wrapped his lips around it and sucked.

Brynnon's hips shot off the bed, her sex pushing against his mouth as she flew into a million pieces. Moving quickly, Grant replaced his fingers with his tongue, licking and sucking every single drop flooding her core.

She was still flying high when she felt him get off the bed. With her eyes closed, she could hear his soft footsteps as he padded across the room, presumably to retrieve the condom. Sure enough, she heard the telltale sound of foil being ripped open.

Greedy, Brynnon opened her eyes back up just in time to see Grant rolling the thin protection over his solid length.

The hard shaft bobbed as he walked back to the bed and crawled over her body again.

Brynnon smiled up at him. "Thank you."

Chuckling, Grant shook his head. "I should be thanking you." He brushed some hair from her cheek. "Seeing you fall apart like that was the most beautiful fucking thing in the world."

For the second time since coming into this room, Brynnon was rendered speechless.

"You ready?"

Brynnon nodded. "Definitely."

With his eyes locked on hers, Grant leveled himself on one elbow. Reaching between their bodies, he lined his hot, blunt tip against her sensitive opening and began to press his hips forward.

Despite the fact that he'd primed her body—twice—Grant was well above-average size, so it took a few tries to get the tip in. Once that happened, he slid his cock all the way inside, not stopping until he was fully seated.

His body stretched hers to the point of a pleasurable pain, and they moaned in unison from the glorious sensation. She'd never felt so full. So right.

With his weight on both his elbows, Grant whispered in her ear. "You okay?"

She nodded, her hair brushing softly against her pillow. "I'll be better once you start moving."

A rush of heated air hit the side of her face as he laughed silently. "Whatever you want," he told her. And then he began to move.

Grant slid himself in and out. Brynnon's fingernails dug into his back, her hips rising in time with his. They moved slowly at first, enjoying the way their bodies felt together…as one.

Soon, Grant's breath became more strained and Brynnon's huffed in and out with more force than before. He thrust inside her with more speed, his movements becoming rougher, but not too much so.

The rooms filled with sounds of sex. Masculine moans and soft purrs of pleasure. Loud exhales and skin slapping together. Wet heat meeting with hard steel.

Though she never would have thought it could happen, Brynnon felt a magnificent pressure building for a third time. As if he could sense it, Grant slid a hand down the outside of her leg and lifted her knee.

Shifting his hips, she gasped loudly when she felt his body rubbing against the exact right spot. Brynnon dug her heel against his taut ass.

"Jesus," Grant panted. "Come on, baby." He slammed into her. "That's it." Another thrust. "Come for me."

"Grant!"

"Ah, fuck!"

Every muscle in their bodies tensed, their climaxes hitting simultaneously. Tiny, white stars flashed behind Brynnon's closed eyes, and she held on tight while Grant finished his ride. Pulling every ounce of pleasure from them both, his movements eventually slowed. Their bodies becoming relaxed.

Brynnon lay there, more satisfied than ever before, while Grant gently released himself and went to take care of the condom. She was still floating when he made his return.

Without a word, Grant lifted her from the mattress, pulled down the covers, and tucked her in. Like before, he crawled in beside her, pulling her body flush with his.

Rough hair tickled her bottom as he leaned over and pressed his lips to her temple. "Goodnight, Princess."

Brynnon's whispered, "Goodnight," was the last thing she remembered before falling into a deep sleep.

Chapter 16

Grant woke to a soft, barely-there touch. Lying on his stomach, he kept his eyes closed and forced himself not to smile. If he did, if Brynnon knew he was awake, she might stop.

Doing his best to control his breathing, Grant remained perfectly still while she continued tracing the tattoo on his back with her fingertip. The large, feathered wing covered the upper right portion of his back and shoulder, flowing seamlessly into the full sleeve encasing his entire right arm before stopping at the wrist.

He knew she'd ask about it the second he woke. Surprisingly, he didn't find the idea of sharing more of himself with her as scary as before. Probably had something to do with the mind-blowing sex they'd had.

Christ, he'd never felt anything like her before. Sure, he'd had his share of women, and always left satisfied, but what he'd felt last night with Brynnon? It was fucking indescribable.

The sex, itself was hands-down the best he'd ever experienced. But it had been more than just sex. Much more.

When Grant slid inside her welcoming body, it felt as if

he'd finally found the one place he belonged. Not only was their physical connection stronger than he could've imagined, the emotions he felt both during and after were unlike anything he'd ever known.

One night, and he was already questioning his ability to walk away once this job was over.

Brynnon's fingertip hit a particularly sensitive spot causing Grant to move away on reflex.

"So you *are* awake." There was humor in her husky voice. "And apparently ticklish."

"Don't even think about," he warned, his own voice rough from sleep.

She giggled but didn't press her luck by tickling him more. Instead, she surprised him with, "You got this for your mom, didn't you?"

Grant swallowed, then nodded. "On the year anniversary of her death."

"It's beautiful." She traced another feather. "Must've taken a long time to do."

"It took a few sessions. Started with the back and worked my way around."

"Is she the one who taught you to dance?"

"She was."

He rolled over so he could see her face, his breath catching in his throat at what he saw. At some point she'd taken her hair down from the style she'd had it in last night. Now, the tussled, auburn waves fell over her shoulders and beyond.

Jesus, she's gorgeous first thing in the morning.

Leaning on one elbow, Brynnon was quiet for a moment before asking, "Why the waltz?"

Grant rolled his eyes, his chest rising with the deep breath he took. "The school I went to had this stupid prom tradition. Every year, the Junior class had to do a traditional waltz as the first dance of the night. Everyone's parents would stay and watch and then leave once it was done. I think it all started in the early nineteen hundreds or something."

Brynnon smiled wide. "I think that's a fabulous tradition."

"You would."

Her jaw dropped. Feigning offense, she teasingly slapped his chest. "Hey!"

Grant chuckled. "*Anyway,* in the weeks before my Junior prom, my mom forced me to learn how to do the waltz." A corner of his mouth curled up at what was now one of his most treasured memories. "Every night after dinner, we'd push the table and chairs against the wall, and dance in the middle of the kitchen."

"She was an excellent teacher. I bet she loved watching you and your date on the dance floor."

A familiar pain struck his heart. "She didn't see me."

She raised a brow. "Please tell me you didn't chicken out."

"She didn't see me dance because I didn't go to my junior prom."

Confused, Brynnon asked, "Why not?"

The memory was damn near as painful as the night it happened. Still, he found himself wanting to share it with her. "I came home from school that day and found her on the living room floor. She was unresponsive."

"Oh, Grant. I'm so sorry."

"I picked her up and carried her to my car. Drove like a bat out of hell across town to the hospital. They made me wait in the hallway even though I fought like mad to stay with her. I sat there, alone and waiting for what felt like hours. Prayed harder than I ever have for her to be okay. But, when the doctor came out of the room, I could see it on his face. Knew even before he said the words that she was gone."

Brynnon's eyes filled with unshed tears. "That must have been awful."

"Yeah. It was."

Her smile surprised him. "Your mother would have been so proud of the way you danced last night."

And just like that, she took some of the sting away. Lifting his head, Grant pressed his lips to hers in a short, sweet kiss. "Thank you."

"This is the SEAL Trident, right?" Her hand brushed across the artwork on his right pec.

"It is," he answered. "Got it right after BUD/s."

Brynnon's eyes fell on the small, broken heart covering his own. Grant prayed she couldn't see how hard it was beating as he wondered what the hell to say next.

"Is that for your mom, too?" she asked, slowly tracing the dark, jagged edges.

His chest tightened. Part of him knew he'd have to talk about it at some point, but he'd always assumed it would be with one of the guys. *She should know.*

The tiny voice was right. If he had any thoughts at all about starting an actual relationship with this woman, she needed to know the truth.

"It's for my son."

A set of wide eyes shot to his. "You have a *son?*"

"Would have."

Understanding sadness washed over her. "You lost him."

No, he was fucking ripped away. "In a manner of speaking."

She hesitated before asking, "What happened?"

The pressure in his chest increased, but soon Grant heard himself sharing the whole, twisted story.

"You asked me once if I'd ever been married. I haven't, but I came close once. About nine years ago."

Grant became focused on a lock of hair brushing against his skin. Taking it between his thumb and forefinger, he concentrated on that. Brynnon stayed quiet, giving him the time he needed to get through this.

"Her name was Baylee. I met her two years before I left the Teams. She was the only serious relationship I've ever been in." *Biggest mistake of my life.* "We'd been dating about eight months when I asked her to move in with me. She'd just started law school, and I was making enough, so I told her I'd cover the expenses so she could focus on her schoolwork."

"That was nice of you."

"I was an idiot."

With a scowl, Brynnon asked, "Why do you say that?"

Grant filled his lungs before letting the air out slowly. "I'd planned to propose on our year anniversary. The week before, our team was granted an unexpected leave. I didn't tell Baylee. Thought it would be fun to surprise her. Turns out, the surprise was on me."

He pressed his lips together, the anger he still felt towards the other woman very much present. "I walked into the house we were renting and found it empty. Furniture, dishes…even the fucking toilet paper was gone."

Brynnon's jaw dropped again. "You're kidding."

"Wish I was."

"What a bitch."

A low chuckle escaped from his chest. "You have no idea."

"Did she at least leave a note or something explaining why she left?"

"Oh, she left a note. Along with a pile of bills she'd racked up while I was off busting my ass, including two credit cards she'd opened in my name and then maxed out."

"That's horrible." Brynnon shook her head. "What did the note say?"

"That she wasn't cut out to be a military wife after all. Or, a mother. That part confused me. She was on the pill and in school and I was always gone, so we figured we'd wait a while. It wasn't until a different bill came to the house with her name on it that I understood what she meant. It was from a women's clinic located a couple towns over." Grant swallowed against the painful knot in his throat.

"She had an abortion," Brynnon whispered the words he couldn't bear to say out loud.

He nodded, blinking away the moisture suddenly forming in his eyes. "I didn't even know she was pregnant. I drove straight to the clinic, expecting them to slam the door in my face, but Baylee had put me down as her emergency contact and had initialed the box stating they could share her information. I don't think she really cared if I found out after the fact, because she knew she'd already be gone." His jaw clenched. "Anyway, they told me everything."

Pausing, Grant gave himself a moment to regroup before continuing on. "She was about ten weeks along, which meant she got pregnant shortly after we moved in together. She'd gotten sick the week before we moved in, and the doctors had prescribed some antibiotics. Apparently, they can affect the strength with which certain birth controls work." He shook his head. "The doctor I spoke to said he was required to do detailed lab work prior to the procedure, in case anything concerning came back. That's how he knew it was a boy."

Twin tears ran down her cheeks. "I don't even know what to say."

"Nothing to say, Princess." He wiped the moisture from her face before tucking some wayward curls behind her ear. "It was a long time ago." With a deep, cleansing breath, he pointed to the small tattoo. "But, that's why I got this. To help me remember."

Brynnon leaned up and pressed her sweet lips to the small tattoo. "And that's why you drew so many lines," she whispered softly. "To protect your broken heart."

A broken heart that, miraculously, was starting to heal. "I've never told anyone that story."

This surprised her. "Not even Jake or Coop?"

"No one knows."

Emotion filled her eyes and she kissed his chest again. "Thank you for trusting me with it."

If he wasn't careful, he'd end up trusting her with everything he had. *You already do.*

Knowing that was one line he wasn't ready to cross, Grant pulled gently on her shoulders. "Come here."

With a smile, she obeyed and for the next hour, he did everything he could to replace the bad memories floating in his head with some that were new. And hotter than hell.

****

Later that afternoon, Brynnon found herself walking aimlessly around the showroom floor looking at furniture she was never going to buy.

Following Grant's emotional memory purge and an hour of toe-curling morning sex, she'd spent several hours locked away in her home office trying to catch up on some work.

249

When the furniture store had called to let her know the bedroom set she'd ordered was ready to be picked up, Grant had offered to load it in his truck and drive them to the cabin.

After a quick session of overnight packing, she was now waiting alone while Grant and a couple of workers loaded everything into the back of his truck. She'd offered to help, but it had gotten noticeably colder, and she'd forgotten to grab her coat. Naturally, her overprotective guard had insisted she stay inside.

Out of the corner of her eye, Brynnon noticed a gorgeous, cherry wood baby crib. Her thoughts immediately turned to Grant and the loss he'd suffered. She still had a hard time imagining the pain he'd felt when he found out what his ex had done.

After he'd told her the story, she'd wanted to ask him whether he'd ever considered having children in the future. In the end, Brynnon had held back, fearing he would assume she was thinking that same future may include her. As much as she loved the idea, the last thing she wanted to do was to scare him off.

More thoughts of lost children had her mind turning to Charles Wright. Brynnon wondered if he'd heard from the private investigator and made a mental note to ask Grant if anyone on his team had found out anything more.

Brynnon was still lost in those swirling thoughts when a familiar voice rang out from behind her.

"I thought that was you."

She turned around and forced a smile. "Lucas. What a coincidence."

Her ex grinned. "I thought the same thing when I saw you. What brings you here?"

"Oh, I'm just waiting for them to load some furniture I ordered."

"Same. You doing some redecorating or is it for staging your next property?"

"Neither, actually. It's for my new place."

His brow furrowed a bit. "You're moving?"

"I am. I bought a cabin a few months ago, and I've been using my free time to fix it up."

"A cabin? Sounds quaint."

He's still a pretentious bastard. "It is. The area's pretty secluded so it's quiet. Very peaceful."

"That'll be a big change from Dallas, for sure."

"We're done loading." Grant said curtly as he approached them both.

Relieved, Brynnon nodded. "Look who I ran into."

"Twice in as many days," Grant observed. "That's quite a coincidence."

"That's what I told him."

Lucas held out his hand. "Grant, right? Good to see you again."

Grant accepted the handshake, though Brynnon could tell he didn't really want to. Without responding to the other man's comment, he looked over at her.

"You ready?"

Sensing he was more than ready to get out of here, Brynnon nodded again. "Yeah. Sure."

The other man tipped his chin. "Hopefully, I'll see you again, soon."

"The truck's running." Grant placed a gentle hand on Brynnon's elbow.

"O-oh. Okay." She looked at Luke from over her shoulder. "Good luck with your furniture."

Lucas gave her a sideways grin. "Same to you."

The second they were out the doors, Brynnon turned to Grant, asking, "Why are you in such a hurry?"

"I don't like that guy." Grant opened the passenger door for her.

"I don't either, but *I* actually have a reason." Brynnon climbed up inside.

Waiting until he was in the cab with her, Grant put the truck in gear and started to drive before responding. "I do, too."

"Yeah. It's called jealousy. And I already told you, I was only being polite for the sake of the charity. Nothing more."

Grant grunted. "I just don't trust him. I don't think you should, either."

Brynnon laughed. "I don't. But not because I think he's out to get me. That man may be a Class-A jerk, but Lucas doesn't have the balls to physically hurt someone. His being here is just a coincidence."

"I don't believe in coincidences."

Brynnon scowled. "Is that a SEAL thing or a R.I.S.C. thing?"

"Both."

Sighing, she settled back against the seat. "Seems like a pretty cynical way to live."

Grant slid his eyes to her then back to the road. "When you do what I do, Bryn, it's the *only* way to live."

She supposed he was right. Not a lot of room for second-guessing in his line of work.

They drove for a couple of miles before he spoke again. "I forgot to tell you, Derek called while you were upstairs working. He still hasn't been able to locate Mitchell, the P.I. Wright hired, so he called his brother." Grant looked over at her. "Eric's a detective with the DPD."

"Okay," Brynnon nodded.

Grant continued, giving her a more thorough explanation. "Derek told Eric about the threats and what happened with the car. He also relayed what Wright shared with us. Eric got in touch with one of his contacts with the Phoenix P.D. and they're working to find Mitchell."

"Sounds good."

"I also gave Derek the address to the cabin so he'd know where we'll be."

Memories of the close call with the car began to seep in. "Okay."

Grant reached over and took her hand in his. "We'll get to the bottom of this soon, Bryn. I promise."

When they got to the cabin, the first thing Grant did was make sure it was safe and secure. Next, they worked together to move the mess from the fallen scaffolding into the small shed located a few feet from the house before finally carrying in the new pieces she'd purchased.

A little over an hour later, her bedroom was set up exactly as she wanted it.

"Well," Grant turned to her from the foot of the bed. "What do you think?"

"I think"—she walked toward him— "we should test it out."

With a knowing grin, he stared back at her. "Test it out, huh?"

Brynnon shrugged. "Sure. I mean, we need to make sure it's secure."

"And just how do you propose we do that?"

"Oh, I have a few things in mind."

Using her fingertip, she reached up and pushed against his

chest. Though he could've easily stood his ground, Grant let himself fall backward onto the bed.

Brynnon lifted her sweater up over her head, letting it fall somewhere on the floor next to her. Heat flooded his eyes. With his hands resting behind his head, Grant watched while she unlatched her bra.

"You gonna do something about those, or do I have to do that, too?" Brynnon asked, referring to his pants.

Smiling, Grant toed off his boots and reached for his belt. Within seconds, the two had discarded every scrap of clothing and Grant was rolling a condom down his long, hard length.

Not wasting time, Brynnon climbed onto the bed, straddling his strong thighs. In the mood to take full control, she put her mouth to his and lifted to her knees. With her hand wrapped around him, she quickly lined the hot, blunt tip to her core and began slowly sinking down.

A low, guttural moan traveled from Grant's throat, combining with her own as she filled herself with his pulsating cock. The position made her feel even fuller than before, something she hadn't thought possible.

Grant's hands wrapped around her narrow hips as he lifted his pelvis to meet hers. Brynnon broke away from the kiss. With her palms pressed against his impressive chest, she pushed herself into a sitting position.

Undulating her hips forward and back, she began riding him in a way that brought them both the ultimate pleasure. With him seated more deeply inside her than ever before, Grant's shaft reached places it had never been.

Moaning loudly, she let her head fall back. Grant's body thrust forcefully against hers, causing Brynnon to cry out in ecstasy.

"Yes!" She praised him. "You feel so good."

Inner muscles quivered. Their bodies began to move faster, Grant forcefully pistoned himself in and out of her soaking heat.

"You're already close," he stated, his voice strained. "I can feel it."

He was right. Brynnon felt the telltale tingling building deep inside her. She was almost there, she just needed a little push.

Lifting one of her hands from his chest, she slid it to where they were connected and began circling her swollen clit with her fingertips.

"Fuck, yeah," Grant grunted with approval. "Jesus, that's hot."

His words encouraged her, the pads of her fingers pressing down harder. Moving faster. Brynnon cried out again and could feel Grant becoming impossibly larger while he continued pumping himself in and out of her body.

Hot breath heaved from their chests as they each worked to bring the other to the edge. Grant's fingers dug into her hips. Brynnon knew he was probably bruising her pale skin, but didn't care. The thought of this man marking her in such a primal way brought her nothing but pure, female satisfaction.

"I'm not gonna last," he warned her, his words escaping with each mind-blowing thrust. "Hurry...make yourself come again."

Obeying, Brynnon rubbed herself faster, her fingertips moving in small, tight circles. A shiver of pleasure ran the length of her spine, her body jerking with impending explosion.

With his eyes locked on hers, he panted out, "That's it, baby. Let go."

Brynnon threw her head back, crying out his name as her climax hit. She could feel her body clamping down over his, the strength of her orgasm sending Grant straight into his own.

"Brynnon!" He growled, his body tensing beneath hers. Grant's hips jerked uncontrollably, thrusting in and out a few more times until he was finally spent.

Falling back onto the mattress, he released a loud, satisfied breath. With him still inside her, Brynnon leaned down and kissed him softly before resting one side of her face over his pounding heart.

"I think you killed me," his voice rumbled against her cheek.

Brynnon smiled. "At least we went together."

A low laugh reverberated inside his chest. The room had just gone quiet again when Brynnon's stomach growled loudly.

"Sounds like you worked up quite an appetite."

"I'm starved." She lifted her head to look at him. "We could leave now and go get something. Or, there are some frozen pizzas in the freezer downstairs. I could go pop in a couple before we head out."

Just then, Grant's phone beeped with a sound she didn't recognize. Though she hated to break their connection, Brynnon climbed off. Reaching down to where he'd left his jeans, Grant pulled his phone from the pocket and looked at the screen.

"Doesn't look like we're heading out anytime soon." He turned the phone so she could see.

"A snowstorm?" Her head swung toward the window. "I

thought there was only a *slight* chance for snow tonight."

Dressing in a rush, Brynnon walked over to the window facing the drive. Sure enough, it had already snowed over half an inch with no signs of stopping. "Well, crap."

From behind her, Grant said, "Pizza, it is."

Chapter 17

With snow halfway up his boots, Grant swung the axe, its blade splitting the log right down the center with an echoing crack.

Not only had the meteorologists gotten the forecast wrong, they'd done so in spectacular fashion. Rather than a dusting to an inch, as they'd first predicted, northern Texas had been hit with a record-breaking snowstorm, forcing them to stay at the cabin for the past two days.

Brynnon had access to plenty of firewood, which helped keep the place warm. She'd been keeping a few extra sets of clothes in her closet already, so she was good in that department. As for him, Grant was thankful she had a washer and dryer.

With enough coffee and frozen shit in the freezer to keep them fed for the foreseeable future, food wasn't much of an issue, either. Although, Grant didn't know how she ate that processed crap on a regular basis.

According to the highway patrol reports, the roads were almost cleared, so he and Bryn were planning on heading back to the city later today. He'd just wanted to make sure she had more wood cut and stacked for the next time she came back here.

A twinge of disappointment shot through him as he thought about having to go back to Dallas. He never thought it would have been possible, but Grant had enjoyed these last few days with her.

For two and a half days, they'd done nothing but make love, sleep, and eat. They christened nearly every space in the cabin.

The bed. The shower. The couch.

Grant couldn't seem to get enough of the fiery woman, and from the way she reacted each time he touched her, Brynnon felt the same about him. Domestic bliss hadn't been anywhere in his future plans, but after being locked away with her these last few days, Grant had to admit...the idea was becoming more and more appealing.

He smiled, cracking another log in two. Throwing the pieces in the pile with the others, he'd just started to reach for another when he felt something hit one side of his ass with a dull thud.

Spinning around, he saw Brynnon standing about five yards away. She was in jeans, her brown work boots, and a spare coat and gloves she forgot she'd left.

Her long hair was down, spilling well past her shoulders and she stared back at him, smiling. The vixen looked guilty as hell, but not sorry in the least.

"Told you I'd get you back for that swat you gave me the other day."

Grant leaned the axe against the large cutting log. "Don't even think about it."

Locking eyes with his, Brynnon bent over and scooped up another handful of snow. "What's the matter, big guy? You scared of a little snow?"

Damn, he loved how playful she was. "You're gonna start something you can't finish, Princess." He knew she was going to throw it before it even left her hand.

Brynnon drew her arm back and let the frozen ball fly. It hit him center mass, exactly where she'd been aiming.

Rolling his lips inward, Grant used his gloved hand to brush the moisture from the front of his coat. "Just remember," he cautioned. "You were warned."

With lightning speed, he picked up some snow, packed it into a ball, and threw it back at her. Brynnon squealed and ducked, the ball skimming the top of her hair as it flew past.

"Ha!" she taunted. "You missed!"

Simultaneously, they both gathered more snow and began lobbing the balls at one another. Some hit their target while others were narrowly avoided. Brynnon moved in closer as she continued her attempt to take down the enemy not realizing her mistake until it was too late.

The second she was within reaching distance, Grant swung his hand out. She screamed, trying to fight him off, but it was too late.

Wrapping his arm around her waist, Grant pulled a laughing Brynnon to him. He was just about to secure his hold when the thick sole of his boot slipped in the wet snow and they both began to fall.

Doing his best to keep from crushing her, Grant threw his other arm out to the side for leverage. The pair landed on the ground, the impact almost silent as the thick, soft snow broke their fall.

With her body beneath his, Brynnon dissolved into laughter. The sound sparked his own amusement, and soon the two were laughing together.

Out of the corner of his eye, Grant noticed an SUV

pulling into the drive. On instinct, he pushed himself up and started to draw his gun, but realized who was behind the wheel.

Adrenaline rushed through him as he blew out a breath and helped Brynnon to her feet. When he saw the look of fear she was giving him, Grant silently cursed. "It's just Derek."

Her relief was palpable and he felt like an ass for scaring her the way he had. Of course, he felt like an even bigger idiot for allowing them both to become so vulnerable.

What the fuck were you thinking?

He couldn't believe how stupid he'd been. Grant had been so busy playing around with her in the snow, someone could've snuck up through the trees or opened fire from the road and they would never have known what hit them.

He looked at her as she smiled over at the other man walking toward them. Pain entered his chest at just the thought of something happening to her. Especially on his watch.

Get your head back in the game, jackass.

"Looks like you two are actually enjoyin' this shit."

"Hey, Derek," Brynnon chuckled. "And yes. I love it."

Derek looked over at him and shook his head. "She's nuts."

"I am not." Grant watched as she looked up at the snow-covered trees surrounding them. "How could you not love this? It's beautiful."

"It's cold and wet," Derek grumbled. "It also makes it damn near impossible for me to drive my beautiful car, which is why I had to borrow one of R.I.S.C.'s."

"Why are you here?" Grant asked bluntly.

Brynnon gave him a look, and he knew she was confused

by his sudden change in mood.

Derek smirked. "Nice to see you, too, buddy."

Rather than call him out on it in front of his teammate, Brynnon covered it with a smile. "Speaking of cold, my pants are soaked. I'm going to go change into something dry. I'll put on a fresh pot of coffee for us while I'm at it."

"Sounds great." Derek grinned. "Thanks."

"No problem." With another quick glance in his direction, she turned and headed back to the cabin.

Grant waited until she was inside before speaking. "You must've found something important, otherwise you would've just called."

"Very perceptive." Derek reached into his coat and pulled out a file. "Our P.I. is officially missin', and it doesn't look good. Eric's contact got back with him. No one's seen or heard from Mitchell in several days. There's no sign of his car, his phone is untraceable, and his mail's stacked in front of his apartment door."

Not wanting to jump to conclusions, Grant said, "Could've gotten caught up with another job."

"That's what I thought until I hacked into the guy's bank account. There hasn't been any activity since the day he was last seen. Not his checking, savings, or credit cards. And there are no records of any recent cash withdrawals, which he would need in order to stay off the grid."

Grant sighed. "Damn. That's not a good sign."

"Nope. Eric's contact is going to keep lookin'. In the meantime, the guy was able to get me access to Hank Mitchell's computer." Derek tipped his chin toward the folder. "That's everything the P.I. had on the bridge collapse and Cantrell Construction. He'd deleted the file, but like most people, the guy didn't realize deletin' somethin' doesn't actually make it go away." He looked back toward the cabin then to Grant. "I haven't had a chance to look through it all, but from what I can tell, Wright was tellin' the truth."

"What do you mean?"

"Take a look at the P.O.'s."

Grant opened the file and glanced over the documents. "Am I supposed to know what I'm looking for?"

"See the dates and company Cantrell supposedly ordered the supplies from? Those are all for the bridge in Kunar."

Grant's brows turned inward. "What's your point? We already knew they built the bridge."

"I accessed the listed buyer's records to see if they matched. They don't."

"What's off about them?" He looked back up at his teammate.

"Everything. There's no record of that company havin' ever received an order for those supplies on those dates. Not from Cantrell Construction or any other buyer I could find."

Grant studied the P.O.'s. again. "So what are you saying? These are fake?"

"Looks that way."

Shit. "The only reason someone within the Senator's company would falsify purchase orders would be to cover something up."

Derek's expression became grim. "Exactly."

"We need to find out where they got the materials to build that fucking bridge."

"From everything I've found so far, that's where Mitchell's investigation was headed when he disappeared."

Grant closed the folder. "We figure out which company actually supplied those materials, they should be able to point us to the person responsible for the collapse."

"Whoever it is knows what we know. Probably more. That's why they're comin' after Cantrell."

"Wrong." Grant's chest tightened as he thought of the her being in danger. "They're coming after Brynnon."

A shadow fell over Derek's eyes, the situation most likely reminding him of when his fiancée was in danger. Thankfully, Charlie and Derek no longer had to worry about her sick-as-fuck ex.

With a slight hush to his southern voice, Derek asked, "Do you want to keep this information a secret for now?"

A big part of Grant wanted to do just that. The emotional side that had only just begun to come alive again wanted to shelter Brynnon from anything that could cause her pain. Physical or otherwise. But he knew she'd be pissed as hell if they kept something like this from her.

"No." He shook his head. "She deserves to know the truth."

Derek nodded in agreement before saying, "Speakin' of the gorgeous redhead. Did my eyes deceive me, or were you actually *laughin'* when I pulled up?"

Grant stepped past him heading for the cabin. "Don't start."

"Oh, come on, man. You had to know I was gonna to ask. So tell me…is it just sex or did the great Grant Hill finally thaw out enough to actually start to care about a woman?"

Turning back around to face him, Grant shook his head. "What's going on with Brynnon and me is none of your goddamn business."

"Whoa." Derek put his hands palms-up. "You don't have to get so defensive."

"I'm not getting defensive," Grant lied.

"The fuck you aren't. Jesus, you sound like you're…"

Derek's blue eyes grew wide. "Holy shit. Are you in love with her?"

"Thanks for the file, dickhead." Grant started to turn, but the other man grabbed the sleeve of his coat.

"You didn't say no. Interesting."

"There's nothing interesting about it. I'm guarding her. Period."

"That doesn't mean you can't fall in love in the process. Trust me."

Grant worked to control his growing frustration. "I'm not having this conversation."

"Oh, my god." Derek covered his mouth in shock. "You *do* love her!"

Grant swung his gaze to the closed door and back. "Keep your voice down, for fuck's sake."

Not bothering to heed his warning, Derek started to laugh. "This is…I don't even…this is *huge*."

"No. It's not."

Glancing down toward Grant's crotch, the smart-ass winced. "It's not? Damn. Sorry about your bad luck."

"Jesus Christ, can you be serious for one goddamn minute?" Fed up with the man's juvenile behavior, Grant got into Derek's face. Forgetting to keep his own voice down he blurted out, "Yes, we slept together. Was it against protocol? Definitely. Was it a mistake? Probably. Does having sex with Brynnon a few times mean I love her? Hell, no."

Before Derek could respond, both men heard the soft sound of someone clearing their throat from behind him. Grant closed his eyes, his hands fisting at his sides.

Shit. Fuck. Shit.

Though he had zero desire to do so, he turned to face her. She was standing at the top of the porch steps with her arms crossed protectively around her midsection. The devastation staring back at him was clear.

She'd heard every fucking word he'd said.

"I just came out to tell you the coffee's ready." Without waiting, she turned her back on him and walked away.

"Damn, man. I'm sorry. I didn't see her come out or I'd have stopped you."

Grant wanted to blame his friend, but it wasn't Derek's fault. It was one hundred percent his.

"Can you stay with her a couple hours?"

"Wait, you're leavin'?"

"It's for the best." He ground his teeth together, more pissed at himself than ever before. "I didn't hear you pull up until you were already parking. Didn't hear her come outside just now."

"Don't beat yourself up, G. You just got distracted for a minute, that's all. Happens to the best of us."

He whipped his head around. "Not to me, it doesn't. I won't put her at risk because my head's not in the fucking game." Grant inhaled deeply. "Besides. I'm pretty sure after hearing me run my mouth, she'll be more than happy to see me go."

"Whatever you want to do, man. I've got your back."

Nodding, Grant mumbled, "Give me a minute."

Once inside, he found Brynnon standing in the kitchen. Her eyes were red and her adorable-as-fuck nose flush, both telltale signs she'd been crying.

Motherfucker.

Removing his gloves, Grant set them on the table before trying to explain his way out of the giant mess he'd made. "Brynnon, I—"

"Don't apologize." She stared up at him, the light in her

gorgeous eyes dimmed. "It's not like we made each other any promises or anything."

He ran a hand over his jaw. "What you heard...I was just pissed at myself and—"

"You don't owe me an explanation, Grant," she cut him off again. "After all, you warned me. From the start, you said you weren't the man for me. I guess I thought maybe..." She shook her head, swallowing back emotions he knew she didn't want him to see. Her smile didn't come close to reaching her eyes. "You know what? It doesn't matter. The last couple of days have been fun, but that's all it was, right? Fun. Now, it's over, and we can go back to the way things should've stayed. With you as my bodyguard and me as your client."

Brynnon turned to dump her coffee down the drain as Grant went to get his things. When he came back downstairs, she was still standing in the kitchen. Staring at the window, she didn't turn around when she spoke.

"You're leaving, aren't you?"

Grant's heart hurt knowing he'd caused her pain, another validation that he was making the right decision.

"I called Coop. Derek will stay with you until I can get to your father's office to relieve him."

Even from behind, he could feel the disappointment rolling off of her.

"Fine."

Goddamn it, he needed her to understand. "I let myself become distracted. By you...by us. I can't"—he shook his head— "I can't risk you getting hurt because I'm too lost in what's happening between us to see the threat." When she remained silent, he added, "I can't protect you like this, Princess."

"Don't call me that." Brynnon spun around, glaring back at him. "And there hasn't been any sign of danger since we spoke to Wright and his daughter, so don't try to pretend you're leaving for anyone else but yourself." She stormed past him, parting with a final, "You know the way out."

Grant stood there, quietly watching as she walked up the stairs. It wasn't until the bedroom door slammed behind her that he made his way out of the cabin.

This is exactly why you never mix business with pleasure. The thought continued running through Grant's mind as he drove his truck away from that fucking cabin. Away from Brynnon.

Not only had he lost his chance with the first woman to break through his defenses, Grant would probably get an ass-chewing of epic proportions once Jake found out what he'd done.

Maybe it was for the best. Hell, he'd warned her. She'd even said so herself. He'd warned her away from him because Grant knew damn good and well something like this was bound to happen. So why had he allowed it to in the first place?

Because you love her.

No, that wasn't it. He couldn't love Brynnon. Grant Hill didn't do love.

Years ago, after Baylee and that whole shitshow, he swore he'd never open himself up to that kind of pain again. Since then, he hadn't allowed himself to imagine laying down roots.

He didn't do strings or think about having kids. He sure as fuck hadn't entertained the thought of growing old with someone. Not until Brynnon Cantrell came along.

Except, after that first night with her, Grant had found himself thinking of all those things…and more. And look where it got him.

With a fucking door slammed in his face. Not to mention potential career suicide. Yeah, he'd done a bang-up job this time.

The farther he got from the mess he'd left behind, the more Grant told himself he was better off this way. He'd help Derek figure out what the fuck was going on with this case and then walk away scott-free.

No attachments. No one to worry about losing. *No one to warm your bed at night, or laugh with, or love.*

Gritting his teeth, Grant continued the drive to Cantrell's office, hoping he could come up with a plausible excuse as to why he'd just left someone else to watch over his daughter. He also prayed the senator couldn't tell just how hard it was for him to walk away from the woman who'd come damn close to being his everything.

Chapter 18

Three days. It had been three long days since Grant left the cabin. Not wanting to deal with the noise of the city, Brynnon had decided to stay here and bury herself in work. Determined to not think about Grant or what Derek had shared with her about what he'd found, she'd used the time to finish the paperwork for the bank, as well as diving back into the search for her next flip property.

Earlier today, she'd made the mistake of calling Angie to discuss which ones she thought were worth looking at in person. The conversation had quickly turned to Grant, at which time Brynnon spilled it all.

Okay, maybe not *all*. She'd purposely left out a few parts. Like the fact that, beneath his rough exterior lay the gentlest, most passionate man she'd ever known. Or, at least that's what she'd thought.

Brynnon did, however, tell her best friend about his shouting out to the world that he most certainly did *not* love her. Right before she told the other woman how Grant had unceremoniously left.

Angie tried to reason it. Her sweet friend had suggested he was probably just worried about his job. Or that maybe Grant felt guilty for starting something with her while she was a client. But, Brynnon had told her what she could no longer deny.

He'd gotten what he wanted, and when it looked like things could possibly become more serious, he'd split. Using his concern for her safety as an excuse, the coward had run off as far and fast as he could.

Which was fine. *She* was fine. At least, that's what Brynnon told herself every time she became lost in a memory of the two of them together.

So many memories in such a short period of time.

For the two days they'd been stranded together, she and Grant had made love in nearly every room. Now, each time she walked into one, pictures of those incredible moments with him assaulted her.

They were everywhere, continuously tainting the one place she'd felt truly at home. It was why she'd decided to go back to her condo tonight. There were memories of the two of them there, too. But somehow, the ones they'd made here seemed more…personal. More real.

After the conversation with Angie and a phone call to her father, she'd worked a little longer before re-packing her bag and tidying things up.

"You about ready to head out?"

Brynnon looked up to find Coop peeking in through her bedroom door. For a second, she still expected to see Grant's face, and it took everything in her not to crumble from disappointment when it wasn't.

"Yep." She zipped her bag. "All set."

The two left, and for the first few miles, Coop did his best

271

to keep the conversation light. He told jokes, filled her in on his family and his crazy, childhood antics. He talked about Mac and some of the crazy sniper shots she'd made in the past.

Brynnon did her best to join in, but found keeping up appearances more difficult than usual.

Sensing her struggle, Coop looked over at her as he drove. "I don't know if you're aware, but Grant's sort of a complicated guy."

"Tell me about it." She snorted.

He gave her an understanding smile. "Hill has a hard time opening himself up to people. I don't know what happened to him, but whatever it was, it scarred him pretty good."

Her chest became tight as she remembered Grant's words. *I've never told anyone that story.*

Grant's heartbreaking confession rang through her mind. "It's okay, Coop." Brynnon sighed. "I appreciate what you're trying to do, but you don't have to. I'm sure Grant's a great guy to have on the team. He's just not relationship material, which is fine, considering he was only supposed to be my bodyguard."

The handsome sniper looked her way, his hazel eyes laser-focused on hers. "He left because he cares about you."

She shook her head. "That's what he said, but—"

"No," he cut her off. "There's no but. Trust me. I've known that man a long damn time, and I've never once seen him as torn up as I did when he walked into your father's office. Hell, he spilled his guts right there to your old man. Told him everything."

Brynnon's wide-eyed gaze swung to his. "What do you mean, everything?"

"He wanted to make sure your father knew he'd crossed a

line with you."

Horrified, she asked, "Why in the hell would he do something so stupid?"

"Not stupid. Honest."

"Oh, God." Brynnon groaned, covering her blushing face with her hands. "My father knows we slept together?"

Coop chuckled. "Yeah, but he actually didn't seem surprised. In fact...and I could be wrong...but your dad looked sort of happy about it."

"*Happy?*" She growled. "Remind me to kill Grant the next time I see him."

"Don't think that's gonna be necessary," Coop chuckled before turning serious. "Look, Brynnon. There's something you need to know about Grant. If there's one thing I've learned, it's that he doesn't like to admit he has actual feelings like everybody else."

"Oh, I know. Trust me."

"Right? The thing is, I was there when he explained his reasoning for the sudden switch in guards. Grant told your dad he left because he cared about you, and was afraid you'd get hurt if he stayed."

Brynnon looked down at her lap. "Really?"

"Really. Look, Grant's not some player looking for a quick score and an exit sign. You've just gotta give him some time. He'll come around."

Brynnon wanted to believe him. She really did. But the fact was, the second things got a little murky, Grant had taken the first chance he had to walk away. She wasn't sure how to get past that.

Glancing out the window, she saw a billboard advertising a realty company, the ad jogging her memory. After a panicked glance to the back seat, she cursed loudly.

"Shit."

"What's the matter?"

"I forgot my computer." She gave him an apologetic grin. "I'm so sorry, but I have to have it for work."

"No worries," Coop looked at the road up ahead. "We can turn around at the next exit."

"I guess I was so lost in my thoughts, I forgot to grab it."

"Seriously, Bryn. It's not a big deal. We'll turn around, grab your computer, and then hit some drive-thru on the way to your condo. Sound good?"

"Thanks, Coop." Brynnon gave him a little smile. "I really appreciate it."

He chuckled. "If this is the worst thing that happens while I'm in charge of your safety, I'll call it a win all day long."

With a grateful smile, she glanced out the window, watching the scenery darken as night began to fall around them. By the time they pulled back into her driveway, the sun had set completely.

Thankful she'd left the security light on, Brynnon reached for the door handle. "I'll just run in and grab it real quick."

"I should probably come in with you."

She looked at the well-meaning man. "I've been here for the last five days and nothing happened. Besides, I'm pretty sure I know where I set it down. I'll be in and out in no time."

He didn't looked convinced. "You've got five minutes. After that, I'm coming in after you."

"Careful, Coop," Brynnon teased. "You're starting to sound like Grant."

"Nah. Grant would probably order you to stay here while he went in and got it for you."

Chuckling, she hopped out of the car and headed for her

front door. Not bothering to flip on the light, she ran up the stairs to her bedroom in search of the computer.

When she didn't find it right away, Brynnon went back downstairs and looked around. Still not seeing it, she made yet another trip upstairs, kicking herself when she found it on the floor of her closet.

Grabbing the bag, she carefully made her way down the darkened staircase. She was about to leave when she thought about how long it had been since she'd gone to the bathroom.

Knowing she had another hour in the car, Brynnon set the bag down by the front door with a groan and weaved quickly between her living room furniture to the bathroom at the back of the cabin.

She took care of business and had just stepped out of the small room when she realized the back door had been left open. The flimsy, screen door was the only thing keeping someone from breaking in.

"Jesus, Bryn. Why don't you just put up a bright, neon sign that says, 'Break In Here'." Continuing to mentally chastise herself, Brynnon went over and closed the door, making sure to lock it.

As she walked through the kitchen toward the front of the cabin, something caught the corner of her eye. The dark, odd-looking object had been left on the floor next to the edge of her counter. With the lights off, she had to get right up on it before she was able to make out what it was.

Staring down at the black duffle bag, Brynnon tried to figure out where it had come from. She didn't remember Grant having one like that, but it was possible he'd brought it in without her seeing.

Curious, she leaned down and unzipped it. Pushing the

two halves apart, Brynnon's heart nearly stopped from what she saw.

Bright red numbers shone back at her from within the bag, their display attached to something she didn't dare pick up. Several wires weaved in and out of the device, and Brynnon froze when she realized the numbers were steadily counting down with every second that passed.

It took a few seconds for her body to catch up to what her eyes were seeing. A bomb. It was a freaking bomb.

"Jesus," she exclaimed, the word barely a whisper.

"I know it's only been six minutes, but a deal's a deal."

Coop! Brynnon's eyes flew back at the display...only eighteen seconds remaining. *Move your ass, Bryn!*

She shot up from the floor and immediately started running for the door. "Move!" she screamed at Coop. "Go! We have to go!"

"What?" Alarm crossed over his shadowed face as he started in her direction. "Brynnon, what is it? What's wrong?"

"A bomb," she choked out. "There's a bomb in the kitchen! It's about to go off!"

Coop's eyes grew as big as saucers. He reached out and grabbed her arm, pulling her with him as they ran for the door.

As a last-second thought, Brynnon scooped her computer bag up as she past by it. She and Coop ran out the door and down the porch steps. They'd only made it a few yards when a deafening sound filled the night air, the powerful rush of heat sending them both flying.

****

"Where is she?" Grant demanded, pushing his way into the

hotel room.

Coop stepped aside. "Bathroom. She just got off the phone with her brother a little while ago. He was pretty upset, which only added to her anxiety level. I suggested she take a shower to help her relax."

"When you called, you said she'd hit her head. Should she be doing that alone?"

Shrugging, Coop smirked. "Sort of figured you'd frown upon my joining her."

It took less than a second for Grant to invade his teammate's personal space. "Do I look like I'm in the mood for fucking jokes? She could've been killed."

"I know," Coop shot back, suddenly serious. "I was there, remember? I'm fine, by the way. Thanks for asking."

Shit. He was right. This was his friend. His teammate. And he hadn't bothered asking if he was okay.

From the moment Coop called to tell him what happened, Grant hadn't been able to think straight. Pictures of deadly scenes he'd witnessed as a SEAL. Along with all the what-ifs, horrific memories from what felt like a lifetime ago played through his mind.

Grant knew the only thing to put it to an end would be to see Brynnon with his own two eyes. To touch her and know for a fact that she was okay.

He could hear the water running from behind the closed bathroom door. Coop had explained over the phone that their boss had instructed him to bring her to a hotel, rather than back to her condo.

Grant looked back at his teammate. For the first time since barging in, he noticed the scrapes on Coop's cheek and chin, stark reminders of just how deadly the explosion could've been.

Coop grabbed his shoulder and squeezed, snapping him away from his thoughts.

"It's okay, man. I get it. But like I told you on the phone, she really is okay. We got thrown by the blast, but landed in the grass. The snow helped break our fall." Though he tried to hide it, a slight shadow fell over Coop's eyes when he added. "We got out of there just in time."

Trying not to imagine how close they'd both come to dying tonight, Grant gave his teammate a jerky nod and took a step backward. "What the fuck happened?"

"Someone blew up your girlfriend's cabin."

Grant snarled. "I'm serious, Sean."

"So am I."

Coop walked over and grabbed a soda from the fridge. With his outstretched hand, he offered it to Grant, but he declined. Closing the small refrigerator, Coop popped open the can and leaned against the kitchenette's counter before giving him the full story about what went down.

"We were about halfway to the city when Brynnon realized she'd forgotten her computer. I turned around and drove us back to the cabin. She ran inside to get it. I waited a few minutes then went in to make sure she was okay. I'd just walked through the door when she came running at me from the kitchen screaming about a bomb and yelling at me to run." He took a sip of soda. "I pulled her with me and hauled ass out of there. Made it to the middle of the yard when it detonated. We've both got some bumps and bruises but are otherwise fine."

Coop's description of what went down left Grant even more shaken than before. Running a hand down his face, he told his friend, "Thank you."

"Don't have to thank me for that. I'm just glad she found

the bomb when she did."

Grant clinched his teeth tightly together. "Where was it?"

"Inside a duffle bag on the kitchen floor. Someone broke in through the back door after we left. At first, Brynnon saw the bag and thought maybe you'd left it. She opened it up and...well, you know the rest. Ryker sent a couple of bomb techs out to the scene. He'll let us know what they find."

"Christ." Grant shook his head. Too worked up to stand still, he walked over to the large window overlooking the city.

He knew all too well the way some bombs worked. Some could be picked up and turned every which way and not go off. Others were designed to detonate with even the slightest of movements. If the one Brynnon found had been like the latter, she would've died the second she began unzipping that fucking bag.

Like when he first heard the news, Grant suddenly found himself precariously close to losing his shit. Tempted to punch a hole in the fucking glass, Grant shoved his hands roughly into his pockets.

Clamping his jaw shut, he took a few seconds to tamper the fear and anger bubbling up inside before asking, "The cabin?"

"Gone. I didn't see the bomb, but whoever built the damn thing knew what they were doing."

Grant's eyes slid closed. He'd seen first-hand the heart and soul Brynnon had put into that place and how happy she was there. His heart physically hurt, knowing the loss was a devastating one.

I'm so sorry, baby.

With a desperate need to find the bastard responsible, Grant filled his lungs and tried to remain focused on that.

"I told Derek to look into Jessica Price. She's the one who

sent the threats and almost killed Brynnon before."

"Yeah, D told me about her, but, uh..." Coop paused. "It wasn't her."

Unhappy with that answer, Grant spun back around. "Who the fuck else would it be?"

"I don't know, but I'm telling you, it wasn't Jessica Price."

"Her father, then. Hell, Charles Wright's the one with a hard-on for Senator Cantrell. He could've—"

Coop shook his head. "It wasn't him, either."

"How the hell can you be so sure?" Grant growled, his frustration building at an increasingly fast pace.

He needed it to be Wright or his daughter. If it was, if the evidence pointed to one or the other, then Brynnon would finally be safe.

I need her to be safe.

Keeping his cool, Coop responded calmly with, "We know it wasn't Wright because the man was admitted to Dallas Regional earlier today."

"When did you find this out?"

"Derek called just before you showed up. Since I was the one still guarding Brynnon, he contacted me rather than you."

"What happened."

"Apparently, Jessica went by to take him to lunch at around eleven and found him unresponsive. Hospital security shows her staying with her father from the minute the ambulance arrived with Wright right up until..."

A sick feeling settled in his gut. "Until when?"

Regretfully, Coop told him, "Grant, Charles Wright never regained consciousness. He died less than an hour ago, and his daughter was by his side the entire time. The team of doctors and nurses who were assigned to him have already vouched for her, which means—"

"Someone else planted the bomb." Grant ran a hand over his rough jaw before sliding it around to the back of his neck. With his fingers pressing against the tense muscles there, he sighed loudly. "Does Bryn know?"

Coop nodded. "I told her."

Damn. "How'd she take it?"

"Not great." The other man shook his head. "Even knowing the guy had spent years trying to prove her father basically killed those soldiers, Brynnon still genuinely felt bad that she hadn't been able to give Wright answers before he died. Crazy, right?"

No, Grant thought. Not crazy. It was kind and loving. It was...Brynnon. His heart broke for her, knowing she'd take Wright's death as a personal failure.

Looking back at his teammate, Grant said, "D's spent the last few days going back through the files on the P.I.'s computer. He's gonna stay with Cantrell until you get there, and then keep at it until he finds something."

Playing musical bodyguards was highly unprofessional, but Grant couldn't bring himself to care about that right now. Nothing—not even the job he loved—would've kept him away from her tonight. Thankfully, the senator had agreed.

Earlier, Grant thought he'd go mad waiting for her to get back to the city. After Coop finally called with the hotel information and to say they'd arrived at their room, Brynnon spoke to her father. Grant had tried to ignore the crushing disappointment he'd felt when she hadn't asked to talk to him, too.

After ending that call, William Cantrell contacted her brother to fill him in on what had happened. Unwilling to stick around another second, Grant had bluntly told the man he was leaving.

Giving permission he hadn't asked for, Brynnon's father simply waved him away as Grant ran out of the office, probably breaking a few land speed records on the drive over. He didn't care.

His only thought had been getting to Brynnon. To be able to see her with his own two eyes and know for a fact, she really was okay.

"Well, it looks like you've got this under control," Coop broke through his thoughts again. The guy tossed his empty can into the trash. "I'm gonna head over and relieve Derek so he can keep doing whatever the hell it is he does."

Making his way back across the room, Grant shook his teammate's hand. "Thanks for keeping her safe. And…I'm glad you're not dead."

Laughing, Coop reached out and gave him a half-hug. "Gee, thanks, Hill. That's the sweetest thing you've ever said to me."

Despite the situation, the corner of Grant's lips curled. Though he may never admit it out loud, he really did love his team.

"Get out of here, jackass." He pushed against his friend's chest.

Grinning, Coop grabbed his go-bag and headed for the door. With a final, shared look, the young sniper left him to face Brynnon alone.

A few minutes later, Grant heard the water turn off. Pacing the room, he waited anxiously. Finally, after what felt like forever, Brynnon walked out of the bathroom.

Wearing a thin pair of pajama pants and a tank top, it came to no surprise when she stopped dead in her tracks at the sight of him. Her eyes landed on his, a giant fist wrapping its unforgiving fingers around his heart when he found hers red and swollen from crying.

Recovering quickly, Brynnon walked over to the room's small desk. Pulling a folder from her computer bag, he waited silently as she began sorting through its contents.

Without looking at him, she sounded hollow when she spoke. "I'm fine. So if you're here out of some misguided guilt from not having been with me, you can leave. The bomb would've gone off whether you were with me or not."

Grant took a moment to look at her. Though he couldn't see her face, he knew she'd rather be anywhere but in this room. With him.

But she was alive. His princess was safe, and she was alive. The rest would hopefully work itself out soon.

Praying she'd listen to what he had to say, Grant licked his dry lips and admitted, "I couldn't breathe." Strong emotions left his deep voice rough. Unsteady.

Brynnon let the papers fall back onto the desk. Turned to face him, he watched as confusion caused her eyebrows to turn inward. "What?"

Grant took in the pure beauty that was his Brynnon and continued baring his soul.

"Coop called to let me know what happened." He paused, needing to swallow past the painful knot in his throat in order to continue. "It was like my lungs froze inside my chest. Everything went numb."

Brynnon just stood there, staring back at him with those mesmerizing eyes of jade. Taking a chance, Grant moved a little closer to her.

"He told me your cabin exploded. That you'd gone inside. For a second, I thought…" His voice broke as he worked to convey the unprecedented terror Coop's words had created.

Some of her anger dissipated as she moved hesitantly

toward him. "I-I'm okay," she said again, her voice much softer than before.

Grant's eyes fell on the fresh bruise darkening one side of her forehead. His vision blurred, the thought of her being violently thrown in the air from the blast creating a sudden, unfamiliar stinging.

Blinking against his unshed tears, Grant moved a few more inches in her direction and tried like hell to say what needed to be said.

"I was standing there, fighting to breathe, and all I could think of was that you'd died believing I didn't care about you." He shook his head, licking his lips to try and stop their quivering. "The truth is I don't know what I'm feeling, but only because I've never felt anything like this before."

Grant took another step, his lungs stuttering as he attempted to fill them. "What I do know is, in those few seconds I thought I'd lost you, I didn't know how I was going to go on."

"Grant." Brynnon's chin trembled.

Unable to keep from it, he closed the remaining distance between them in two long strides. He placed both hands on her bare shoulders, thankful as fuck when she didn't pull away.

"Baby, when I got that call, I felt like my entire world had ended." Raising a gentle palm to her face, he brushed his thumb back and forth over her flawless skin. "I don't know what you've done to me, but I can't"—he swallowed hard—"I *won't* walk away from you again."

A tear fell down her cheek, the silver streak hitting his thumb. Grant brushed it away gently.

With a hand to his chest, Brynnon looked up at him, the love in her eyes damn near bringing him to his knees.

Blinking, she set more tears free.

"I don't want you to walk away, Grant. I never did. I want you with me." She bit her bottom lip nervously before adding a quiet, "Always."

Thank. Fucking. Christ.

Taking her face between both hands, Grant looked her in the eye and promised, "I'm here, Princess. And I'm not going anywhere."

Meeting each other halfway, their mouths came together in a powerful explosion of emotion and heat. Grant's heart filled to the point of near combustion.

His lips moved against hers as he spoke. "I'm sorry I left."

"Why did you?" she asked breathlessly, nibbling his bottom lip.

"I thought you'd be better off with someone else."

Speaking between ravishing kisses, Brynnon's uttered words were music to his ears. "I don't want anyone else." She pulled away, leaning back in order to look him in the eyes. "I only want you."

With her arms wrapped around his neck, Grant lifted her off her feet. He carried her to the bed where they fell together, their hands working in an almost wild frenzy to rid each other of their clothes.

Grant slid his belt loose and undid his button and zipper. He was just about to push them down with his boxers when Brynnon pushed against his chest to stop him. His stomach dropped.

Despite what she'd just said, he found himself terrified she'd finally come to her senses. From the moment he first saw her, Grant had known she could do a hell of a lot better than him. Maybe now, she did, too.

With his body hovering above hers, Grant waited with

bated breath for her to speak. By the grace of God, his fears were quickly put to rest.

"Where's Coop?"

Grant exhaled with relief. "On his way back to your dad's."

He watched as Brynnon's perfect, bow-shaped lips curled into a seductive smile.

"Good."

Seconds later, with their clothes tossed haphazardly around the room, Grant slid into her hot, wet core. Overwhelming emotions clouded his ability to think about protection until he was already fully seated.

"Shit," he breathed. "Condom."

Brynnon shook her head. "No. I want you like this. With nothing between us."

His cock twitched inside her, the sensation of her velvet lips encasing his bare skin unlike anything he'd felt before. Though they hadn't talked about a future together, Grant knew in his heart, he was in it for the long haul. She was it for him.

Grant had spent the last several years avoiding the sort of pain and loss loving someone could bring. Never wanting to feel that way again, he'd shut himself off to the possibility of building a future with someone.

He'd welcomed the knowledge that he'd never have children of his own, convincing himself he didn't want them. Not with anyone.

Then he met Brynnon.

As he lay over her now, their bodies connected in the most intimate way possible, Grant found himself wanting to see her round with his child. His heart swelled at the thought of spending the rest of his life with this woman. Raising a family with her.

The knowledge sent a shocking jolt to his heart. *I love her.*

With a silent promise to share his feelings and desires with her soon, Grant put those thoughts aside and began to move. Without words, he used his body to show Brynnon everything he felt in his heart.

Chapter 19

Hours later, after Grant made love to her in the sweetest, most affectionate way, Brynnon woke to the sound of a phone ringing. Lost in a sleep-riddled haze, she heard him answer. She thought he uttered a low curse before mumbling something else and ending the call.

With a hand to her shoulder, Grant gave her a gentle nudge. "Sweetheart, wake up. We have to go."

The alarm in his voice broke through the fog. Looking up at him, Brynnon blinked against the last remnants of sleep. "What is it? Did something else happen?"

"Coop just called. It's your brother."

"Billy?" She sat up quickly, her heart beating faster as her hands swiped at the wild hair in her face. "What happened? Is he okay?"

Regret filled Grant's tired eyes. "He's been shot."

"*What?*" she gasped. "Oh, my god!"

Wide awake now, Brynnon threw the covers off her legs and jumped out of bed. Dressing like a mad woman, she began firing out questions as she slid on a pair of jeans and the nearest T-shirt she could find.

Her chest heaved with rapid, shallow breaths as she spoke. "I-is he okay? Do they know who did it? W-where was he?

Did someone break into his apartment, or was he—"

"Brynnon!" Grant spoke sharply. Dressed in only his boxers, he wrapped his large hands around her shoulders, forcing her to stop and look at him. "Sweetheart, take a breath."

Her eyes shot to his. "It's my brother." She tried worming her way free from his grasp.

"I get that, but you're no good to him if you're passed out cold."

His words resonated within. Following his example, she drew in several slow, deep breaths.

Grant gave her a nod. "Good girl. Now, all I know is that Billy was found shot in his apartment a few hours ago and taken straight into surgery."

"Okay." Her mind whirled. Licking her lips, she repeated herself. "Okay. Dallas Regional isn't too far from here, right?"

Seeing she was no longer on the verge of hysteria, Grant let her go, dressing as he spoke. "Your father arranged for him to be transported to Homeland's private medical facility rather than the public hospital. Coop's headed there now with your dad. I told him we'd meet them there."

She hastily slid on her boots. "Homeland has a private hospital here?"

"They do. It's southwest of the city, near the Dallas Executive Airport."

Brynnon finished tying the last shoestring and stood. Running a hand through her untamed hair, she blew out breath. "Okay. I'm ready."

Not wasting any time, Grant shoved his gun into his waistband at his lower back, his wallet into his back pocket, and threw on his coat. Grabbing his keys, he headed for the door with Brynnon in step behind him.

The ride to the hospital was one of the longest of her life. Staring out the window, memories from when she and Billy were just kids plagued her mind as they sped through the night.

Her heart filled with love when she remembered all the good times they'd had together...before their mom had passed. Sadness tore at her when Brynnon's thoughts turned to the dark times after. When Billy struggled with drugs before straightening himself out.

A more recent memory struck, along with overwhelming guilt.

"I saw him arguing with someone," she spoke woodenly.

Grant's gaze spun toward hers. "When?"

"The night of the ball." She turned to face him. "I was waiting for you to get our coats, and I saw him through the glass doors. He was standing across the street, and he looked upset."

"Who was he arguing with?"

Brynnon shook her head, tears welling heavily in her eyes. Emotion leaving her voice rough. Raspy.

"I don't know. He was wearing a dark coat and hat. His back was to me. I thought about going over there, just to check on him, you know? But I was too selfish."

Reaching over, Grant covered one of her hands with his. "Why do you say that?"

She gave Grant a sad smile. "I had a feeling things were finally about to happen between us. I didn't want..." Brynnon put a hand to her trembling lips. After taking a few seconds to compose herself, she glanced out the window again. "I didn't want Billy's never-ending drama to interrupt our night."

"You're allowed to have a life, Bryn."

"What if it was the person who shot him? What if I could've done something to keep this from happening? I should have gone over there. I should've—"

"Hey," he squeezed her hand. "Look at me."

Brynnon swiped the tears from her face, but continued staring out the window. Grant refused to let it go. Speaking more sternly, he gave the order again.

"Brynnon, look at me."

Reluctantly, she did.

There was an unyielding certainty in his eyes when he told her, "This is not your fault."

"You don't know that."

"Yes," he stated with confidence. "I do. If you'd gone over there, it could've escalated the situation. You told me before, Billy had a tendency to hang with the wrong crowd, so—"

"Are you saying this was his fault?"

"Maybe," he answered bluntly. "Maybe not. I can't tell you that, but what I do know is whatever happened tonight is *not* on you. So get that shit out of your head right now."

Brynnon still wasn't convinced, but she also wasn't in the mood to argue. Instead, she told him about the conversation she'd had with Billy when he'd called her earlier.

"He seemed agitated. I thought he was just upset about what happened at the cabin, but..." She swallowed back more tears. "Do you think the person who shot him also set the bomb?"

"It's possible," Grant told her honestly. "What did Billy say to you?"

Brynnon thought a moment. "Not a lot. H-he asked if I was okay, and then told me again and again how sorry he was.

He kept repeating it. I thought it was because I'd lost the cabin, but now, I'm not so sure."

Grant's spine straightened. "You think, maybe he had something to do with it?"

"No," she adamantly denied the question, despite the fact that she'd just been wondering the same thing. "Billy and I had our fair share of issues, but he'd never try to hurt me."

Though the statement came out with unquestionable certainty, a sliver of doubt began creeping in as Brynnon thought back to the way he sounded on the phone.

At least, I never thought he would.

With a sideways glance, Grant squeezed her hand. "You're probably right. He probably just felt bad because he knows how much you loved the cabin."

"Yeah," Brynnon nodded absentmindedly. "After the explosion, I was sure Jessica Price had decided to come after me again. But then Coop told me about what happened to her father today, so I know it wasn't her." She got choked up again. "That poor man. I really wanted to help him find some peace before he passed."

"We'll figure this out, Bryn." He lifted her hand and kissed her knuckles. "No matter how long it takes, I won't stop until we have the answers we need."

Several minutes later, after showing his I.D., Grant pulled his truck into the secured parking area. After opening the passenger door, he took her hand and helped her out of the truck.

Wrapping her arms around herself, Brynnon shivered against the cold wind. She'd rushed out in such a hurry, she hadn't thought to grab her coat.

With a low curse, Grant shrugged out of his coat and wrapped it around her shoulders. She thanked him for the chivalrous gesture as they walked toward the building's entrance.

"I've driven by this place a handful of times, but I had no idea it was a hospital."

Grant gave her a tiny smirk. "That's because Homeland doesn't want people to know."

Once inside, Brynnon couldn't help but notice how familiar Grant seemed to be with the facility. Not only did he know exactly where the elevators were located, he'd also lead her straight to the Intensive Care unit, where he'd been told her brother's room was located.

"You've been here before," she stated the obvious.

"A few times." He looked down at her as they walked. "Someone at R.I.S.C. gets hurt badly enough to see a doctor, this is where we come. Also, Olivia, our boss's wife, is a nurse here. She won't be working tonight, though. They're expecting their first kid in a couple of months. Liv had some issues with the pregnancy early on. As a precaution, she took a few months off from work. Jake's also been taking a lot of time off from R.I.S.C. to be with her."

The big guy was talking way more than was his norm, and Brynnon had a sneaky suspicion it was for her benefit. He knew she was terrified at the thought of losing her brother and was making every effort to take her mind off it. Even if only for a few moments.

If she wasn't already hopelessly in love with the man, that small act of kindness would have tipped her over the edge.

Seeing the guards standing by one of the ICU room's doors, Brynnon instinctively knew it was her brother's. Recognizing Grant, the serious men allowed them entrance with a tip of their heads.

Sitting in a chair next to the bed, her father's puffy, red-rimmed eyes met hers the second she walked into the room. Heaviness pressed down onto her chest when she realized the powerful politician had been replaced by the sad, hopeless man before her.

To her left stood Coop, his arms crossed at his chest as he leaned against the room's sink. His expression was grim.

Unable to put off the inevitable, Brynnon tried hard not to react when her gaze fell upon her brother. Lying in the middle of the stark white room, he looked pale and small. Several tubes and cords ran from his body to the many machines surrounding the head of the bed.

A heart monitor beeped with the steady thrum of his pulse and a breathing tube had been inserted and was taped to his mouth, providing some much-needed oxygen to his lungs.

"Billy." Releasing Grant's hand, Brynnon shrugged out of his coat and handed it back to him before rushing to her brother's side.

Her father stood, leaving the chair he'd been using to go to her. With an arm around her shoulders, he did his best to comfort her while sharing the grave news.

"The doctor said he's critical. Apparently, the bullet nicked his aorta. He'd already lost a lot of blood before anyone found him. Crashed twice during surgery. We should know more in the next hour or two, but should prepare ourselves for the worst."

"Oh, God." Brynnon hugged her father as they stood there, crying together. When the two parted, she wiped her face dry and asked, "Do they know who did this?"

Before her dad could answer, Martin Downing came rushing through the door. "Sorry, it took me so long to get here, sir." He looked at Billy then eyed the others in the room. "I-I would have left sooner, but I had to make a couple phone calls first. Damage control with the press."

"It's fine, Martin." Her dad looked warily at his chief of staff. "I was just filling Brynnon in on Billy's condition."

Barely able to look at his friend, Martin asked, "How is he?"

"The doctors aren't hopeful," Brynnon said tearfully.

"Damn."

"To answer your question, Bryn"—Coop continued the interrupted conversation—"no. We don't know who did this. But we will soon."

"How can you be so sure?" Martin asked anxiously. His eyes bouncing back and forth between Billy and Coop.

Brynnon actually felt sorry for the man. It was no secret they merely tolerated each other, but personal feelings aside, Martin and her brother had been best friends for years. It was no wonder the guy was upset.

"Billy was shot inside his apartment," Coop backtracked to give them a full picture of the night's events. "A neighbor heard the shot and called it in."

Martin put his hands into his pockets. "Did the neighbor happen to see who shot him?"

Coop shook his head. "Unfortunately, no. According to the woman's statement, she heard a gun go off. A minute or so later she heard Billy's door slam shut. The woman was afraid whoever shot the gun would come back, so she waited several minutes longer before calling apartment security."

"That still doesn't answer my original question," Martin challenged, his normal state of arrogance even stronger than usual. "How can you say with certainty you'll find the guy who did this? The neighbor didn't see anything. Do the police have another lead, or are you just assuming your team is that good?"

Coop stared back at Martin, his lips rolling inward. From what she'd seen, Sean was a very laid-back kind of guy. Currently, however, Brynnon could tell the guy was working hard to keep his demeanor as calm and professional as possible.

"Derek's on his way here, now," Coop finally answered. "He's been working with apartment security to access the footage from the cameras in the building."

Brynnon caught the look Coop gave Grant and understood perfectly. Derek would have no problem gaining full access to the building's security footage…but he'd be doing it alone.

"That's great and all." Martin continued on. "But unless they got a good look at the guy's face as he left the apartment, I don't see how that will be of any help."

"Martin, I'm sure Mr. Cooper and the rest of his teammates know what they're doing."

Coop smirked. "It's okay, Senator." He looked at Martin. "Derek West is the smartest man I've ever known. Trust me. If anyone can figure out who shot Billy, it's him."

Martin's gaze slid to his injured friend then back to Coop. With his entitled chin in the air, he nodded, "Good. That's really good news."

"Martin, you don't look too well," Brynnon stated. "Are you okay?"

"What?" He looked back at Brynnon. "Oh, yeah. Sorry. I guess all of this is starting to sink in."

In a rare form of affection toward the other man, Brynnon walked over to Martin and gave him a hug. "I know you're scared, but Billy's strong. He can still fight this, I know he can."

Martin pulled back, giving her a tight smile. "You're right.

If anyone can beat this, it's him."

"First, someone puts a bomb in my daughter's cabin and later that same night, my son is shot. That can't be a coincidence."

All eyes went to her father, who was staring expectantly at Grant.

"I agree," Grant spoke for the first time since entering the room. "That's why as soon as Derek gets here, I'd like to set up a command post."

Brynnon's stomach clenched. "You're leaving again?"

Cursing under his breath, Grant ate up the distance between them. Uncaring of the audience around them, he cupped her face with his hands, his eyes locking with hers.

"I'm not leaving the building, Princess. I'm just talking about finding private office somewhere here in the hospital. A place for Derek to set up all his tech crap so we can have some privacy to work while you and your father spend time with your brother."

"Oh." Suddenly embarrassed by how needy she'd sounded, Brynnon looked away and whispered, "Sorry."

"Hey." He used his thumb and forefinger to tip her chin, gently forcing her to look at him again. "You've been through hell tonight, so no apologies. Got it?"

Biting her lip, she nodded as best she could. "Okay."

With a quick kiss to her forehead, he released her chin and turned to her father. "Whoever did this is still out there, and I won't stop until I find them. Now, every person on staff is a Homeland employee. Same with the guards standing outside this room. No one can get in or out of the building without clearance, so you'll be safe. This way you and Bryn can remain here, with Billy, while we work to find the son of a bitch responsible."

"I like the way you think, son." Her father gave Grant a look of approval.

The door opened and Derek walked through. With a black bag hanging over each shoulder and two smaller ones in his fists, the shaggy-haired man scanned the room before looking to Grant.

"Hey, man."

With a tip of his chin, Grant responded with, "I was just explaining how we'll be in one of the other rooms so they can have some privacy."

After glancing toward the bed, Derek looked at Brynnon with genuine sympathy. "Sorry to hear about your brother. How is he?"

"Not good." More tears began to form but she pushed them back.

Derek frowned, his expression turning fierce when his eyes met Grant's once more. "You ready to get started?"

"Faster we get started, the sooner we'll find answers."

Martin chose that moment to start for the door. "I'm going to go find a restroom."

Sliding to the side, Derek gave the other man plenty of room to move past. After, Brynnon watched as the three men she knew to be warriors turned their focus on finding the shooter.

Before leaving, Grant turned to face her. "Don't worry. You're safe here." Then with a wink, he was gone.

Taking advantage of the privacy, Brynnon turned to her dad. "I know it's a bad time, but there's something we need to discuss."

For the next several minutes, Brynnon proceeded to share her thoughts—ones she'd not been able to quiet since Billy's phone call last night—with her father. When she was finished, she sat quietly and waited for his response.

"I may lose one child tonight, Brynnon. I don't want to lose you, too."

"You won't. And I don't want to do anything that will hurt you. So if you tell me to drop it, I will. I'll go find Grant right now and tell him and the guys to stop their search."

Her father raised a trembling hand to her cheek. "You are just like your mother." He smiled. "She would be so proud of you. I know, I am."

Brynnon covered his hand with hers. "Thanks, Daddy."

"You know in your heart what's right, sweet girl. So do what you need to do, and don't worry about me."

"But, your career—"

"Isn't worth covering up for whoever caused those soldiers' deaths. No career is worth that. Besides, Derek may find that our company had nothing to do with it. But you won't know unless you keep looking."

"Grant won't stop until he finds the truth."

Her dad smiled. "That man loves you, you know."

Brynnon blushed. "Maybe."

She watched as he stepped away to pull one of the plastic chairs next to his. He sat down and patted the empty seat.

"Come sit for a minute."

Brynnon did, wondering what sort of worldly wisdom he was about to bestow upon her. It didn't take long to find out.

"Your mother was about your age when she and I met. I saw her from across the room, and I knew." Her father smiled at the memory. "From the second I saw her, I knew she was the one."

Sharing his need to think about something other than bombs and shootings, Brynnon's lips curved. "I know.

You've told me that story a hundred times, but I always love hearing it."

"I suppose I have." His rough, aging hand held hers. "But there's something I haven't told you."

"What's that?"

"Do you remember the philanthropy ball I hosted a few months back? The one where you and Grant first met? He was working as extra security for me, then."

"I remember." She nodded. *How could I forget?*

"Well, the thing I haven't told you before now is that night, when you walked through those doors, I saw Grant look at you the exact same way I did your mother."

Her eyes rushed up to his. "I think you were mistaken, Dad."

"Think about it, sweetheart. I had several guards there that night. Many of whom, you didn't know."

"Is there a point to all this?" Brynnon shifted in the uncomfortable seat.

"Of the men working security, how many did I introduce you to?"

She thought back to that night, her heart stuttering when she realized, "Just one."

Her father nodded. "Ever wonder why?" When she shook her head, he went on to explain. "I knew the two of you would somehow find your way to one another."

Brynnon slid a glance to her brother's still form. "This doesn't really seem like an appropriate time to—"

"It's the exact right time." Her father looked down at Billy before his sharp gaze found hers once more. "What happened tonight, first with you and then your brother...it's a stark reminder that none of us know how much time we have here. Grant's a good, solid man, Brynnon. From what I've seen, he loves you very much."

Brynnon's heart swelled with a knowledge her mind had yet to accept. "He doesn't…w-we haven't said…"

"The words will come, dear, but actions? Those are what matter most." Turning to face her more directly, he took her other hand in his and added, "Life is short, baby girl. If you have the chance to experience the magic your mother and I shared, grab onto it with both hands and never let go."

She'd lost her mother far too soon. Her brother was fighting for his life before her very eyes, but she couldn't have asked for a better father than the one she'd been given.

"Thanks, Daddy." She hugged him tightly. "I love you."

Holding her close, he whispered back, "I love you, too, Brynnon."

"Oh, sorry. I can come back."

Both Brynnon and her father turned to see Martin standing just inside the door. He was fidgety, and the guy looked like he was about two seconds from throwing up.

He's taking this really hard. Brynnon offered him a tiny smile. "You're fine."

Martin's gaze skittered from hers, to her fathers, and back to hers. "You know, this is really a family thing. I-I should probably just go."

"No." Brynnon stood quickly. "Stay."

She couldn't quite place the expression on Martin's face when he asked, "You sure?"

"You're his best friend, Martin. Billy will want to see you if he wakes up. Besides, Grant and the guys should be back soon, hopefully with the shooter's I.D. I'm sure they'd welcome any help you could give once that happens."

The other man gave her a shaky smile. "All right." He

took a step forward, but then stopped suddenly. "You know, I was thinking of going to go find some coffee. Would either of you like some?"

"I'm good," her father answered. "But thank you."

"Brynnon? What about you?" His eyes met hers with slight desperation.

Assuming he wanted company but was too afraid to ask, Brynnon offered, "How about I walk with you? We'll probably be here awhile, and it'll do me good to stretch my legs."

Nodding, Martin's smile widened. "Great idea."

She gave her dad a quick kiss on the cheek, took some cash from her purse, and she and Martin left the room. Walking down the hall toward the elevators, Brynnon took her phone out to text Grant. However, when she hit send, the message failed to go through.

"That Grant?"

Brynnon scowled at her phone. "Yeah. I thought I'd send him a text asking if he wanted coffee, but it won't go through."

"The signal's spotty in this place."

She put her phone back into her pocket and sighed. As they came to the elevators, she told Martin, "I'm just glad R.I.S.C. is involved in the investigation."

"Why is that?" Martin hit the button to bring the elevator to them.

"They're the best." She looked over at him. "I mean, the private investigator working for Charles Wright has spent the last six *years* trying to validate Wright's claims against Dad's old company. It took Derek less than a handful of days to figure out Charles was right all along."

The elevator dinged and Martin's brow furrowed as they

stepped through the open doors. "W-what do you mean, he was right?"

"Apparently, there's a discrepancy on some of the documents relating to the job in Kunar. Derek has connections far beyond even my father. Plus, the guy's a literal genius. It's only a matter of time before he figures out what really happened. Once he does, the person or people behind it all will most likely be charged in the deaths of those poor soldiers."

Martin nodded but remained silent as he reached out and pressed the button with the big 'G' on it.

"It doesn't matter how long it takes," Brynnon continued. "Grant and I are going to see those responsible are brought to justice."

Martin cleared his throat. "You know, Bryn. I get that you and Grant are a thing and you have a lot of faith in his team's abilities, but you shouldn't get your hopes up too high."

"What do you mean?"

"Just that, with Charles Wright dead and the private investigator he hired missing, it seems to me the case has reached a dead end."

"I have to do this *because* Wright is gone."

The elevator stopped and the doors opened. Stepping out, Brynnon followed Martin down the hall, trying her best to make him understand.

"Don't you see? Martin, there is a very good chance someone who worked at Dad's company, probably someone you and I both know, tampered with those documents. Why would they do that, unless it was to cover something up?"

Agitated, Martin shot back with, "Like what?"

"A direct link to the bridge collapse. I don't know for sure yet, but I'm telling you, there's something there. We just have to find it."

As he continued down the long corridor, Martin thought a moment before speaking again. "Fine. We can keep looking, but let me handle it."

"You?" Brynnon frowned.

"Sure. I worked for Cantrell Construction, remember? And as you know, I'm very familiar with the way things were done. Why don't you give me the documents. I can look them over and see if I notice anything unusual. Maybe I can figure out what it is you think you're missing."

Brynnon shook her head. "I can't."

"Why not?"

She stopped to look at him. "Because I think whoever's responsible is the same person who put that bomb in my cabin. I also think they shot Billy. If I involve you, then you could end up being the next target."

He ran a hand over his jaw. "I'm sure whoever did those things is long gone by now. Besides, I can take care of myself."

They turned down another hallway. Seeing a doctor and two nurses walking toward them, Brynnon waited until they'd passed and were out of earshot before continuing.

"I think you're wrong," she said bluntly. "I think the person is closer than we realize. And I think that same person shot Billy."

"Why would they go after him?"

Brynnon shook her head, sick to her stomach from what she was about to say. "I think my brother knew about the cover-up. I also think he may have even been involved."

This time, it was Martin who stopped. Going pale, he asked, "Why would you say that?"

"He sounded off when we spoke last night. There was

something in his voice." She swallowed down the knot of guilt she felt for even thinking these things about her own brother.

"So why shoot him?"

"That, I don't know. Maybe the shooter was trying to tie up loose ends. Or, maybe Billy threatened to tell the truth. All I know is I can't stop now. If I do, that means the cabin and Billy...it was all for nothing. I have to see this through to the end."

"Even if it kills you?" he challenged.

Brynnon looked back at him with conviction. "Even if it kills me."

Martin studied her for a moment before he began walking again. "What about your father? A scandal like that could ruin his career as a United States Senator."

And there it was. The real reason Martin wanted her to walk away from the investigation. He didn't give a shit about her safety. All he was concerned about was her father's career. Or, more accurately, his career.

"I've already spoken to Dad about it. He said no career was worth covering up the wrongful deaths of those American soldiers. He wants me to keep digging." Brynnon looked around, wondering just how far the coffee shop was. "Are we close, or did we take a wrong turn?"

With an odd look, Martin gave her a small smile. "Actually, I remembered seeing Grant as I was coming out of the restroom. He told me they were going to be in a conference room located on this floor. He told me how to get there, in case you needed him for something. I thought, if you want, we can go by there first to see if they could use some coffee."

Surprised he'd actually thought of someone other than

305

himself, Brynnon said, "Oh. Okay."

They went down hallway after hallway until finally, Brynnon heard Martin say, "It's down this way."

They'd passed by several staff members since leaving her brother's room, but this hallway was completely empty. An odd feeling began to settle in Brynnon's gut, but she brushed it off as emotionally-induced paranoia and kept walking.

He pushed open another door. When they walked through it, a rush of cold air nearly took her breath away. The winter air sent a flurry of goosebumps over her exposed arms and Brynnon stopped in her tracks.

Looking around, her heart thumped a little harder when she saw the concrete floors, walls, and pillars. A large, metal sign attached high on one of the walls caught her eye. It read, 'Employee Parking Only.'

Already shivering, she glanced back at the door they'd just walked through. "Martin, I think we took a wrong turn. This is the employee parking garage."

He smiled wider. "I know. Grant told me about a short cut. It's right through there." He pointed to a door on the opposite side of the garage. Giving her his prized, politician's smile, he said, "Trust me."

Brynnon wrapped her arms around herself to help fight off the cold as they made their way across the open space. Temperatures had dropped drastically in the short time since they'd arrived, and a strong wind whistled eerily as it traveled passed the garage's dark opening at the top of the ramp.

Martin smiled over at her. "I know Derek's good at what he does, but I really don't see how a couple of doctored P.O.'s are going to lead you to the person you're after."

Brynnon's steps faltered, her heart stuttering inside her chest.

Noticing, he looked over at her with concern. "What's wrong?"

A gnawing feeling settled deep inside her gut as she stopped moving. "I never said the documents that were falsified were purchase orders."

Martin stopped as well. He thought for a moment before smiling again. "Sure, you did. You said Derek found something off with the P.O.'s for the Kunar job."

Pulling a pair of black leather gloves from his pocket, he began slipping them onto his hands. That same, gnawing feeling she'd experienced seconds earlier grew teeth. Their bite painful and shocking.

"No." Brynnon shook her head. "I didn't."

Calling him out on his bullshit here, in the middle of a freaking parking garage with no one else around, was stupid. Unfortunately, Brynnon realized this a second too late.

Quickly trying to recover, she smiled back at him. "You know what? I'm sure you're right. It's been a long few days, and with everything that's happened, I probably just forgot I'd mentioned the P.O.'s."

Martin stared back at her. His lips were still curved into a smile, but his eyes held no humor. "I'm sure that's it."

Suddenly fearful of a man she'd known half her life, Brynnon took a step backward. "I'm really not in the mood for coffee anymore. I-I think I'm just going to go back to Billy's room."

Turning around, she started walking back in the direction they came. She made it three steps before hearing the metallic sound of a bullet being chambered.

"No. You're not."

Brynnon spun around, her heart leaping into her throat at what she saw. Martin, her brother's best friend and a man she'd known over half her life, was holding a gun. And it was pointed directly at her heart.

Chapter 20

"What exactly am I supposed to be looking for?"

Keeping his eyes glued to the financial report he was scanning over, Grant answered Coop's question. "Anything that seems odd or out of place."

"You're kidding, right?" Coop held up the report Derek had given him to check. "All this shit looks odd to me." When Grant didn't respond, his teammate griped, "It's like looking for a needle in a damn haystack."

Patience wearing paper fucking thin, Grant sent Coop a look. "That needle tried to kill Bryn and her brother tonight, so keep fucking looking."

The other man wisely chose to remain quiet and continued searching for something that would give them a clue as to who the hell they were after.

Grant couldn't really blame Coop for being frustrated. For nearly an hour, now, both he and Coop had been scouring through page after page of supply orders, bank statements, and other financial documentation from Cantrell Construction and its employees.

In the meantime, Derek worked to hack into Billy Cantrell's building camera feed. According to D, the system was much more sophisticated than he'd first expected, requiring him to jump through several more hoops than normal.

So far, they hadn't found a single fucking thing.

"By the way, where the hell is Mac, and why isn't she here helping us go through all this shit?"

"Jake has her working on something else with Trevor."

Coop frowned. "What?"

Derek shrugged. "No idea. When McQueen called earlier for a SITREP, he just said she was hanging back to go over some stuff with Trev."

Grant could tell Coop wanted to know more, but the guy knew it was useless to hound D for information he couldn't give. A few minutes passed before the younger man spoke again.

"I've been thinking."

"Oh, great." Derek smirked, his fingers incessantly clicking away on his keyboard. "This should be good."

Flipping him off, Coop glanced over at Grant. "I don't think whoever set that bomb actually meant for Brynnon to get hurt."

"Why do you say that?"

"Think about it." Coop abandoned his files and rested his elbows on the table. "You two were there, what, three days? Then after you left, she and I were there another three."

Grant's gut tightened. He'd already cleared things up with Brynnon on that front. Still, he hated thinking of the way he'd left her that day.

"Your point?" he bit out the question.

"Whoever it was waited until after we left to break in and set the bomb. He couldn't have known we were coming back. Hell, *we* didn't know until half an hour later."

Grant thought for a moment. "You think it was meant to

be a warning?"

"Makes sense."

Derek looked at them from over the top of his computer. "Why go after the brother?"

Shrugging, Coop asked, "Are we sure the two incidents are related?"

"Huge fucking coincidence if they're not," Grant grumbled.

Coop's wheels turned. "Okay. So maybe Billy is involved. After all, his signature is on the P.O.s."

"Those could've been forged," Derek pointed out while typing.

"Maybe," Coop agreed. "Maybe not. Hell, for all we know, he's the one who built the damn bomb."

Jesus, Grant prayed that wasn't the case. Brynnon had been dealt enough shit lately. The last thing she needed was to discover her own brother had blown up the home she loved, almost killing her in the process.

"That's the whole fucking problem." He stood abruptly, sending his chair rolling across the floor behind him. "We're in here making guesses while Brynnon's sitting with her father waiting to see if her brother's gonna pull through."

Sympathy clouded Coop's hazel eyes. "I get that, but until we have more to go on, that's all we can do."

Grant wanted to scream. He was sick and tired of grasping at straws. Worse, he hated seeing Brynnon scared and upset.

Her tears fucking gutted him, and he refused to sit around with his thumb up his ass hoping the answers would fall in their goddamn laps while she was forced to sit and wait for the next attack.

"We're better than this." He went back to the papers in front of him. "There has to be something here. Some piece of evidence that will explain what the hell is going on."

"I don't know, man." Coop sounded less than hopeful. "Derek's looked over this shit already and we've looked at it three times. There's nothing there."

"Doesn't really surprise me."

Both men turned their attention to Derek. "What do you mean?"

"Hill's right." He stood. "We need to quit guessin'."

In full geek mode now, Derek began pacing the room and talking through his thoughts. Grant and Coop both watched and waited for the former SEAL to do his thing.

"For argument's sake, let's assume everything is related. The bridge, the bomb, the shootin'…all of it."

"Okay," Coop agreed, his voice leaving a trail.

"Let's also assume Wright's missin' P.I. was on the right track, and someone in Cantrell's company *did* falsify those P.O.s. The most plausible reason would be so they could spend less on supplies and launder the extra money."

Still sitting in his seat, Coop looked up at Grant. "No offense to Brynnon, but from what I've seen of her brother, that sounds like something he'd do."

Knowing what she'd shared about Billy's past, Grant couldn't really argue against the comment. "Okay." Grant went along with the scenario. "Say, for whatever reason, Billy ordered shit supplies and pocketed the extra cash."

Derek nodded, adding, "No one's the wiser. Then news of the bridge collapse hits. After that, he'd have to rush to cover his ass."

"Not to be the only asshole in the room"—Coop jumped in— "but Billy doesn't exactly strike me as the cunning type. Player, yes. Bullshitter extraordinaire, absolutely. But to get away with something like this? That would take a hell of a lot more than his boyish charm."

"He'd need help," Grant surmised.

"It would have to be someone with deep fuckin' pockets and a lot of pull," Derek thought aloud.

"Wait." Grant thought of something. "I can see him covering this shit up on the business side, but how the hell could Billy Cantrell cushion a military investigation involving multiple casualties?"

"Same way you or I would." Derek grinned. "Find whoever's in charge and bribe them."

"That's it!" Grant snapped his fingers. He began rummaged through the papers again, finally finding the report he'd already read. "This is the official results of the investigation Ryker got for us." He flipped through the stapled packet to the last page. Honing in on the signature, he read off the name of the man in charge.

Derek immediately began working his technical magic, and within minutes, he'd accessed the guy's bank account records from the time of the investigation.

"Bingo. What's the date of the report?" Derek smiled when Grant told him. "This has to be it."

On the edge of his seat, Coop asked, "What is it? What did you find?"

"A wire transfer to the account in the amount of ten thousand dollars." Derek's eyes met Grant's. "It posted the same day the investigation officially closed."

Grant's heart sped up. "We find out where that money came from, we find who was responsible for the bridge collapse."

Coop nodded. "With any luck, it'll lead us to whoever shot Billy."

Derek's computer beeped again, the sound different than

his earlier message alert. He rushed over to check it.

"That's odd." His brows turned inward as his fingers moved with rapid speed.

"What?" Both Grant and Coop asked in unison.

Still focused on his keyboard, Derek said, "I got into Billy's apartment building feed, but there was another security server detected. One that runs off a completely separate network."

"Can you figure out where it's coming from?" Grant asked.

His friend's blue eyes narrowed. "I'm going to pretend you didn't just say that." Derek looked back at his computer. "It's more advanced, but the network it's connected to is one I'm familiar with." A few more clicks of the keyboard and, "Holy shit."

"Find something?" Coop asked unnecessarily.

"You could say that." Derek's gaze slid to Grant's. "It's connected to Billy Cantrell's apartment."

Grant looked across the table expectantly. "So the guy had a security system installed. What's so strange about that?"

"Not just any security system. This one is on a twenty-four hour recording setup. Not for the hallway, but"—Derek spun his laptop around for the other two men to see—"inside the apartment."

"Holy shit. Can you rewind it to earlier tonight?"

Derek's expression turned deadpan. "I swear, it's like y'all have no faith in my abilities whatsoever."

Sighing dramatically, Derek turned his computer back around and began working to rewind the feed. Talking while he worked, he said, "If we can get a clear shot of the shooter's face, we can nail the son of a bitch."

"Shouldn't be a problem. This feed runs through the

entire apartment. Including the bathroom."

"Jesus," Coop spoke beneath his breath. "Paranoid, much?"

Grant and Coop both walked around to the other side of the table. With Coop's help, Derek was able to narrow down when he'd spoken to Brynnon on the phone. Using that as a starting point, he found that portion of the recording and hit play.

The screen came alive. Divided in equal squares, they could see every inch of Billy's apartment, all at the same time.

Clearly upset, they watched as Billy spoke to someone on the phone. The feed didn't have audio, but Grant could tell he was apologizing repeatedly.

"He's talking to Brynnon," he stated for clarification.

A few minutes later, after ending that call, Billy went into his bedroom and removed a second phone from a safe he kept under his bed.

Stating the obvious, Derek said, "It's a burner."

Again, they couldn't hear the conversation, but there was no doubt Billy was upset about something. His facial expression and other body language suggested he was yelling at whoever was on the other line.

With a look of resolve, Billy ended that call, slammed down the phone, and walked over to a desk butted up against one of his bedroom walls.

"What's he doing now?"

Billy opened a drawer and pulled out a sheet of paper. His hand flew across the blank sheet as he hastily wrote out something. The camera angle didn't allow for them to make out what he was writing, but Grant had a feeling he already knew.

"It's a confession." Both men looked at him. "Brynnon

told me he kept apologizing over and over again when he called her. She thought he felt bad for her having lost the cabin, but I think it was because he felt responsible."

"I spoke to Eric before I came here," Derek said of his detective brother. He pointed to the screen. "If that's a confession, the police didn't find it."

Grant continued to watch as a desperate man wrote down his greatest sins. "That's because the shooter didn't want them to."

Sure enough, after fast-forwarding to the hour EMS was called, Grant's prediction was proven accurate. He wasn't surprised when the man who shot Billy picked up the letter and shoved it into his pocket. What he hadn't been expecting was the face he saw staring back at them.

"No way." Coop stared at the frozen screen, slack-jawed.

Beside him, Derek whispered a disbelieving, "Jesus Christ."

Grant remained silent. He studied the man's face, his blood turning hot with fury knowing the son of a bitch was under their noses the whole time.

"Of course, it's him." Derek ran a frustrated hand through his hair. "Should've fuckin' seen it."

Shaking his head, Coop looked at the frustrated man. "Nah, D. No way you could've known."

"But I *should* have. Think about it. The guy worked side-by-side with Billy at Cantrell Construction. He would've had access to the paperwork and the connections required to pull off a cover up of this proportion."

Still attempting to placate their teammate, Coop said, "He's also been a part of the senator's family for years. Hell, the guy is Billy's best friend. No one suspected him."

The image of Martin Downing pulling that trigger was

permanently burned into Grant's mind. After a late-night visit to Billy's apartment, the two men had argued. Tempers flared, Martin appeared to have panicked and shot Brynnon's brother.

"He had no idea the cameras were there," Coop stated softly.

Derek shook his head. "Nope. He avoided the ones in the building entryway and hallways but didn't bother trying to hide his face once he got inside the apartment." Taking a deep breath, he asked, "Who wants to tell the senator?"

Coop's eyes bounced between Grant's and Derek's. "Rock, paper, scissors?"

"I'll tell him," Grant offered. With one final glance at the man who'd been a part of Brynnon's family for years, Grant headed for the door.

"I want Brynnon out of the room and away from Downing first. He could get desperate and do something stupid." The last thing he wanted was for her to get hurt. "When we get there, I need one of you to come up with a reason for her to leave."

"Like what?"

Grant thought for a minute. "Say her friend, Angie, is waiting downstairs or something. I don't give a shit what excuse you give I just don't want her anywhere near the prick when he realizes we know the truth."

His heart broke for Brynnon, knowing this was just one more blow she'd have to endure. As Grant and his teammates made their way back to the ICU, he made a silent vow to be there for her. Every fucking step of the way.

****

"Martin, what are you doing?"

"What I should've done a long time ago. Now, walk toward me, slowly."

Brynnon's mind raced, her heart beating hard and fast. As she took a tiny step forward, she wondered if it might actually explode from fear.

Rubbing her cold arms with her hands, she glanced up toward the ceiling. "Martin, there are cameras in here. This is a secured Homeland facility, for Christ's sake. How the hell do you think you're going to get away with this?"

"Easy, actually. The staff schedule is posted on the wall in the emergency area for all to see. Shift change doesn't happen for two more hours. Cafeteria's closed for the night and security is surprisingly minimal. It's still dark outside, and I parked around the corner, as far away from the nearest light post as I could. The security gate is a couple hundred feet away, next to the road, and with the sound of that wind, there won't be anyone around to hear you if you scream."

Brynnon felt herself grow pale.

"See? That, right there is the problem with you." Keeping the back of the gun pulled in snuggly against his chest, he moved toward her, instead. "You've always underestimated me. Always thought you were smarter and better than me. Still do."

"No." Brynnon shook her head. "I-I didn't. I don't."

"Yes, you do!" He clenched his perfect teeth together. "Your brother did, too."

A sickening realization began to seep in. "It was you, wasn't it?" Nauseated, Brynnon stared back at the man who'd claimed to be like family. "Y-you shot Billy."

"I had to!" he yelled. "It was his own fault. He's the one who started this mess in the first place. All I ever did was try to protect him and your father."

Martin shook his head, erratically pacing the immediate area before her. The entire time he moved, the gun remained pointed directly toward her.

"Billy got scared after the bomb destroyed your cabin," he continued on. "He called me after he spoke to you. Said he was going to tell your father everything." Dark eyes pleaded with her to understand the unforgiveable. "He would've ruined both our lives, and I couldn't... I couldn't let that happen."

He moved back and forth some more before stopping directly in front of her. An almost hysterical laugh escaped the back of his throat. "You want to know the most ironic part? *I'm* the one who set the bomb in the first place."

Anger worked its way passed her fear, Brynnon forgetting for a second about the gun. "*You* blew up my cabin? Martin, I could've been killed!"

"I didn't have a choice!" he shouted back, his voice echoing off the concrete structure. "Besides, you weren't even supposed to be there."

"Oh." Brynnon couldn't contain her sarcasm. "I'm so sorry for nearly ruining your plan."

"No one was supposed to get hurt." The crazy man shook his head, then looked back at her with an apologetic frown. "I never really wanted to hurt you. Y-your father mentioned you were coming back to the city, so I went there and waited. I watched you and Coop leave." He laughed again. "I even waited an extra ten minutes to make sure you hadn't forgotten something."

"I *did* forget s-something, asshole. And if I h-hadn't seen the b-bomb when I did, Coop and I both would've been k-killed."

"I know!" The gun shook in Martin's hand as he yelled. *Jesus.* The man was clearly unstable. With no one else around, Brynnon knew she was on her own.

"Where'd you even get the bomb?"

His shoulders shook with silent laughter. "You'd be surprised at how easy it is to acquire something of that nature."

Feeling like she'd stepped into some sort of alternate universe, Brynnon forced herself to calm down and try to buy herself some time. She was freezing, but if she could keep him talking long enough, someone else would come by. If not, she'd try to get the gun from him herself.

"Tell me what happened, Martin." She took a cautious step closer. "Tell me what Billy did, and I promise, my father and I will do whatever we can to help you."

As she spoke, Brynnon started to slide her hand in her back pocket, thinking maybe she'd have a signal now that they were outside.

"Don't!" Martin screamed, immediately changing his mind. "On second thought, yeah. Take out your phone."

Shivering worse than before, Brynnon did as she was told.

"Now, throw it over there." He tilted his head toward the space behind him.

More tears escaped. With no other choice, she tossed it over his shoulder, glass and plastic shattering into pieces as it landed. Still, she tried reasoning with him. "M-martin, please. Why are you d-doing this?"

He scowled in anger. "Why? Because of you."

"Me?"

"Yes, *Princess.* You."

Hearing him spit out Grant's nickname for her made Brynnon want to shove her fist down the asshole's throat.

"What the hell are you talking about?"

He took another step closer, the barrel still pointing back at her.

"You just couldn't leave well-enough alone, could you?" he seethed. "Had to keep sticking your nose in where it didn't belong. I thought when Jessica Price nearly ran your ass over, you'd stop snooping around. Instead, you made friends with the bitch and her father. Then you got your boyfriend and his little friends to start helping, too."

"Wait." Brynnon pushed past her fear to try and understand what was happening. "You're t-talking about the b-bridge."

"Ding, ding, ding!" he shouted loudly. "Give the lady a prize!" Martin's lip curled in disgust. "Jesus Christ, of course I'm talking about the fucking bridge."

"Martin, w-what did you d-do?"

"What I've always done. I protected your family."

"I don't..." Brynnon shook her head. "I d-don't understand."

"Of course, you don't. No one ever has."

Body shaking, Brynnon pleaded with him to make sense of what he was doing. "So tell me. Let's g-go inside, and you can explain what h-happened. Whatever's going on, m-my dad and I can help you f-fix it."

"It's too late for that, now."

Ignore the cold and keep him talking. "W-what did Billy d-do?"

"The dumbass borrowed money from the wrong people. They'd threatened to kill him if he didn't pay, so he laundered money from your dad's construction company."

Brynnon felt as though her world was shattering around her. Fearing she already knew the answer, she still had to ask, "How?"

"He was in charge of the supply orders, so he made it look like the company had ordered the better, more expensive materials. Instead, he got them from some fly-by-night company that went bankrupt less than a year later."

The picture of Jordan Wright and his father flashed through her mind. Her stomach churned. "The cheap materials were used to build the bridge in Kunar."

Martin nodded, shocking the hell out of her when he started to cry. "Your brother had no idea that would happen. He just wanted to pay the man he owed off so he could start fresh." He sniffled. "Billy knew what happened in Kunar was his fault. He came to me, panicked. He was terrified your dad would find out what he'd done, or that he'd be sent to jail. So I did what I always do." He looked back at her sadly. "I fixed it."

"H-how? Martin, the m-military looked into it. How were y-you able to—"

"I knew the guy in charge of the investigation. I also knew he'd been having an affair for years. If his rich wife ever found out, he'd not only lose his military pension, he'd lose every dime he ever had. So I paid him off to keep quiet and then—"

"C-covered it up on the c-company's side," she concluded for him.

Martin nodded. "I made fake purchase orders to cover up what Billy had done. Used my own fucking trust fund to pay off anyone else who could blow the whistle on us. And it worked, too." He chuckled humorlessly. "That is, until Wright's P.I. contacted me a few weeks ago. I didn't know what else to do, so I offered to meet with him. I kept thinking I could figure out a way. Maybe bribe him, too. But everything got out of hand."

A sinking feeling knotted in her gut. "Y-you k-killed him." Martin started to cry again, his mood swings bouncing from one extreme to the other. "I didn't mean to. We met at night, down by the river. I swear, I just went there to talk. I thought I could pay him off like the others, but he wouldn't listen. He got his phone out and started to call the police. I had to shoot him."

Sadness filled the man's eyes as he stared back at her. The lines on his forehead smoothed, and when he spoke again, his voice held a tone of acceptance.

"I had no choice, Brynnon. Not then, not now."

Martin had been a part of her family for years, and her brain struggled to believe he'd killed one man, shot her brother…and had just confessed everything to her.

"I didn't go to Billy's apartment tonight with the intentions of killing him. In fact, it didn't even cross my mind to bring this in with me."

From his other pocket, Martin pulled out a long, black tube. In less than a second, she realized what it was for.

"I did, however learn a thing or two after."

Brynnon watched as he attached the silencer to the end of the gun's barrel. *Oh, god. He's going to kill me.*

Feeling as though she had no other choice but to fight, Brynnon reached for the gun.

"No!" Martin fought back hard.

With her hands wrapped around the cold metal, growling as she attempted to break it loose from his grasp. When Martin's finger slid down to the trigger, Brynnon used all her strength to turn the barrel away from her body.

The gun went off, a sharp zipping sound passing by her just before the bullet hit the concrete wall behind her.

"You stupid bitch!"

With surprising strength, he forcefully ripped the weapon from her grasp. Before she could protect herself, Martin swung the butt of the gun toward her head, the hard metal slamming against her temple.

Brynnon dropped to the ground, blood immediately beginning to run down the side of her face. Its warmth was an almost welcomed sensation.

"Get up!"

She felt a rough pull on her left arm as she was yanked back up to her feet. Stars danced before her eyes, the dizziness making it hard to fight back. But she still tried.

"Let me go," Brynnon pushed against him.

"Knock it off!" Martin yanked her body close to his. "Try a stunt like that again, and I'll shoot you right here."

Pushed forward, Brynnon winced when she felt the gun's barrel being pushed against her ribs.

Forced to walk quickly up the smooth ramp, she groaned, "You're gonna shoot m-me anyway. Doesn't really m-matter where you d-do it."

"You'd just better pray the wind muffled that gunshot enough for no one to notice. And don't even think about screaming for help. Anyone comes to your aid, they'll be shot, too. Don't think you want that on your pretty little conscious."

Good god. The man had gone from being her father's trusted chief of staff to someone who didn't blink at the thought of killing an innocent person.

"What's the p-plan? Y-you take me somewhere else and shoot m-me. Then what? N-not like you can just v-vanish."

"Actually, I can." He smirked. "Unlike your brother, I think ahead of the game. I made a contingency plan. Invested well and made a nice little nest egg for myself with a new I.D.

and everything."

"You'll have every p-police department s-searching f-for you."

"Not in Mexico, I won't." He glanced over at her, disappointment shadowing his expression. "After all this, you're still underestimating me."

A blustering wind whipped through her hair, it's below-freezing temperature stealing the breath from her lungs as they cleared the garage's entrance and onto the open parking lot.

If she felt cold before, it was nothing compared to now.

With his free hand, Martin pulled the keys from his coat pocket and pressed the fob. An SUV parked a few spaces up beeped, its brake lights flashing to indicate the doors had been unlocked.

If you get into that vehicle, you're dead.

Brynnon tried—and failed—to come up with a way to get herself out of this unbelievable situation. Between the intense, wintry air and the shock of what she'd learned, her mind felt as though it was shutting down. Protecting itself from what it knew would inevitably happen.

Fear, unlike any she'd ever felt before, consumed her as she realized her only chance of escape would be to run from the man she now knew was planning to kill her. He may still succeed, but against the odds or not, she damn sure wasn't going to make it easy for him.

Before she could change her mind, Brynnon used all the strength she could muster to shove him away from her. Not wasting a second, she spun on the balls of her feet and began to sprint as fast and as far away as she could.

Though she'd anticipated it, the painful force from the bullet was a shocking surprise. Brynnon cried out as she flew forward, her legs crumbling beneath her as she fell.

Fire filled the entire left side of her back, it's burning tentacles spreading throughout the rest of her torso. She tried to move, but the pain was too much, and this time, even the warmth from her blood did nothing to fight off the ice-cold pavement beneath her.

A string of curses barely reached her ears as Martin stormed over to where she lay. Rather than putting a bullet in her brain—as she'd assumed he would—the man reached down and wrapped his gloved hands around her wrists.

Unceremoniously, he began dragging her limp body across the rough asphalt, rock salt and the occasional rock digging into her abs as they went. Brynnon opened her mouth to scream for help, but the pain from her gunshot wound and the bone-chilling air stole her ability to scream.

Stopping in the shadows between two cars, Martin released her arms, letting them fall onto the ground above her head. He squatted down next to her, his voice barely audible over the strong wind.

"I would've made it quick, you know." He gently moved some hair from her face. "I was going to take you someplace secluded and be done in one shot. Because you didn't listen, you'll have to lie here in the cold, waiting to die. Don't worry." He glanced at the wound on her back. "From the looks of it, you'll probably bleed out soon."

"P-please…" she begged.

"I'm sorry, Brynnon." Martin stood. "Just remember, it didn't have to be this way." Then he left her there. Alone and bleeding.

She thought of her father, her heart breaking for what he'd be forced to live with if both she and her brother died tonight. Brynnon prayed Billy would pull through.

He'd most likely spend the rest of his life in prison, but at least he'd be alive, and her father wouldn't be left completely alone.

Grant's face filled her mind, her tears freezing against her cheeks before they could fall to the ground. Her greatest regret was that she hadn't told him she loved him.

Brynnon continued to lay there, helpless. Dying. She wasn't sure how much time had passed, but soon felt her muscles relax and the violent shivers subsiding.

Her breathing shallowed and her pulse weakened. Oddly, she no longer felt cold and the unbearable pain from before had become nothing more than a dull ache. Even on the verge of unconsciousness, Brynnon knew she was dying.

When her eyelids became too weighted to keep open, she gave up the fight and slowly let them close. Using the last of her remaining mental strength, she brought forth her most cherished memory.

Picturing the way Grant looked as he danced with her, she let go and drifted off to sleep. Before the last sliver of consciousness gave way, Brynnon whispered a silent prayer her death wouldn't push him over the edge for good.

Chapter 21

"Where's Brynnon?" Grant scanned Billy Cantrell's room, but she wasn't there.

"She and Martin left a little while ago." William Cantrell stood. "Why? Did you find something?"

"They left the hospital?" Fear threatened to choke him as he pulled out his phone and tried calling her.

"No. Just the room. Did you find the shooter?"

Derek scoffed. "You could say that."

"Where'd they go?" Grant demanded, a tidal wave of fear threatening to take him over when he couldn't get the call to go through.

Surprised by the alarm in Grant's voice, the senator's gaze bounced between them. "Who was it? Who shot my boy?"

Forcing himself to remain calm, Grant ignored the man's questions. Knowing he needed to keep a clear head, he did his best to treat this like any other job and think of their best course of action.

They could wait for Brynnon and Martin to come back to the room. Logically, Martin had no way of knowing they were onto him, so there'd be no reason for him to be suspicious and take off.

Earlier, however, Coop had made it pretty clear they'd find the person who shot Billy sooner, rather than later. If the guy did get spooked, there was a chance he'd either use Brynnon as a bargaining chip while he made his escape, or the asshole could try and get rid of her, just like he did her brother.

Fuck. That.

Pointing to Derek, he ordered, "Access hospital security. See if you can find where they went."

"How long ago did they leave?" Derek asked Cantrell as he sat his laptop down next to the sink and began typing.

"I don't know. Half an hour ago, maybe? Will someone please tell me what the hell is going on?"

Grant didn't pull any punches delivering the bad news. "Downing shot Billy."

"What?" Brynnon's father shook his head.

"We're pretty sure it had something to do with what happened in Kunar, which means as long as Brynnon's with him, she's in danger."

"That's impossible."

"Unfortunately, Sir" —Coop looked at the shocked man— "it's not."

"Martin's like a son to me. He's Billy's best friend. He'd never—"

"Well, he did!" Grant practically shouted. When Cantrell started to argue again, he closed the distance. "I know it's hard, but I need you to listen to me. Derek discovered an extra security system set up in your son's apartment. There's a camera in every room, and it's constantly recording and sending that data to a private server. We were able to access the recorded footage from tonight, when Billy was shot. You can see Martin's face clear as day."

The senator shook his head. "I-I don't know what to say."

"You don't have to say anything. I just need you to trust me."

"Oh, my god." The senator dropped back into his chair.

"I know it's a lot to take in, and we don't have all the answers yet. But right now, my focus is on finding Brynnon and getting her as far away from that bastard as possible. So is there anything you can think of that would help us do that?"

Cantrell nodded woodenly. "They were going to get some coffee."

"We could split up," Coop offered. "Start looking for them."

Grant shook his head. "This place is too big. It'll be a goddamn goose chase. D?" He swung his gaze to Derek.

"I'm on it," his teammate responded.

The seconds rolled by at a nauseating pace until finally, Derek stopped typing. He spun around, the expression on his face grim.

"I found them. He took her into the parking garage after they left here." Derek looked over his shoulder, his next words struck with fear. "Downing pulled a gun on her."

"*What?*" Both Grant and Brynnon's father spoke at the same time.

"Here." Derek rewound the footage and stepped aside for Grant and Brynnon's father. "See for yourself."

Grant watched as Brynnon and Martin entered the garage beneath the building. Martin smiled and said something to her, but Brynnon stopped walking. They exchanged a few words before the fucker pulled out a gun.

"Jesus," Coop whispered from beside him.

Bulldozing past his fear, Grant forced himself to look at the scene with the eyes of an operative, rather than a lover.

As much as he wanted to race to the garage that very second, chances were they were no longer there.

Needing to see as much as they could in order to determine where they went after this moment in time, Grant continued watching the heart wrenching footage.

Brynnon stood stoically as Martin put a silencer on his gun. They went back and forth, talking and yelling at one another, and then all of a sudden, she went for the gun.

"Oh, God," Cantrell groaned.

Baby, no!

Grant's throat closed up and he held his breath, praying he wasn't about to witness her death.

Downing regained control of the situation. He didn't shoot Brynnon, as Grant had feared, but his relief was fleeting.

Instead, the bastard pistol-whipped her on the side of her head. A violent rage unlike any Grant had ever felt soared through him as he watched her fall to the ground.

"Motherfucker," he hissed between clenched teeth. Fists shaking at his sides, Grant vowed, "I'm going to fucking kill him."

"Get past this so we can figure out where the hell they are now," Coop encouraged.

The sped-up version showed Downing yanking Brynnon off the ground and hauling her up the ramp. When they got to the top, they turned left, and out of the camera's viewpoint.

"Where the hell did they go?" Grant shot Derek a look."

"I'm working on it." Derek squeezed himself back in front of the screen. A few clicks of his fingers and then, "Here. He took her around the corner."

Grant kept watching not willing to take his eyes off her.

Less than a minute into the new feed, his world began to shatter.

All four men, including Brynnon's father, watched as she pushed herself free and started to run. Grant's legs nearly gave out from beneath him when he saw Martin raise the gun, the bullet hitting Brynnon a fraction of a second later.

"No!" Grant reached out toward the screen, as if he could somehow save her.

"Ah, fuck." Coop ran a hand through his hair.

Cantrell started to cry. "He shot her. That son of a bitch shot my baby girl!"

Tears pricked the corner of his Grant's eyes, but he held them in. The only way to help Brynnon now was to watch the rest of the footage and find out where she and Martin were now.

Ignoring Cantrell's cries of anguish—along with his sudden urge to vomit—Grant remained silent as they saw Downing drug the woman he loved out of sight.

Less than a minute later, Martin came back into the camera's view, walking casually to his car and driving off. Without Brynnon.

Grant could hear Derek speaking to someone but he couldn't make out what he was saying. It was as if everything around him had suddenly become muted.

For the first time since being with her, he felt himself shutting down. Walls only she'd been able to break past began rising again, and emotions Grant had finally allowed himself to feel started to fade.

Before that happened, Derek's excited voice broke through.

"She's still out there!"

Grant slid his cold gaze to his teammate. "What?"

Derek's hopeful eyes turned to his. "Snap out of it, man! Downing didn't take Brynnon with him. H-he must've left her outside somewhere. She has to be close."

Grateful his teammate was still thinking straight, Grant shook off his numbing fear and ran from the room. With him in the lead, all four men shot down the hall toward the elevator.

"As soon as we get outside and I have a fuckin' signal again, I'll call Ryker and give him everything we have, including a description of Downing's car and license plate."

Good. Downing shot an innocent woman on Homeland's turf. Grant knew Ryker would send every agent available to take his ass down.

Coop slapped the button, but Grant refused to stand and wait. "Fuck this. I'm taking the stairs."

The rest did the same, falling in line right behind him.

"I just checked the temp." Derek ran into the stairwell. "The good news is, it's only thirty-five with winds moving at fifteen miles per hour."

"How the fuck is that good news?" Grant growled, running down the stairs two at a time.

Derek explained himself as the group of men continued hastily making their way down to the ground floor.

"She's been out there long enough, hypothermia's probably already set in. That will slow her heart rate, causing less blood loss."

The fact that they were now praying her body temperature had dropped low enough to slow her heart told Grant just how dire the situation was.

Hold on, baby. I'm coming.

Grant's legs moved even faster, as though he was running for his life. In a lot of ways, he was.

He couldn't lose her. Not now. He'd finally opened himself up again, and it was all thanks to her.

After what felt like an eternity, Grant threw open the door leading into the parking garage. Running at full speed, he didn't bother to wait for the others as he made his way up the ramp. Following the same path Downing had taken, he went left. His mind raced to remember the cars he'd seen on the footage.

"Brynnon!" he screamed. "We're here, baby. Where are you?"

Ignoring the cold, night air, he screamed her name again, pleading for her to call out for him. The only thing he got in return was the sound of the bitter wind.

"Here." Derek heaved a breath from behind him. When Grant looked over, he realized his teammate had brought the laptop with him.

"You really are a genius."

Derek pulled up the frame where Martin started dragging Brynnon out of the camera's viewpoint. "Remind me later to make a huge fuckin' deal about the compliment."

They studied the frozen image, committing to memory the cars surrounding Downing and Brynnon. Almost simultaneously, they began scanning the parking lot in search for those same vehicles.

Coop pointed to a red car several spaces down from where they stood. "That's the Honda on the screen!"

Grant looked back to the computer, and sure enough, that same car, along with the ones parked beside it, were those Downing had passed.

"Let's go!"

About that time, four security guards came running up behind them. Having already been filled in on the basics, Coop quickly explained they were searching for Brynnon.

The group of men ran against the wind, yelling out as loud as their lungs would allow. With every second that passed, Grant grew closer and closer to a complete fucking meltdown.

"Spread out!" he ordered roughly, desperate to find his woman. His knees nearly buckled as an unimaginable thought hit.

This whole time they'd been assuming she was still alive. But what if…

No! He couldn't start down that path. Grant knew in his heart—one he'd only recently discovered he still had, thanks to her—Brynnon was still alive.

Along with her father, the three R.I.S.C. operatives searched between the cars and beside the building. They hollered her name, Grant praying he'd hear her voice calling for him. But, he didn't.

Claws of doubt began digging their way into his core, and he was about to give up hope when Coop shouted, "I found her!"

Grant swung his head up to see his teammate standing in the shadows between two cars. Coop was waving his arms and yelling, "Over here! Hurry!"

Moving faster than he ever thought possible, Grant took off in that direction. His heart stopped when he saw her.

With Coop squatted next to her, Brynnon was lying face down on the ground. And she wasn't moving.

His teammate's tormented eyes flew up to his. "She has a pulse, but barely. We've got to get her inside."

Grant all but pushed Coop out of the way. A strange,

guttural sound escaped his chest as he saw where she'd been shot.

Kneeling down next to her, he lifted the hem of her shirt. The blood-soaked material stuck to her skin as he slowly peeled it up and away from the wound.

Grant closed his eyes, allowing himself only a second to fight off the consuming rage within before putting the shirt back down.

Though they wouldn't know for sure until she got into surgery, he felt confident the bullet had missed her spine. With paralysis the lesser of two evils—the other being death—Grant took the chance and rolled her over onto her back.

Sliding his hands beneath her cold body, he quickly lifted her into his arms and made his way out from between the cars. Once they were clear, he took off like a bat out of hell toward the emergency entrance around the corner.

Carrying her limp body through the automatic doors, he began shouting for someone to help. A doctor about the size of Trevor's tiny wife, Lexi, and two nurses came running up to him.

Knowing Brynnon didn't have time for a long-ass story, Grant told them what they needed to know in order to save her...She'd been shot and left in the cold to die.

Practically ripped from his hands, the team of medical professionals transferred her to a gurney and began taking her vitals. One nurse shouted out her low-as-fuck blood pressure and a bunch of other shit he didn't recognize. After that, the doctor rambled off a shit ton of tests she wanted ordered, plus something about a warming system.

In the midst of that chaos, another staff member came and got Brynnon's father, stating there was something going on with Billy.

Knowing the man was torn between staying with his daughter and going to his son, Grant said, "Go. Be with Billy. I've got her."

With a weary nod, the man followed the gentleman down the hall toward the elevators.

The team working on Brynnon quickly pushed her through a set of opened, double-doors and into a room. When Grant started to follow, the doctor put a hand to his chest. "I'm sorry, but you'll have to stay out here."

Memories of another hospital—another hallway—assaulted him. Now this doctor wanted him to go through that shit again?

Like hell.

"I'm not leaving her."

Coop pulled on his arm. "Come on, man. Let them do their jobs."

"He's right, G," Derek chimed in. "Trust me, I get it. It was hell waiting for Charlie to get out of surgery after that bastard of an ex nearly beat her to death. But you have to give them room to work. It's what Brynnon needs most right now."

Glaring at his teammate, he jerked away from his grasp. "I'm not fucking leaving her."

The brunette opened her mouth to argue when a voice he recognized cut her off.

"Go take care of your patient, Sophie. I'll deal with these guys."

They all turned to see Jason Ryker, R.I.S.C.'s Homeland handler, walking toward them. "Thanks, Jason." The doctor's eyes softened a bit. She turned to go back into the room, stopping long enough to tell Grant, "I promise I'll do everything I can to save her."

With a final, sideways glance at Ryker, the woman walked into the room, shutting him out.

"How is she?"

Grant stared at the closed door, ready to break the fucker down. "Alive. For now."

"Soph's one of the best doctors here. Your girl's in good hands."

Even the best doctors fail. He knew that all too well. And if they did this time...if he lost Brynnon for good...there wouldn't be a god powerful enough to save Martin Downing's soul.

For the next hour, Ryker, Coop, and Derek all hung out in the hallway with him. Upon Ryker's insistence, a nurse brought him a set of clean scrubs to change into, since the front of his shirt was covered in Brynnon's blood.

Their topic of conversations moved from one thing to the next, but Grant didn't listen to any of it. Instead, he spent that time planning.

Driven by his need for revenge, his thoughts were quickly consumed with bloody, gratifying scenes. In his mind, he saw himself torturing Downing with the most excruciating methods he could imagine.

Every once in a while, a comment was made about how strong Brynnon was. How, if anyone could make it through this, it would be her.

Grant appreciated what his friends were trying to do, but the idea of inflicting insurmountable pain on the bastard responsible was more comforting than any platitudes his teammates or Ryker could give.

Downing may think he'd gotten away, but with his team by his side, Grant knew they'd eventually find him. And when they did, when he finally got his hands on the motherfucker, he was going to show Downing just how big a mistake hurting his Brynnon had been.

Sometime later, Grant wasn't sure how long it had been, Jake and Olivia came rushing through the doors. Olivia's large baby bump caused a slight waddle to her step, but she was still able to keep up with her husband's long stride.

"Boss." Grant looked at the dark-headed man.

"We would've been here sooner, but there was a wreck and we had to take a detour."

His team leader's words made Grant think of the night of the dance and the detour they'd taken, too. It was the first night he and Brynnon—

"How is she?" Jake's voice grabbed his divided attention.

He ran a hand down his rugged jaw. "I don't know. They've been in there a while. I'm not really sure how long."

A shared understanding flowed into Jake's blue eyes as they slid toward Brynnon's room and back to him.

"Sorry I didn't call." Grant didn't even try to make excuses. "I should have—"

Jake's supportive words cut him off. "You were doing exactly what you needed to."

"I'm so sorry, Grant," Olivia reached up and gave him a hug. Her pregnant body made the move a bit awkward.

"Thanks," he patted her gently on the back. Grant was afraid if he said much more he'd break down like a baby.

Trevor arrived next, Mac walking in seconds behind him.

"Got here as soon as I could," Trevor told him somberly. "There was a wreck, and the detour was a bitch."

"S'okay."

Mac's worried eyes found his. "She's going to be okay, right?"

Emotions threatened to break through the protective wall he'd begun to rebuild. Though not everyone on the team had even met Brynnon, they'd all showed up...for her.

No, big guy. They're here for you.

Grant barely held back his reaction to hearing Brynnon's comforting voice in his head. He knew it was just his imagination, but the words were still startling, all the same.

Christ, he needed to hear it again. Like he needed his next breath.

"I heard she took a hit to the back."

Jake's voice tore Grant away from his thoughts. Feeling almost numb, he nodded. "Downing shot her. The bastard shot her, and then dragged her off into the shadows."

His nostrils stung, and warm tears filled his eyes. An enormous knot swelled in the back of his throat to the point he thought he'd choke. Though he had no idea how, Grant managed to swallow down the painful emotions seconds before they could burst free.

Sniffling, he told his team leader, "He just left her there to die, Jake. Like a fucking dog, Downing just...left her."

Jake stared back at him with utter certainty. "We'll find him."

Jaw clenched, Grant nodded. "I'm counting on it."

Ryker's phone rang, the sound echoing off the pristine, white walls.

"Excuse me," the Homeland agent muttered before taking a few steps away from the rest of them.

"Have they given you any updates on Brynnon's condition?"

Grant looked back over to Olivia. "Not yet. The doctor won't..." His voice cracked. "She, uh, won't let me go in."

With an understanding smile, Jake's sweet wife said, "I'll

go see if they'll give me an update, okay?"

He nodded, his chest tightening from the love he knew Olivia shared for everyone on the team. "Thank you."

"Well, I just got some good news," Ryker rejoined the group. "Downing's no longer an issue."

Grant perked up at that. "They found him? Where is he?"

His fists tightened from just imagining getting his hands on the bastard. Once he knew for sure Brynnon was going to be okay, he planned to pay the fucker a visit.

"On his way to the county morgue."

Chapter 22

"He's *dead?*"

Grant waited for Ryker to answer Coop's question, certain they'd heard the man wrong. Unfortunately, they hadn't.

"My guy just confirmed it." The other man nodded.

Grant huffed out a disbelieving breath.

"What the hell happened?" Grant asked a little too loudly.

"State police spotted him on the highway not long after the BOLO went out. Tried pulling him over, but Downing took off. Ended up losing control on a curve and rolled his car."

Derek shot Ryker a look. "You've gotta be kiddin' me. A fuckin' *car wreck?*" He shook his head. "The bastard got off too damn easy, if you ask me."

"Actually, the wreck isn't what killed him."

Confused, Mac frowned at their handler. "Then what did?"

"Bullet to the head."

"The cop?" Jake asked from beside Grant.

Ryker shoved his hands into his suit pants. "According to my guy, Downing spouted off some bullshit about how he'd rather die than go to prison." Ryker's dark eyes slid to

Grant's. "A second later, guy shoved his own gun into his mouth and pulled the trigger."

A few of the others began wishing Martin Downing good riddance. Muffled by the sound of his own blood rushing past his ears, Grant thought he heard someone say the world was better off without the son of a bitch.

The conversation carried on and other comments were made. Ones like how Downing had saved the taxpayers a shit ton of money, and by taking himself out, the fucker had done everyone a favor.

As he stood there, half-listening, Grant understood why they were all relieved by the news of Downing's death. But he wasn't.

All he could think was that he'd been fucking cheated.

He'd wanted to confront Downing himself. Wanted to beat the man within an inch of his life. Make him suffer for every ounce of pain he'd caused Brynnon and her family.

After, when it was over and Grant felt the man had been punished enough, *he'd* wanted to be the one to put a bullet in Downing's brain. Now, he'd never get that chance.

Olivia came back out of the room, quieting his murderous thoughts.

Grant shot toward her. "Is she okay?"

With hopeful trepidation, she said, "Her temperature is steadily rising, and her pulse has gotten a bit stronger. They're going to go ahead and move her into surgery to remove the bullet, keeping the warming system on her as much as they can."

"That's good, right?" He searched her round, hazel eyes for reassurance. "If she's well enough for surgery, that means she's going to be okay?"

With a sympathetic smile, Olivia gently grasped his

forearm. "She's not out of the woods yet, Grant. So far everything's gone as well as could be expected, given the circumstances but…"

The door behind Olivia opened and an unconscious Brynnon was pushed into the hall. Pinpricks of fear ran the length of his spine, sending him rushing to the gurney's side.

A thick, almost industrial-looking blanket covered her from the neck down. It was connected to a machine that was resting at the foot of the bed between Brynnon's legs and the railing. *The warming system.* His eyes flew back to her beautiful face.

Long, delicate eyelashes rested on her flawless skin and dried blood covered the area near her hairline from where the son of a bitch had struck her. Grant's fists clenched the cold railing.

The bluish tinge of her lips had faded some, but he knew she was still too cold. Too pale.

Leaning down, Grant pressed his warm lips to hers. "Keep fighting, Princess." He kissed her again. "Please, baby. You have to keep fighting."

"I'm sorry, sir." A male nurse looked over at him. "But we really need to get her to the O.R."

Trevor put a hand on his arm. "Come on, man. She needs to go."

Grant let go of the railing.

Stumbling back, he watched the group of people he didn't know take the woman who'd become his everything away.

"She's a fighter, G," Derek spoke up from behind him.

Coop shared the sentiment. "Hell, yes, she is."

Grant nodded but said nothing. He just kept watching them push Brynnon farther down the hall until they turned a corner, and she was gone.

She could be gone forever. How am I supposed to do this without her?
It was crazy. They barely knew each other, yet in a lot of ways—the most important ways—she knew him better than anyone ever had.

After years of being alone, Grant finally found a woman he wanted a future with. One who could die any minute.
Ah, Christ. I could lose her tonight.
He couldn't even take it out on the man responsible because the fucker had taken the chicken shit way out and ate a goddamn bullet.
Rot in hell, you motherfucking cock sucker.
"Hey," Mac rested a hand on his arm. "You okay?"

Concern was etched all over the tiny blonde's face. When Grant glanced at the others, he realized they were all staring back at him with that same, sorrowful expression. All, except Jake.

When Grant locked eyes with the other man, Jake simply gave him a tip of his chin. "Go. Do what you need to do. We'll come get you if anything changes."

Grant thought back to the conversation he and Jake had shared once, in a bathroom just down the hall from where they were now.

Jake had completely lost his shit when Olivia was taken to surgery after having been kidnapped by a man who'd damn near tortured her to death. The former Delta operator had tried his damnedest to destroy the men's restroom. Until Grant finally went in and talked him down.

Now, *he* was the one who wanted to break something. To demolish anything and everything in his path, not stopping until some of this goddamn fear went away.

His breathing shallowed and his focus tunneled.

Knowing he was seconds away from a complete

meltdown, Grant didn't say a word. He just turned his back on his friends and walked away.

Not one person tried to stop him.

Woodenly, he shuffled down the hall and through the ER doors. His vision blurred, but Grant ignored it and kept going.

Each step brought with it a new, agonizing thought. He pictured Brynnon on that operating table. Thought about how, in this very second, she was lying in there fighting for her life.

For *their* life.

Grant's mind whirled with the lifetime of memories they'd created over the span of only a few days. Pictures of her smiling back at him and laughing flashed before his watery eyes.

As if he'd somehow been transported back in time, Grant swore he could feel the warmth from her touch as they'd danced that night at the ball. The way her body had writhed sensually beneath his as they made love.

Having been moving almost robotically, he suddenly found himself around the corner, on other side of the building. When the moisture pooling in his eyes became blinding, he stopped.

He felt his chin quiver as his tears fought for release. Grant denied them, at first, determined to remain the strong, stoic man everyone expected him to be. But his emotions were too strong. Too powerful.

Trails of warm tears poured over his lids and down his cheeks as Grant Hill—the man who'd been called more machine than human—lost the battle miserably.

A loud, unrecognizable roar echoed through the night, and it took him a second to realize it was coming from him.

As the gates flew open and his heartache poured out in waves from his body, Grant turned to the one thing he knew would break the spell.

Pain.

With only one available target, he rammed his balled-up fist against the wall beside him. Again and again, Grant punched the unforgiving bricks, his throat becoming raw as he finally let go of the pain and anger he'd kept bottled up inside.

He'd lost his mom. His child. And now, he may very well lose the only woman he'd ever loved.

In the short period of time they'd spent together, Brynnon had somehow burrowed a permanent place deep inside his soul. She'd seen him at his worst. His best. And everything in between.

And by some miracle, the crazy, amazing woman had still chosen him.

I can't lose her. Ah, god...I can't lose her.

As his grief set in and his strength quickly became depleted, Grant turned and slid down the rough wall. His ass hit the cold, hard ground below with a thud.

Knuckles bloody and throbbing, he rested his forearms on his bent knees and dropped his head between his shoulders. Then for the first time since his mom died, Grant began to sob.

He wasn't sure how long he sat like that, but eventually his tears began to dry up, and his stuttering breaths became even. Exhausted, Grant pushed himself back onto his feet.

"You good?" The deep voice startled him.

Swinging his watery gaze up, Grant saw Jake standing by the corner's edge. His hands were shoved into his pockets, and though Grant knew he'd seen at least part of his emotional meltdown, there was no judgment in the man's eyes.

"Yeah." Grant nodded. His voice sounded thick and hoarse. With a loud sniff, he wiped away the last remnants of tears and walked toward his boss.

"If you need more time, I can go back inside."

He shook his head. "Thanks, but I'm good."

Jake stared back at him with an understanding Grant knew the other man felt to his core. "I'm sorry you lost your chance to deal with Downing on your own. I know what having that taken away from you means."

Grant licked his cold lips. "It's all I've thought about since they took her into that room. Making him suffer…it's what got me through that first hour. But when Ryker told us Downing was dead, I…" He shook his head and swallowed. "I don't know. I guess I just lost it."

"Trust me." Jake took a step forward. "I get it. So do Trevor and Derek. Taking down the bastards responsible for causing the women we love so much pain…that kind of satisfaction is indescribable."

As far as pep-talks went, Grant thought this one was pretty fucking shitty.

"But," Jake continued on. "Revenge like that? It's not everything. Not even close."

The two men stood silently in the cold, their breaths escaping in puffs of white smoke as they became lost in their own thoughts. Grant finally broke the silence a few minutes later.

"I knew this would happen." He looked back at his boss and teammate. "I knew if I let myself care about someone, I'd lose them."

"You haven't lost anyone yet. Brynnon's still in there,

fighting to stay with you. Don't give up on her, now."

"Losing my mom..." Grant shook his head. "That shit was the hardest thing I've ever had to go through. But this...I don't know. It's different."

"I know."

Grant swallowed hard. "I can't get this fucking pain in my chest to go away." He rubbed the area covering his heart to try and ease the pressure. "It feels like something's got ahold of my heart, and it won't let go."

"That's because you love her."

"I didn't want to," Grant admitted quietly. "I didn't want any of this."

Jake smirked. "Unfortunately, my friend, that's not always up to us to decide. Come on." The other man slapped his shoulder. "Let's go back inside and wait for the doctor to come give us the good news. I'm freezing my ass off out here, and that hand of yours could probably use a band aid...or a cast."

Though he wouldn't have thought it possible, one corner of Grant's mouth lifted. As the two men walked back to the building's emergency entrance, he turned to his boss.

"Thanks, Jake."

"For what?"

"Not firing me, for starters."

Jake gave him an incredulous look. "Why the hell would I fire you."

Blunt as always, Grant said, "I slept with a client."

"Meh." Jake shrugged. "Technically, Brynnon's father was the client." He waited a beat before adding, "Unless he's the one you were referring to."

He huffed out a silent chuckle. "Funny."

Jake smiled. "I try."

****

The first conscious thought Brynnon had was that she was finally, blessedly, warm.

After that, her body woke in stages, her mind trying to make its way through the odd murkiness to remember what had happened.

She remembered feeling cold. Colder than ever before. And the pain...God, the pain had been excruciating.

It was still there, on the left side of her back. But instead of the sharp, burning pain she remembered, it had become more of a dull ache. She could feel all her fingers and toes, which was a huge relief because it meant the bullet had missed her spine.

Brynnon tried opening her eyes, their lids heavily weighted. While she lay there, struggling to peel them apart, strobes of memories flashing behind them.

Her cabin. The bomb. Her brother. Martin.

He'd confessed to so much. Shooting her brother. The private investigator. He'd shot *her.*

Brynnon couldn't reconcile the man she knew as her brother's best friend and her father's confidant with the cold blooded killer who'd left her in the cold to die.

He tried to kill me.

More memories assaulted her. Martin dragging her across the rough pavement. The way he'd sounded just before he walked away. Cold and emotionless.

What if he comes back?

Fear that he'd return to finish the job left her shaken. Terrified, Brynnon tried calling out, but the only sound she could make was a low moan.

Somewhere in the background, the incessant beeping sound she'd barely registered from before grew faster. More intense.

She attempted to move, to get someplace safe where Martin could never find her, when a deep, soothing voice broke through the panicked fog.

"Easy, Princess. You're okay."

Clearing her dry, scratchy throat, Brynnon was finally able to speak. "Grant?"

There was a slight pause and then she heard, "I'm here. I'm right here."

He sounded funny, his voice thicker than normal.

Brynnon's pulse slowly returned to normal, coinciding with the steadying rhythm of what she realized was her heart monitor. She licked her lips, the delicate skin there stinging as though they were chapped.

You laid in the freezing cold for who knows how long. Of course, they're chapped.

Feeling stronger by the second, she worked her eyes open. The sight before her damn near overwhelming.

Holding her left hand in his, Grant was sitting as close to the bed as possible. His gray eyes shone with profound relief.

Brynnon immediately noticed something different about the way he looked. It had nothing to do with his rumpled clothes and scraggly hair. Nor was it the exhaustion reflecting back from his weary gaze.

The man was still sexy as sin, of course, but something just seemed different. If she didn't know any better, she'd say he almost seemed...lighter.

"Hi, Princess," Grant whispered with a smile.

Brynnon's chin trembled and a tear escaped the corner of her eye. "H-hi."

With sweet understanding, he used his free hand to gently wipe the droplet away. "Damn, you're a sight for sore eyes."

"So are you."

Reaching over to the metal tray beside him, Grant poured her a cup of water. Using great care, he put the bendable straw between her lips and held it there so she could take a much-needed drink.

Once she'd had her fill, he set the cup down and exhaled a slow, shaky breath. Carefully cupping one side of her face, he said, "I thought I'd lost you."

Brynnon reached up and took hold of his thick wrist. "Me, too." Despite fearing the answer, she asked, "Martin?"

"Dead." Grant's answer was instant and final.

Her eyes landed on the white bandage wrapped around his knuckles. "You?"

He shook his head. "Downing got cornered by the police and shot himself."

"Oh, my god."

She tried to fight it, but in the end Brynnon couldn't help but shed a few tears. Not for the man who'd tried to murder her, but rather the one she thought cared about her family. Now, however, she knew that man never really existed at all.

What saddened her the most was knowing her dad had lost his right-hand man. Her brother, a best friend.

Billy!

Feeling horrible that she hadn't thought about him first, Brynnon asked, "Billy?"

Sadness filled Grant's eyes. "I'm so sorry, baby. He didn't make it."

This time, when the tears began to fall, they didn't seem to want to stop.

Brynnon's face crumbled. She began sobbing

uncontrollably as all the pain and loss she felt was set free.

Careful of her wound, Grant slid onto the thin mattress beside her and held her closely. With his strong arms wrapped securely around her, the gentle giant stayed like that until finally, the gut-wrenching sobs subsided.

As he pulled back, Grant brushed some hair from her forehead. "Whatever you need, I'm here."

"Thank you," she whispered with a sniffle. "You know, it sounds awful, but part of me thinks Billy would have preferred it this way."

"What makes you say that?"

She smiled sadly. "You met my brother. He never would've survived going to prison."

Brynnon knew her thoughts were twisted, but they stemmed from the love she felt for Billy. It tore her heart in two to know she'd never see him again, but he hadn't been the same since their mother passed. Maybe now, he would finally find the peace he'd spent years searching for but never found.

Take good care of him for us, Mama.

"How's my dad?"

"As good as can be expected. He's been in and out of here this morning, trying to check on you while dealing with the fallout from Martin's actions."

Brynnon's heart ached. "It must be awful for him."

"Yeah, he took it all pretty hard. I think the only thing keeping him going is the fact that the doctors told us this morning they expected you to make a full recovery." Grant smirked. "He wanted to stay but I kicked his ass out."

Her brows rose high. "You did?"

Grant nodded. "I know sitting around here wasn't helping him, so I told him to go take care of whatever business he needed to attend to, and I'd keep him updated. He's been checking in through texts and phone calls. He'll be by later this afternoon."

"He trusts you," she smiled.

With a wink, Grant said, "Your father's a smart man."

The two sat in silence for a moment before Grant took her by complete surprise by blurting out, "I love you."

Brynnon blinked quickly, her heart skipping. "W-what?"

He cringed. "I'm sorry. I know my timing's shit. But I've wasted so much of my life." He squeezed her hand. "I've spent years avoiding the type of pain and loss I felt when my mom died, and again when I found out about my son. My entire life, I've tried so hard not to get hurt that I...I forgot how to actually *live*."

"Grant," Brynnon whispered back, shocked by the man's emotional confession.

"Then I met you," he whispered, his voice cracking at the end.

Unshed tears filled the fierce warrior's eyes as he continued filling her heart with more love than she could've ever imagined.

"You make me feel whole, Brynnon." His Adam's apple bobbed. "Because of you, I've known happiness again. I've laughed for the first time in years, and I've...I've loved." He blinked, sending two silver streaks racing down his rugged cheeks. "I love you, Princess. God, I love you. And I know we have a lot to work through with everything that's happened, but I swear I'll do whatever it takes to make sure you're happy and safe from here on out."

She thought she understood, but just to be sure, Brynnon asked, "W-what are you saying?"

Grant's lips curved up into that sexy, half-smile she loved

so much. "I'm saying, I want to spend the rest of my life with you."

Brynnon nodded against her pillow. "Okay," she answered quickly.

Grant's broad shoulders fell as he sighed a breath of relief. "Thank Christ."

His reaction to her response made her giggle. She hid a wince when a twinge of pain pulled in her back, refusing to let anything ruin this crazy, wonderful moment.

Very gently, Grant leaned down, pressing his lips to hers. When he pulled back, his smile widened, lighting up his entire face…and her world.

"In case you're wondering," she smiled back at him. "I love you, too."

With cocky wink, he said, "I know."

Brynnon laughed, immediately groaning from the pain. "Oh, God. Please don't make me laugh."

His whispered apology was followed by another sweet kiss. Looking her square in the eye, the bossy man let her know, "Just so we're clear, I want it all. Marriage. Babies. The works."

The beeping increased again, her new tears filled with happiness. "I want that, too, Grant. More than anything, I want that, too."

Epilogue

Five weeks later...

"Aw..."

"Oh, my gosh! That is so freaking adorable!"

"I love it so much. Thank you!"

From the back of the room, Grant took a sip from his beer to hide the smile working its way to the surface.

If someone had told him two months ago he'd be attending a baby shower, he would've told them they were crazy. If they'd asked if he ever thought he'd *enjoy* one, his answer would have been an immediate, "Fuck. No."

Yeah, well...a lot of things can happen in two months.

His eyes slid to where Brynnon was sitting with the other women of R.I.S.C. With Charlie—Derek's fiancé—at the helm, they'd all banded together this past week to throw Jake and Olivia a surprise baby shower.

Despite Grant's objections, Brynnon had insisted on setting up and decorating for the day's event. The doctor had recently declared her fully healed, but when it came to his wife, Grant refused to take chances.

My wife.

Married nearly three weeks, now, he still wasn't used to

calling her that. God, he fucking loved the sound of it.

In the days following the shooting, Brynnon had been inundated with answering questions and giving her official statements for both Homeland and the DPD. During those times, Grant never left her side once.

When he thought it was becoming too much for her, the questions ended. Immediately.

Once she was released from the hospital, Grant had moved into her condo, paying the extra to get out of his lease. His apartment was too damn small for the two of them, and after everything she'd been through, he'd wanted to bring some sense of normalcy back into her life.

The condo, however, was only temporary. They were breaking ground on the new cabin next week. The one she'd lost had been her dream home, and he had to admit it suited him just as well.

As for the wedding, they'd chosen against a big one…for several reasons. The most obvious being the media circus surrounding Martin's shocking murder spree and subsequent suicide, and Billy's death.

Brynnon's father was still dealing with the aftermath of the whole fucked-up shit show, both personally and professionally. Even though he had no knowledge of what Billy and Martin had done, William Cantrell felt responsible for those soldier's deaths.

As a matter of principle, he'd resigned his position as senator and was doing everything in his power to help the surviving families deal with the truth of what really happened. Between the evidence found on the P.I.'s computer and Martin's confession, it was clear Brynnon's father played no part in the cover-up.

The military had taken swift and immediate action against

the man who'd falsified the original investigation report, ensuring everyone involved paid for crimes they had committed.

The final bit of closure came when Hank Mitchell's body was recovered. He'd been shot, his body and car dumped in the water. Just as Martin had said.

Originally, Brynnon had wanted to wait to get married. Once Grant found out it was because she'd been worried her still-healing body would be a disappointment on their wedding night, he'd put a plan into action.

After making a few phone calls, he took a few days to get things together. As soon as everything was ready, Grant had promptly hauled her happy ass here, to Jake's ranch.

The second they'd stepped foot into the ranch, Max, Lexi, Charlie, and Gracelynn had whisked Brynnon away where a dress and flowers were waiting for her. While the amazing women helped get her ready, he and the guys quickly changed into a matching set of tuxes.

Less than an hour later, Brynnon had walked down the make-shift aisle in Jake's decorated living room—courtesy of Lexi and the others. Grant could still see the love she felt for him as she'd made her way to where he'd stood, waiting to make their unbreakable bond official.

The ceremony lasted all of five minutes, but when it was over, they were married. And that was all either one cared about.

"Damn, man," Coop muttered beside him. "You've got that look again."

Grant turned to his teammate. "What look?"

"You know, the one that says, 'I want to take my wife home and have my way with her.'"

He just grinned.

"Pretty sure I wear that expression every time I see my Gracie." Nathan Carter slid Coop a narrowed look. "You got a problem with that?"

Coop smiled back at the Bravo Team member. "Not at all, Nate. Hell, I'm used to seeing it on the rest of your ugly mugs. Just shocks the hell out of me every time I see it on *Hill's* face. That's all."

While the other men laughed, Grant flipped his teammate the bird and smirked. "Just wait, smart-ass. Your time's coming."

With a shake of his head, Coop snorted. "After seeing the shit you all have gone through? No, thanks, man. I'm good."

Despite the guy's word's, Grant noticed the almost indiscernible way Coop glanced at Mac from the corner of his eye. Whatever was going on between those two wasn't any of his business, but Grant had a feeling it would come to a head soon…one way or the other.

Later, after the presents had been unwrapped and the food eaten, the group sat around the fire shooting the breeze. When he noticed Brynnon trying to hide a yawn, Grant made the executive decision to call it a night.

"Come on, Princess. Time to head out."

She smiled up at him. "I'm good. We can stay a longer, if you wa—"

He pressed a finger to her lips, cutting her off. "You're tired. So we're leaving."

"Grant." She moved his hand from her mouth. "I love that you want to take care of me, but I'm a big girl." She'd no more gotten the words out when another yawn hit.

"A big girl who's dead on her feet." He grinned. "Come on. Let's go home."

She frowned. "You're bossy."

Leaning down next to her ear, Grant whispered, "You like it."

He saw the shiver race down her spine as Brynnon looked back up at him with a heated gaze. "Yeah," she whispered back. "I do."

Smiling from their secret conversation, they said their goodbyes and headed for home.

A few miles down the road when Brynnon spoke up. "You know, bossiness is sort of pre-requisite for parenthood."

Confused, Grant looked over at her. "I suppose it is."

His gorgeous wife bit her lip nervously. "So I guess it's a good thing you've already got that part down so well."

He chuckled. "Just try to remember that when we have kids someday."

"Someday." Brynnon shrugged. "Nine months from now…"

Her voice trailed off, and it took Grant half a second to catch what she was trying to tell him. His eyes flew to hers, the joy there confirming his suspicions.

Nearly jerking the car to the shoulder, he slammed the gearshift into park and turned to her. "Seriously?" He didn't even bother trying to hide his shock. "You're *pregnant?*"

She nodded. "Yes."

Grant couldn't seem to catch his breath…or construct a coherent sentence. "What…how…when…"

With a soft giggle, Brynnon reached across the truck's bench seat and covered his hand with hers. "Take a breath, big guy. To answer your questions, yes, I'm pregnant. Pretty sure you know the how. As for the when, the doctor estimates I'm about two weeks along."

The doctor. She'd gone to the doctor yesterday for her

final check-up. Grant had been to all her other appointments, but had been called into the office to discuss something related to their next op. Brynnon had gone to the doctor alone.

As if reading his mind, she explained. "After the doctor cleared me physically yesterday, she ran a blood panel, just as an added precaution. It's still really early, and I don't want to tell anyone else yet, but my HCG levels were already high enough to be detected."

"The pill?" Grant asked, his mind whirling.

She looked chagrined. "Apparently, the antibiotics they put me on after I was shot diminished my birth control's affect."

Grant's mind whirled.

Brynnon was pregnant.

He was going to be a father.

"We're having a baby."

His whispered words of awe must have worried her, because Brynnon sounded nervous when she asked, "Are you mad?"

"Mad?" He looked back at her as if she'd lost her damn mind. "Fuck no, I'm not mad. I'm...I'm..."

Shit. He was screwing this whole thing up. Inhaling slowly, Grant blew out a slow, controlled breath before unbuckling his seatbelt and sliding over to her.

Taking her beautiful face between his, Grant kissed her softly. "Baby, mad is the furthest thing from what I'm feeling right now."

"Really?"

He kissed her again. "Really."

"So you're happy?"

Grant shook his head. "Happy isn't a strong enough word

for what I am." Kissing her again, he took his time, doing his best to show her without words exactly how the news she'd shared had affected him. When he pulled away, he asked, "What about you? Are you happy?"

Brynnon's smile made her eyes dance. "Very."

"We're going to have a baby," Grant whispered to his wife.

"Yes." Brynnon nodded. "We are." She leaned up, initiating the next kiss. "I love you so much, Grant Hill."

"I love you, too, Princess." Grant slid his hand down to her flat belly and smiled. "I love you both."

****

Coop watched through the curtain as Trevor and Mac stood outside on Jake's porch. He was hoping to figure out just what in the hell was up with those two, but they were both speaking two low for him to hear anything through the window.

Damn.

He didn't know what they were up to, but something was definitely going on. And from the look on Mac's gorgeous face, it wasn't good.

The pint-sized blonde was staring up at Trevor, her long ponytail swaying back and forth as she shook her head at something the former Delta operator was saying.

As a sniper—first in the Army and now with R.I.S.C.— Coop had studied enough faces through his scope to recognize fear when he saw it. And Mac looked terrified.

What the hell?

Mac was the strongest, most courageous woman he'd ever met. Like him, she was a former Ranger and, though he'd never admit it, was an even better sniper than he was.

The five-feet nothing spitfire could outrun, outshoot, and outsmart most men he knew. She didn't flee in the face of danger. She thrived on it. So seeing the fear clouding her eyes now? That turned his blood cold.

As Coop continued to watch the odd exchange, his mind raced to think of what she and Trevor could be talking about so intently. An affair was out of the question. No way were Mac and Trevor involved romantically.

One, Trevor loved his wife to the moon and back. The guy would sooner lay down his life than hurt Lexi.

Two, the former Delta operator may be good looking as fuck—the bastard—but Mac sure as hell wasn't a home wrecker.

Something was definitely going on, though. And as her partner, Coop intended to find out what. Starting now.

Having had enough of the pair's covert crap, Coop stepped out onto the covered porch and shut the door behind him. "All right." He crossed his arms at his chest. "Spill it."

His team members swung their heads around, both wearing a deer-in-the-headlights expression.

"Spill what?" Mac asked too innocently.

Coop rolled his eyes. "That girl-next-door act doesn't work on me, remember? Now, what the hell is going on?"

Mac slid a quick glance to Trevor before looking back at him. With a shrug of her delicate shoulder, she said, "Nothing's going on."

"Bullshit." Coop dropped his arms to his sides. "You two have been sneaking around for the last two weeks, having your private meetings and these little side conversations. I've kept quiet up to now, but enough is enough."

Trevor looked to Mac, as if he were waiting for her to say something, but she simply broke eye contact and remained silent.

Throwing his hands to his hips, Coop's eyes narrowed to thin slits. "Seriously? I'm your fucking partner, Mac."

Angry blue eyes flew up to his. "Being partners on the team doesn't mean I have to tell you everything."

"No." Coop shook his head. "It doesn't. But it sure as hell means we should trust each other."

Mac's expression softened. "I do trust you."

"Then tell me what has you so scared."

Admission flashed behind her eyes before she could stop it. Still, the stubborn woman said, "I...I can't."

Refusing to let his disappointment show, Coop shot back with, "Can't or won't?"

Mac bit her bottom lip nervously. Ignoring how much he wished it were his teeth nibbling her there, Coop sighed. "Come on, Mac. Part of being partners is knowing you have someone to lean on when you need it."

Clearing his throat, Trevor spoke up. "He's right, Mac."

Coop's gaze slid to the other man's. From behind her, Trevor gave him a single nod before heading for the door. Looking back over his shoulder, he said, "Told you before, the story is yours to share. Tell him or don't tell him. The choice is yours." The guy shrugged. "Just remember...you're not alone in this."

With those parting words, Trevor went back into the house, leaving the two of them alone.

Coop shoved his hands into his pockets. "Well, that sure as hell didn't make me feel any better."

A corner of Mac's enticing mouth turned up for only a second before falling back into a straight line. Swallowing hard, she looked back up at him. "I trust you with my life, Sean. You have to know that. I always have."

"So trust me with it now."

Her hesitation was palpable. "I'm leaving tomorrow."

Coop took a step back, the shock from her words damn near knocking him on his ass. "You're leaving? Where are you going?"

"I can't tell you."

"Goddamn it, Mac." His anger swelled. "You *just* said you trusted me."

She closed her eyes. "You're right." Inhaling deeply, his partner opened them back up and met his stare. "I could tell you. But I won't."

Pain stabbed him in the heart. "Why the hell not?"

"Because it isn't safe."

"For you?"

Mac shook her head. "For you."

Coop ran a hand over his short hair. "Okay, you're going to have to explain that one."

Walking over to the edge of the porch, she looked out at the snow-covered lawn. "I'm working a solo op."

If she'd punched him in the jaw, he wouldn't have been more surprised.

"The fuck you are." He went to her side. "R.I.S.C. doesn't do solo ops. Not ones that are known to be dangerous, anyway." When she opened her mouth to argue, he shut her down. "I'm talking about more than the occasional solo bodyguard gig, and you know it. Whatever this job is, it has you scared to death. I can see it in your eyes."

Mac's shoulders fell in an uncharacteristic show of defeat. "You're right." She looked back up at him. "I am scared."

When Coop saw the way her body shivered, he

instinctively knew it wasn't from the cold. "Jesus, Mac." He took her shoulders between his hands. "You're shaking like a leaf."

She swallowed nervously. If he didn't know any better, Coop would have sworn there were fresh tears trying to fight their way free.

She's scaring the hell out of me.

"Talk to me, McKenna. Please."

"This job…it has a personal connection." Mac licked her lips. "One from my past."

Mac had always kept her time before R.I.S.C. close to the vest. Out of respect for her, Coop had never pried. Now, he wished like hell, he had.

"Okay," he nodded. "Whatever it is, I can help."

"You can't."

"Sure, I can. Jake will give me the green light if I ask. If not, I'll put in for vacation time."

"It's not about getting permission, Sean."

"Then let me go with you."

She shook her head. "I can't."

"Why not?"

Yelling, Mac blurted, "Because I care too much about you!"

Okay, so he wasn't exactly expecting *that* answer.

"I care about you, too, Mac. A lot."

She squeezed his arm. "I know you, do. Our partnership…our friendship means more to me than you'll ever know. It's one of the biggest reasons I have to do this alone."

"You're not making any sense, McKenna."

"I know." She smiled sadly. "I wish I could tell you more, but I can't run the risk that you'll get hurt. Not because of me and my fucked-up past."

Coop was still trying to understand what the hell she was talking about when Mac leaned up and kissed him on the cheek. "Take care of yourself, Sean. And...thank you."

He frowned. "For what?"

"For being the best partner a girl could ever have." Pulling the keys to her Jeep Rubicon from her pocket, Mac turned and walked down the porch steps.

Coop shouted her name, ordering her to come back, but she ignored his pleas. A minute later, he was still standing on that damn porch, feeling as though her goodbye had been final.

It was a loss he felt to his soul. One that damn near brought him to his knees.

The utter terror he'd seen in her eyes and the trembling of her voice when she'd admitted how scared she was damn near brought him to his knees.

Fuck that.

McKenna Kelley may be the epitome of strength and female independence, but she was also the woman who owned his heart. Even if she didn't know it, yet.

She was his partner. His friend. And, even though he'd never admitted his true feelings for her, his woman.

So screw invasion of privacy. He was going to dig as far and deep as he had to in order to figure out where she was going and what the hell she was getting herself involved in.

Whether she liked it or not, Mac was his to protect. And the first chance he got, Coop was going to make damn sure she knew it.

****

Want more Coop and Mac?

ULTIMATE RISK (R.I.S.C. Book 6) will be released **May 2020!**

Be sure to keep scrolling to see how you can keep up to date on all of Ms. Blakely's new releases!

Want to read more from Ms. Blakely's R.I.S.C. Series?

See how it all started with Jake and the rest of Alpha Team by checking out the other books in this series:

Book 1: Taking a Risk, Part One (Jake & Olivia's HFN)
Book 2: Taking a Risk, Part Two (Jake & Olivia's HEA)
Book 3: Beautiful Risk (Trevor & Lexi)
Book 5: Unpredictable Risk (Grant & Brynnon)

Check out R.I.S.C.'s new Bravo Team! Click below to read the first in Ms. Blakely's new R.I.S.C. spin-off series in Susan Stoker's Special Forces: Operation Alpha World:

Book 1: Rescuing Gracelynn
(Nate & Gracelynn "Gracie")

Coming Soon:

Book 2: Rescuing Katherine
(Matt & Katherine) – March 2020

Keep reading for an excerpt from Rescuing Gracelynn…

Rescuing Gracelynn Blurb

(Book 1 in Ms. Blakely's new R.I.S.C. spin-off series, Bravo Team)

"Anna Blakely has another hit book! This exciting story is filled with action, drama, excitement, romance, terror and much, much more. If you want a book that pulls you in and keeps you excited to turn the next page, over and over again, then I highly recommend reading RESCUING GRACELYNN!"
— *Bookbub reviewer*

HE NEVER BELIEVED IN TRUE LOVE...
UNTIL HE MET HER.

Bravo Team's technical analyst and confirmed bachelor, Nathan Carter, is happy being single and has no intention of falling under the spell of a woman. Ever. Then, he meets Gracelynn. Before he knows it, the sweet, tenacious woman has Nate questioning his long-standing doubts about love, soul mates, and happily ever after.

Gracie McDaniels is happy with her new life and loves her new job. Working closely with the hunky guys on R.I.S.C.'s Bravo Team, including her future brother-in-law's best friend, doesn't seem as if it'll be an issue. Then, she meets him.

Nate's smart, funny, and handsome...everything she's ever wanted in a partner. But just as they start to grow close, an innocent friendship from Gracie's past comes back to haunt her. When her life is threatened, Gracie instinctively turns to Nate for protection and soon he and the other members of Bravo step up to keep Gracie safe.

With help from Ghost and his friends, the Delta Force and Bravo teams find themselves racing against the clock to save the only woman Nate has ever loved...before it's too late.

Excerpt from Rescuing Gracelynn

"Are you okay?" Her question came out much softer than she'd meant for it to.

Nate gave her a humorless smirk as he shoved his hands into his pockets. "I should be asking you that question."

"I'm...better." And she was. The pounding in her head had quieted to a dull ache, and the intense trembling had subsided.

When he continued to just stand there, staring without saying another word, Gracie realized he was probably waiting for an apology. One that was well-deserved.

Standing, she laid what was left of the ice pack down onto her seat's cushion and began to say what needed to be said. "I'm really sorry, Nate. We never should have left the building without one of you. Or, at the very least, we should have checked with you beforehand."

She waited, but he remained silent. *Okay.* Apparently, more groveling was going to be involved.

Stepping toward him, Gracie nervously continued. "I-I know it wasn't very smart of us, and you and Kole have every right to be upset. It's just that, I was exhausted from going over everything with Jake and the others, and then doing the sketch with Dalton. Sarah mentioned coffee and I..."

She let her voice trail off, hoping he'd say *something.* Instead, he simply began walking slowly toward her, a muscle in his strong, sexy jaw bulging as he moved. The look he gave her was so intense, Gracie half-expected to see steam to start shooting out of his ears.

"Okay, look," she said defensively. "I get that you're upset, but we just wanted to go grab a quick coffee. That was it. I mean, you saw us, right? We were coming straight back. Yes, it was stupid, but you can't seriously stay mad about this forev—"

The rest of the word were cut off when he grabbed both her upper arms and slammed his mouth down onto hers.

A tiny squeak escaped the back of her throat just before he used his tongue to pry her lips apart. Apology forgotten, Gracie opened her mouth and let him in.

Standing in the middle of their boss's office, she held on tight as Nate began to devour her. He took and she gave. It was the most sensual, raw-emotions moment of her entire life.

When he was done feasting, Nate pulled away slowly and rested his forehead against hers. They remained locked in each other's arms, their chests moving in sync as they both attempted to catch their breath.

Regaining some control, Nate lifted his head and locked his eyes with hers. "I thought I'd lost you."

He sounded different than before. His voice was low and there was this dark edge to it she'd never heard before. "Nate?"

"You scared the shit out of me, baby." He swallowed hard and shook his head back and forth slowly. "Don't ever do that, again."

You can grab your copy of Rescuing Gracelynn today!

373

Made in the USA
Coppell, TX
12 February 2022